Shattered Fate

Linda Fagala and Karen Pugh

Ruth
Thank you and enjoy the
Read!

PF KARLIN PUBLISHING
SUGAR LAND, TEXAS

Karen Pugh
Linda Fagala

ISBN: 978-0-9890247-2-3
Library of Congress Control Number: 2013903909

Shattered Fate

By Linda Fagala...a.k.a. l. fagala
Karen Pugh...a.k.a. k. pugh

Copyright © 2014 by Linda Fagala and Karen Pugh

Published by:

PF Karlin Publishing
Sugar Land, Texas

This is a work of fiction. Characters, places, and events portrayed in this book are either a product of the authors' imagination or used fictitiously, with the exception of certain towns and locations which were used to provide the reader with a sense of locale of the story line. Any similarity to actual places, events, or persons, living or dead, is coincidental and not intended by the authors.

ISBN: 978-0-9890247-2-3

Library of Congress Control Number: 2013903909

Printed in the United States of America

In memory of a dear friend,
who helped inspire me to write this novel

ACKNOWLEDGEMENTS

We owe a world of thanks to everyone who took the time to help us with the writing and publishing of our first romance novel. Without their help this project would never have been completed.

A special thanks to our husbands:

Gary Fagala, Linda's at-home editor, for his countless hours of answering questions, reviewing our words, giving his opinion, cooking meals so we could keep working, and for making our book the first romance novel he has ever read.

Joseph Pugh for keeping a light on so Karen could find her way home.

A huge thanks to our editor, **Vicki Barber**, for her patience and help given to first time authors who needed assistance with improving their manuscript.

Many thank to everyone else who assisted with the completion process:

Doris Davidson for being the first to read an early version of the manuscript and for her encouragement to continue.

Brian Fagala for his opinions that helped us get started and without whose computer knowledge we would have been lost.

Jessica Figueroa for her opinions that helped us kick start the endeavor.

Nancy Kaminski, her last reading gave us the push we needed to stay excited.

Larry McGee for your input to improve Chapter 1.

Heather Metcalf for giving Karen a weekend with the grandchildren while she read the complete book and pointed out areas needing improvement.

Dwight Murray, who gave up many hours of his time to help us muddle through the nuts and bolts of the book publishing business.

Lane Simmons for giving the manuscript a face by assisting with the design of our book cover and for other design work.

Henri Socha, who took the late night calls when our frustration level with the computer program became too much.

Shattered Fate

CHAPTER 1

THERE WAS TOTAL darkness as I attempted to open my eyes. My body wouldn't respond to any of my commands. I shouted in my mind for it to move, but nothing happened.

I could feel my blood coursing through my veins until it pulsed in my ears. My heart was racing so fast I thought it might beat its way out of my ribcage. What was happening to me? Frightened and paralyzed, all I could do was lay there and listen to the sounds around me…rushing footsteps, the low hum of motors, and the beep, beeping of machines.

In the midst of the noise, I heard muffled voices, indecipherable, like in a crowded restaurant. I strained to hear, making every effort to comprehend what was being said. My mind couldn't recognize all of them, but one stood out— my mother. Her words were garbled, but I could hear her sobs. I wanted to reach out to her. I tried to open my mouth, to formulate words, to make any kind of a sound to let her know I was there, but nothing happened.

Like a wildcat clawing to be free, I fought to maintain my awareness, the only thing left of me, but my brain just wanted to go to sleep. The experience was like drowning, with rushing water coming over me. The more I tried to swim to the top to release myself, the more the sinking feeling took me deeper and deeper. I was plummeting into a bottomless cavern as the fog in my mind was getting thicker. It was winning the battle when the silence fell over me. Exhausted, I gave in to the onrushing darkness. The fog took over and my body relaxed, but into what?

CHAPTER 2

I HAD NEVER been in love. Oh, the concept was familiar enough. My parents and best friend Abbey all loved me. I returned their love, but that was of a different kind. Having never experienced the touch of another person who was in love with me, I didn't understand the affection two people can give to each other. The emotional excitement was unfamiliar to me. So, at twenty-two years old I, Belinda Davies, would've liked to experience that tenderness before the darkness took me....

***

Even though I was on an East Texas college campus, it was not commonplace in the twenty-first century to see someone on horseback, especially on a magnificent animal like Beau. From the first time Matt, the guy I was dating, let me take a ride on his chestnut gelding, I found it exhilarating.

Beau was such an easy and comfortable horse to ride. He was accustomed to the sounds of humans around him. I trusted him. On Saturday mornings, we would head for the trails behind the college, retreating into my sanctuary amongst the trees. The woods on either side of the paths created an illusion of total isolation. I used this time to free myself from the tensions of school and to reminisce about the course of my life to this point.

I grew up very shy and reserved, and when I saw pictures of myself as a kid, I'd throw in "just plain homely." The resulting feelings of insecurity controlled my life from early childhood through my second year of college. Of course my parents gave me all the attention a child could ever wish for. They made me feel loved and beautiful, and like most children, I saw myself through their eyes as their perfect princess.

However, my princess delusion would be crushed upon starting school. My parents attempted to build me up for my new adventure, but, though excited, I never realized how ill-suited I was to take on my new social experience.

At first I saw myself just like all the other children, with the exception of being a bit shy. Slowly, as the weeks went by, things began to change. I noticed my classmates making friends. The girls would whisper to each other in the classroom about great secrets only they were privy to. At recess, they seemed to naturally be attracted to each other. They would gather in groups and rush to their favorite spots in the yard. No one ever invited me to participate. It embarrassed me, but my lack of self-confidence prevented me from trying to join in.

As the years passed, being alone became...comfortable. By the time I was an adolescent, my lifestyle had become more of a safety net. It was easier to not be involved with my fellow students on a social level. There were acquaintances, just no close friends. Content with that, I accepted my fate and continued to mold it. I did very little to enhance my natural assets, such as they were. I wore no makeup and lived in jeans, t-shirts and loose comfy clothes.

When other girls my age were hanging out talking about boys and dating, I was in the library or in my room. No boy ever asked me out. In high school I never went to a dance or my prom. I told myself I preferred not being like the other girls, trying to convince myself being different didn't matter. This became my tactical choice, a sort of self-imposed invisibility which made my life less complicated—that is until my mother interfered.

Mom meant well, but she always overstepped her bounds with multiple attempts to socialize me. She would drag me to every type of lesson she could think of—cooking, painting, and lamest of all because of my two left feet, ballet.

I would attend the first few times to appease her—it made my life easier. To get out of going, I'd find a built in excuse, like signing up for a school project that would take too much time to complete. Voila! Problem solved.

However, one time she did get it right—with singing lessons. It was something I could do that involved only my voice coach and me. I could practice all I wanted at home, in private. The few people who did hear me sing told me I was good, but of course, I always had my doubts. I'm sure Mom was hoping that I'd join the school or church choir which meant I'd be hanging around with more of my peers. Sadly for her, I never had any intention of taking my singing any further than my own private concerts.

Now, I belt out a few tunes in the shower or on girls' night in with Abbey Curtiss, my friend and college roommate since freshman year. She is an attractive girl who is a couple of inches shorter than I. She has a nice figure and slender legs. Her thick dark auburn hair is worn shoulder length and curled under, with a wispy thin bang that frames her pale, smooth face. Abbey has great skin and uses very little makeup. Her eyelashes are naturally long and thick, accentuating her bright green eyes, giving them a seductive look. Unlike me, Abbey never had trouble securing dates all through high school nor in college.

Compared to Abbey, I was on the opposite end of the attractiveness scale. Before college, my hair was shoulder length and parted down the middle so it would hide my face. In my freshman year I decided to let my hair grow longer so it would also cover up more of my body. Most of the other girls my age were developing a figure. *Not* me. With small breasts and no hips, I still had the humiliating shape of an adolescent boy. So when Abbey met me our freshman year of college, that's what she saw.

Abbey had always just accepted me for who I was. It was like she never even noticed my ordinary looks or lack of self-confidence. When we first became roommates, it took her a few weeks to figure out that I wasn't dating. She would become so thrilled about the weekends and ask who I'd be going out with, assuming I had a date. I'd always have an excuse that I was behind on a project and needed to stay in to complete it. College was good in that sense. There was always something to study for.

After she figured it out, she gave up dates to stay home with me on several Saturday nights. We would "obtain" a bottle of cheap wine, make popcorn, and settle in to watch a good chick flick or comedy. Once the full effect of the wine kicked in, the CD's would come out and the real entertainment began. Singing along to the music, we'd let our inhibitions melt as we became wanna-be rock stars. Those Saturdays we spent together were a lifesaver for me, making Abbey my best friend and the sister I never had.

Like most best friends, we kept in touch even over the summers, especially between our sophomore and junior years. Abbey lived outside of El Paso, Texas, and I lived in Sugar Land, Texas. To see each other during the summer would've meant a sixteen-hour drive one way, so phone calls, texting, and emails were the best we could do. There was always excitement in her voice when we talked about the changes I was noticing. I actually developed breasts and just enough hips that gave me something that resembled a figure.

That same summer, my mother had one more trick up her sleeve. For her, I think it was the last straw. She could see the changes in me and was determined to release me from my shell once and for all. So without any discussion, she enrolled me in a modeling class with the edict that I was going to participate. So, on the first morning, I begrudgingly attended with crossed arms and rolling eyes. After two sessions, I decided to stick with it. To my surprise, the class taught me all sorts of tips on how to emphasize myself while improving my posture.

During one session, we were taught a "runway walk"—a strut with one foot crossed over in front of the other—like walking on a tight rope, but strutting and faster. The whole idea was such a joke to me because when was I ever going to use that kind of walk.

There was a brief practice session before everyone was instructed to line up and strut our stuff. Stupidly, I chose the end of the line thinking it would give me time to mentally practice and calm my nerves. Big mistake! When my turn came, I had every pair of eyes on me. My nerves churned as I scanned their faces and took the first step heading down the catwalk. At the midpoint, my two left feet tangled and sent me sprawling. To this day, I still feel the humiliation from the ear splitting laughter that turned into thundering applause.

I recovered from my appalling performance and decided I liked the way the walk looked, minus the strut. Determined to master it, I practiced it in the privacy of home. I'd sneak into mom's bedroom whenever she was downstairs, and sashay in front of her full-length mirror. The walk looked sophisticated, but it was hard to keep my balance. So, acting silly, I exaggerated it by swishing my hips from side to side. It looked sassy, thus developing my signature "Sassy Sashay."

So, at the start of my junior year, I was a different person on the outside and when Abbey saw me, she flipped. I stood taller and actually picked clothes that flattered my body. But beneath that polished exterior, I was still a shy, reserved little girl riddled with doubt, insecurity, and little knowledge of men.

My dating experience during my first two years of college could only be described as a farce. I attracted boys because of my academic standing, but only when they were desperate because they were about to fail a class. Apparently death by parent was more frightening to them than hanging around me.

I think this was Matt's motivation after we met on a blind date that had been arranged by Brent, Abbey's boyfriend. Matt was having trouble with a math class, stuff I took in high school, so I agreed to help him if he'd let me ride Beau.

During my time tutoring Matt, he would only invite me to do something that didn't involve a crowd and was never on a weekend. We'd go out to eat and sometimes a movie. I soon became very aware I was a low priority in his social life—an afterthought, not the girl on his arm at the many parties he attended. I found myself being invisible and that hurt because now I no longer wanted to be. With all my heart, I wanted to be that girl on his arm.

What I found interesting was that Matt seemed oblivious to how I felt that year. I knew I just didn't matter to him. During the fall semester of my junior year, after my transformation, Matt changed his tune and was trying to become more exclusive with me. All of a sudden I had what I'd longed for, but now I wasn't sure I wanted it.

For the first time in my life, I thought I was ready to experience a real romantic relationship, something different from what Matt and I had. I wanted a relationship where I mattered.

I came to rely on Abbey and her knowledge of dating. She seemed so comfortable with the whole thing and I was such a rookie. To prepare me for any scenario, she would endure endless questions. She would just laugh and answer all my silly queries to the best of her ability. Sometimes we'd talk all night, but I did learn and was starting to have fun. I was on the adventure of a lifetime and for once excited to be me.

But despite all of Abbey's mentoring, I still lacked the emotional maturity and self-confidence needed for a successful social experience, especially with men. This caused me trouble and now I refer to my lack of social graces as my "Monster." When confronted with an uncomfortable situation, I would panic and literally run. The need to protect myself, to make myself invisible, would take over. This was a facet of my personality that still overpowered me, one that I was frantic to manage. But how?

***

If I had to summarize who I had become, I could describe myself with one word: SAFE. I was not what you would call a real risk taker and since starting college, not much had stopped me from staying focused, not even my new look. My life and my college career were going according to my plan, I thought...*until I met HIM.*

CHAPTER 3

EVERY YEAR, ON the first Saturday of April, there was a Spring Carnival at the college. All the student organizations would set up game booths down a barricaded portion of the street that split the campus in half.

Matt was a Theta Kappa and I knew he'd be working on their booth that morning. So, I'd decided to stroll over to see how it was coming along, hoping he had ridden Beau.

It was a perfect day for a carnival. The breeze was mild and brushed my face as I ambled toward the booth construction area. Matt and several other fraternity brothers were there working hard, taking advantage of the cool sunny morning to do the physical labor. Approaching, I scanned the area searching for Beau and spotted him tethered to a nearby tree.

"Hey, how's the booth coming along?" I surveyed the project and pieces of lumber lying on the grass around Matt. Only a few boards had been nailed together, making it difficult to determine what the structure was meant to be.

He looked up from the board he was sawing and huffed out an exasperated sigh. "We still have a lot to do." He glanced at my jeans and shoes. I seldom wore tennis shoes and they were a telltale sign I was interested in only one thing.

"Are you going to be finished in time?" I was trying to make conversation, so it wouldn't be so obvious that riding Beau was my priority. His project didn't interest me at all.

"I hope so." Shaking his head, he looked doubtful. "I suppose you really came to ride Beau, didn't you?" He nodded his head in the horse's direction then peered down at my shoes.

"No, I didn't know you rode him here," I fibbed. He rode Beau every Saturday morning and I hoped today would be no different. "But...can I?" He could see right through me and knew exactly what I wanted.

He half grinned as he turned back to his task of sawing. "Sure...go ahead.

Just don't overheat him and make sure you water him before you come back."
I wasn't an idiot when it came to Beau. I loved him too.

Strolling toward Beau, I retrieved some baby carrots from my pocket. He
saw me and lifted his head, anticipating his tasty morsels. I reached out and
said my usual greeting. "Hey Beau. Carrot?"

Soon we were off trotting around the campus. About thirty minutes into the
ride, my attention was diverted by a tall, nice-looking stranger waving his arms
frantically in the air as he motioned me to come over. So, I did.

The closer I rode, the more I realized the angle of his gaze was fixated on
only one part of me, my boobs. Riding up to a stranger was nerve wracking
enough and this added distraction fed into my self-conscious nature.
Fortunately, his obvious gaze finally shifted from me to Beau as he scanned the
horse seconds before I reached him.

"Beautiful horse. Is he yours?" His eyes shifted to my face, briefly
slipping down to my cleavage, then drifted back to my face. He took hold of
the bridle with his strong-looking hands, then stroked Beau's neck with his
right one. Most people who approached me never gave Beau a second glance
or touched him. This guy was different. He had a confidence about him I
admired because I had so little. I tended to be attracted to confident people,
perhaps hoping some of it would rub off on me.

"No, he belongs to someone I'm seeing." He intrigued me with his
boldness.

"He's a fine specimen." He continued to look the animal over and
instinctively combed his fingers through Beau's mane as he turned his attention
back to me. "You're a pretty good rider. Been doing it long?"

"Thanks. For awhile."

He extended his right hand to me while looking straight into my eyes. "I'm
Garrett Barnett."

"Nice to meet you. I'm Belinda Davies," I lilted, extending mine. As he
took my hand, I noticed my first assumption was correct—his grip was strong,
yet gentle, like with Beau. He gave me an intense look as I studied his soft
brown eyes and decided he was someone I'd like to know better.

He never let up on his grip of my hand. This was a nice technique. It kept
all of my attention on him in an effortless, flirty way. "Nice to meet you....So,
you're just dating this person—it's not serious?"

"Yes—just dating," I casually said, hoping he would ask me out.

He released my hand and resumed stroking Beau's neck. "Good. How
about going out with me tomorrow evening?"

"Hmmm." Placing my hand on my cheek and looking above his head, I acted as if I needed to think about all my other plans. I returned my gaze to him and tried not to sound too eager. "I'll have to check my calendar, but I think I'm free."

"We'll start with dinner. Do you like Mexican food?" A wide grin spread across his face.

He sounded eager, like he had the whole evening already planned and I hadn't even said yes yet. "Yeah. It's my favorite."

Releasing Beau's bridle, he asked for my phone number and input it into his cell phone. "Great, I'll call later this afternoon after you've had time to check your full calendar. If you're free, I'll pick you up tomorrow at 5:30. That okay?"

"Sure."

"Now make sure to check that calendar." He had a modest ribbing tone, as a crooked smile formed on his face. He knew very well I was free, but the flirt was fun.

"Gotta go. I'll check as soon as I get back to my place." With a slight smile on my face, I rode off in a canter, not giving him a chance to continue our conversation.

I knew we had been gone too long and Matt would be anxious if we didn't make an appearance. I rode toward the pond located in front of the administration building to water Beau. A small group of guys walking across the grass were about to cross my path. I pulled on the reins to slow Beau's pace, but instead he stopped and reared up. I held on for dear life as the horse placed me in a perilous position. *Luckily*, I didn't fall off. That would've been really embarrassing.

Seeing the horse must have surprised the guys because they stopped and were staring my way. Once Beau settled down, I looked up, scanning their faces. There amongst the group was the most gorgeous face I had ever seen. My eyes were drawn to his. I don't know if I believe in love at first sight, but when he smiled, it took my breath away and my heart started racing. We stared at each other for several seconds until one of his friends encouraged him on. He took a few steps to move out of my way then stopped and watched me. Our eyes stayed fixed on each other's as I rode past, giving him a bashful smile. With my back to him, I tucked my chin into my shoulder as I glanced back to look at him. He was still watching me. He winked. Stunned by his subtle flirt, I smiled as a warm sensation came over my face. Quickly, I turned my head away with a jerk so he wouldn't notice me blushing.

Clutching my hand over my chest, I took a deep breath and released it slowly. I was filled with an unexplainable excitement—a sensation I'd never felt before, a type of thrill. My heart was still pounding as I realized I was experiencing something I'd never had in my relationship with Matt and I wondered how a perfect stranger could do this to me with just a look.

It was a short ride to the pond where I allowed Beau a long drink. The reins extended in my hands as the horse dipped his head. I stared across the water, haunted by a pair of eyes that belonged to a stranger. Looking back over my shoulder, I scanned the area hoping to get another glimpse of HIM, but he was nowhere in sight.

Beau gave a quick jerk of his head, diverting my attention back to him. I pulled up on the reins and headed back to Matt, praying the whole time my ride would not end after I checked in.

Once Matt was satisfied his orders had been carried out, he gave the okay to keep riding. My heart jumped as I rode off hoping to see HIM again. I took a shortcut between two buildings to return to the place where the group had been and like before, HE was nowhere in sight.

I continued to ride around campus searching for HIM. My heart hammered at the thought. I was drawn to HIM, obsessed with seeing HIM again, until the ringing of my cell brought me back to my senses. It was Matt asking me to return. He needed a break from booth building and wanted me to go along to the Cave, a small food court in the Student Center.

My route to meet Matt took me past the Delta Lambda Nu or Delt booth. Beau rambled by as I attempted to figure out what the frat brothers were building. My attention was on the half-built structure and not the guys who were all bent over working. I was observing it when, in the middle of the construction site, one guy stood up. It was HIM. As he turned toward me, a slow smile crossed his face. My breath hitched as our eyes connected. He stood there, fixed, as he watched me ride by. I couldn't stop staring but managed to crack a smile. My heart picked up speed as Beau continued taking his time and I did nothing to encourage the animal to move faster. Liking what I saw, I wanted to enjoy this moment as long as possible. The closer I rode to my destination, the more my mystery man faded from my view.

Matt grabbed Beau by the reins and led him to a nearby tree, securing him to allow me to dismount. He came toward me with his arms outstretched. "Let me help you down." I threw my leg over the saddle horn and slid down into his arms. He gripped me around the waist and swung me around playfully. When we stopped, I noticed HIM standing near the street watching us. Matt leaned over and gave me a quick kiss. Before I knew it, he gripped my waist and tossed me over his shoulder. I was bent over, hanging there facing his back.

"Put. Me. Down! MAAATT! Please put me down." He just popped me on the butt and walked toward the Student Center. Looking up from my precarious position, I noticed Mr. Gorgeous was still observing us and grinning. I was so embarrassed, I went limp—just hanging there like a corpse swinging from side to side as Matt walked into the building.

After our break, we were leaving the Student Center when I noticed HE was across the street at a sorority booth talking to a petite girl with shoulder length blonde hair. They didn't look right for each other. He was tall, about 6' 2", nice physique, not too muscled, broad shoulders, with dark brown hair and hypnotic clear blue eyes. He was *so* handsome it made my heart flutter.

The closer we walked toward the pair, the more I had to control my compelling need to stare. I forced myself to look at the ground, watching my feet move nearer to HIM. Unable to stand it any longer, I glanced up to see HIM looking at me. He half smiled. Quickly my gaze fell back at my feet. Summoning up enough nerve between my shortened breaths, I lifted my head, smiled, and winked. My heart skipped a beat when he returned the gesture. Fortunately, the blonde and Matt never noticed our indiscretion.

Back at the booth, Matt resumed his work and I took off running to find Abbey. She was lying on a blanket studying under the big oak tree in the front yard of the house where we rented a room. Out of breath, I yelled, "Abbey! Abbey!" and plopped down next to her. "I just saw the most *gorgeous* guy and he flirted with me. I wish you could've seen him. I'm dying to meet him," I sputtered out then rolled over on my back placing my hands behind my head, still gasping for air. After a few seconds, Garrett popped into my head. "Oh yeah, I met another guy. He's kinda cute and I have a date with him tomorrow night."

Abbey just stared at me with a dumbfounded look. "How do you do that? I want to know your secrets."

I tilted my head to the side, puzzled by her comment. "Secrets? You should know. You're my teacher."

The sound of male voices and laughter coming from the yard next door interrupted our conversation. The two houses were separated by a tall thick hedge about seven feet high. Both were rentals with one difference—our house had a landlady living in the residence with us. The one next door was just filled with a bunch of guys living on their own. The two houses had very different atmospheres. Ours was quiet and managed, while theirs was louder with more traffic.

Abbey and I had never met any of our neighbors, so we decided to sneak a peek through the bushes. My breathing faltered. HE was standing less than ten feet away. I shook Abbey's shoulder, never taking my eyes off him, as I pointed him out. "Surely he doesn't live there," I whispered. "Have you ever seen him before?" I could hardly contain myself.

"No, jeez, we spend too much time in class and the library," Abbey murmured while peeking through the hedge. Her eyes were as big as saucers.

HE was standing sideways, so only his profile was in view. Frustrated, I started to seek a better vantage point. Before I moved another guy joined the group. As HE turned to make room, he faced the hedge. For a short time, I was able to study his facial features. He was clean-shaven and his eyes were nicely set. The eyebrows were dark, but not too thick. He had a strong jawline, yet his face was gentle with the most compelling smile. Turning, he walked out of sight and my heart sank.

"WOW! He's hot." Abbey feigned a swoon, touching the back of her hand to her forehead and leaning back, and that made us giggle.

Realizing we had been too loud, we darted for the blanket to resume our studying facade. A few minutes later a guy came walking up the driveway toward us. Abbey and I glanced at each other surprised, watching him warily as he approached. She murmured from the side of her mouth, "Who the hell is that?"

Before I could say anything, the intruder was upon us. "Hey…I'm Brian. I live next door. We heard some strange noises coming from this side of the bushes, so I was sent over to investigate." He gave us a questioning look, most likely in reference to our giggling. We offered no explanation. His eyes scanned me. "Hey, weren't you the girl riding the horse on campus today?"

"Yes, why?"

"One of my frat brothers was just asking about you. No one knew who you were." He pointed a thumb over his shoulder to the house next door.

"Oh! Really?" I was praying it was the gorgeous one who was so interested.

"What's your name?"

"Belinda, and this is Abbey." My throat went dry. Keeping my voice monotone, I tried to mask my excitement. "Who wants to know?"

"Robert. I'll have to tell him that you live here. So I guess you didn't see anything over by the bushes?" Abbey and I shook our heads, denying everything. "Well, it was nice meeting you. I have to get back. See you around." As he turned to go, I noticed he half smiled, and assumed he knew we were the spies they heard laughing.

Full of excitement, I tugged at Abbey. "I wonder if it was HIM asking about me. How can I find out?"

"You could always pry it out of Brian the next time you see him. Just bat those baby blues at him and he'll tell you anything." Abbey was teasing in her usual witty way as she closed her book to head inside.

"Oh yeah." I rolled my eyes and head. "I'll probably never see him again. Look how long we've lived here and today was the first time we've ever met anyone from over there," I grumbled, pointing toward the hedge.

"I have a feeling you'll be meeting Mister Gorgeous pretty soon. Let's go get ready for the carnival."

Abbey and I attacked the closet, yanking clothes off hangers. I'm a blue jeans girl. That's all I like to wear. So my wardrobe consists of several styles of jeans, a variety of knit tops and blouses, and two dresses. Picking out something didn't take long, since we had decided to turn some heads by wearing our form-fitting jeans, V-neck sweaters, and three-inch mules. This look would complement our sassy sashay. I had decided to wear my hair down in soft curls that framed my face. The process of fixing hair and makeup, the little I wore, took up most of the time. During the dressing ritual, I stopped to glance over at Abbey and found her smiling like the proud mentor she was.

I taught Abbey a few things as well. One big side benefit of the modeling class was the development of my "sassy sashay." I was proud of it and excited to teach it to her. It went great with three-inch heels and snug jeans.

While I was putting the finishing touches on my hair, my cell phone rang. It was Garrett. "Hey there. Have you checked your calendar yet?"

"Oh, hi, umm...hold on for a second." Picking up the nearest book, I ruffled through the pages close to my phone, pretending to check my calendar. "Nope. It looks like tomorrow evening is clear. Should I pencil you in?"

There was a snickering on the other end. "Yes, but please use a pen. I'll pick you up at 5:30." He briefly paused. "Exactly how much time will you be able to spare?"

"We can't make it too late. I have an early class in the morning." I liked that he had a good sense of humor and could play along with me.

"Okay, we can manage that."

"Will you be at the carnival tonight?" I was curious if I'd see him there.

"I'm actually at my parents' home right now, but I'll be back tomorrow afternoon."

Abbey and I headed straight for the Theta Kappa booth. Brent and Matt, our dates, were busy with the final set-up. I wanted to walk around and check out each booth, but Abbey preferred to hang with Brent. I told her I'd hook up with her on my second go-round so we could play some of the games and check out the band.

The Theta Kappa booth, a dart game, was near the end of one side of the street. I walked past the last few booths, checking them out, and then crossed over to the other row of booths, looking at each one as I strolled by.

I was almost halfway down the row when two fraternity brothers approached me. One of them said that I was under arrest and had to go to jail for five minutes or until I "made bail." Someone had paid them to put me in there. Toy plastic handcuffs were fastened on my wrists. Giggling, I played along. They led me over to the Delt area and put me in the jail-like enclosure I had seen being built earlier.

I wondered if Matt might have done this as a joke and I'd see him smiling or laughing at me. Curiosity got the better of me, so I moved to the front right corner of the structure to look in his direction. To my surprise, his attention was zoned in on a group of giddy females.

Suddenly, I felt a strange new feeling as a hand touched my arm. It was like an electric pulse. It didn't hurt, but was rather a pleasant, arousing sensation. However, it did surprise me and I jumped back just as I heard a male voice. "Sorry, I didn't mean to startle you." I looked up just as he pulled his hand back through the bars. He was studying his palm with a confused look on his face. My heart skipped a beat and then started racing. I froze, speechless. It was HIM. He was absolutely magnificent. I could only imagine the flabbergasted look on my face with my eyes wide and my mouth agape.

When he looked back at me, his expression changed to one of concern as he gripped the bars. "Are you okay?"

I took a deep breath. "Yes, but when you touched me it…oh, never mind." I bowed my head as I felt myself start to blush, wondering how you'd tell someone you don't know that his touch is…arousing?

He furrowed his brow. "What were you going to say?"

I looked up at him and just stared. His gaze captivated me and I didn't answer him for a few seconds. I just took in his expression until I realized he expected an answer. "Ah…oh, nothing," I stammered, too embarrassed to tell the truth.

He appeared baffled as the corners of his mouth slowly turned up into a smile. "You're the girl on the horse this morning. I was hoping I'd get to meet you. I'm Robert Pennington."

"Hi." I shyly glanced away, then looked back into his face. "I'm Belinda Davies. I was also wondering who you were. I've been here two and a half years and have never seen you around campus before."

"I've been here three and a half years and have never seen you either. How strange." He raised an eyebrow and grinned. "You'd be hard to miss." He paused to size me up. "I thought I'd already met all the beautiful young ladies on campus." He hesitated, studying my face. "Was that your boyfriend you were with earlier today?"

"No, he's just a guy I'm seeing."

He cocked his head to one side. "Exclusively?"

"No." I beamed with excitement at what might be coming next. My heart leapt as I waited in anticipation.

"Would you like to go out sometime? Say, tomorrow evening?"

Yes! My insides were jumping around in circles as I tried to keep my outside calm. *Oh nooo.* Realizing that I already had a date, my tone saddened. "I can't. I've already made plans. Sorry."

He looked disappointed but jumped right in with his next question. "What about dinner on Tuesday?"

"That'll work for me." I had to restrain my excitement. *Play it cool. Keep it light.* My tutor Abbey's little voice was in my head warning me.

"What's your favorite food?"

"Mexican and Italian."

"My favorites as well. I'll take you to my favorite Mexican restaurant. Is five okay?"

"Yes."

Our conversation was interrupted when one of the jailers told me that I was free to go. As I turned to leave, he reached through the bars taking hold of my arm and asked for my cell number. His touch caused that pleasant electric feeling within me again, surprising me. I attempted to pull away.

Quickly, he released me. "Did I hurt you?"

"No." With a sense of excitement, I grasped my arm where he touched me. I wasn't about to tell him it was so titillating. After giving him my cell number, I hesitated, wanting to stay there talking to him, but knew there was no reason to linger. So I ended our encounter. "Bye."

I flashed him a bashful smile and strolled as casually as possible toward Matt's booth, occasionally looking back. When I was out of Robert's sight, I ran to Abbey, pulling her aside so Matt and Brent couldn't overhear. I was ecstatic. "Abbey, I met HIM. Someone had me put in the Delt jail and he talked to me. I have a date with him Tuesday."

We hugged each other, jumping up and down, squealing like junior high girls. "What's his name?"

"Robert Pennington."

Abbey's eyes widened. "The 'Robert' that was asking about you?"

I shrugged my shoulders. "I guess. He said he was hoping to meet me."

"Do you think he had you put in there?"

"I'm sure Matt didn't do it. So, maybe it was him. Something strange happened every time he touched me." I rubbed my arm where he made contact.

"What?"

I made my voice as low and sexy as I could. "A kind of exhilarating feeling. It's kinda scary. Nothing like that has ever happened before."

Abbey was about to ask a question, I'm sure exploring for more details, when Matt and Brent hollered for us to come back to the booth. They wanted to know what was going on. "Oh, nothing," we answered, grinning at each other as we approached them.

"We're going to play some games. See you later." I waved as we walked past without stopping to offer any further explanation.

We made our way around from booth to booth trying different games. At the Delt jail, Robert wasn't there. So, feeling impish, I paid the Delt police to find and arrest him. I asked them to tell him one word – PAYBACK. Abbey and I made the rounds of the remaining booths, but stayed within close proximity of the jail so I could see Robert being placed in confinement. Almost finished with the bean bag toss, I glanced over my shoulder and saw the Delt police with their next prisoner. Once imprisoned, Robert walked to the bars and peered out. Within seconds his gaze met mine and it flustered me. A smile spread across his face when he raised his hand pointing his right index finger as if he were shooting me. I returned his gesture with a smile. My eyes stayed fixed on him until I felt Abbey tug my arm, pulling me away to go listen to the music playing at the end of the street.

We decided to go check in with our dates first, but they were busy flirting with some girls, which was fine with me. Matt and I weren't exclusive and his other interests made it easier for me to explore my own pursuits. So Abbey and I just continued strolling toward the band.

Our path took us past the jail that temporarily housed Robert. When he spotted me, he smiled and winked. I flashed a coy wave, peering over my shoulder with a smug smile across my face. The whole time my attention was locked on his clear blue eyes. Our gaze broke only after I walked out of our line of sight. I took a deep breath to refocus, then turned and caught up to Abbey who had walked ahead.

We stood as close as we could to the band, swaying to the music, until Brent showed up and asked Abbey to dance, leaving me alone. I continued to move back and forth to the rhythm when a hand rested on my arm. Immediately my body flooded with electrifying sexual awareness from the touch, telling me who it was before I heard, "May I have this dance?" I looked around and up to see Robert and, of course, I said yes.

His touch took my breath away as he slid his hand down my arm into mine and led me into the crowd. When we stopped, he placed his other hand at my waist. He held my hand close between our chests. I hoped he couldn't feel my heart racing. I put my arm around his shoulder and slid my hand up the back of his neck into his thick hair. He leaned his head back into it, closed his eyes and exhaled before he focused his eyes back on mine. I think he enjoyed my touch.

I was locked on his questioning eyes as we moved as one to the rhythm of the music. With every sway, I could feel a strange new sensation creep into my soul. At first I wasn't sure what was taking place. I was searching my mind trying to figure it out. Slowly, a hint of awareness crawled into my consciousness. I was feeling a new emotion that was exhilarating. Never had I felt anything like this before…with anyone. I never took my eyes off Robert and when the song ended neither of us let go. We just stood there in silence with him peering at me, his head cocked to the side.

The next song the band played had a hot tempo. "I don't know how to dance to this."

He had a seductive look and a mischievous grin. "I do." With my hand clutched in his, he spun me out away from him and pulled me back into his chest. With his hand at my waist he pulled me closer with a quick tug. His alluring blue eyes held mine as our bodies moved in tandem. Again he spun me out, then pulled me to him with my back to his chest. I could feel his warm rapid breath on my neck as he ran his hands down the sides of my body. Suddenly I was back facing him, his hand at my waist holding me close, our other hands clutched between us. With his lips inches from mine, I lusted for their taste. His sultry blue eyes peered into the depth of my soul. Heat pulsed through my veins and at that moment, I knew I was his.

Rhythmically, I moved with him. His body seemed to be communicating with mine. Overwhelmed by my feelings, I thought my heart would leap out of my chest. To break the trance and gain control of myself, I glanced away for a second and noticed people were staring at us. I whispered, "We're being watched." He looked up into the crowd and smiled, mumbling something about being lost in the moment. He started to return his gaze to me when he saw something or someone and abruptly stopped dancing.

He glanced around the dance area in haste, then took my arm leading me to the opposite side as he spoke into my ear over the loud music. "I thought you said you couldn't dance to this music. You were great."

"I can't. You're a good leader." I gave that feeble excuse not wanting to admit to him it was like his body was telling mine what to do.

Seeming nervous, Robert scanned the crowd and grumbled, "I have to go.

See you Tuesday." He disappeared as fast as he'd arrived, leaving me standing there wondering what the hell just happened. I replayed the dance in my head. He obviously was into it as much as I was. His swift departure confused me.

I needed to talk to Abbey without worrying about Matt overhearing us. Hoping he wouldn't be there, I was relieved he was nowhere in sight as I made my way through the crowd to her and Brent.

"HOT mama!" Brent then gave a catcall as he looked me up and down with exaggerated, seductive eye movements.

With a wide-eyed look, Abbey took hold of my shoulders, giving me an excited shake. "Where did you learn to dance like that?!"

"I *don't* know how to dance to that. It seemed like his body was telling mine how to move." I was still trying to figure out what exactly just happened.

"I thought you two were going to make out, the way you were looking at each other. Steamy! Where did he go?" Abbey's eyes were searching through the crowd as she rubbernecked, attempting to obtain a better view.

I joined her in her search, looking around. "I don't know. He just said he had to leave." Suddenly it hit me. "He probably saw his date heading our way."

Matt made his way toward me. Clutching his hand, I led him into the crowd before Brent could mention my dance with Robert. As we moved to the music, Matt leaned toward my ear so I could hear him. "Are you ready to head to the frat house?"

"I guess so." I became painfully aware my interest in going out with Matt had disappeared. All my thoughts were on Robert and how he made me feel.

As we were leaving, I saw Robert with a petite blonde. She didn't look happy. He had a frown on his face and was doing all the talking. I wondered if she had seen us dancing and now he had some explaining to do.

CHAPTER 4

IT WAS SUNDAY morning and it was going to be a glorious, warm sunny day. Abbey was still asleep, so I decided to go lay under the big oak tree in the front yard for some serious study time. After dressing in a knit top and shorts, I picked up a blanket and my textbook then headed out and made myself comfortable. I sat back enjoying the peaceful environment, immersing myself in my required reading.

The campus was usually void after a night of heavy partying, with students still too hung over to get out of bed. I was making good use of the quiet until the silence was broken by the familiar sound of hooves on pavement. It was Matt on Beau galloping toward me. Matt leaped out of the saddle, snatching me up in his arms and planting a smack on my lips. "Hey, Babe. I need to kill some time."

During his impulsive move, my book was tossed into the air. It landed in the grass, inches from Beau's front hooves. Bending down to retrieve it, I took Beau's reins and started stroking his nose while talking in a gentle voice. "Hey Beau. Sorry, I don't have any carrots today." The animal nuzzled my hand searching for his usual treat.

"I suppose you'd like to ride Beau around the campus?" Matt half grinned.

"Can I?"

"Sure, take off." He gave me a leg up into the saddle and told me not to ride too long or I could get saddle sores. After all, in shorts and barefoot, I really wasn't dressed for riding. Matt walked to the tree and plopped down on my blanket. "I'll just lie here and wait for you. Anything good to read?" He picked up my textbook and frowned, tossing it aside.

"Hey, be careful with that." Scowling, I lifted Beau's reins to head for campus. I hadn't ridden far when someone called my name through the crisp spring air. I looked over my shoulder to see Garrett waving.

Garrett was about six feet tall with light brown hair which he wore spiked on top, just enough to give him a hint of the "bad boy" look. In my opinion, he could never pull off that persona. He had the sweetest face and gentle brown eyes that lit up when he smiled. His body was well-muscled with nicely defined arms.

"Are we still on for tonight?" He took hold of the bridle and stroked Beau's neck like he did before.

"Yes, of course." He seemed at ease around Beau. "Have you been around horses much?"

"I've been around a few in my life. I grew up on a ranch….Is 5:30 still okay?"

I smiled and nodded. "That's fine."

"How about a ride to the Student Center?"

"Sure, climb on." As soon as my foot was removed from the stirrup, Garrett hoisted himself up. He locked his powerful arms around my waist, then pressed his chest against my back and held me very close. His body against mine felt warm and inviting, but nowhere near the sensation I felt when I was in Robert's arms the night before.

Garrett was a good rider. He moved with the rhythm of Beau's gait. I moved along with the both of them and soon realized I wasn't the one controlling Beau even though I had the reins. Garrett had taken over using his legs and the horse was responding. I was just along for the ride.

When we arrived at the Student Center, I saw the Delt jail being torn down, but Robert wasn't around. I dropped Garrett off and took control of Beau.

"See you later." Garrett waved, walking toward the building.

Watching him leave, I knew I had a big problem because of the nagging memory of Robert in my brain. It insisted on rattling around in my head and always seemed to be there. I knew I would enjoy my date with Garrett, but now there would be three of us attending. I realized my thoughts of Robert would interfere, no matter how hard I tried to keep him out.

Beau and I were taking our time back to the house and were in front of my neighbor's when I saw Robert standing in the front yard talking to Brian. My heart immediately sped up and my stomach churned with excitement. From the corner of my eye, I saw him stare my way with an enduring smile. I smiled back but rode past, controlling my impulse to linger and possibly make a fool of myself.

Fortunately, my emotional switch turned off when I passed the hedge that shielded Robert from my view. The thrill of seeing him was now overshadowed by Matt dozing, propped against my favorite oak tree.

He opened his eyes as the clomping of hooves came closer to him. With a lazy stretch followed by a gaping yawn, he acknowledged my presence. "Well, I hope I've waited long enough so that they won't need my help tearing down the booth. I guess I'd better go check." He mounted Beau and was about to ride off. "How about coming to the fraternity baseball game tomorrow afternoon?"

I gave him a nod of approval.

As soon as Matt was gone, I studied the hedge, the only thing that stood between me and Robert. The sound of a car starting caused me to glance toward the street and see Robert drive by. He looked my way and nodded as he sped up, squealing his tires. Just the sight of him sent my insides into a frenzy.

My busy morning killed my interest in studying, so I gathered everything up and went inside to see if Abbey was awake. She was lying across her bed with her nose buried in a textbook. "Where've you been?"

"I was outside reading when Matt stopped by on Beau. He was trying to avoid helping with the booth teardown, so he let me take a ride on Beau while he napped under the tree. On my ride, I saw Garrett and confirmed my date." I paused, coming up for air. "I just saw Robert and he flirted with me."

Abbey momentarily broke her concentration to look at me. "Boy, you had a busy morning." She pointed toward my phone. "You need to check your cell—it rang two times while you were out."

"Oh. I forgot I left it up here." My phone really wasn't forgotten. Sunday morning was a quiet time for me, so I usually left it in my room. Besides, up until this school year, the phone rarely rang. It was something I used to stay in touch with Abbey or my parents. Now I found the need for my phone increasing as my social life picked up. I still couldn't quite grasp it being a necessity. My inner self liked having the control to have quiet time, and not having the phone with me every minute assured that.

Now, I had two calls in less than an hour. Go figure. The first one was from Robert. *Well, shit*! The second was from Garrett. The time indicated that he had called before I saw him. He was probably just confirming our date.

Standing there, I looked at the missed call alert from Robert. I thought about returning it, but didn't want to seem too eager. I was interested in him and after our encounters, I just couldn't stop thinking about him. With all the strength I could muster, I ignored the call, placing my cell in my purse, then headed for my closet to pick out an outfit. He would have to wait. I had a date tonight to get ready for.

***

I sat at the window waiting for Garrett. At 5:30 on the dot, he pulled into the driveway. Hearing the door bell, I bounced down the stairs and swung open the door. "Hey. You're right on time." He gave his head a single nod in recognition of his punctuality. With his hand on my back, we walked to his car, a shiny jet black Mustang. "Nice car."

Garrett glanced at me. "You like Mustangs?"

"Yeah, they're one of my favorites. They're horses." I smiled as I slipped into the seat. He chuckled.

While we were driving, our conversation was consumed by our majors and decisions that led to our chosen fields of study. Garrett was very proud of himself because he had just been accepted into grad school. He said he was surprised that he had never seen me around campus until now. I explained that my study habits made me somewhat reclusive, but there didn't seem to be the need to tell him about my lack of a social life the first two years because of my appearance. Chances are he had seen me, but didn't remember or chose not to.

When we arrived at the restaurant, he opened the doors and seated me. He asked what I wanted, then ordered my meal. He was a perfect gentleman, however, if he tried to cut up my meat, that's where I'd draw the line.

"Where are you from?" He took a bite of a chip.

"Sugar Land. It's a small city southwest of Houston. Where are you from?" I picked up a chip.

"Athens…Texas," he clarified. "You know, I have a friend from Sugar Land. Well…his parents live there. He never has."

"Oh. Who?" I popped the chip into my mouth.

"Robert Pennington."

I almost choked on my tortilla chip. *Oh crap*! Dating friends would *not* be a good idea. Now I had a dilemma on my hands. I managed to recover from the news by changing the subject to Garrett's family. We continued conversing after our food arrived, never returning to the subject of Robert, but he remained in my head, teasing me and interfering with my time with Garrett.

As we walked to Garrett's car, he asked, "Do you like to play pool?"

"Yes, but I haven't played for a while."

"You up for a game?"

"Sure. Are we going to the rec room at the Student Center?"

"No, the frat house."

I glanced at him. "Which one?"

"Delt."

Wide-eyed and mouth agape, I stopped dead in my tracks and spat out, "You're a Delt?"

Garrett was a few steps ahead of me by then, when he turned back in my direction, appearing perplexed. "Is there something wrong?"

"I didn't know you're a Delt." Now, I had a *real* dilemma on my hands, having made dates with two frat brothers who also were friends. "Ah, I have a big problem." My heart sank like a stone from the news.

"What?"

"I accepted a date with one of your brothers. I didn't know, so I'll just cancel. That will take care of it." *Well, damn*!

Our drive to the frat house was relatively quiet with spurts of superficial conversation. I could tell Garrett was very curious about the other frat brother, but he continued to be a gentleman and didn't bring up the subject.

The first thing I did when we arrived at the Delt house was scan the place for Robert, who thankfully wasn't there. Garrett was watching me check out the room as we headed for the pool table. "Is he here?"

I gave him a stern look and ignored him by setting up the balls. "Do you want to break?"

Garrett picked up a cue stick, chalked the end, and broke. One ball went into a pocket. He sank three more, then missed.

Bending over the table to take a shot, I heard Robert's voice. Taken by surprise, I froze. My face and hair were hidden behind Garrett. All Robert could possibly see were my long legs and butt in a tight pair of fitted jeans.

Robert let out a small grunt. "How about a challenge, us against you two?"

"You're on....Hey, I'd like you to meet my date, Belinda." Garrett stepped aside. "Belinda, this is Robert and his girlfriend, Lora."

Girlfriend? Taking careful aim, I sank my shot, then looked up at them and smiled, still bent over the pool table. "Nice to meet you." I hoped he'd play along and not let Garrett know he met me earlier.

Lora gave me a once over and snooty half-grin. Robert had a surprised look on his face that broke into a smile as he eyed my position. He let out a barely audible chuckle as he extended his hand to me. "Nice to meet you."

Standing to face him, I looked at his hand, then backed up a step from him. I tightened my grip on the cue stick. I still wasn't sure what I felt when we danced and this was not the time or place for me to try to figure it out, so I evaded his touch, avoiding any sensations. "Nice to meet you too." By the look on his face, he seemed to understand and dropped his hand to his side.

Garrett was already racking the balls. "We'll let the girls start. Who wants to break?"

"No, you guys start. You can probably break better than we can." I wanted to see how skillful they were. Garrett told Robert to break. He sank four balls. Garrett sank three. Lora sank one.

Now it was "show time." I kicked off my espadrilles, then named the ball color and which pocket it would sink in. I had balls ricocheting off sides and dropping in. Pretty soon, my playing skills attracted the attention of other people who were encircling the table to watch. I sank all the remaining balls with everyone in awe of my little side show.

Garrett looked amazed. "How did you do that?"

"A guy I used to hang around with taught me."

***

Pool had become a real pastime for me during the first two years of college. I first noticed Gary in the recreation room. I would sit somewhere close to the pool tables acting like I was studying. Instead, I watched his every move as he struck the balls so they would dramatically hit the sides of the table before sinking into their intended pocket. When he left, I'd try to copy his moves. To my surprise, some of the balls would sink in, but not enough to make a real difference between luck and skill. Something was missing.

After a few months of just watching, Gary startled me one afternoon by walking up to my table. I nearly fell out of my chair and didn't know what to do. He laughed a little at my reaction, then sat down. From that day on, he became my pool buddy. He taught me the final piece of the puzzle, the physics of pool. When he graduated, he left me with the skills to challenge anyone to a decent game.

***

"Garrett, you're dating a pool shark." Robert was standing there with a sweet grin on his handsome face.

I was lost in Robert's expression when Garrett planted a surprise kiss on me. He pulled me closer and kissed me more passionately. My thoughts moved from Robert back to Garrett, long enough for me to enjoy our encounter. The kiss was nice, but nothing else. Still in Garrett's arms I mentioned, "It's getting late. I think I should go home." I glanced back at Robert, but he had turned away from us and was talking to Lora.

As we were leaving, I told Robert and Lora it was nice meeting them and I had enjoyed the game. Robert just shook his head. "Amazing."

Garrett was full of pool questions on the way home. Thank goodness my house wasn't very far away. He walked me to my front door and said he had a great time, and then he kissed me with his warm firm lips. The kiss was pleasant and that was all. "I'll call you soon. Good night." He had walked down a few steps off the porch when he hesitated and turned back. "Was he there tonight?" I just smiled and went in.

Running upstairs, I burst open the door to our room to tell Abbey about my night…and the complications. "Abbey. Garrett and Robert are friends and frat brothers. I can't date both of them. I have to break my date with Robert. Shit! He was the one I wanted to go out with. Why is life so comp…"

My cell phone rang before I could finish my sentence. It was Robert. I answered, feeling my world was about to end.

"Belinda. Hey. I'm sorry, but I have to cancel our date. A problem has developed."

"I know. I'm sorry. I didn't know you both were Delts and friends when I accepted the date."

"When did you meet Garrett?" He sounded somewhat disappointed.

"Saturday morning, while riding Beau around campus."

"Garrett's my best friend. I can't date you while he is. Sorry."

"I know." My heart was breaking. This guy was getting under my skin and I couldn't shake off the thought of him. Even if I did continue seeing Garrett, Robert would be right there with us, preoccupying my mind.

"Well, I guess that's it. I'll see you around." There was a long pause then he ended with, "Good night."

I sighed. "Good night." I wanted to cry. Throwing the phone on the bed, I looked at Abbey. "How can this be happening to me? I go two years without a real date, get a date with two guys on the same day, meet the guy of my dreams, and then dream guy and the other guy are friends and frat brothers to boot." I threw my hands up in the air. "Then, I have to cancel the date with the guy of my dreams because he asked me last. I can't catch a break!" I dropped down on my bed and glanced at the ceiling. The room went silent.

Abbey's voice turned soft, almost cautious-sounding. "How'd the date go with Garrett?"

I rolled over, taking a deep breath before continuing to tell her about the night and how my pool lessons paid off during the challenge against Robert and his girlfriend, Lora. With Abbey satisfied with the details, I went to the bathroom to get ready for bed.

Turning off the bathroom light, I entered a dark bedroom. Abbey was asleep. I crawled into my bed. The light from the street lamp outside our window filtered through the lace curtains causing shapes to form on the ceiling. As I stared up, the day's events flowed through my mind. Sleep came, but it was restless because my heart was breaking over a guy I didn't even know.

CHAPTER 5

AFTER CLASS ON Monday, I strolled along my usual route to the library, but was intercepted by Matt who invited me to go to the Cave. The tables there were staked out by fraternities in a self-assigned manner. Matt seated me in the Theta Kappa section. While he went to purchase sodas for us, Garrett and Robert came in. Robert was staring at me while he walked to the Delt area. I tried to ignore him. When I did look up, he had seated himself facing me and our eyes met. My heart immediately went into overdrive as my breathing increased. But our gaze was soon broken when Matt returned and sat blocking my view.

Matt noticed me peering over his shoulder. He glanced back and scowled. "Two Delts are looking over here. One's Pennington. Do you know him?"

"I've met him. We were supposed to go on a date, but it was canceled. The other one is Garrett Barnett. He's a friend."

"You were going to go out with Pennington? I'm glad it was canceled. I've heard he dates a girl until he bags her and then dumps her."

"You know he won't get it from me," I boasted, feeling a bit insulted that he thought I couldn't handle myself around Robert.

Matt half smiled and nodded, then continued on his soapbox a little longer. Garrett saw me glance toward the Delt table and waved me over. "I think I should go say 'hi'. Thanks for the drink." I raised my cup to Matt and headed across the room. "I'll catch up with you at the game."

"Hey. Why are you sitting over there?" Garrett offered me a chair between Robert and him. It was difficult being so close to Robert, but I had no choice. I had to try to be cordial to both of them. Robert repositioned himself, accidentally brushing his arm against mine. A pleasant sensation hit me, and I jerked back, scooting my chair away from him to avoid a recurrence. Garrett noticed my reaction. "Uh, what just happened?" Robert and I looked at each other, but said nothing. Garrett told Robert to touch my arm. Robert slowly raised his hand and ever so gently slid his fingers over my forearm. I instantly tensed, feeling the sensation come over me. Robert's touch was light, smooth and lingering which caused a stronger response. My breath hitched as a slow pulse ran up my spine. Robert tensed. Glancing at his hand, he looked puzzled flexing it.

Garrett's eyes widened, seeming mystified. "O…K." I just sat there trying not to be obvious. I hoped he would drop the subject, but I wasn't so lucky. Garrett touched my other arm, appearing baffled when nothing happened. He kept looking back and forth at Robert and me. "What's going on?"

In unison, Robert and I said, "I don't know." He appeared to be as bewildered as I was.

"I seem to be extra sensitive to his touch. That's the best way I can describe it. He's the first one I've ever experienced that with." I looked shyly at Robert then back to Garrett. This conversation was too uncomfortable and I needed an out. I glanced at my watch. "I need to go to class." Standing, I picked up my things to leave.

Garrett followed suit. "I'll walk you there."

We walked outside in silence, then he asked, "He's the other Delt who asked you out, isn't he?" I didn't respond, gripping my books just a bit tighter across my chest. "I heard about a steamy dance between him and a knockout with long golden brown hair. That was you, wasn't it?"

"The date was canceled." This situation had me so confused. Garrett was a nice guy. He would be a good catch for someone, but I knew that someone wasn't me. I couldn't get my mind off Robert.

"When did you two meet?"

"The Delt jail. He introduced himself and asked me out."

He put his arm around my shoulders as we walked. "I really like you, but you two seem to have something going on here." He stopped and turned me toward him. Placing one hand under my chin, he lifted my face to his. "I don't want to fall for you and then lose you later. I'll tell him to ask you out, so the two of you can figure out what's happening."

"You sure?" My eyes began to moisten because he had just handed me the opportunity of my life.

"Yes. I'll take my chances."

"I just heard something about his reputation."

He looked at me baffled. "What?...What did you hear?"

"That he dates a girl until he gets you-know-what and then moves on."

He cocked his head and spat out, "What? Robert's a great guy! Girls throw themselves at him. He's like a magnet. Besides, he just hasn't found the right girl yet. He's only been dating Lora, but I guess that's ending now since he met you. Go out—give him a chance."

When we reached the library, I turned to Garrett and hugged him. "I hope he knows what a good friend you are. Thanks. See you later."

***

Opening the door, I stepped out and found myself in the cool dry air of a Texas spring afternoon. I paused to take in my surroundings. The sun was just starting to set behind the taller buildings, casting shadows that gave a romantic mystique to the pathways. All over the campus there were flowering trees blooming in their splendor and shedding petals like snowflakes on the passers-by. This was the type of afternoon I wished I could share with someone special. Robert was first on my mind.

From the steps of the library, I saw Robert and Lora leaving the Student Center together. I wished I could've been a fly on the wall to hear what their conversation was about. I wondered if he would break up with her to date me. My walk home took a little more time than usual. There was a lot on my mind.

Abbey wasn't at the house when I arrived. I tossed my books on my bed and left to go to the Theta Kappa baseball game. Since it was a nice afternoon, I decided to walk.

The large, freshly mowed field was busy with three fraternity baseball games. The area was crawling with frat brothers and their girlfriends, sorority sisters and others like me, invited guests. As I approached the Theta Kappa side, Matt saw me and came running over. "Hey doll, I'm glad you came." He picked me up and swung me around as he hugged me.

"Who are you playing against?"

"The Delts." Just as he answered, I saw Robert and Lora standing off to the left of home plate. Robert was watching me. I smiled at him and nodded before turning my attention back to Matt.

I leaned close to him. "What position do you play?" Matt explained he was the catcher and his team was doing very well this year. They had won three out of four games.

He looked toward his frat brothers gathering at home plate. "Stay here, I'll be back after the game." When Matt left, I turned and looked Robert's way. He had his arm around Lora's waist and was leaning over listening to her. She wrapped her arms around his neck. Allowing her a brief kiss, he then pulled away and walked over to his frat brothers at home plate.

An umpire flipped a coin. From the Theta Kappa's reactions I surmised they won the toss as the teams moved into position. Each side had good players and their abilities provided the spectators an exciting, fast-moving game. I cheered aloud for Matt, but silently and truly for Robert because that was all I could do when he made a hit or scored a run.

Robert was the Delt third baseman, positioned in direct sight of where I was standing. During the course of the game I caught myself staring at him, admiring the fit of his team t-shirt. It was snug to his body, accentuating his upper arms and shoulder muscles. Our eyes met often. It was very hard to look away from him. He must have had the same problem because he let a hard grounder down the third base line get past him, costing his team a run. Lora eventually noticed him looking at my side of the field. With a scowl, she started eyeing everyone then stopped when she reached me and gave me a dirty look. Her glare was scary and it made me feel very uncomfortable. I tried to avoid looking at Robert after that, but I just couldn't.

When the game ended, the score was very close—THETA, 7; DELT, 6. After celebrating the win, Matt returned and invited me to go eat with him and his friends. I congratulated him on the win, but declined the invitation. He offered to drop me off at the house on his way to the restaurant.

As we walked to his car, I noticed Lora watching me. When she saw me glance over, she threw her arms around Robert's neck and gave him a kiss, then glared spitefully over his shoulder at me. I wondered how she knew it was me he was looking at. I wasn't the only girl standing over there. There was something evil about her stare that made me uneasy.

Abbey was home studying when I walked in. "Where've you been?"

"Oh. I forgot to tell you. I went to Matt's game and guess who they were playing and who was there with his girlfriend?"

She blurted out, "The Delts? And Robert brought Lora? Awkward!"

"Extremely. They seemed rather cozy together. Then she noticed Robert glancing over to our team's side and started scanning until she stopped at me." I shuddered. "She's crazy scary." I changed the subject telling Abbey about earlier in the day when Robert touched me at the Delt table in front of Garrett. "He told me to go out with Robert. Can you believe it?"

"I agree with him. There might be something there and you need to find out what. Besides it sounds like it could be fun exploring." Abbey raised her brows in a devilish manner."

"Abbey!" I squealed. "Okay, enough of that! I'm going to bed."

After cleaning up, I crawled onto my comfy mattress. Abbey continued studying. "Good night." I turned off my light on the nightstand and barely heard Abbey say good night as I fell asleep.

About ten p.m. Abbey shook my shoulder, awakening me from my dream of Robert. "Belinda, wake-up. Your cell phone is ringing. It's Robert!"

"What? Who?" I croaked, half-awake.

"Robert's calling," Abbey repeated, handing me the phone.

"H-hello," I stuttered.

"Belinda, its Robert. Come outside."

"Come outside? I'm in bed." His request was confusing.

"Get dressed and come outside...*please*."

"Okay. Give me a minute." I slipped into my robe and bunny slippers, and was about to leave when a thought came to me. Putting my hand to my mouth, I checked my breath, then stopped in the bathroom for a quick touchup.

To avoid waking up my landlady, I tiptoed down the stairs. Once on the porch, I scanned the yard until I located Robert standing next to the big oak tree off to the side of the house. "What's up?" I clutched my robe tightly around me.

"I'd like to try...." He trailed off his statement as his eyes made their way to my feet. "Are those bunny slippers?" He snickered.

"They are bunnies. What were you saying? You'd like to try what?" I was confused and impatient. "What do you want? I'm getting cold and my bunnies are getting wet." I stomped my feet and glanced down at them.

He returned to his reason for waking me up. "I want to try something."

"Try what?" Now I was more confused than ever as to his motive for this late visit. My eyes roamed over his face. He was so good-looking and in the moonlight, he looked even better. His face and demeanor were distracting me, making it difficult to concentrate.

"Let me explain. I also..." He lowered his head, obviously having difficulty trying to explain what he came to tell me. Taking a few seconds and without looking at me, he started again. "I also feel something. Your touch excites me...I mean...ah...I feel....Oh, I don't know." He gave me a quick glance. When he saw me just standing and listening he continued. "I want to kiss you and see what happens." Now he was observing me. Our eyes connected and I stood listening for what was to come next. I nodded my head toward him, but didn't say a word. "So, are you up for experimenting? But don't tell Garrett about this, okay?"

I gave him a curious look at his strange request. "I...I guess so."

He moved closer to me, making a motion to put his arm around my waist then stopped. "You're shorter than I remember."

I pointed to my bunnies. "No heels."

"Of course, cute slippers by the way."

"Thanks." I was trying to play it cool on the outside, but inside I was a nervous wreck. My mind and heart were running a mile a minute.

He put one arm around my waist pulling me close as he lifted me off my feet. With his other hand, he raised my face up to his as I softened and molded to his body. His touch gave me that pulsating feeling inside, but when his lips touched mine—Oh God! The intense desire that came over me was overwhelming. Strange feelings I had never experienced before. I gasped as an electrifying surge raced up my spine, firing every neuron in me. My back arched as my body stiffened, my hands slid up the back of his neck and my fingers entwined into his thick hair. I couldn't pull his body close enough. With a surge of emotion, I seemed to meld to him. My heart pounded wildly. When I wrapped my legs around him, his breathing became more ragged and he pushed me up against the tree. My back arched again as he peppered kisses over every inch of my neck. I tightened my grip around his neck, finding his willing mouth then kept him lip locked. His hands were kneading my upper thighs when suddenly he pushed them away, then pulled at my wrists, until I was no longer in his arms. Feeling a rippling sensation inside, I braced myself against the tree as Robert backed away.

Looking dazed, he shook his head. "Whoa! That's never happened before." He was panting like he had just run a race.

"I can't believe I did that. I'm so embarrassed." My chest was heaving as fast as his. "It was like I didn't have any control over my body. I need to stay away from you." I turned to run, but he seized me, pulling me back into his arms, and kissed me again. All the sensations started again with more intensity.

I found myself losing control in the arms of a stranger and struggled not to let that happen. I pushed him away. We stood staring at each other—panting, sucking in air. He appeared puzzled, his brow drawn and his head cocked. As panic came over me, I repeated, "I *have* to stay away from you," then turned and ran into the house leaving him standing there with no further explanation.

I ran up to my room and rushed over to look out the bedroom window. Pulling the lace curtain aside, I saw him just standing in the front yard with his back to the house. His silhouette was backlit in the filtered light of the street lamp. Broad shoulders, strong arms, and slender hips were visible as I relived the events that took place just moments ago. He turned and looked up at me. My heart skipped a beat and I froze. We stood watching each other, neither one of us moving. And then he turned and walked to his car, shaking his head.

Abbey came to the window. "What's going on?"

I watched Robert as he drove away. Still reeling and stunned, I continued staring out the window. "He kissed me and my body went berserk. I attacked him. It was like...like I had no control." Bewildered, I turned toward Abbey.

"Are you alright?"

In a muted voice I answered, "He just came over to kiss me. I didn't want it to end." Abbey's eyes widened and I knew she would want more details. Still dazed, I couldn't talk about it right then. My heart was pounding from the thought of him and how he looked in the light, watching me from the yard. "I'm tired right now. I'll tell you about it later."

There was disappointment in Abbey's eyes, but she knew not to press me if I didn't want to talk. "You promise. You have to tell me everything." Excitement rose in her tone as her eyes enlarged.

"I promise." I tried keeping my voice calm considering I was in turmoil over a person I barely knew. This was one time I didn't think I could tell her everything. She would get an abbreviated version.

After crawling back into bed, I lay there reliving the kiss over and over again in my mind. Every replay of the event caused my heart to race and my breathing to accelerate.

About half an hour later, my cell chirped, indicating a text message.

Robert:	Garrett called. Date back on?
Me:	NO
Robert:	Why?
Me:	I can't.
Robert:	Why? ☹
Me:	Afraid.
Robert:	Promise not to take advantage.
Me:	No, me.
Robert:	???
Me:	My control.
Robert:	Promise, won't do anything. Give me a chance. ☹
Me:	Promise?
Robert:	YES
Me:	Ok
Robert:	☺☺☺

I looked at Abbey. "My date with Robert is back on. I'm not going to be able to sleep." My eyes went back to the phone that was clutched tight in my hand. At the present time, it was my only direct link to Robert.

I kept replaying the kiss in my mind, not wanting to forget the feelings. Every hour on the hour, I looked at the clock. My alarm buzzed before my eyes even closed. After it was turned off, I fell asleep from sheer exhaustion.

CHAPTER 6

"BELINDA! WAKE UP. You're going to be late to class," Abbey called out from across the room while she was dressing.

Leaping out of bed, I hit the shower, dressed and took off running to class. My cell started ringing. I was digging in my purse looking for it when I plowed straight into Robert, almost losing my footing. My cell stopped ringing. When I looked up, he had his phone in his hand turning it off, and slid it into his pocket. Me bouncing off his chest must have been amusing because he was grinning from ear to ear.

"Oh, hey. I can't stop. I'm running late for class." I had turned away from him and was walking backwards, putting distance between us.

"Meet me outside the Student Center after you're finished."

"Okay." Turning, I started to run again. There were only a few minutes left to reach the classroom. I was *never* late for class. I ran as fast as I could, sitting down just as the professor started his lecture, which turned out to be the most boring one of the day.

Thank heavens class let out twenty minutes early. I headed to the Student Center but didn't want to stand around outside waiting for Robert. So, I went into the Cave, intending to come back in plenty of time for our meet.

Garrett was sitting in the Delt section, so I asked if I could join him. "Sure, you know you're always welcome." He pulled a chair out for me.

"Thanks. My date with Robert is back on for tonight, but I'm still nervous to be around him."

"Don't be. Everything will be alright. If he doesn't behave, he'll have to answer to me." He smiled, putting up two fists. One look at Garrett's arms convinced me Robert would be outmatched.

About fifteen minutes into our conversation, I looked at my watch and realized I was going to be late for my rendezvous. I glanced toward the entrance and saw Robert walking in with Lora. Stunned and fully aware of my royal screw up, I focused on Garrett. "I have to go. I forgot to review for a quiz for my next class. See ya."

I needed to leave before they reached the table because I didn't want to be in close proximity to Lora. To avoid any contact with the couple, I skirted around the interior of the room and headed for the door. My attempted stealthy escape was not successful. As I approached the door of the food court, Robert saw me. Our eyes met. Shaking off his gaze, I slipped out.

At the steps of the library I heard, "Belinda, hold up." I stopped as a hand made contact with my arm. A momentary sense of excitement stirred me. I pulled away from his grasp and sighed as I turned to gaze into Robert's clear blue eyes. I took a deep breath. It was hard to control my urge to stroke his face. I just wanted to kiss him, but held back. After a few seconds the spell was broken when Robert stiffened up ever so slightly. The expression on his face changed. He became more serious. "Belinda, I waited for you...."

"My class let out twenty minutes early and I didn't want to stand outside that long, so I went in. My plan was to go back out and I was on my way when I saw you and Lora coming in. I don't want to cause any problems." I was rambling, but couldn't tell him my real reason for leaving was to avoid Lora.

"Lora just showed up. I came in looking for you and she followed me." He hesitated for a few seconds. "Look, I'm trying to let her down easily. She doesn't make me feel...like you do." He looked shyly at me with a half-grin and raised one eyebrow. My heart melted.

I didn't question the hesitation. We both probably felt the same way. Yet it was obvious from my observations that Lora was more attached than Robert was. How was I going to fit into this awkward little threesome? Judging from the way Lora leered at me at the game, my life was on the line.

I looked around for her, expecting her to pop up. "Where is she?"

"I gave her an excuse that I forgot something. Do you *really* need to go to the library?"

"Yes, this professor loves to give pop quizzes. I don't have much time to study before class."

He looked disappointed. "Okay. See you at five." He walked back toward the Student Center and I went into the library, still unnerved from his touch.

Abbey was already there reviewing. Pulling out a chair across from her, I made myself comfortable and dove into my book making an attempt to study, but Robert was taking over my mind.

It was almost time for our next class when Abbey's whispering broke what little concentration I was able to maintain. "Are you excited about your date tonight?"

"I'm really nervous. I just saw him outside on the steps and when he touched me…I thought I was going to faint! I felt that arousing pulsation again. I just wanted to reach up and kiss him. Abbey, what is going on with me?"

She looked very concerned. In her infinite wisdom, she reminded me to take it slow and keep it light.

"But there *is* some kind of connection here. I know he feels something."

Abbey hesitated for a second, then gave a quick wave of her hands in front of her face. "It's nothing but hormones, nothing more than physical attraction."

Irritation shot through me. How could she think that? "NO IT'S NOT! Something more is happening here." A soft "shhh" from one of the library assistants was her way of politely requesting I keep my voice down. I got her point and gathered up my books, giving Abbey a dirty look for not understanding.

As I rose to leave, Abbey whispered, "Keep it light," and without hesitation, she followed me to class.

***

Laying my head on my pillow, I was hoping for at least a few hours of snooze time before my date, but I had trouble falling asleep. Robert was burned into my head and the memories of the kiss haunted me as they stirred feelings deep within me. What was happening to me was foreign territory— something I was more than willing to explore, but I couldn't figure out exactly what *it* was. Finally, I closed my eyes and sleep came all too late.

Having forgotten to set my alarm, I awoke at 4:33. Twenty-seven minutes wasn't enough time to be ready, so I texted him.

Me:	Change date to 5:30? Took nap w/o alarm. Just woke up.
Robert:	Ok
Me:	No sleep last nite ☹
Robert:	No sleep? Me either. CU@5:30 ☺

I took a quick shower then put on my little bit of make-up, fixed my hair and went to my closet to decide what to wear. It wasn't too hard a decision to make from my limited wardrobe. I finished dressing just as there was a knock on the door at 5:30. I flew downstairs and opened the door. There stood Mister Gorgeous with his captivating smile. My heart started racing, butterflies attacked my stomach, and I was speechless. I couldn't believe we were going on a date. Was I his new challenge? I wondered. At the moment I didn't care and the only word that came out of my mouth was, "Hi."

"You ready to go?"

"Yeah." I could hear the nervousness in my voice.

We walked across the lawn and I had to make a conscious effort to keep a little distance between us. It was killing me because all I wanted to do was taste his luscious lips again!

My attention shifted when I saw the royal blue, two-seater, sports car parked in the street. "Nice car—what is it?"

"BMW Roadster." He gave the car a lingering once over as if it were a beautiful girl.

"Your parents *bought* you a BMW Roadster?" I was freaking out because I'd heard how expensive they were.

"No, Dad decided he wanted a sedan. So, he gave me his car and traded in my old one. I always get my parents' cars when they're tired of them, but I think I'll keep this one for a while. I like driving it, especially with the top down. It's a chick magnet." He arched a brow and smirked, still keeping a polite distance.

"Like you really need a chick magnet," I interjected, shaking my head. "You'd be one even if you were driving an old beater." He gave me a cocky grin as if he knew it wasn't the car that attracted the girls.

Robert was about two feet behind me as I arrived at his car. I slid my fingertips over the passenger-side front fender and across the door, all while exaggerating my sassy sashay. As my hand reached the edge of the door, I turned to face him. He stood there with a soft half-smile and sparkling eyes. I fell back against the car as his gaze left me breathless. He came within inches of me as he reached for the door handle. "Excuse me." As he requested, I inched my butt down the side of car so he could open the door.

As I went to slide into the seat, I turned toward him. "Thank you." I paused and had an incredible urge to kiss him, but fought it off with all my might. He leaned in closer to me when I decided this would be a good time to slip into my seat.

As soon as I heard the click of Robert's seatbelt my anxiety level rose and I started to rattle on. "I hope I'm dressed okay. I live in jeans. My whole wardrobe consists of jeans and a variety of tops. I don't like baggy pants. I like stretch jeans that fit just right." Horrified at how I must have sounded, I stopped talking and inhaled a deep breath to calm myself. "I'm sorry. I'm rambling. I do that when I'm nervous."

He glanced at me and smiled. "You wear'em well. You're fine for where we're going."

"A Mexican restaurant?"

"No, since Garrett took you to one Sunday night, I thought we'd go to Uvabianca Bistro. Is that okay with you?" Backing out of the driveway, he turned to look out the rear window as he placed his right arm over the back of my seat. It put his face in close proximity to mine.

I almost stopped breathing. Hesitating to look at him, I had a slight crack in my voice. "That's fine."

"So, why are you nervous?"

"Look in a mirror. I can't believe I'm on a date with you."

He straightened back up in his seat and put the car in drive. "You also need to look in a mirror." He glanced in my direction with an approving look on his face. I could feel my cheeks flush. He changed the subject and I was glad the attention was off of me. "Garrett said you're from Sugar Land. My parents moved there when I started college." He gave me a darting look as he repositioned his right elbow on the back of my seat and rested his hand on the headrest. "I go home occasionally on weekends and holidays. I've never really lived there though."

"What else did Garrett say about me?" Suddenly I became aware of his fingers playing with my hair. It was a gentle touch and I didn't mind at all. I liked it, so his subtle technique could be practiced any time he wanted.

"Oh, when Garrett told me to call you back, he just told me a few things. Nothing personal. Delts don't kiss and tell."

Accepting his explanations, I changed the subject back to where this all started. "My family moved to Sugar Land the summer before I started high school. They wanted to downsize to save money, so they could put me through college. Thankfully no college debt for me." Our conversation led to sharing information about each other with no mention of the kiss.

We arrived at the restaurant and, with both hands on the steering wheel, he whipped the car into the parking lot almost on two wheels. Instincts kicked in causing me to grab the door rest and hang on for dear life so I wouldn't fall into him. Maybe that was his plan, which I foiled. Thank heavens he slowed down to pull into the parking space. He got out, opened my door and offered his hand. I took it hesitantly, my insides somewhat astir. He closed his eyes and chuckled.

I gave him a bashful look wondering if he was feeling the same. My thoughts raced back to our kiss in the moonlight under the oak tree. My knees almost buckled, but I managed to keep upright. No need to embarrass myself in front of him any more than I already had.

When the hostess approached, Robert requested a quiet booth. She led us to the back of the restaurant where it was more dimly lit. It had a romantic feel.

She must've read Robert's mind. Then again, I had a feeling most females could since he seemed to get whatever he wanted from them.

After receiving our menus and placing our orders, we continued our conversation. "I still can't believe you've been on campus all this time and I've never seen you. And then this past weekend, I saw you everywhere. Strange." He appeared puzzled as he leaned back against his seat with his arms crossed over his chest.

"Perhaps I haven't seen or heard of you or your reputation because I spend all my time in class or the library studying. In the past, I rarely ever went to the Student Center. That's probably why you haven't seen me, either."

He zoned in on my statement. "My reputation? What have you heard?" he hissed, leaning forward, resting his elbows on the table.

"That you only date a girl until you get you-know-what and then you leave her." He frowned, tight-lipped. Maybe I shouldn't have said anything, I thought.

He *was* upset. His voice became harsher. "'Til I get you-know-what? Sex?" He was glowering when he unfolded his arms and slammed his clenched fists on the table. I flinched. "That's not true. I'm always respectful."

I was now desperate to recover some credibility after my last verbal screw up. "Garrett stood up for you. He said you weren't like that."

"You talked to Garrett about this?" His frown deepened along with his sharp, angry tone.

I sank down in my seat trying to become visibly smaller and answered cautiously. "Yes, he said I needed to go out with you. And I told him I was a little nervous because I'd just heard about your reputation. He said you're a great guy and to give you a chance. Sorry."

Robert was dead silent as I watched him. He just sat there with balled fists still on the table staring out into the room. I was afraid to say anything else. I had upset him enough. He relaxed his hands and took a deep breath, appearing calmer as he looked up at me with an icy stare before he spoke. "Are you still nervous?"

My voice became quiet and timid. "No, now I'm scared." I reminded him of our text from the night before. "I'm not sleeping with you or anyone."

He leaned in closer to me from across the table. "Belinda. Do you think I sleep with every girl I'm with?"

Afraid to answer, I curled into the back of the booth like a frightened mouse as I gave him a quick nod to verify what I'd heard. This conversation was tanking more every time I opened my mouth.

Now appearing even more frustrated, he took a minute and looked around the restaurant before he relaxed his shoulders. He rested against the back of the booth and took a deep breath. He looked at me in astonishment, I assumed, when he realized I was intimidated by his reaction. Robert rubbed the back of his neck and appeared embarrassed. "I guess I can get a bit forceful."

"You think?" was all I could reply.

"I'm really sorry. I'm not upset with you. It's just I've heard this before and it bothers me when I hear the lie all over again. Who told you this?"

Unsure if I should even answer him, I opted for a little white lie. "I heard some girls talking in the restroom." I didn't want to get Matt in trouble. As his face and voice mellowed, I began to unfold from my mouse-like posture, feeling more relaxed yet very stupid. I never seemed to get anything right. How could I be so smart, yet not have a brain cell that would allow me to carry on an intelligent conversation with someone of the opposite sex that I was attracted to? This one was different from any of my other dates. Maybe that's why I was acting like such a total airhead.

After our food arrived, we ate for a short time without talking. He broke the silence with a very strange question. "So, you…ah…haven't done it? You've never?" He had a curious look on his face.

I felt my cheeks heat and answered honestly this time. "No, I haven't."

"You're one of a kind." He appeared shocked, but also amazed as his eyes studied my face.

Feeling a bit uncomfortable, I lowered my eyes from his face and peered down at my plate. "I've never been in love." I looked back at him. He just stared at me with those piercing blue eyes. It made me even more uncomfortable. I broke the gaze by looking back at my plate and stirring my fork in the spaghetti.

Keeping my eyes fixed on my food, I changed the subject. "Another reason you didn't notice me before is probably because I didn't look like this my first two years. I changed last summer. I kinda came out of my cocoon. I developed." *Oh no, not again with the stupid words.* I briefly closed my eyes and shook my head, then glanced up to see his expression.

He stopped eating and looked at me as a broad smile spread across his face. "It's hard to believe that you haven't always been this beautiful."

"You can ask my roommate Abbey. We became best friends my freshman year."

His brows slightly pulled together. "Do you believe in fate?"

I tilted my head and shrugged. "I don't know. Why?"

"Maybe fate kept us apart, so I wouldn't hurt you. My first three and a half years, I had fun dating around—I guess I played the field. I dated any girl I wanted and may have hurt a lot of feelings." I was looking at him questioning his statements now. He must have understood because he clarified his explanation. "No, I did *not* go to bed with every girl I dated." He gave me a stern look to make sure I got the point before continuing. "Now, I've been accepted to grad school and I'm just not as interested in dating around anymore. So fate seems to have brought us together. It's something to think about." He ended on a serious note taking another bite of lasagna.

"So you think we're meant to be together? I don't know you." I nudged a strand of spaghetti with my fork, wondering if it could be true.

"I'm just trying to piece all this together. This is rather strange."

"I agree." Since I had never been in love before, I wasn't sure how love affected you mentally and physically. I leaned closer to him with my elbows on the table, not sure if I should ask my next question. I figured I'd go for it since I was on a roll for the dumb question award. "I feel like I lose all control when you kiss me. Why?"

He moved in closer, with a sincere look about him. "I haven't a clue. It hasn't happened with any other girl. Angel, you're the first."

Angel?

When we finished eating and paying the bill, he got up and extended his hand. "Do you need to go home now?" I ignored his hand and stood up.

"No, I still have time." I wanted to stay out with him as long as possible.

He dropped his hand and smiled, seeming pleased with my answer. "Good. I have one more place in mind." With his hand at my waist, he led me out of the restaurant.

"Where?"

"Surprise." A grin slowly spread across his face.

He drove in a direction that was unfamiliar to me. As we headed down the road, we left the lights of the town behind us. All of a sudden, the stars brightened and filled the cloudless night sky. He turned along a winding road that opened to the top of a hill. At the crest, you could look out over the town and college campus, all lit up. The lights flowed up to meet the stars. They were everywhere. It was breathtaking. A few other cars were parked there. Their steamy windows gave me a good idea of what was on Robert's mind.

"Where are we? It's so beautiful." I was admiring the sight presented before me.

"You haven't been brought here before?"

"No. Is this like 'Lovers Lane?'" My voice cracked from nervousness as I quickly glanced at him.

"Yesss. It's known as 'Make Out Ridge.'" He used a slight impish tone.

I whipped my head toward him and frowned. "Why did you bring me here? You promised."

"Look at my car." He was motioning around the inside of his vehicle. "Do you think we could do anything in this small space?"

I observed our surroundings. "I…guess not. So why?"

"Privacy. I want to spend some time with you and you have to admit this fits the bill." He made a grand gesture to the front windshield and the magnificent light display outside. He then turned to me. "I'll keep my promise."

Robert moved the steering wheel out of the way and adjusted the seat back as far it would go. His touch thrilled me as he pulled me over across his lap and cradled me in his arms. But, when his lips touched mine—intense feelings of desire rushed over me. I threw my arms around his neck as a flash of heat radiated throughout my entire body. My muscles constricted and my back arched. His body tensed and his hand slid up my neck, his fingers knotting in my hair pulling me closer. My heart pounded as his lips moved against mine. I was praying he'd never stop. I pressed my hand against his chest, and could feel his heart hammering. When his tongue pressed between my lips, I parted them and his tongue plunged in exploring, then caressing and twisting around mine.

Tantalizing pulses surged through me until he abruptly pulled his mouth away. He was breathing hard and his eyes were lustful as we came up for air. Thank God we were in a small space. Robert leaned his head back against the headrest, closed his eyes, and took a few breaths. "Holy shit, Belinda…." He sucked in air then released it slowly. "I have never experienced anything like this before."

With my arm around his neck, I rested my head against the hollow of his shoulder—breathless and dizzy—and breathed a sigh. "Me either."

I lifted my head to watch him as I finger-traced around his face, across his lips then kissed him softly. His eyes opened full of desire. Robert's arms tightened around me and the kiss became more vigorous. My fingers locked in his hair, holding him close as I slipped my tongue into his mouth to savor his taste. He groaned deep in his throat as our tongues explored one another. I hummed as he swept his through my mouth. The feeling was thrilling and I didn't want it to end, but I had to take control. I pulled away.

"What's wrong?" He appeared surprised as he was catching his breath.

"Nothing. Just an early class tomorrow. I need to go home," I fabricated. I knew if I stayed any longer, it would be very easy for me to give in, even in this confined space. I wasn't ready to go there.

We peered into each other's eyes, moving our lips closer with every frantic breath. I was afraid I would find myself lost in his embrace, unable to escape if we made contact again. But, I didn't want to stop. As he moved in, he gave me one quick kiss. "Okay." With a hint of a smile on his face, he helped me sit up and return to my seat. My feeling of utter shock turned to disappointment, but I knew it was for the best. He seemed to know exactly what he was doing. On our way home, there was total silence.

Looking in his direction, I decided to interrupt the void. "Is everything okay?"

"Yes, just thinking." He flashed me his flawless smile.

At my place, he opened the car door and extended his hand to help me out. Before I could take it, he pulled it back to his side, I guess to help avoid arousing my emotions. He then walked beside me to my front door.

"I had a great time." I moved closer to him putting my hand on his chest.

"Me, too. Good night." He turned and left, leaving me standing on the porch as he walked away.

What just happened? A feeling of insecurity came over me. I felt a button being pushed and "Monster" began to stir as I ran up to my room. Abbey was asleep. I undressed and crawled into bed, but sleep evaded me. I kept thinking about what had happened. What went wrong? Boy, now I really needed to talk to Abbey.

Again, I tossed and turned all night and peeked at the clock hourly. Around three a.m. I sat at my window, looking up at the stars, just thinking about Robert. I imagined him standing in the yard the first night we kissed. He was creeping into my soul and I didn't know how to get him out, nor was I sure I even wanted to.

When morning came, I was too tired and sleepy to get up. I told Abbey I was skipping my morning class and would explain later. After turning off my cell, I went to sleep, skipping Wednesday entirely.

CHAPTER 7

THE NEXT MORNING, Abbey woke me up. "Are you going to class today?"

"Of course." I looked at the clock. Sitting up, I stretched my back and let out a big yawn, then rubbed my eyes. "Why wouldn't I go?"

"What happened to you yesterday? Are you alright? I got worried—you never miss class."

Confused, I looked around the room. "What day is it?"

Abbey was combing her hair. She spun around with a dazed look on her face when she realized I didn't know. "Seriously? You missed a whole day. It's Thursday morning." She turned back to the mirror. "That must've been one helluva date." With a half-turn back, she looked at me. "So, when are you going to tell me all the juicy details about Mr. Wonderful?"

Trying to get my bearings, I glanced around the room. "Did I really sleep a whole day?" I shook my head amazed I could actually sleep that long. "I guess I needed to catch up on my beauty rest."

Abbey was in the final stages of dressing. "I couldn't get you on the phone and when I got home, you were passed out, dead asleep….So, how was your date?" She had an earlier class and would leave before me. I could linger a bit longer before getting a move on.

"I thought it was great. Evidently, I was the only one. He left me standing on the front porch. All I saw was his backside walking away."

Abbey was checking her hair, fluffing it. She stopped in mid-fluff and turned to me with those wide eyes of hers. "What happened?"

I started to give her a brief rundown of the night. I told her about the conversation we had at the restaurant and how he got extremely upset over the rumor I heard regarding him.

Abbey's eyes became even bigger as she briefly covered her mouth. "Why did you tell him that?! First rule of dating is never give out too much information. TMI! Oh, Belinda, tell me more."

I sighed. "It just kinda slipped out. Anyway, he did get a little upset, but seemed to get over it when I told him I was a virgin."

By now Abbey was sitting on my bed with her head in her hands saying, "Oh my God! TMI! Then what happened?" She waved her hand in a circular motion to encourage me to continue.

"Then, he took me to 'Make Out Ridge.'" Abbey's eyes grew even wider. "Oh Abbey, when he took me in his arms and kissed me, I thought I would die." Abbey was listening, hanging on every word. "There's something else. I never felt this before. The only way I can describe it is...I feel this very enjoyable pulse of electricity race through me when we touch. It intensifies when we really get into it." I studied her face hoping she didn't think I was crazy.

Abbey sat there for a few seconds. "Oh." She looked at the clock. "We need to talk about this. You've got me interested, but I have to go. Are you doing anything Saturday night?"

I shook my head, no.

"Plan for a girls' night in. We need to do some serious talking before you get into any more trouble." Abbey scowled as she shook her finger at me and walked out of the room.

I sat up, turning in bed to look out the window. It was like I'd never dated before when I was with Robert. I thought I was doing so well with the dating cues Abbey had taught me and had managed to maintain control over those situations with the other dates I had, but Robert was so different.

***

After class, I headed for the library. "Belinda, hold up." Matt was running to catch up with me. "Haven't seen you lately. Are you free tomorrow night to go to a party with me? My date canceled on me. I need a fill in."

"Sure." After all, what else did I have planned?

"You look upset. What's wrong?"

"Long story." I waved him off.

He grasped my hand. "Come with me to the Cave. Tell me about it. Maybe I can help."

"Okay, but you're not going to like my story."

When we arrived, I sat with my back to the Delt area and didn't even look to see who was there. Scooting his chair closer to me, Matt put his arm around my shoulders. "What's wrong? Tell me." He sounded sincere.

I huffed. "Pennington...I went out with Robert Pennington." I looked up at Matt. He was frowning as I went into a good enough explanation of my evening. Finished, I laid my head down in my arms on the table.

"You shouldn't date him. You're too good for him."

"You think?" I was trying to avoid looking over there. "Do you see him at the Delt tables?" Sitting up, I put my head on his shoulder.

Matt glanced over there. "Nope, but the other one is looking this way."

"Garrett?"

"Yep and now Pennington's walking in. I'll show him you don't have to put up with him. Play along with me." Before I could say anything, he pulled my chair out and turned it toward him. He placed his hand behind my head, pulling it forward as he leaned in and kissed me. Not a peck, but a long kiss. His plan of action took me by surprise, but I played along.

"Will you walk me to class? I just don't want to deal with him now."

"Gladly. Do you want to leave now?"

"Yeah."

Matt stood up and in a grand gesture, bending at the waist in a slight bow, extended his hand to me. He looked so chivalrous standing over me, it made me giggle. I put my hand in his, then stood up and curtsied. He put his arm around my waist and led me out.

When we were in front of the Fine Arts building he asked, "Do you want me to walk you home after class?"

"No thanks. I'll be fine. What time tomorrow night?"

"I'll pick you up at seven. Oh, I almost forgot. It's a pajama party."

"Okay. Sounds like fun."

"I have a pair of leopard print men's pajamas. You wear the top and I'll wear the bottoms."

I looked at him puzzled. "Any top for you?"

He laughed. "You'll have to wait and see. And you? Any bottoms?"

I lifted an eyebrow and sashayed away, not responding.

"I'll bring the top to you tomorrow morning. Meet me in the Cave," he yelled as I continued on my way. I just gave him a wave of acknowledgment and walked toward my class.

Approaching home after class, I saw the signature blue BMW parked next door, but no Robert. I crossed the street and headed for my porch. At the steps, I heard my name being called and turned to see Robert walking across the lawn. He was wearing a pressed light blue oxford shirt and jeans that fit very well, as they always did. He always looked so perfect and handsome. "I've been trying to call you."

"You have?" I pulled my phone out of my purse. "It's turned off. I'm not used to using this thing."

"You turned it off? Why?" He looked baffled.

"So I could sleep. I slept all day yesterday."

"Oh. That explains why I didn't see you. I saw you with Matt today. Garrett said you looked upset earlier. Are you alright?"

"I'm fine," I snapped.

He cocked his head, looking a bit surprised at my tone. "What's wrong?"

Now, it was my turn to have icy blue eyes as I glared at him. "What's wrong?!" My tone was full of sarcasm. "You just walked off the other night."

He shoved his hands into his pockets and looked at the ground, then shot me a glance without fully picking up his head. "Sorry. The date was sort of…I was trying to process everything that happened—the kisses, our reactions." He stared at the ground, appearing nervous.

I was observing him closely, curious if he would be willing to tell me what he was feeling when we kissed. "So, have you figured it out?"

Robert looked up and walked toward me, placing his hands on my shoulders. We stood there gazing at each other. I wondered what he was thinking. I dared not ask. Abbey's voice kept repeating in my head, *TMI! TMI! TMI!* So, fearing I'd start my telltale rambling or stick my foot in my mouth, I just stood and waited for him to reply.

"I know I feel really close to you…more than any other girl and I definitely want to date you."

My heart skipped a beat. I couldn't believe what I was hearing. I guess I didn't screw up as badly as I thought. I sensed he wasn't going to offer any more on his emotional state, so I responded to his second comment. I flung my arms around his neck as his dropped to my waist. "Me, too."

"Can we start tomorrow night?" His intonation had a hint of excitement.

Oh crap! My happy face melted away as I looked him dead in the eyes. "I can't, I already have plans."

His eyebrows drew together. "With Matt—the Theta Kappa pajama party?"

"Yes, how did you know that?" I could tell he wasn't happy.

"I just put two and two together. Tell him you changed your mind."

"I can't do that!"

"Okay, I thought it was worth a shot." He half smiled and went on. "I have a swim party to go to Saturday afternoon. How about coming with me?" Robert's manner was very direct, almost business like. I guess he figured he'd better close the deal now or lose out.

I gave him a curious look. "Sure, but isn't it still too cool to swim?"

He gave out a slight chuckle. "The pool is heated but no one ever seems to actually get in. The Hindses have a 'Pool Party' at least four times a year." He exaggerated the term by making quotes with his fingers. "Sometimes we're all out there with jackets just having a good time."

"Is it okay if I want to swim?"

"That shouldn't be a problem. Just bring a big towel to wrap up in to keep warm. Then again, I'd be more than happy to help you out if you're cold." He had a mischievous look on his face, and then he hugged me.

I dismissed his last comment. "Good. What time?"

"I'll pick you up about three." His face lifted with my acceptance.

"Okay."

…"Do you have plans for dinner this evening?"

"Noooo."

"Is six o'clock okay?" He didn't even wait for a response. A take-charge kind of a guy or just wanting to stake his claim? Either way, it was charming.

I smiled to myself. "That's fine."

"What are you hungry for?"

"Surprise me."

Robert hesitated again then looked at his watch. "Are you free now?"

"I guess so. Why?"

He squeezed me a little tighter in a playful manner. "Because I want to spend as much time as I can with you."

"Oh. Alright, let me take my books inside." I hurried in and ran upstairs. Abbey wasn't home. I tossed them on the bed and rushed back to Robert.

He took hold of my hand. Even the slightest touch from him was exciting. It took all I had to keep walking. I just wanted my lips pressed against his. He must have known what he was doing to me. He looked at our hands, gripped a bit tighter and smiled from ear to ear as he walked me to his car.

"Where are we going?"

"To get a view of the city during the day." With an anticipating, devilish look, he brought my hand to his warm lips and kissed it.

Half excited by the suggestion, I was about to agree when my logical side kicked in. I knew a repeat of our first encounter on 'Make Out Ridge' would put me in a situation I wouldn't want to get out of, thus putting me on the same level as some of his other girlfriends. I stopped walking and pulled my hand from his. Not saying anything, I just stood there and looked at him.

His brows knitted and he cocked his head. "What's wrong?"

It would've been so easy just to go with him. I longed for the feeling of his lips against mine and that scared the hell out of me. I stood my ground. "I don't want to go there now."

Appearing more somber, he shrugged his shoulders. "Okay. Don Reynaldo's it is. We'll sit in the bar until we're ready to eat."

I didn't know if I was reading the dating cues the right way. His mood had definitely changed, so before we had driven too far, I figured I'd give him an out. "I know I'm not what you're used to dating. You can take me back if you want. I'll understand."

"How do you know what I'm used to dating or want to date?" He exhaled in a big gust as he frowned at me.

Did I put my foot in my mouth again? If so, my foot didn't stop me from continuing. "Your reputation." I wished Matt hadn't told me about it.

"My reputation? Damn that rumor!" He hit the steering wheel with his fist before darting a glance in my direction. He took a deep breath and softened his voice before he began again. "Look, I want to date you. You're not like the other girls—you're special to me. Okay?"

We drove the rest of the way in silence. Why couldn't I keep my mouth shut? Maybe I should just stay home on Saturday with Abbey for "Girls' Night" instead of going out with him.

I glanced over at Robert. He appeared to be mulling over our conversation. His head was slightly shaking, and his jaw was tensing as he let out a snort. When we arrived at the restaurant, he chose a parking place in the rear of the restaurant, passing up empty ones in the front. After turning the engine off, he leaned over and kissed me on the cheek. I felt that all-too-familiar sensation and quickly turned to kiss him. As my lips met his, a shot of electricity ran up my spine. My heart started racing. I gently pulled away and murmured, "You're special to me too."

He grinned, then exited the car and came around to help me out. When I took hold of his hand, he pulled me up into his arms and kissed me passionately. That zingy feeling happened again, but before it took complete hold, I pushed him away. When I was out of his reach, I started walking while shaking my finger at him. He hesitated, but complied by walking next to me into the restaurant.

We sat at a table in the bar to talk and drink until we were ready to eat. "What would you like?" Robert gazed at me, never looking at the waitress who was waiting for our order. I requested White Zinfandel. He ordered my wine and a house beer on tap for himself. He never took his eyes off me. It was like he was trying to figure me out. Relaxing in his chair, he crossed his arms over his chest. "So tell me, what's your major?"

"Art and Education."

"Double major. Why did you pick those two?"

I explained how I liked to draw and paint and appreciated the many aspects of the art world. I told him I thought teaching would be fun and felt the combination of both fields would be a good fit for me as a career.

"So, what's your major?" I took a sip of wine. He was someone I wanted to learn more about and this was an opportune time.

"Business Management and in two years, I'll have my master's." Robert became very serious as he divulged his reasons for his major. It was a family decision. His grandfather had started a financial firm and with his passing, his father took over. Robert was expected to do the same. He further divulged he was looking forward to passing the business to his son someday.

"So, you plan on a family of your own?"

"Yeah, isn't that what everyone wants." He took a swig of his beer. "I have good parents. They taught me well and I think I would make a good father."

I looked him dead straight in the eyes. "What about a good husband?" I really wanted to see how he answered this one.

He delayed his answer as if he had to ponder it. "I think I'd make a very good husband to the right woman." He chuckled. "Are you game?"

I shot up straight in my seat. "Did you just ask me to marry you?"

Robert started snickering and broke into a huge smile. Under the smile came a chuckle. He covered his mouth with his hand as he tried to control his muffled laughter.

"I'm glad I amuse you so much. Besides, I wouldn't marry you anyway, at least not with such a lame excuse for a proposal like that. You'd have to give me a big rock for my dainty finger." I gestured waving my hand in front of his face. "Then, you'd have to get down on your knee. No mister, I get the whole nine yards or no deal." Dramatically, I crossed my arms and put my nose in the air as I glanced over at Robert.

He was just sitting there with his arms crossed over his chest, shaking his head. "Did you ever think about changing your major to Drama?"

I wadded up a napkin and threw it at him.

After talking for the next hour about anything and everything, he asked, "Are you ready to eat? We need to stop drinking on empty stomachs."

"Yes. My wine is starting to make me feel a little light-headed."

Robert asked the hostess if we could order food in the bar area. She gladly handed him two menus. I looked at her, but her attention was on Robert. He politely took them, thanked her and turned his attention back to me as if nothing out of the ordinary happened. The hostess got the message and left.

After ordering, he started up the conversation again, leaning forward with his elbow on the table and his head resting on his fist. "The swim party Saturday is at Russell and Cheryl Hinds' house. They're alums and he's a Delt. Nice couple. I think you'll enjoy it." He paused momentarily and stared at me. His next statement bewildered me. "Have you ever thought about modeling?"

"NO!" I leaned up against the table. "I don't know if I'd be able to strut down a runway with hundreds of eyes watching. Kind of unnerving. I'd probably fall and make a fool of myself." My mind flashed back to my hideous display in modeling class. No, that was one episode I never wanted to repeat. Once was more than enough.

"I think you'd be a good model. Your long hair would be a great feature. I really like it. Don't ever cut it." Robert reached across the table and gently fiddled with a few strands. "It's so soft." He then relaxed back into his chair.

"I don't plan to. I hated my hair when it was short."

As we ate, our conversation drifted from subject to subject effortlessly. He had a good sense of humor and I found myself opening up to him, telling him things about myself that I had never shared with another human being.

It was a convertible type of evening, dry and clear. There wasn't a cloud in the sky. In the east, there was a huge full moon rising, as orange and blue bands appeared in the western horizon with the setting of the sun. The temperature was warm enough that a sweater wasn't needed. Yeah, this was perfect convertible weather. We drove off with wheels squealing. I gave him a disapproving look, but had to giggle because he was just being such a guy.

After he parked in front of my house, he reached over to pull me closer. I leaned away. "I can't. I have an assignment due tomorrow. We'll end up taking too long." Robert hopped out, opened my door and offered me a hand. Without thinking, I took it. He pulled me up into his arms and kissed me. All my reactions began. *What homework?* crossed my mind.

Tenderly he ended our kiss. His eyes were still closed and his breathing heavier than usual. I watched him as he stood there in his moment of silence—statuesque in the streetlight. He paused a few seconds, then walked me to my front door and kissed me very sweetly on my lips.

"I had a nice time. Thanks for dinner." I placed my hands on his shoulders and reached up to kiss him.

Smiling, he pulled back avoiding my advance. "Good night."

I closed my eyes, knowing he was right, but didn't release him right away. Looking back into his eyes I just thought, *Oh my God, he is sooo gorgeous.* My heart was thumping. I couldn't believe he wanted to date me. I turned to go in. This time, he didn't leave until I was inside the house.

I ran upstairs to tell Abbey about my day, but she wasn't home. After preparing for bed, I started my homework, finishing about eleven. Falling asleep was difficult, but when I succeeded, my dreams were filled with Robert.

CHAPTER 8

WE WERE RUNNING late in the morning and there wasn't time to tell Abbey about my date with Robert. In her consistent fashion, she wanted all the details, so I filled her in as we meandered to the Student Center after class. The most fun I had was watching her mouth drop open when I told her Robert proposed to me.

"Are you going out with him tonight?"

"No, I'm going with Matt to the pajama party, but I'll see him Saturday afternoon. We're going to a swim party. I guess our date for girls' night is off." I checked out Abbey's face as we walked up the steps, she seemed unfazed.

"That's okay. We can get together later."

Walking into the Cave, we headed for the Theta Kappa tables where Brent was waiting for Abbey. Robert caught my glance toward the Delt tables and motioned me to come over. I discreetly shook my head. He frowned. We didn't take our eyes off each other. To make my staring less obvious, I flipped my hair over the side that faced everyone at the table. Placing my elbow on the table, I rested my chin on my hand. I could see Robert and he could see me. His face softened, apparently amused by my subtle flirting technique.

Robert's facial expression changed as his eyes followed someone walking across the room. Before I could turn to see who it was, Matt surprised me by hugging me from behind. I gave Robert a fleeting glance. He didn't look happy.

Again Matt distracted me by handing me the pajama top crumpled in a plastic bag. I pulled it from the bag and shook out the wrinkles, then stood up, holding it against me. The top was about ten inches above my knees. Across the pocket was embroidered Wildcat. I laughed as I fingered the stitching and felt a warming of my face. With a subtle glance in Robert's direction, I winked. Robert responded with a forced half-grin.

Trying to be polite, I listened to Matt ramble about something until it was time for Abbey and me to leave for our next class. Sometime while I was distracted with Matt's raving, Lora came in. She was sitting next to Robert running her hand through his hair as they talked. I tried not to stare. I didn't want him to think I was jealous, but I was. As we passed, I glanced toward Robert. He looked my way. Time became suspended as I scrutinized him. I felt I was moving in slow motion. Our gaze seemed to last forever, but it really only took a few seconds. Robert looked away with a smile as Lora commanded his attention. I knew I had no right to be envious, but I wished I was in her place right then.

I had two hours to finish my art assignment and turn it in before the end of class. The project didn't require much brain power, which meant too much time for me to think about Lora showering her affections on Robert. Fighting with myself to keep on task, the ear-piercing sound of the dismissal bell was a welcome relief as I hurried to turn in my work. I had one thing blazing through my head, Robert. I glanced at Abbey, gathering my things before I turned to run out of class. "I'm going back to the Cave to see Robert."

She managed to grasp my arm. "Don't be too eager." I nodded my understanding. "Okay. I'm going home to take a nap." She released her hold on my arm but not before shooting me an austere glare.

"See you later," I shouted back, scurrying down the hallway. As I reached the building next to the Student Center, I saw Robert and Lora leaving. He had his arm around her shoulder. I had enough time to conceal myself behind a brick column, sure he hadn't noticed me. I could peek out enough to watch them. They looked like I imagined we appeared together—at ease. *Does he make all the girls he's with comfortable? Am I like all the other girls?* The thoughts made my stomach churn. I turned my back against the column, tilting my head back as they came into view. Lora was looking at him with admiration as Robert stared ahead. My need to run was almost unbearable. As soon as they were out of sight, I ran as fast as I could to the house and the safety of my room.

Abbey was fast asleep, so I decided to take a nap to clear my mind. It was hard to rest. The sight of Robert and Lora together kept repeating like a broken record. Sleep came, but it wasn't restful.

About four p.m., hunger awoke me. It took a few seconds before Robert invaded my mind again, lifting my spirits. The thought of him made me smile until the memory of how nonchalant Lora and he looked made my heart sink like an elevator dropping out of control. I lay in my bed, tormenting myself, when a rumble in my stomach interrupted my thoughts. I sat up and looked at Abbey. She was sitting on her bed reading. "How does pizza sound?"

"I don't know—I've never heard a pizza make a sound." She giggled at her lame joke. "Sounds great to me." We ordered our usual.

While we waited for the food to arrive, we started getting ready for the pajama party. I was preoccupied and still upset until Abbey interrupted the silence. "Did you see Robert?"

I stopped and sat on the bed. "*Yeah.* I saw him leaving with Lora."

"You sound upset." She had a look of concern.

"I guess I am. Abbey, why is this bothering me so much?"

She sat next to me and took hold of my hand. "Forget about him tonight. We're going to a party. Keep things light and let's go have some fun." After a gentle pat on my hand, she stood up and headed to the closet. She came out holding my outfit, the pajama top. "Now get ready." With a determined look on her face, she tossed it at me.

"Okay." She was right. I needed some fun.

Abbey and Brent were also sharing a pair of pajamas. Abbey wore a blue and white striped top with white tights. I was ready, wearing my Wildcat top and black tights.

Brent arrived first, honking his horn as he drove into the driveway. Abbey picked up her purse, saying, "See ya at the party." I watched from the window as she met Brent halfway across the yard and jumped into his arms. I admired her. She always seemed so comfortable with the opposite sex.

Shortly after they left, Matt arrived. I opened the front door and, placing my hand on my hip, struck a pose to show off my outfit. Matt was dressed in the leopard bottoms and a black muscle t-shirt. His well-formed upper arms did him justice as he acted like a body builder showing off. We both laughed at the same time and for a moment I managed to forget about Robert and Lora.

My peacefulness was short lived. Looking over Matt's shoulder I caught a glimpse of the signature blue BMW as it passed by with two people inside. Like a shot, Robert and Lora were back on my mind as I pondered if she was the other person in his car.

The party was a great distraction and to my surprise, I enjoyed myself. When Matt took me home, he walked me to the front door and planted a juicy wet kiss on my cheek, trying to be funny. "Thanks for going with me. I had a great time."

"I enjoyed it." I wiped the spittle off my face with the sleeve of the pajama top and smirked at him before heading inside.

While I lay in bed, thoughts about the two people in the blue Beamer crept back into my head causing my mind to race.

CHAPTER 9

IT WAS TEN o'clock Saturday morning. I just lay in bed imagining what my evening with Robert would be like, until my mind wandered and the reality of what I saw last night invaded my fantasy. *Was that Lora with him?* I couldn't be upset. After all, I had been with Matt. Stopping myself, I shook my head to clear all the negative thoughts and was determined nothing was going to spoil my date with Robert. Not even me.

To stop my obsessing, I had to keep myself busy so I rummaged through my dresser for my bathing suit and cover-up. My suit was a sea foam green bandeau-style two piece, not an itsy-bitsy bikini. The cover-up was a two-piece terry cloth set—shorts and short-sleeved jacket in the same color. I decided to wear my mules.

Why did our next date have to be so challenging? I hated the thought of a bunch of scantily-clad females strutting around him, and didn't need the competition. *STOP! Get those thoughts out of your head.*

Thank heaven Abbey woke up and interrupted my fixation. "I'm hungry. Let's go grab something to eat." She jumped out of bed, bright-eyed and bushy-tailed. She had entirely too much energy in the morning. I liked to linger and wake up slowly, but not Abbey. She hit the floor running.

"Me too. How about pancakes?"

We hurriedly threw on comfortable clothes and decided to go to a small diner on Main Street. It was an unusually warm day, so we walked the few blocks needed to procure our breakfast. We were standing on the corner waiting to cross when the blue roadster, with two people in it, flew by and turned toward campus. I clearly saw Robert, but couldn't make out who was with him. My heart sank and my thoughts went berserk as they swirled around in my head. I wondered if he had spent the night with Lora. My preoccupation with the sight of the beamer caused my unsettling thoughts to intensify as we entered the diner.

I managed to order my food without drawing too much attention from Abbey, and then descended into my own world of torment.

She snapped her fingers in front of my face. "Belinda, what are you thinking about?"

I looked at her. "Two heads last night, two heads this morning. Who was with him? The same person?"

Abbey squinted her eyes. "What are you talking about? I'll bet this has something to do with Robert."

"When I was leaving with Matt last night, Robert drove by and there were two people in the car. Then when we were standing on the corner, I saw the Beamer, and I'm certain I saw two people."

"Could you see who was with him?" I shook my head. "It was probably two different people. Quit thinking about it. You're going to drive yourself crazy. You know he lives with a bunch of guys at the frat house. It could've been one of them."

"You're right. Today is my day with him." I attempted to brush off the feelings, but my nagging thoughts still haunted me.

We were headed home, crossing the street to the house, when I noticed the roadster was parked next door. Abbey spotted it too. "Are you going over there to see him?"

"No, I'll see him at three." My first impulse was to run over there, but I had to maintain control. He was no different from any other guy I had dated so far this year. Yet, in my heart, I knew that wasn't true.

Abbey walked into our room first and pointed at my bed. There lay my cell, right where I left it, its little red flashing light indicating I had missed a call.

"Who was it? Robert?"

"Yep." I flopped down on my bed, scrutinizing the phone.

"Are you going to call him back?"

"Nope. If he wants to talk to me, he can call back." I tossed it on the bed and stared at it, wishing the stupid thing would ring.

"Playing hard to get, huh?" Her smirk reeked with satisfaction.

I was trying to control my impulse to pick up the damn thing and return the call. Not only was I tormented, I had to kill time. I thought about sitting and reading under the oak tree. Instead, I chose to stay indoors and keep myself busy with studying, painting my nails, and anything I could think of to keep my mind occupied.

Time passed too slowly and when I couldn't stand it any longer, I got dressed. With my suit on and hair styled, I sashayed out of the bathroom.

Abbey was lying on the bed reading a romance novel. She looked up and chuckled at my exaggerated display as I stood in front of the full-length mirror. I wanted to look my best and make a lasting impression on Robert. Examining myself, I saw the reflection of someone who was told she was attractive, but inside there was a girl who couldn't convince herself that was true.

Abbey broke my concentration. "You look terrific in that suit. You'll keep his attention, along with all the other Delts. And you'll have all their girlfriends wanting to strangle you."

Shifting my weight from side to side, I ignored her warning about my possible demise. "Does it really look okay?"

"Definitely. You need to quit seeing yourself as the old you. Focus on what you see in that mirror."

"It's hard. I was that invisible person for so long it's hard to believe what I see is me."

The first few bars of "Forever in My Mind," my favorite song and the ring tone I assigned to Robert, played from my cell. I waited a second and took a deep breath before answering sharply, with attitude. "Hello Robert."

"Are you back home? I saw you and Abbey on the corner this morning."

"Yes. We were on our way to breakfast."

"Will you be ready by three?"

"Yes!" I wasn't going to tell him I was ready now. I didn't want him thinking I was eager.

"Is everything okay? You sound...."

I interrupted. "Yeah, I'm fine. I'll see you then." And with a push of a button, I ended the call.

Folding her arms across her chest, Abbey looked up though her lashes, furrowing her brow. "Be nice." She reminded me that I didn't have any claim on him, and I also had a date last night, in pajamas no less.

She was right. I needed to be nice if I wanted to keep him around. He could have any girl he wanted, so why should he put up with me and all my insecurities?

My digital clock next to my bed kept me informed of how much time I had left until Robert's arrival. I sat close to the window, but not so close that he could see me. At three o'clock sharp, Robert walked across the lawn. My heart skipped a beat when the doorbell rang. As I stood up to leave, Abbey mumbled, "Keep it light. Be nice, have fun and strut your stuff."

"Bye, see you later." I picked up my bag and towel as I dashed out.

At the front door, I paused taking in a deep breath to calm myself. Like an actor, I plastered a broad smile across my face and opened the door. There he stood wearing his trunks and unbuttoned sport shirt, which displayed the most attractive tanned six-pack ever. *Be still my heart.* I thought I'd faint right then. I was starting to think a swim party may not be the best idea. There was just too much exposed skin between the two of us.

My attention was diverted when he took off his sunglasses and flashed me a drop-dead smile. He looked at me the same way he looked his car over, making me feel very self-conscious. "Aaah, you look *great.*" He had a slight crook to his smile as he gave me a second once-over, but this time his eyes traveled slower down and up.

"Thanks." I made a conscious effort to avoid his chest while I gave him a quick kiss. The thrill of arousal welled in my soul, nevertheless. I briefly shut my eyes, maintaining control, then headed down the steps toward his car.

Neither one of us said anything at first as we drove to the party. Robert broke the silence. "Did you have fun last night?"

"Yes. *Did you?*" I barked, watching him. He gave me a curious look. "I saw you with Lora." I was guessing it was probably her.

"We just went out to eat and to a movie. Then I took her home." His tone was defensive, matching his raised brow and slightly tightened grip on the steering wheel.

"Did you have fun?" Of course I was fishing for more information. It upset me that he was out with her last night, but I had to keep myself calm. I didn't want him to know how much his association with her was driving me nuts. I was flat out jealous.

"No! I kept thinking about you in that short top at the pajama party with him," he spat out as he glanced at me with a frown.

I didn't know what to say. His response surprised me, so I kept my mouth shut the rest of the way until we drove up to a two-story house surrounded by huge pine trees. I broke the silence. "What are their names? I forgot."

"Russell and Cheryl."

"Russell, Cheryl. The man is Cheryl and the woman is Russell?" He looked at me like I was crazy, but I managed to keep a straight face. Bursting out with a short laugh, more like a grunt, he evidently realized I was kidding around. It helped break the ice and his mood changed after my ridiculous attempt at a joke, but it worked.

We walked around to the back where a crowd had already gathered on a nice-sized patio. Robert introduced me to Russell and Cheryl, a very pleasant and attractive couple. We shook hands and I used their appropriate names. As we walked away, I nudged Robert and smirked. "Got the names right." We laughed. Laughing felt good.

In the past twenty-four hours I had managed to make myself miserable thinking about all the scenarios that could play out in my story with Robert. This was a flaw of mine. I was good at stirring up turmoil within myself. I had to work at keeping things light. Most of the time I was successful, but with him my mind was on overdrive and I couldn't stop it.

We claimed two lounge chairs next to the pool. Removing my jacket and shorts, I heard someone yell, "Robert, she's HOT!"

Ignoring the comment, I turned my attention back to Robert. He was standing with his arm crossed and a hint of a smile on his face, staring at me. "WOW! You do look hot."

"Thanks, I'm glad you like it. You're pretty hot yourself." After stepping out of my mules, I sashayed to the deep end of the pool, dove in and swam back to where Robert was now sitting on the edge. I extended my hand as if asking for help. Instead, once he took hold, I gave him a yank. He hit the water with a splash and went under. When he came up, he had a devilish grin and I knew I was in for it. Lunging at me, he missed as I swam out of his reach.

Halfway across the pool, Garrett scared the daylights out of me as he popped up from the water next to me. My first reaction was to dunk him, but he was too fast for me as he took off swimming for the other side. Bound to pay him back, I went after him.

When I came up for air, my exuberant mood changed after noticing Robert's attention had shifted. He didn't follow me, he was talking...no, flirting...with two girls who were sitting on the edge. Feeling as green as my swim suit, I let "Monster" out of her lair. I climbed out of the pool, snatched up my towel, and walked toward the house. Garrett yelled, "Hey, where are you going?" I ignored him.

Cheryl was in the kitchen, so I offered her my services. She encouraged me to go back outside to the party and my date. "Robert's preoccupied *right now*." I guess I looked like a puppy dog with my wet hair and sad eyes.

"Girls always seem to flock around him. Don't let it bother you. Here, put the chips and dip on this plate."

About five minutes later, Robert walked into the kitchen. "Belinda, here you are. Why'd you come in here?"

"You were *obviously* busy," I hissed in my most sarcastic tone. "So I came in to help." I couldn't give him the real reason, that I was riddled with jealousy and felt the need to run, letting "Monster" escape her hole. So I retreated to the safest place, the house.

With pleading eyes, he grimaced and extended his hand. "Sorry, come back out with me."

"No, I'm helping. You go talk to your *girlfriends*.

He appeared perplexed by my attitude and snapped back, "No!" He turned his attention to Cheryl. "What can I do to help?"

Cheryl seemed to be studying the two of us, trying to figure out what she was getting herself into. She did the best thing she could and very nicely ordered us out of her kitchen under the ruse we were both helping. She handed him a tray and told him to put it on the table outside, pushing him out the door. Turning toward me, she handed me a tray and said she'd finish the rest. "Go be with him." Her eyes grew larger to emphasize the point.

Reluctantly, I followed him to the table where we left the trays. Robert slipped an arm around my waist, then lifted my chin and gazed into my eyes. "Sorry I upset you." Pressing his lips to mine, I got a shooting feeling up my back, but pulled away. He understood and raised his hands as he took a step back, giving me more room. I thanked him with a nod.

"I missed you Friday."

"I came back to the Student Center, but I saw you leaving with Lora." I didn't want to tell him I watched as he put his arm around her and how that made me feel.

"Her class is in the building next to mine." He stared into my eyes commanding my attention. "Look...I know you're having fun dating around, but I don't like it. I don't want to share you with other guys."

I was stunned and heard myself responding impulsively, but it felt right. "I feel the same way. I...I don't like seeing you with other girls." I wanted to add, *especially Lora*, but held my tongue. With her on my mind, and his recent flirting incident, I pointed out, "You know, I can do what you do. We don't have any tie on each other." He scowled and shook his head, seeming to understand what I meant.

Without saying a word we walked to the pool and waded to the deep end where it was quieter. I wrapped my legs around his waist and my arms around his neck, fusing myself to him. His arms encircled me, only our heads were above the water. His lips touched mine and my body went crazy reacting to the tantalizing zingy feeling flowing within me. When the kiss became more intense, he took us underwater....We came up gasping.

Robert studied my face as he pushed some hair aside. "I love how we respond to each other. I get this very pleasant electric pulse when I touch you. But when we kiss, it's like every nerve in my body comes alive."

Now I no longer had to wonder if Robert felt something unusual when we touched. He just validated what I'd thought all along. "I feel exactly the same way....I've never felt this way with anyone else."

"You can't imagine how…how hard it is to stop like I promised." His eyes were sinful. He reached up, placing his hand on the back of my head and pulled my face close to his. "Belinda Davies, I'm in love with you." He leaned away and waited for my response, never releasing my head.

I was overwhelmed by his words. Abbey's "keep it light" speech entered my head. I knew he expected a reply, so I decided to heck with it. I fell in love with him the first day I saw him and knew I wanted to be with him the rest of my life. "I love you, too." It passed my lips in a velvety tone.

Our eyes were intent on each other as he placed his lips to mine. He pulled my head closer, crushing our lips together. With a searching tongue, he explored my mouth heightening my lust for him.

My heart accelerated as my breathing became heavy. I was about to forget we weren't alone when Robert took us underwater. We continued kissing for as long as we both could hold our breath.

The need for oxygen overrode the desire for our touch. When we surfaced, I pulled away and raised my hands, backing up to give us more room, the same way he gave me some space a few minutes earlier. He acknowledged the gesture with a nod. My heart was beating so fast I felt as if I had run a marathon. Taking short, uneven breaths, I mouthed, *I will always love you*, before turning to swim across the pool to where Garrett was sitting on the edge of the shallow end.

Robert caught up and stood behind me with his arms wrapped around my waist, resting his head on my shoulder. "Garrett, I never thanked you for stepping aside and letting Belinda and me date. I owe you bro." A smile stretched across my face as I leaned my head against Robert's. His voice got very quiet, almost a murmur. "Garrett, have I told you I'm in love with her."

Needing some reassurance that Robert was being sincere, I looked up at Garrett as he stared at us with his mouth gaping. "You're his best friend. Is this for real or a ploy to lure me into bed?"

I could feel Robert shake his head in response.

"As long as I've known him, he's never said those words to any girl." Garrett looked at Robert then back to me. "I really believe he means it."

Now Robert was nodding, his chin digging into my shoulder.

Turning to face Robert, I looked him straight in the eyes to make sure I had his full attention. "Are you sure? We've only known each other for a week. Can you be with one girl?"

"I've never been more positive of anything in my life. You're on my mind constantly. As I said before, I don't like sharing you." He gave me a slight tug, pressing our bodies together.

"I love you too. No doubts." Filled with joy, I planted an open mouth kiss on his lips. My body reacted and we collapsed back, underwater. We came up chuckling and gasping for air.

"Would you accept a sweetheart pin?"

Again, without giving his question a second thought, I responded in an almost inaudible voice. "Yes, absolutely."

Garrett was still perched on the edge of the pool watching the show unfolding in front of him. "He wants to pin me. Am I dreaming?" Garrett only shook his head. A little voice in my head interrupted as it warned me, *keep it light*. Without a further thought, I dismissed it. I didn't care.

"Garrett, let's keep this a secret right now. I'll arrange for a pinning ceremony." Robert looked at me for approval. We both agreed, but I had one stipulation. I wanted to tell Abbey and bring her. Robert agreed and made me promise she would be the only one I'd tell for now.

Russell announced that the grilled hamburgers were ready. The hungry partygoers converged around the tables picking out their choices of the available foods. During the meal, Russell changed the tone of the music. His selections were more romantic, befitting the digestion of food and fostering conversation. Later he would raise the volume and tempo to enhance the dancing experience.

The three of us were sitting on our lounge chairs eating when curiosity got the better of me. "Garrett, why didn't you bring a date?"

"I haven't met anyone else I'd like to date." He looked at me and half smiled, wolfing down a bite of hamburger.

I swallowed my bite of food. "I'm sorry. You know, I think you'd like my roommate, Abbey. She's dating someone, but I don't think it's serious. I'll talk to her about you. Is that okay?"

"She's pretty. You've seen her with Belinda at the Theta Kappa tables. She's tall and slim, auburn hair." Robert described her to Garrett with just a hint of too much enthusiasm. "Nice green eyes." I stopped eating and glared at Robert. He responded innocently. "What?"

Garrett laughed. "You two sound like an old married couple, and yes, talk to Abbey."

After the used plates found their way into trash cans, Russell changed the music to a lively tempo. The beer, wine, and anything else the frat brothers sneaked in was flowing freely and the excitement of the night heightened. The swimming pool lay abandoned with the guests utilizing the dance area, moving to the beat of the music.

As a slow song started, I reached for Garrett's hand and pulled him up to dance. "Robert thanked you. I also need to. Thank you for bringing us together."

"If things don't work out, I'll be here for you." He tightened his grip around my waist and glided me around to the music.

"Not if you and Abbey get together." I smiled and laid my head against his shoulder.

The song ended and a hot tempo piece started. Robert jumped out of his chair and took me out of Garrett's arms. "This is my dance." Just like the first time, we moved together as one.

His hypnotic eyes made me tingle all over. He didn't know how hard it was for me to say NO to his advances. My mind was still saying NO, but my body was screaming YES. *But* maybe it was time to show him how much I loved him. Surprising him the night we're pinned would make the event more special and memorable. This decision would need more consideration. It was a big step I didn't know if I was ready for.

Little was said as we drove to my place. Robert broke our silence. "Stay with me." That one statement set off an alarm within me.

"I can't. I'm not staying in a frat house." I didn't want the brothers thinking I was like his other conquests. Then it dawned on me—if I surprised him by giving in after the pinning, our only other options would be his car or a motel. *No way*!

"Yeah, you're right." Robert hit the steering wheel with both palms. "I need to move into an apartment."

I wasn't too worried. It wouldn't be easy finding an apartment mid-year in this college town. This would take him some time. I was confident my virtue was safe until I was ready.

After parking the car in the usual spot in front of the house, he moved the steering wheel out of the way before he slid the seat back as far as it would go. Lifting his arms, he had a silly grin on his face as he invited me across his lap. I made him button his shirt before maneuvering myself into his arms.

Fog was forming on the windows from our heavy breathing. Robert rested his head back, filling his lungs. "I need to go. I'll call you in the morning." We arranged what little clothes we wore, making ourselves presentable for the outside world. He helped me out of his car and walked me to the door. "I do love you." He gave me a quick, gentle kiss. "Good night."

"I love you, too. Good night." I hugged him and didn't want to let go, but as with all good things, our night together had to end. Against every fiber of my soul, I released him and went into the house.

Abbey was awake reading her romance novel. "How was the party?"

I could hardly contain myself. I threw my stuff on the bed and jumped on it, folding my legs underneath me as I faced her. "Unbelievable! Great! Terrific! You'll never guess what happened! But first, how would you like to go out with Garrett sometime? He's a senior and he'll be going to grad school, so he'll be around for at least two more years. He's not dating anyone in particular and he said he'd like to go out with you. You interested?"

"Sure. From what you've told me, he seems nice and he's cute."

"Great! Now for the unbelievable news...." I stalled trying to build up the excitement. "Robert said he's in love with me and we're getting pinned. I'm so excited!" I shrilled. "I'm crazy about him and he feels the same." I was bubbling over with joy. "Do you want to come to the ceremony? I'm not sure when it is. I'll let you know later."

Abbey sat with a dumbfounded look on her face. It seemed to take her a few minutes to grasp what I'd just said. She looked down at the bed. I could tell she was trying to figure out what happened to the "keeping it light" part of my relationship with Robert. She looked up beaming, jumped off her bed and rushed over to give me a big hug. "You bet I want to come. Who cares if you can't keep it light. I'm so happy for you."

I was glad Abbey responded the way she did. It would've been very upsetting if she had disapproved. Our conversation just dwindled as sleep overtook my best friend. After a quick shower, I slipped into bed. I didn't think I'd be able to sleep, but I closed my eyes and drifted into a peaceful slumber.

CHAPTER 10

MY WAKING THOUGHT Sunday morning was of Robert and the events of the night before. I closed my eyes, letting my mind wander so I could relive every wonderful second. He was in love with me and I with him. Despite everything he told me and what I knew of him, I still found it hard to believe all of this was happening. After all, we'd only met a week ago. I couldn't believe this gorgeous guy loved me. My daydream was interrupted when a familiar sound from my cell indicated I had a text message. I replied then lay back on the bed and waited.

Within seconds Robert texted back. He asked me to meet him in thirty minutes at the frat house to help him move to an apartment. His text stunned me. How on earth did he get an apartment so fast? I could be in BIG trouble. Was I ready to give in? I didn't know if I'd be able to control myself if we had a bed and privacy at our disposal. He had to be moving in with someone else, and a roommate could always be used as an excuse for not spending the night. I decided I had nothing to worry about.

Putting my fears aside, I jumped out of bed, pulled my hair back into a ponytail, and threw on shorts, a knit top and tennis shoes as quietly as possible so I wouldn't awaken Abbey. I left her a note, *With Robert*, then picked up two large suitcases for packing, flew out the door and was on my way.

"You're late." Robert pointed to his watch and grinned. "It's been thirty-three minutes." He grasped me around the waist, swung me around, and then kissed me tenderly on the lips as I took in the pleasant sensation of his touch. "Let's go for breakfast first."

"Good. I'm starving. I didn't get to eat much last night. Someone kept me busy with other things," I joked, poking him in the side as we walked to his car. I was dying to know about the apartment, but decided to wait and see if he offered the information.

"What do you want?"

"Pancakes. I love pancakes."

"As much as you love me?" he teased. "Pancakes sound good to me too."

I was hungry, so it was good the order came quickly. I was about to take a bite when I stopped, cast a glance his way, and asked, (since he hadn't bothered to mention the apartment yet) "How'd you get an apartment so fast?"

"I remembered Paul wanted to live in the frat house. He was there last night when I arrived home. I asked if he'd be interested in swapping and he was. He thought it would save him some money. So we decided to switch today."

"So, are you going to have a roommate?"

"Nope. I have the whole place to myself. That is…unless you're interested." I slowly turned my head toward him. He looked at me rocking his eyebrows in a rapid motion. "We can have all the privacy we want."

My heart skipped a beat. His gaze was intense. He expected an answer. My earlier fears were coming true. Now I knew I was in trouble. The roommate excuse just went out the window. I wouldn't be able to say no to spending the night with him any longer. Shoving a bite of pancake into my mouth, I chewed as long as I could, giving me more time to think. I glanced over at him as he waited patiently for me to swallow. Robert wasn't joking around like he did on the first date. When I couldn't chew any longer, I just swallowed and sat there. I really didn't want to address the awkward suggestion about us being roommates and he seemed to have figured it out. I was grateful he didn't push the issue—he just smirked.

I changed the subject back to the move. "I brought two large suitcases you can use."

"Thanks for helping. My car doesn't hold much. It would've taken all day moving a few things at a time. With your car and help, we'll finish faster. Then I can spend more time with you."

"Glad *we* could help. Where is this place?" I put another bite in my mouth.

"Close to campus—walking distance. I think you'll like it."

When we arrived at the frat house, I noticed Paul's things were piled up in the hallway. Robert had helped him vacate the apartment before he contacted me. We packed all of Robert's belongings and loaded everything into the two cars. Robert was right. His car was a joke. He put the top down to load more stuff in the seat next to him. He barely fit, leaning over as far as he could into the driver's side door.

Thank heaven the apartment was only a few blocks away. We pulled up in front of a large Victorian-style house. Robert tossed me the keys and told me his apartment was the first door on the right just inside the building. While he started to unload boxes from his car, I took hold of the two suitcases and wheeled them up the path.

The house was rather impressive. One could easily imagine its grandeur in its day. There was a huge wraparound front porch with rocking chairs. The front door had ornate etched glass windows surrounding it which made the door look bigger. The doorknob was solid brass with a beautiful floral motif.

Robert's apartment was furnished. There was a decent-sized room that served as the living, dining, and kitchen area. To the left of the kitchen was a small but adequate bedroom and bathroom. Most of the wood trim was stained, not painted, creating a warm feeling that blended with the hardwood floors.

The living room was at the front of the building and had a real wood-burning fireplace, which would come in handy for cold days and romantic nights. The kitchen had everything needed to cook a great meal, yet the flavor of the Victorian style was maintained, complementing the rest of the house.

This apartment was a place I could feel comfortable in. It was a place I could call home, but it wasn't mine, it was Robert's. I was here to help him move in and, from the looks of things, give the place a good cleaning.

As I walked around the living room, I noticed a single rose on the table in front of the windows. Propped next to it was a piece of paper. The note was handwritten with a few small red hearts drawn on it. It simply read, *To New Beginnings, Love Robert*. My heart raced. This was the sweetest thing anyone had ever done for me. No one in my entire life had ever given me flowers of any sort. Robert instinctively knew how to touch my heart.

I was captivated by Robert's thoughtfulness when the door flew open. There he stood struggling to manage the door and several boxes. I ran over and held it open. After he put them down, he faced me with a big smile. "Good, you found it. I hope you like it."

"I love it as much as I love you." I sashayed over to him and put my arms around his neck. We kissed. That familiar electric surge rushed up my spine and then we kissed again. I didn't want to let go and as far as I could tell, Robert didn't want to either.

Things could have gotten out of control, but I broke the mood by getting our focus back to the task. "While you're unpacking, I'm going to clean the kitchen and bathroom."

He looked at me and whispered, "Later," as he attempted to pull me close again. I put my hands on his chest holding him off. Tilting my head, I raised an eyebrow to let him know I meant business. He complied with a sigh, dropped his hands and walked toward the door. As he went out, he turned and mouthed, *Later*. This time it had a totally different meaning.

I found some rubber gloves and cleaning solution under the kitchen sink and started to work. Robert was trying to unload everything as fast as possible. There was rain in the forecast for the early evening, and the gathering clouds were becoming darker. "You don't need to do that. Relax, you're not here to be my maid," Robert puffed as he brought in another load from my car.

"*Oh, yes I do.* Have you seen everything in here?" I rubbed my glove-clad hand over the kitchen counter and made a face at the grime I lifted. "I even had to wash all the dishes, but I found a vase." I pointed to my beautiful rose now feeding in a glass container of water sitting on the table.

Robert smiled at the rose, but could've cared less about the dishes. He shrugged his shoulders. "I don't cook." He left to retrieve the last load he had placed on the front porch.

I finally finished cleaning about 4:30. "Your maid is starving and exhausted." Sighing dramatically, I peeled off the rubber gloves and tossed them in the trash can. I muttered, "I never want to see those things again."

Robert stepped out of the bedroom where he was unpacking his clothes. "What are you hungry for?"

"I'm too tired to go out—just order anything."

I walked into the bedroom to help unpack. I took some t-shirts out of a suitcase and walked over to the dresser to put them in. When I opened the top drawer, Robert became anxious and told me to put them in the third drawer down. They were placed in the third drawer as instructed. I picked up some of his shirts he had on hangers and walked over to the closet. I opened the door and was told to place the hangers on the right side of the closet—the whole left side was empty. As instructed, the clothes were placed on the right side. The rest of our time unpacking was spent in the same manner. When everything was done, the two top drawers of the dresser remained empty and the left side of the closet had nothing hanging in it. His place. His clothes. He told me to go relax while he finished unpacking his stuff in the bathroom.

By then, rain was hitting against the windows in a rhythmic pattern. It was darker than usual because of the thick black clouds. The only lamp on in the living room cast a dim glow, giving the room a warm and cozy aura. I let my hair out of the ponytail and went to the couch to stretch out. It was well-worn leather, comfortable, and clean, *Thank Heaven*. It didn't take long to fall asleep.

"Belinda, Angel—the food is here. Wake up." Robert was kneeling next to me, gently pulling my hair away from my face.

I slowly woke up and looked around without lifting my head. I was confused. For a second, I forgot where I was. It was spring and with the rain, the night turned cooler. Robert had lit a fire in the hearth. Turning onto my back, I looked at his face and studied his outline in the dim light of the flickering flames. I reached out to touch his cheek and ran my fingers down the side of his face. A sensual awareness moved me and I closed my eyes. When I opened them, Robert was bending down to kiss me. Unsure whether I'd be able to control myself if we made contact, I put my hand on his chest to stop him and murmured, "I'm starving." He stopped in mid bend and studied my face before he stood up.

We ate in front of the fireplace and drank most of the bottle of wine Robert picked up earlier. We talked and laughed, asking each other questions about one another. After we ate, I lay on the couch with my head on his lap watching the mesmerizing flames flicker and dance as he stroked my hair.

"Thank you for all your help." His voice was soft and tender.

"My pleasure. I enjoyed it."

"Will you stay here tonight? I promise to keep my promise."

I hesitated and stopped breathing with a small gasp. He stopped stroking my hair. Feeling him looking at me, I had to ask myself if I could keep my hands off of him. I rolled over onto my back and gazed into his eyes. I knew I would have to muster all the strength I had, but I couldn't say no. I thought for a several seconds longer then answered. "Okay. But I don't have any clothes for tomorrow or my books."

"Let's go get them now."

I smiled. "You're so anxious to have me stay with you."

"Who me?" Robert was grinning innocently. "Come on, let's go."

At my place, he waited in the car while I ran upstairs to pack my clothes, books, and toiletries. Abbey wasn't home, so I left her a note. When we returned, I threw my stuff on the bed and headed for the bathroom. "I get the clean shower first."

"Can I join you?" I slammed and locked the door in his face. I think he understood the message.

After showering I discovered that in my haste with my haphazard packing job, I didn't bring anything to sleep in. "Robert, I forgot my pajamas. Can I borrow one of your t-shirts?" I shouted from behind the door.

"Sure, help yourself."

"Can you please get me one?"

"NOPE. You know where they are. They're in the same place you put them earlier," he teased.

"ROBERT PENNINGTON JR! Please get me a t-shirt."

Again, a simple "Nope."

I wrapped a towel around me, took a deep breath and opened the door.

Robert was lying on the bed nonchalantly looking through a magazine, ignoring me. Keeping an eye on him, I tiptoed quickly over to the dresser. He didn't move. I snatched a t-shirt from the drawer and ran back into the bathroom, slamming the door behind me. After putting on the tee, I picked up my stuff.

As I walked into the room, Robert pointed to the chest of drawers without looking from the pages of his magazine. "Put your things in the first two drawers. They're yours."

Not knowing how to respond, I stood silent for a moment. I went over and placed my clothes in the top drawer. I turned around, but before I could say anything, Robert was off the bed proclaiming, "My turn," as he headed for the bathroom. He shut and locked the door behind him.

While he showered, I crawled into the fresh clean bed, laying claim to the right side. I was so tired I fell asleep. When he came to bed, he pulled me over next to him. I curled up over his side. He whispered, "Sexy t-shirt. It never looked better."

"I thought you were too busy with that magazine to notice."

He kissed my forehead. "I love you. I took a peek while you were putting your things away. I did, however, prefer the towel look more." He kissed my forehead again. "Good night, Angel." I felt a slight shiver inside. I slept all night, better than I could ever remember, and Robert kept his promise.

I was deep in a dream when I became aware I was being sexually teased. There were lips brushing kisses up my neck. And then I heard a soft loving voice. "Wake up, Angel. How did you sleep?"

Opening my eyes, I stretched. "I've never slept better. Do we have to get up?"

"Come on." With his strong arms, he pulled me off the bed and pressed me against his bare chest. "You feel so good." His voice deepened. "Now get ready." A quick slap on the butt made me jump as he left for the bathroom.

My heart felt like it had been yanked from my chest. I had to steady myself to keep from losing my balance. Lying back on the bed to regroup for a few minutes, I wondered how long I would be able to resist him.

The morning was clear and crisp. The sun was just coming over the buildings as we stepped onto the porch. Taking a deep breath, I allowed myself a few moments to enjoy the fabulous spring day. Raindrops still clung to the leaves of the trees from the showers during the night. As we walked along the sidewalk, they splattered on our heads. We laughed, trying to dodge our attackers from above, weaving from side to side.

"Where are we going anyway?"

"For my favorite breakfast."

I realized we were going to the bakery when we turned onto Main Street—the aroma of the pastries hit me well before we arrived. In front of the store, Robert threw his arms up. "TA DA! Blueberry bagels and coffee." He was such a goof with a good sense of humor.

We were eating our food when Robert swallowed and looked at me. "Oh. I almost forgot to tell you, the pinning ceremony will be at the frat house before our meeting tomorrow evening at 7:30. The ceremony doesn't take long." With breakfast finished, we headed for campus and began our busy day of classes.

I saw Robert a few times during the day, but he never mentioned being with me tonight. At the end of the day, Abbey and I headed for home to work on an assignment. We walked in silence halfway before she could no longer contain herself. "So, did you stay at the frat house last night?" She jabbed me in the shoulder with her finger.

"No, his apartment." I was laughing inside.

"His apartment?" Abbey listened intently as I explained how Robert acquired his love nest in less than a day. Satisfied with those details, she moved on. "What else did you do?"

I knew what she was fishing for, but I wasn't ready to give her that information yet. "Dinner."

Abbey shot a piercing glare my way. "Okay! Did you seal the deal?" She stopped, refusing to take another step. "Come on, Missy. Give it up! What else did you do?"

By now I was laughing. "Nothing else happened. Robert was a perfect gentleman. He promised he wouldn't put any moves on me and he didn't." I knew deep down that Robert, at some point, would want to move our relationship to the next level. I had to be prepared in every respect, for what was inevitable. The thought of the unlimited possibilities of our love made me nervous, yet excited.

I was jarred back to earth when Abbey hit my arm. "I don't believe you! Tell me all the details."

"When we get home. We have to be comfortable." Before she would move, Abbey made me swear. I crossed my heart, but boy was she going to be disappointed. "By the way, the pinning ceremony is tomorrow evening. Can you still come?" I glanced at her. "I can introduce you to Garrett."

"Yes, of course."

The minute we arrived in the room, Abbey started in on me. "Okay. Now for the details." She dropped her books on the floor and jumped on her bed, sitting Indian style, anticipating what I wasn't going to tell her.

I felt bad for leading her on like I did. "Abbey, there really isn't anything more to tell you. He was a gentleman. Really he was."

It was getting late, so with no word from Robert, Abbey and I decided to take a break from our homework and go eat.

We were walking back when she nudged me to get my attention. I looked at her as she pointed toward the house. Robert was sitting in his car with the top down, just waiting. Abbey walked by giving him a quick wave.

"I've been trying to call you."

"I haven't heard my cell." I retrieved it from my purse. "It's dead. Sorry." I gave the phone a shake in my hand. "If you haven't figured it out yet, I'm not used to this thing."

He hopped out of his car and wrapped his arms around me. "Stay with me tonight?"

"I can't. Abbey and I are working on an assignment that's due. I'll see you tomorrow evening at 7:15."

His expression turned sad and pouty. "I liked holding you last night." His eyes scanned my face and hair. "I'll miss you."

"I'll miss you holding me, but I have to get back to my assignment. I need to go. Good night." I ran my hands up the back of his neck and into his hair. He pulled me close and kissed me. Kissing was more of a thrill than just his touch alone. I shuddered and pulled away. "Good night—love you."

"Love you too, Angel." Almost in his car, he looked back. "You sure you don't want to come with me?"

"Byeee."

Abbey and I finished our assignment late. I was exhausted, but sleep didn't come easy. I kept thinking of Robert and how much I missed having his arms wrapped around me.

CHAPTER 11

AFTER AGONIZING HOURS of class work and growing anticipation over this evening's event, it seemed to me that Tuesday afternoon would never come. Abbey and I hurried back to the house to prepare for the pinning ceremony.

My dress was strapless with a belted waist and short pencil skirt in a blue and lilac floral print. With it I wore my white three-inch heels. It was 6:30, and I was as ready as I'd ever be. So was Abbey, in her hot pink dress.

I paced the length of the room several times, biting my lower lip. On my last pass, I turned to Abbey. "I don't know anything about this ceremony. Do you?"

"Nope. Not a clue." She pursed her lips, shaking her head. "Relax. Everything is going to be fine."

My faithful digital clock finally read 7:15 and there was a knock on the door. As Abbey and I went downstairs, I pulled some of my hair in front of my shoulders so Robert couldn't see that my dress was strapless. I didn't want him to notice until he started to pin me. I opened the door and paused, taking in the sight of him. "WOW! You look so handsome." Wearing a sports coat, slacks, dress shirt and tie, with dress shoes, he looked a model.

Abbey elbowed me in the ribs then stood there looking at the ceiling. "What?" I looked at her and she nodded her head toward Robert. Suddenly I realized they had never met. "Oh. I'm sorry. Abbey Curtiss, I'd like you to meet Robert Pennington. Robert, this is Abbey." I apologized, a little embarrassed by my lack of social skills.

Abbey extended her hand. "Nice to meet you, Mr. Pennington. I've heard a lot about you." She gave a quick glance in my direction.

Robert politely took hold of her hand. "Nice to meet you as well, Ms. Curtiss. I likewise have heard nothing but good things about you." Now the two were playing the introduction past where it needed to go. Robert seemed to sense my impatience and took a step back. A smile grew across his face as he shook his head. "You two look absolutely gorgeous. I'll have a beauty on each arm." Turning to proceed down the steps, he extended an elbow for each of us. "Ladies."

The minute Robert and I walked into the frat house, Michael, the Delt chapter president, made an announcement. "May I have everyone's attention?" A hush came over the group. The brothers and their dates were curious to find out the answer to the question on all their minds. "Everyone please gather in the living room." Michael then dropped the bombshell. It was announced that Robert was pinning me. The sound of muffled voices erupted as a room full of eyes followed us when we walked toward him.

The ceremony wasn't very long. Words were spoken, and then it was time for him to pin me. He pushed my hair back behind my shoulder, grinned and shook his head. My plan to embarrass him backfired. Robert pinned me without any problems, but his fingertips slid under the bodice and touched my breast. A powerful feeling of arousal came over me—I quivered. He took hold of both of my hands as soon as the sweetheart pin was secured. At first I didn't understand. When he reached over to kiss me, I glued my lips to his. The kiss was passionate enough without me entwining myself around him. Robert kept hold of my hands the entire time, I assumed, to control me so I wouldn't embarrass myself. After a few seconds, he ended the kiss and let my hands go. I was still embarrassed by the sensations and wasn't sure if anyone else could tell. I whispered, "I'm sorry," as I hid my burning face in the hollow of his shoulder.

"Nothing to be sorry about. We handled it," he murmured back as he nuzzled my hair.

The moment was broken when we were rushed by the fraternity brothers. Some hugged me while others shook Robert's hand. I heard "beauty" and "Lora" mentioned several times.

When things settled down a bit, I found Abbey surrounded by a group of guys. "Hey, I need this lady to come with me."

Grasping Abbey's arm, I led her over to formally introduce her to Garrett. "Garrett Barnett, this is Abbey Curtiss, Abbey—Garrett." They smiled and acknowledged each other. By the way Abbey looked at him, I knew she was impressed.

An announcement was made that the meeting was about to start. Robert handed me the keys to his car. "Come back in forty-five minutes."

"You're going to let me drive your car?"

"Sure, why not?"

"Great! Come on Abbey, we're goin' cruisin'."

"Be careful."

"I promise it won't end up on the scratch and dent aisle," I joked as I rolled my eyes up while jingling the keys.

"I don't care about the car…only you."

Hugging, I promised I'd be careful. He was always so concerned about me. I was in love and if everything worked out as I planned, tonight would be a perfect time to elevate our relationship to the next level.

I took Abbey by the hand and we dashed to the car. Driving the beamer around campus was fun, but the need for quenching our thirst became a priority. So we stopped for sodas at the local drive-in to solve the problem. Several minutes after our arrival, a car parked next to us. Abbey and I were talking when I glanced past her at the girls in the next vehicle. To my horror, I saw an all-too-familiar face. There was Lora, staring at me with a look that could kill. Here I was sitting in the only blue BMW Roadster in town and it belonged to Robert Pennington. If she didn't know before that something was going on between Robert and me, she knew now. By tomorrow the rumor mill would have confirmed the pinning. I was frozen as I returned her glare.

Abbey looked around to see what I was staring at. "Oh shit! Is that Lora?" She swung her head back toward me.

"Yeah, let's get out of here." Lora never released her fixed stare from me. I don't know what possessed me or why I even felt the need to do what I did next. I guess it was that look of disdain she was giving me, a look that was all too familiar from my high schools days. As I backed out, I turned to see if any cars were behind me. With my bodice in her view, I pointed to the pin on my dress. The look on Lora's face was priceless and paid me back for all the ridicule I had taken for years.

Abbey's mouth dropped open when she realized what I was doing. "Belinda, I never thought you had it in you."

We finally headed back to the Delt house. Robert and Garrett were standing out front talking. Robert walked over to the car and opened my door. "Did you have fun?"

"Yeah, we enjoyed ourselves." I chose not to tell him about my encounter with Lora. I figured he'd have to handle her all by himself.

He pulled me close and bent over to my ear. "Stay with me tonight."

"Okay."

Abbey was being helped out of the car by Garrett. I turned toward them when she said, "Garrett is going to take me home. See you there." She gave me a quick thumbs-up when Garrett wasn't looking. I hoped things worked out for them. I liked the idea of two best friends dating two best friends.

During the ride to my place, I held on to his arm with my head on his shoulder. When we arrived, I ran upstairs to pick up some clothes and books. Abbey wasn't there, so I left a quick note on the desk where I knew she would see it. *Staying with Robert. See you in class. Mum about Lora.* I hopped back in the car and we drove the few blocks to his apartment.

I put my things on the couch. Robert took off his jacket and tie and laid them on a chair. He was looking over his mail that was on the table. Slowly I walked toward him, regaining all of his attention before wrapping my arms around his neck. I gave him a long enticing kiss. The mail fell to the floor, scattering around our feet as he clutched my waist, tugging me close. I trembled. This time I reached behind me, grasped his hands, and pulled them in front of us. He gave me a questioning look and was about to say something. I put my finger across his lips and looked into his clear blue eyes. He kept quiet. "Robert, I've made a decision. I…I want you to be my first—first love—first time to…." I nodded toward the bedroom. His eyes widened and for the first time since I met him, he said nothing. I took his hand and led him to the bed. He followed willingly.

I turned and started unbuttoning his shirt. He grasped my hands and frowned. "Belinda, we don't have to do this now. I didn't pin you so you'd have sex with me. I *am* in love with you. I can't imagine my life without you."

My face flashed hot. "I want tonight to be a memory I'll always cherish."

"Angel, I didn't expect this. I'm not prepared."

Knowing exactly what he meant, I rubbed my hands over his chest. "I started taking the pill right after we began dating." A look of astonishment came over his face. "I wasn't sure I'd be able to resist you. I wanted to be ready." Gripping the back of his neck, I pulled him close, and kissed him. My neurons went crazy. He pulled me closer. I felt my heart racing as his kiss melted me into his body.

He pulled away. "You know that's not enough."

I walked to the dresser and produced five foil packets from the top drawer. Holding them between my fingers, I sashayed back to him.

He grinned widely. "You're optimistic….Are you positive you want to do this?" Concern was evident on his face.

Removing my belt, I felt the heat rising in my body. "Very positive." I grabbed my hair, dividing it as I pulled it forward, letting it fall over my breasts. Turning my back to Robert, I coyly requested, "Unzip me." I wrapped my arms under my breasts to hold the dress in place as I felt him slide the zipper down my back. Taking a deep breath to gather enough nerve to make the next move, I relaxed my arms just enough to let my dress slip down to the floor. I stepped out of it and slowly turned to face him. He had an understanding smile as he pulled my arms down to my sides and gently brushed my hair aside. Shivering inside and feeling my face heating up, I stood there in only lace bikini panties and high heels.

Robert's face lit up as he studied me from head to toe. "You...*ARE* the most beautiful woman I've ever seen." His voice was quiet and gentle. His eyes were both sensitive and seductive at the same time, if that's possible.

He studied every move I made as I unbuttoned and removed his shirt. I was unbuckling his belt when he started feathering kisses down my neck. Heat flashed through my body as my head fell back in submission. I hummed and trembled from them. He picked me up and placed me on the bed, then removed my high heels, one by one. Sitting on the edge, he slid the bikini off and began kissing each place his hands explored down my body. I gripped the sheets when an electric feeling intensified, shooting up my spine. My back arched as my body stiffened then melted. I threw my arms around him drawing his body close. In one fluid motion, he pulled away, was undressed, and lying next to me. He rolled over partially on top of me and captured my mouth in a long, sultry kiss. I could feel my heart hammering. Our lips were locked as he slid over on top of me, settling between my thighs. I gasped then moaned. With one steady motion...we were one. For an instant, there was a slight sensation of pain, but I didn't let it ruin our pleasure. A soft groan escaped from deep in his throat. Being connected to him was like we were two halves of a whole— fitting perfectly, moving together in rhythmic motion. I have never felt so loved. It was *pure ecstasy*!!!

The night was fabulous with four empty packets on the floor. I didn't want it to ever end. He turned on his back and had a lustful look in his eyes as his chest rose up and down in rapid motion between breaths. "Never in my wildest dreams did I think it would be so...*mind-blowing*."

"Did you really enjoy it?"

He was still breathing hard when he looked at me. "Yeah! Absolutely! It was beyond words." He pulled me close to his side. I slid myself on top and straddled him, pressing my rotating hips against him. He sighed. "Ooou...Aaah...Angel."

I kissed his forehead, then his nose, and then his lips as I raked my fingers over his well-defined muscles, kneading them, increasing my awareness of him. His hands began roaming my body. I wanted more of him as I ripped open packet number five.

CHAPTER 12

I FELT SOMETHING light and soft tracing all over my face and then my body. Opening my eyes, I gazed upon my handsome boyfriend with a single red rose in his hand. "For you love." With his other hand he stroked my face, down my neck and over my body. His feathery touch was sending chills through me. I trembled. He smiled with every wave that engulfed me.

He shook his head. "We need to get moving or we'll be late to our classes."

I locked my arms around his neck. "Thank you for the rose." Now I was breathing heavier and full of desire for him. "Do we have to go?"

He reached down and retrieved a discarded foil packet. "Are there any more of these?"

With regret, I shook my head. "Can you stop and pick up a box today?"

Grinning, Robert nodded his head. "I can do that." He gave me a quick peck on the lips. "Come on. Get up. We can't get in the habit of skipping class." He took my hands from around his neck. "What time do you have to get out of here?"

"My early class was canceled. I don't have to be there until one."

"Okay, I'll shower first and you, lucky lady, can fix me some breakfast." He paused and watched my face. "Any regrets about last night?"

"No. Remember I was the one who came prepared." My voice was sexy and low as images of Robert naked flooded my mind. "It was wonderful. Will it be like that every time?"

"God, I hope so. We'll see what happens tonight." Robert winked, laying the rose on the pillow next to me before heading for the bathroom. He paused in the doorway and turned toward me. "On second thought, I think I should pick up a few boxes."

After putting on a robe, I picked up my rose and went to the kitchen. I was about to place it in the vase next to the first one when I decided it was time to dry my wilted gift. Rummaging around the apartment, I took a lace from one of Robert's gym shoes. I tied it around the stem of the rose then hung the flower upside down, tying the other end of the lace to a knob of one of the upper kitchen cabinets. There it would remain until it was dry enough to place in a box. After my task was complete, I made breakfast.

Robert came in and with a questioning look on his face, pointed to my hanging rose. "Yeah, it's a girl thing. I'm drying it." I walked over, put my arms around his chest and looked up at his apprehensive face. "I want to save them. Then when I need a reminder of how much you love me, I'll have them to look at if you're not around." I gave him a gentle, well-placed kiss on the lips. My body heated in seconds and the kiss lingered as Robert wrapped his arms around me, tightening his hold. The kiss became more passionate and I hoped our desire would continue.

He cupped his hands on my shoulders and leaned away from me. "I need to eat and leave for class, Angel."

Reluctantly, I released my hold and with a sweep of my hand, pointed to the table. "Your breakfast is served, sir."

Robert looked back at the dangling treasure. "What do you do with it after it's dried?"

"I'll find a box for them. It will be my treasure box of love reminders." In a sexy voice I emphasized the word "love." Robert just shook his head.

Over breakfast, we planned our day. It was agreed I would spend the night with him for the third time. He decided he'd walk to class and leave me the car since my day would start later. This allowed me time to go back to my place to collect some things I needed. Afterwards, I'd pick him up so we could have lunch at a restaurant off campus. With breakfast finished, Robert left.

After a quick kitchen clean-up, I showered and dressed. I was going to take advantage of Robert's car and drive around with the top down. When I arrived at my place, Abbey was gone. I gathered up what I thought I'd need for the next day. And then I jotted down a short note for Abbey, *At Robert's tonight. Habit forming!* and left it in our usual place on the desk.

It was a glorious spring day to be driving around campus. On Main Street, I stopped for a red light. At the corner waiting to cross was Lora. Our eyes met. She never took her glare off me as she made her way across the street. There was hatred in her face. As soon as the light changed, I sped away. Glancing in the rearview mirror, I noticed she was still watching me. I was glad when I finally turned onto the campus drive and lost sight of her.

Arriving a few minutes early gave me some time to recoup from my brief encounter with her. I was having a hard time getting her eyes out of my head. I knew what it felt like being ignored when I was growing up, but being hated by someone was a whole new experience. I thought about telling Robert, but decided to keep it to myself. I wasn't going to let my insecurities get in the way of our budding relationship.

My thoughts were broken when Robert leaped into the car without opening the door. "Hey there Angel. Where're we having lunch?" He was grinning broadly. His smile washed away the unpleasant thoughts I was having after seeing Lora.

Arriving back on campus, we walked to my class. "Meet me in the Cave."

"Okay." I went to give him a kiss, but he quickly stepped away.

"Not in public, Angel." He cupped his hand over the side of his mouth and murmured, "I don't think I'd be able to stop with a kiss." He had a pleading look of longing in his eyes. Walking into class, I just shook my head and smiled, but I knew *exactly* what he was feeling. I don't know if I could've stopped with just a kiss either after what I experienced last night.

When class was over, I hurried to the Student Center. As I was entering, I heard, "Belinda!" Matt was right behind me, so I stopped to let him catch up. He noticed the pin immediately. "A Delt sweetheart pin. Do I dare ask whose?"

I closed my eyes as a smile came over my face. "Robert ...."

"Pennington?" He took hold of my arm and led me to the Theta Kappa area. Robert was sitting at a Delt table and watched us enter. I half smiled at him and then looked away.

"When did this happen?" Matt's tone told me he was upset.

"Last night." I wiggled away from his grip. From the corner of my eye, I could see Robert start to get up. I gave him a stern look and shook my head for him to stay put. "I love him. He loves me. It just happened."

"You sure he loves you?"

"He says he does and I believe him."

"Be careful. I don't trust him." By this time Matt was very serious.

"I'll be careful, but it's really none of your business." I didn't wait for his response as I turned and walked away.

When I reached Robert, he pulled me down across his lap. "Why were you over there?"

"Matt wanted to know about my pin."

"And?"

Looking down, I picked at my thumbnail. "He warned me to be careful."

He lifted my chin so our eyes met. "Did he put doubts in your mind? I'm not going to hurt you. You'll always be a part of my life. I love you." He kissed my forehead and a warm thrill stirred inside me.

"No, I trust you." I laid my head on his shoulder.

"Move in with me."

I shook my head. "I can't—my parents would disown me."

"You're practically living there now."

"That's different. I'm not moved in and they don't know. Sorry."

"I love holding you when you sleep." He squeezed me. "Okay. I can wait, but I won't like it."

I stayed on his lap with my head on his shoulder. With his arms encircling me, he moved slightly from side to side in a rhythmic motion. I don't think anyone watching would have noticed, but I could feel the sway along with the beat of his heart. Neither of us said anything for several minutes. It was nice just sitting there with him. I felt safe and loved in his arms.

Robert broke the silence. "It's time for class." He picked me up by the waist and planted me on my feet, took my hand, and walked me to class.

After class, I waited at his car for him to arrive. When Robert saw me leaning against the trunk of the Beamer, a huge smile spread across his face. He gave me a quick kiss on the cheek which surprised me. I guess he figured since we would be going to the apartment he had nothing to worry about. Of course I responded with a pulse up my spine as I took him by the collar and pulled his lips close to mine. I stopped just millimeters away and hesitated long enough to increase the excitement, then ever so gently pressed my lips to his. My reactions were beginning to intensify when he stepped back. "Naughty girl." He opened the door for me. "Let's go home." His eyes had a twinkle as they roamed my face. "I stopped at the pharmacy earlier and we're all set." He pointed to a small brown paper bag on the passenger seat.

I hated to break the mood with a reminder. "We can't go home. Remember, you have a game." I looked at my watch. "In about fifteen minutes." I saw the lust in his eyes fade as his thoughts turned to the game.

"Okay. Let's go." He gestured for me to get into the car. As I started to move past him, he put his arms around my waist and pulled me close with a tug. "But after the game…you're mine."

While we were driving, I felt guilty about what I needed to tell him. "I have to study for a test tonight. I'll use the bedroom so you can watch TV."

He tsked and heaved a sigh. "Okay."

At the field, Robert walked over to his brothers at home plate and I went to stand in my usual spot so I could see his face during the game. I waved at him and he returned the gesture with a smile and a wink.

The Delts were playing the Omega Tau's. The score was close in each inning. The game was heating up. In the eighth inning, the game was tied three to three. All the spectators on either side were screaming. The Omega Tau's were up first and failed to score a run. Then it was the Delts' turn. Paul was at bat first. The first pitch was a strike. The second pitch was a foul right into the crowd. All the guys scrambled to retrieve the ball as the girls ran for their lives. The third went right over the center fielder's head for a home run. Paul ran the bases as the Delts' crowd went wild.

I was jumping up and down wildly. Abbey and Garrett arrived at the game and were standing next to me. I hugged her as we continued jumping and cheering. The next three batters made outs. We started to settle down to watch that last inning when, out of the corner of my eye, I saw Lora. I looked at her as she looked at me. Her eyes were slits, almost closed as she glared at me. She didn't even try to conceal her hatred.

She was with the same girls that were in the car when I flashed my newest possession at her. The group was in a heated discussion and I surmised I was the main topic by the alternating pointed stares that came my way. But what bothered me the most was the crazy scary way she glared at me.

I managed to ignore her, turning my attention back to the game. The Omega Tau's again scored a run, tying the game. Brian was up to bat. He hit a ball to left field where the Omega Tau player dropped it and kicked it away. Brian made it to third base. Now it was Robert's turn to bat. He hit the ball to center field and took off running. With the encouragement of the crowd, both he and Brian scored before the Omega Tau's could throw the ball back in, finishing the game with a Delt victory.

I ran across the field to join my hunk of a boyfriend. Flinging my arms around his neck, I gave him a huge kiss which was followed by my usual tantalizing feeling. He responded by swinging me around. His adrenaline was pumping. When he put me down, I noticed Lora standing with her arms crossed over her chest as she watched me with her icy glare. She stood there for what felt like minutes, then turned and stomped away. I clearly understood she meant trouble for me.

Robert could do nothing but talk about the game on the way back to the apartment. "Let's stop for burgers before we go home. All I want to do is eat, shower, and relax with you under me....If that's alright with you?" He flashed a glance my way.

"That's fine, but remember I have to study."

When we walked into the apartment, I headed straight for the bedroom. He followed—pharmacy bag in hand.

"I need something." He wrapped his arms around my waist and pulled me close, his lips touching mine. I gasped as my body was given a kick start.

It was hard, but I pulled away. "I need to study. This has to wait 'til later."

"If it has to, but a kiss was all I was after." He grinned.

Pointing to the door, I demanded, "Out!"

"Can't, need a shower and I have to put these away." He opened his nightstand drawer and deposited the contents of the bag, then walked to the bathroom. "Would you like to join me? I could just bring one of those with me." He winked. I crossed my arms over my chest and tapped my foot. "Guess not, but I'll leave the door unlocked." I picked up a pillow and flung it at him. His instincts were too fast, still pumped from the game. He managed to close the door before the pillow made contact.

After studying, I looked at the clock and was shocked it was after midnight. Robert stayed in the living room and had fallen asleep on the couch. To awaken him, I knelt next to the couch and gently traced a finger over his lips. "Robert, come to bed."

When his eyes opened, he grabbed me around the waist, pulling me over on top of him. "Baby, we were up late last night and you must be tired from the game. Would you mind if we just went to sleep? You know we're both exhausted."

He huffed out a big sigh. "O...kay."

I don't know if he was being cooperative or relieved he'd be getting more sleep tonight, but he walked with me to the bedroom very passively. He slid in next to me, and I cuddled at his side. He kissed me. "Love you. Good night, Angel."

Curiosity got the better of me. "Why do you call me 'Angel?'"

"Why? Because...it was like you descended from heaven into my life. You...just appeared one day." He nuzzled my hair.

"Oh." That was the sweetest thing anyone had ever said to me. "I love you too."

CHAPTER 13

I NEVER IMAGINED anything could've ever prepared me for how wonderful it would be waking up every day beside the man of my dreams. The next morning, reality took hold as Robert and I rushed around the apartment getting ready. It would be a quick ride to the bakery for blueberry bagels and coffee. We wouldn't even have time to sit and talk. It was grab, eat, and go.

Both our schedules were packed. I had two morning classes followed by a break, then my test in Art History in the afternoon. My exam had me concerned. Usually I had enough time to study several days before a test. This week I was too busy—there was no library time. I only studied the night before and hoped it would be enough.

"I won't be coming to the Cave after class. I'm going to the library to review. I'll come after my test," I told Robert as I reached for my books stashed behind the front passenger seat.

He gave me a quick, "Love you. See you later," before driving off. I barely had time to close the door before he left.

My first class was a breeze. In the second one, I didn't pay too much attention to the lecture. My mind kept wandering to my upcoming test. I had to continually refocus on what the professor was saying. I was glad it was over and, as soon as we were dismissed, I ran to the library. Abbey had the same test, so I was hoping she'd be there so we could study and quiz each other.

Swinging open the door, I immediately looked for her. Thank heavens she was there. "Hey, I'm glad you're here. I need help studying?"

Abbey looked up from the Art History book she was poring over. "Hey stranger. Where've you been the past few nights?"

"I've been kinda busy." A twinge of warmth flashed across my face.

Leaning closer to me, from across the table, she whispered, "So you *have* done it with him."

Biting my lower lip, I buried my head in my notes ignoring her conclusion.

"I need to review for the test right now. Will you help me?" I gave her a pleading look, but Abbey didn't waver. Her glare told me she wanted more. "Okay. Okay. I promise I'll fill you in later."

"You swear, or I won't help you." Abbey threatened with a stare.

"I promise or my name isn't Belinda Davies." She was happy with that response. I opened my book and we started reviewing and quizzing each other. My nervousness over the test calmed a bit. To my surprise, I knew the answers to most of the questions. I'd be safe as long as the professor stuck to his lecture material and didn't pull any fast ones.

The test was long and harder than I expected. I was one of the last to turn in my exam, making me late to meet Robert at the Student Center. As I entered the Cave I saw him, but he wasn't alone. Lora was sitting across his lap and they were *kissing*. I froze. I couldn't believe my eyes. "Oh my God!" How stupid could I be? The rumor was true. He got what he wanted from me, and now he was going back to her.

I didn't wait to see what happened next. "Monster" reared her ugly head big time. I whirled around and ran out as fast as I could, oblivious to anyone around me. Once outside, my tears came so hard I could barely see. I wanted to run somewhere that he couldn't find me, if he even bothered to look. I heard Garrett call my name, but I kept moving. I didn't know where to go, so I ran and hid behind a building next door. Now Robert and Garrett were calling my name. Their voices were getting close. Through my veil of tears, the wooded area behind the student parking lot came into view. I made a mad dash to it. I knew I could find someplace to hide in there.

Deep into the woods, I ran oblivious to the occasional slap of low hanging branches until a protruding root caught my foot. Like a fallen tree, I toppled to the ground. Pain shot through my ankle as I landed on my face covering it with dirt. I tried to stand up, but the pain caused me to fall again. I just stayed on the ground and scooted under a nearby bush. The drooping branches concealed my location. As I lay curled in a fetal position crying, my cell rang. It was Robert. I didn't answer and shut it off so its sound couldn't be used to track me. Sobbing, I had trouble catching my breath as the picture of them kissing looped through my head.

Time escaped me. A rustling noise in some nearby bushes startled me, making me nervous as I became aware of the potential danger of my hiding place in the fading evening light. To make matters worse, I realized I didn't know which way it was to the parking lot. The light was disappearing fast and my sense of direction was failing me. As panic set in, I picked a path and started hopping on one foot from tree to tree. Between the pain and the effort it took to hop, I was exhausted. Luckily, I picked the right route and finally made it.

I sat just inside the tree line, out of sight. Retrieving my cell from my purse, I called Abbey. She didn't answer, so I left a message. "Call as soon as possible. I need your help, and don't talk to Garrett or Robert."

My ankle was throbbing. I waited awhile and tried again. This time she answered.

"Abbey, don't talk to Garrett or Robert." Now tears were rolling down my cheeks.

"No, I haven't. What's wrong?"

"I need you to come pick me up. I've sprained or broken something in my ankle. I can't walk. Are you at the house?" I asked between the sobs.

"I just got in. I was with Brent all day. Garrett's been calling all afternoon, but I didn't want to talk to him while I was with Brent, so I turned my cell off. Where are you?"

"Just inside the wooded area behind the student parking lot. Can you come get me now? My spare car key is in the second drawer under my pajamas."

"I'll be there in a few minutes."

The parking lot only had a few cars left in it and the lights were just bright enough for me to spot my CRV approaching. I hopped out to where Abbey could see me. She helped me into the car and we drove off.

"My ankle is killing me." Wincing in pain, I reached down to rub it.

"I'll take you to the Emergency Room. What happened?"

I started to tell her through my sobs. "Robert was kissing Lora. I'm so stupid. I shouldn't have slept with him."

"Belinda, I'm so sorry."

"I love him and he said he loved me. I trusted him." My heart was breaking. The pain I felt in my chest was as bad as the pain from my throbbing ankle. I couldn't tell which was worse.

"This isn't the time to talk about Robert. Let's get your ankle taken care of, and then we can talk when you're not so upset." Abbey seemed to be doing her best to try to comfort me.

We arrived at the hospital and Abbey went in, returning with a wheelchair. She helped me out of the car and into the chair, then wheeled me in so I could explain what happened to the ER staff. They x-rayed and wrapped my ankle. Fortunately it wasn't broken, only sprained. I was given a pair of crutches with instructions for no weight-bearing for the next week and told to make an appointment with the orthopedic doctor. If everything was fine, the next phase would be a stabilizing boot to use until the sprain was healed.

I hobbled out on my crutches to the parking lot with Abbey helping me as much as she could. She didn't want to interfere too much. All I needed was to fall again from her accidently tripping me.

Struggling to maneuver on the crutches, I looked up and saw Robert walking toward me. Abbey was with me the entire time in the ER, except when I was having the x-rays done. She must have talked to Garrett or him. Full of anger, I started yelling. "Go away! I don't want to see you!" I pulled off my sweetheart pin and threw it at him.

He stopped and picked it up. Looking upset, he pleaded, "Angel, I need to talk to you, to explain. It wasn't …."

I put my hands over my ears and repeated, "LA LA LA LA LA," while trying to stay upright on the crutches.

When he was in range, he reached out and pulled my hands down, nearly toppling me over. I regained my balance and jerked away, screaming, "Don't touch me! Leave me alone!" Tears were streaming down my face. I yelled hysterically, "You got what you wanted, just go back to Lora! Go away!"

He grimaced, shaking his head. "Angel, please let me explain."

"Go away!" I yelled again, crying.

Helplessly, he stood there and said to Abbey, "Take her home." He walked to his car, slid in and left.

We drove home in silence. I felt so stupid for believing him. How was I going to talk about this to anyone? It felt as though I'd been kicked in the stomach and ached all over from the emotional and physical pain.

Abbey hesitantly spoke. "Belinda, you should let him explain. Garrett said it wasn't Robert's fault. It was Lora's."

"I don't want to hear excuses. It didn't look like he was trying to avoid it or push her away. I don't want to talk right now. Okay."

We parked in the driveway and I was making my way across the yard when Robert's car raced up, stopping behind mine. He was rushing toward me when I yelled, "Go away!"

He reached over and cupped his hand over my mouth. "*Shut up.*" He gave me a stern, persistent look. "You're going to listen to me," he spat out, apparently determined to make me hear what he had to say. My tear-filled eyes widened. His eyes locked on mine and he spoke calmly. "If I remove my hand, do you promise to hear me out?" I nodded my head in assent. With caution, he moved it. "It wasn't my fault. She plopped herself in my lap and kissed me. She caught me off guard. I was expecting you and when I realized it was Lora, I pushed her away. I told her I was pinned to you."

"Right, *WAS* pinned," I snapped back.

He flinched. "Abbey, I'm taking her home with me."

"No you're not!" I screamed. I tried to push him away, but he still managed to pick me up and carry me to his car. He surprised me with a passionate kiss. As his lips touched mine, my emotions heightened and I went limp. He knew how to control me. It would've been useless for me to try to resist because I knew I couldn't. My body betrayed me—it reacted to his sultry kiss. He sat me in his car and knelt next to me. With pleading eyes, he looked at me. "I don't want Lora. I want *only* you. I love you. I don't want to lose you over this."

We didn't talk on our way to his apartment, but he kept glancing over at me. In my mind, I compared what I saw with what he told me. I didn't see the complete incident. Surely, he wouldn't lie to me. Now I was beginning to feel foolish for my actions.

He carried me in and sat next to me on the couch, then tossed my pin on the coffee table. "Please promise me that you won't run away like that again. Confront me next time something upsets you. I was frantic. Where did you go? I looked everywhere." His brow furrowed with concern.

"The wooded area behind the student parking lot."

He grimaced. "What if you were knocked unconscious? You could still be in there. Who knows what's lurking in there? Who knows how long it would've taken to find you, once someone even thought to look there. Please don't do that again." Robert was really distressed—his voice cracking and his hands trembling.

Seeing him this upset caused me to start crying all over again. I didn't like seeing him this way, no matter how angry I was at him. Through my tears I stammered, "I...I'm sorry I worried you. I didn't think you cared anymore. All I could think of was how stupid I was for giving in. I just wanted to get out of there."

"How many times do I have to tell you that I'm in love with you before you believe me? Please, don't let my so-called reputation come between us. I can't imagine living without you."

I couldn't stop crying. Robert pulled me across his lap and cradled me in his arms. I felt the pleasant stir inside me as he nestled my head against his chest. He held me tight and kissed the top of my head as he started the rhythmic motion like he had when I sat on his lap in the Cave. I could feel myself relaxing. "Monster" was back in her lair. The gentle sway of his body and his regular heartbeat would've put me to sleep if it wasn't for the throbbing in my ankle. "Ow. My ankle is killing me. Would you hand me my pills out of my purse?"

"Have you eaten? You shouldn't take a pain pill on an empty stomach."

"Not since breakfast."

"You need to eat. I'll fix something for you." Robert stopped rocking me and headed for the kitchen. "What do you want?"

"I don't care, anything." I was absorbed in my own self-pity and felt foolish. I knew Robert was upset with the whole situation, yet he had a gentleness and strength about him that made me feel everything was going to be alright. I believed his story about Lora. She hated me and I knew that. Unfortunately, I fell into her trap and was now paying dearly for it. I could imagine her sitting with her spiteful sisters gloating over her victory at my expense.

A shooting pain from my foot forced me to think of more immediate needs as I reached down to rub my ankle. "I need to shower, but how am I going to with this ankle wrapped. How am I going to get to my classes? I've screwed everything up."

He came back, sat next to me and hugged me. "We'll figure something out. The showering problem is easy to fix." Robert picked me up and carried me into the bedroom where he sat me on the bed. He went into his closet and came out with a clear dry-cleaning bag. Next, he found some wide tape in his desk drawer. He helped me remove my jeans, and proceeded to wrap my ankle and foot with the plastic bag, taping it to my skin. He picked me up and carried me to the shower, placing me down on the built-in bench. Before leaving, he made sure I had everything I'd need.

"Thanks." I must have looked pitiful. I didn't have a chance to look in the mirror, but imagined I was a wreck. I felt dirty and disheveled.

"Your food will be ready when you're finished."

Exhausted and not wanting to move, I just sat there. Finally, I mustered what energy I had left and took off my remaining clothes. The warm water felt good running over what I imagined to be tear-swollen eyes. When finished, I used the crutches to maneuver over to the sink. I was right. I was a mess. After removing what was left of my mascara, I tried to repair the damage as best I could. There wasn't much to be done about my puffy eyes. Nature would have to take its course there.

I staggered to the kitchen on my newfound friends, my crutches. To my surprise, there was another red rose in the vase next to my plate of food on the table. He had prepared us each a fried-egg-and-cheese on toast sandwich and a glass of orange juice.

I looked over his handiwork and pointed to the rose. "Where did that come from?"

"After Abbey called, I knew how upset you were. So on the way to the hospital I stopped and picked it up."

"It's pretty. Thank you." Leaning the crutches against the wall, I hopped over and sat down. Robert pulled up a chair, placed a pillow on it, and propped up my leg. He packed my ankle with ice packs. "That feels good."

The smell of the food sitting on the table caught my attention. I didn't realize how hungry I was until I took the first bite. "This tastes delicious. I thought you said you don't cook."

"I said I *don't*, not that I can't. Why should I when I can have it done for me, but I'll do it for you." He slid a pain pill over to me. "Take this before you drink all the juice."

"Thanks." I took the pill, then remembered I hadn't called my parents. I was so tired, but I knew this would be the best time. I reached for my cell and hit speed dial. Robert seemed apprehensive until he heard, "Hi Mom." I filled her in on the events of the night, giving her enough details to satisfy her concerns. Now feeling the effects of the pill, I told her good night.

"I'm going to bed. Can you hand me the crutches?" I stood up from the table and wobbled on my one good foot. He came around and swept me up into his arms, carrying me to bed.

I was half-asleep when I felt him next to me. He pulled me over into his arms and held me tight. "Good night, Angel, my love." He followed it with a soft kiss on my forehead. I was too exhausted to respond.

CHAPTER 14

AS WE WERE about to leave for class, Robert looked down at the coffee table. "Haven't you forgotten something?"

I saw my sweetheart pin. "You still want me to wear it? I feel really bad about yesterday."

"Of course I do. Yesterday is in the past." He half grinned. "Let's leave it there."

***

When we reached the Fine Arts building, I located the handicap ramp. I was amazed to see how far it was from the stairs and how long it was. Taking a deep breath, I started toward it.

Robert was right by my side when he noticed the ramp. "That sucker is all the way over there. Hang on to the crutches." With that said, I was in his arms and up the steps. I was amazed at his physical ability. With me in his arms, plus all our books, he took the steps two at a time. At the door to my class, he put me down, made sure I was steady on my feet with the crutches, and carried my books to my seat. "Wait here and I'll be back ASAP after my class."

"Okay, thanks." With that, he turned and raced out the door.

I didn't think class would ever end, and it didn't help that my ankle was throbbing.

Robert was standing outside the door, as promised, when I exited. "Just help me to the library. It's too far to the Student Center."

"Okay, but I'm staying with you." He reached for my backpack.

"No, you don't have to. Go visit your friends."

"Nope, I'm not leaving you. I have some studying I can do."

I was getting a little better on the crutches. Robert took my backpack, making it easier for me to maneuver. Apparently I was still too slow. He rolled his eyes then picked me up and carried me down the stairs to the sidewalk. After repositioning myself, I started to hop one slow painful hop at a time.

Staying at my side, Robert kept pace with his snail of a companion as long as he could stand it. Exasperated, he took a deep breath, I guess from frustration. "This is taking too long. I can carry you faster than this. Get hold of the crutches." He carried me the rest of the way to the library.

Robert found an empty table near the first row of stacks. While helping me scoot my chair to the table, Robert said in a hushed tone, "There's a party at the frat house this weekend. We can go if you want to, but I think we should stay in so you can keep your leg elevated. We can relax in bed and do some studying." He paused then raised an eyebrow and smirked. "Angel, we still have those unopened boxes in my nightstand."

"Staying in sounds good to me, *but* I want to start with the studying first." I winked. "You know which subject I mean." I gave him a coy look. He beamed and gave me a thumbs-up.

***

After our last class, we headed to the Student Center. Entering, I insisted that he put me down so I could use the crutches. I was feeling self-conscious enough. Robert carrying me around outside was fun and people didn't seem to pay any attention, but in the building it was more obvious. In there, I wanted to just be a girl on crutches.

Desperately needing to use the restroom, I headed for the one nearest the Cave and mouthed to Robert, *Ladies room*.

He nodded and went to make himself comfortable, leaning against the wall. "I'll wait here."

There were two girls primping in front of the mirror and talking as I hobbled in. One girl said, "I can't believe he pinned some girl after only knowing her for about a week." It took me just a few seconds to figure out who they were gossiping about. The other girl uttered, "Lora is really mad." The first girl sneered, "Lora heard that his new girlfriend trapped him by getting pregnant. He's doing the honorable thing." The other girl harrumphed. "Really. I'll bet they don't get married. He probably doesn't even love her."

They continued their chatting as I hobbled out of the stall and washed my hands. I was smiling to myself as I listened to their remarks and speculations. Unable to contain myself any longer, I chimed in, "He says he *is* in love..." They gazed at me. I turned to leave and was halfway out the door when I stuck my head back in and finished with, "...and I'm *not* pregnant."

Seeing me, Robert scooped me in his arms and headed for the Cave. I happened to look over his shoulder as the two girls came out of the restroom. Their eyes were fixed and huge, and their mouths agape. I grinned, flashing them a wave. Robert gave me a curious look. "What's this about pregnant?"

"See the two girls standing by the door? They said Lora is saying that you pinned some girl because she's pregnant. I told them I wasn't. You should've seen their faces." We gave a glance back in their direction—both were still just standing there watching us. Robert flashed them his signature smile and nodded in a polite manner to sarcastically acknowledge them.

With a concerned look, he refocused on me. "I hope that rumor doesn't get spread around. Lora is being such a bitch."

He carried me to an empty table. There were six Delts at another one in a game challenge on their cell phones. They were noisy and very preoccupied. Robert walked over to check out who was winning. I hopped to another table that was farther away where it was quieter.

Robert joined me, placing his elbow on the table and resting the side of his head in his palm. He gestured for me to do the same. We sat there face to face enveloped in our own world. "I've been mulling something over." His mood was reserved and more serious than I'd ever seen. "I'd like you to meet my parents."

I leaned back slightly, surprised because his invitation was so unexpected. *"Really?"*

"Yes, really." He was beaming.

"Okay…when?" Life was moving so fast with him. Here was another reason for the butterflies that had taken up permanent residence in my stomach.

"We can decide that later. We need to check our schedules first. I know I have a couple of games coming up." He winked and gave me a sweet thoughtful look. "I love you, Belinda Davies."

I smiled, but before I could respond, Garrett sat down across from us. "Am I interrupting anything? Should I leave the two of you alone?"

Robert motioned for him to stay seated. "We were just finishing up."

Garrett glanced back and forth from Robert to me. We looked at each other. I could tell Garrett wanted to say something, but was having trouble trying to find the right words. Suddenly he quietly blurted out, "Belinda, are you pregnant?"

I nearly gagged. Robert started laughing so hard he couldn't contain himself. Twisting up a corner of my mouth, I looked at Garrett then turned back to Robert. "So much for the rumor not spreading." I rolled my eyes in disgust, turning back to Garrett to explain. "Lora is *not* happy about us and she started the rumor."

Garrett looked relieved. Robert came up for air from his laughing spell and added, "Since I knocked her up, I have to take her home to meet the parents."

Not pleased with his comment, I reached over and punched Robert in the arm. "That's not the reason we're going." I looked back at Garrett and noticed his confused reaction to what was transpiring in the conversation.

"Okay, I got that there's not going to be a Robert look-alike running around anytime soon, but what's this about meeting parents?" He was panning from Robert to me and back again.

"I'm taking Ms. Davies home to meet my folks." He reached over, placing his arm around my shoulders and pulled me close. His attention returned to Garrett, obviously very smug about his decision.

Garrett's mouth was open as he seemed to be processing what Robert just confirmed. "You're the first. I've known him since our freshman year. He has never taken anyone home to meet *Mom*."

Wow! I couldn't believe it. I would be the first to meet his parents. *I guess he does love me.*

"By the way, how are you doing? You had me and Robert so worried." Garrett appeared concerned. "We looked everywhere for you."

"I'm fine. Everything is okay." I turned toward Robert. "Can we go home now? I'm tired and my ankle is starting to throb again." My stomach growled making me aware of its presence. "I'm hungry, too."

"What are you hungry for? How about your favorite?" There was a quick lift of his brow. "Mexican food? We can stop on the way home for take out."

"That would be great. I can take a pill and prop my foot up while we eat."

"Bye," I said to Garrett as Robert prepared to sweep me off my feet.

When we arrived at Robert's apartment, he carried me in and sat me on the couch. After propping my foot up on a pillow on the coffee table, we ate dinner and looked over our schedules. We decided we'd leave next weekend for the visit home. Finished eating, he stood and turned toward me. "You sit here and relax while I shower. I'll be back shortly."

"Take your time." I was about to curl up on the couch when I noticed a white box on the end table with a card. It read, **To my beloved Belinda, my Angel. Love Robert.** I opened it. Inside was a decorative box with a lid, that was about nine inches long, four inches wide, and four inches deep. Inside was a single red rose, a new package of shoe laces, and another note, **For Your Keepsake Roses**, followed by several hand-drawn hearts. Sighing, I studied my new treasure. I was making this guy's life miserable and he buys me a present. I put the box on the coffee table then lay down on the couch. The exhaustion from the day before, the physical strain from the crutches, and the pain meds proved too much for me. I fell asleep.

I felt the rhythmic motion of Robert carrying me to the bedroom. With my head against his chest, I heard the sound of his beating heart echo with every footstep. The motion and the heartbeat relaxed me even more. After sitting me on the edge of the bed, he helped me undress before I lay down. He pulled me to his side and held me tight. Before drifting into oblivion, I thanked him for my new rose and treasure box. "I love it as much as I love you." I felt him kiss me on the side of my head.

"Good night, Angel. Now can I have my shoe lace back?"

"Yes, Baby." I drifted off into a deep sleep, wrapped in his arms.

***

We spent the weekend relaxing in bed, watching movies and actually studying. Robert never left my side. However, at every chance we got, we indulged in our newest interest, human anatomy.

Several times I caught him staring at me. Each time I looked at him, he just half smiled. Something was bothering him. I curled up over his side and he instinctively wrapped his arms around me. I looked up at his narrowed eyes and creased forehead. He seemed deep in thought as he gazed at the ceiling.

"You look troubled. What are you thinking about?"

"You." He turned his head and stared down into my eyes.

"Me?" I was surprised. "About what?"

"How close I came to losing you—once over a misunderstanding because you believed the rumor about my reputation, and then over an accident because of how you reacted." He was upset. He tightened his hold on me, kissing my forehead. "I've been concerned about the misunderstanding part, but I never considered an accident. The second one worries me the most."

"Don't worry." I propped myself up on my elbow so I could look him in the face. "I'll confront you like you asked. I promise." I tried comforting him by running my hand gently down the side of his face.

"You better. I don't know what I would do if you got seriously injured because of me." He was very solemn as he reached up to stroke my hair.

I needed to change the subject to cheer him up. "Are we going to Sugar Land on Friday or Saturday?"

"Saturday morning. I don't want to sleep without you for two nights. I assumed you'd be staying with your parents?"

"Yeah, but I sleep better with you holding me." I leaned over and kissed him. As our lips met, our reactions excited us so much that we were compelled to practice our new home study course for the next few hours—human anatomy.

CHAPTER 15

BEFORE I KNEW it, Saturday morning was here and we were on our way to meet each other's parents. On Friday of that week, I had my follow-up appointment for my ankle. It was healing nicely, so I was given an ugly black support boot to wear. The crutches were no longer needed as long as I wore it. The worst part about the whole affair was not being able to wear heels. Due to the thickness of the bottom of the boot, my gait was uneven when I wore a tennis shoe on the other foot. Even though I had the very unattractive boot, I felt it would make a better impression on Robert's parents than the clumsy crutches.

It would take several hours to drive from school to Sugar Land. The closer we got, the more nervous I became. I felt out of my league being with Robert, but he loved me for who I was. What would his rich parents think of me— common everyday me? "Do you think your parents will like me?"

"Don't worry. They'll love you as much as I do. Relax. Just be yourself. What if yours don't like me?" Now he appeared anxious. "What have you told them about me?"

"I only told them I'm in love with a great, handsome guy who makes me very happy." I was sincere. There was no way I'd tell them about his so-called reputation.

"So, I'm Mr. Wonderful, huh? No pressure there!" Robert looked a bit unnerved. "I've never been home to meet a girlfriend's parents before. This is new territory for me, too."

He shocked me with his honesty. "Do I sense fear? My parents don't bite and they've had all their shots." He gave me a dirty look.

The sun was shining. The sky was big and blue with occasional white fluffy clouds passing by. Since it was a great day for a road trip, we drove with the top down the whole way to Sugar Land. We made our way through Houston and to the southwest side of town where Sugar Land is located. It's a bedroom community, with modest homes and estate subdivisions. Robert's parents lived in one of the estate neighborhoods.

He turned off the main highway and down what could've been a country road. Even though I'd lived in Sugar Land since high school, I never knew areas with such large houses existed. We drove for what seemed like minutes on a lane that curved back and forth. There were trees scattered along the sides of the road hiding many of the massive homes from full view. My head was bobbing around as I tried to catch a glimpse of the structures. Robert made one last turn, and then his parents' home came into sight.

"There it is." He pointed to a huge mansion.

"Oh. My. God! Your house is *fabulous*." It was an enormous brick-and-stone Tuscan-style house, sitting angled on a corner lot with a circular drive.

After pulling in the front of the house, he parked the car. Since the top was down, Robert came over and just lifted me out of the Beamer. He carried me to the front door and rang the bell. "Don't you have a key?" I was curious. How would we have gotten in if they weren't home?

"Sure I do, but it's in my pocket. My hands are occupied right now." He bounced me up a few times.

"Do you want me to reach in and get it?" I smiled mischievously at him. I was only teasing.

He looked me squarely in the eye. "I dare you."

I reached about halfway into his pocket watching his expression, but lost my nerve and pulled back. "Well, you could put me down and get it."

"Chicken."

When the door opened, an attractive lady appeared and smiled at us. "Robert, did you forget your key? Come on in. Welcome to our home." A man who was obviously Robert's father, joined her.

"It's in my pocket. I didn't want to put her down."

Robert set me on my feet in the foyer. "Mom, Dad, I'd like you to meet my girlfriend, Belinda Davies. Belinda, this is my mom and dad, Sandra and Robert Pennington."

Robert's parents had this air of sophistication about them. They were wearing designer clothes. His mom's hair and make-up were perfect. His dad—well, he looked a lot like Robert, just older. I couldn't imagine what they must've thought of me. My hair was in a braid and I had on blue jeans, a knit top, a tennis shoe, and yes, of course, my boot—definitely not in their league.

His mom shook my hand, cupping it in hers. "It's so very nice to meet you. Robert never brings young ladies home for us to meet." She frowned at Robert. Then she noticed the very obvious boot. "What happened to your foot?"

"It's very nice to meet you. Your home is lovely." I was looking around, astonished. We were standing in a very large foyer. There was a horseshoe-shaped stairway that wrapped around either side of the room meeting in the middle, forming a balcony on the second floor. There were matching ornate Bombay chests on either side of the stairs flanking the entry way to the formal living room. On the chests were oversized, hand-blown, cobalt blue vases. A magnificent crystal chandelier hung in the middle of the twenty-five foot ceiling. I could see what looked like a study off to the left behind two closed French doors. The dining room was to the right and hosted a grand oval table that had ten chairs placed around it.

I must have been standing there for several seconds in a daze at the magnificence of the interior, when I felt a nudge. It brought my attention back to Robert. He nodded his head toward his mother. I looked at her and she had the most delightful smile on her face. I then remembered she asked me a question I never answered because I was so enthralled by my surroundings. My face felt flush from embarrassment for ignoring her. "Oh. My foot. I sprained my ankle running in three-inch heels."

Robert grimaced at my statement.

His dad caught his expression, obviously an observant man. "Robert, are we missing something? Did this involve you?" He nodded his head in the direction of my attractive boot.

"Yes, it's a long story and I'd rather not think about it, okay?" Robert grimaced again shaking his head.

Mr. Pennington shook my hand. "Welcome, it's nice to finally meet you."

"It's nice to meet you too sir."

Robert helped me to their family room where I sat on the couch. "I'm going to go get my duffel out of the car. I'll be right back."

"I've fixed the guest bedroom that's across the hall from yours for Belinda." Sandra started walking toward the foyer.

"Oh, I'm sorry. My parents are expecting me home tonight. But I appreciate your thinking of me."

"Can you join us for dinner? We were planning to take you both out for your favorite, Mexican food. There's a really good restaurant near the mall."

"That would be great."

Robert came back in from the car and headed upstairs with his duffel. His mother excused herself and followed him. Mr. Pennington and I sat in the family room, neither of us speaking. The silence was awkward. Looking around the room was my way of dealing with the piercing quiet. It was absolutely beautiful and I assumed it had been professionally done. Mr.

Pennington sat in a chair next to the couch. I finally broke the silence. "Your home is beautiful."

He looked relieved that I said something. "Thank you. My wife had some help, but not much. I'm sure she'd like to give you a tour later."

Having seen only a few rooms, I got excited as I imagined what I would behold in the rest of this palace. "Yes, I'd love that."

After a brief silence, he said, "Robert has told me a lot about you, except how you got injured." He frowned. "What did he do?"

"Umm, it's nothing." I shrugged my shoulders. "My fault—I overreacted."

His dad gave me a curious look. "Overreacted?"

"Yes, I mistook something I saw." I was looking down at my hands clasped in my lap, face warming from embarrassment. Foolishly, I thought changing the subject might help relieve my emotional discomfort. "So Robert has told you about me?"

"Robert and I have a good relationship in that respect. We do talk frequently and he does confide in me....That's why I'm surprised he didn't tell me about your injured ankle."

I bit my lip nervously. We were back on my ankle again. To my surprise, Mr. Pennington's face softened. "Tell me what happened." He reminded me so much of Robert, I felt the anxiety release in me.

I smiled and dove into the story of my unfortunate accident. When I finished, I showered Robert with all kinds of praise for the wonderful care and attention he'd been giving me. I painted a picture of how perfect his son was and attempted to make sure he knew this whole mess was entirely my fault. Upon completing the story, I just sat there in silence. Mr. Pennington took a deep breath, releasing it loudly, and sat back in his chair.

Sandra and Robert walked in, joining us. They had been gone for a while. Whatever they were doing upstairs seemed to put Robert in a good mood. "What have you been talking about?"

Robert's father stood up from the chair and walked over to him. "Her ankle." Robert's mood changed. His smile vanished when his mouth slightly opened as he looked at me in astonishment. Mr. Pennington laughed at Robert's reaction and put a well-placed hand on his son's shoulder. "Don't worry, she didn't sell you out. In fact, she sang your praises." He then followed that with, "She's a keeper." He changed the subject. "What were you two up to? You were upstairs for quite some time."

I wondered what was going on when Robert's face changed. He looked like he was hiding something. "Same as you...just catching up." He turned to me. "Let me take you on home so we'll have some time to visit with your parents before we go out to eat." He looked toward his parents. "I'll be back in a little while."

"See you later," I added.

On our way, I was staring out my side window, pondering, when I finally spoke. "Your parents are so nice. I really like your dad." I paused and looked at him. "Robert, I don't fit into your sophisticated lifestyle. I feel out of place. Y'all look and live like royalty." Concerned, I meant every word.

Robert pulled into a parking lot and turned off the engine. He leaned over toward me and gently ran his fingers down my cheek keeping them at my chin. "I love *you* the way you are—sweet, kind, generous, caring, loving. I could go on and on. I want you. You fit in just fine."

I hugged him. "I love you too. You make me feel so special."

"You are special. So, no more of this 'I'm not good enough' thinking. It's me that's not good enough for you."

"Not true." He was perfect in my eyes.

***

My parents' home was a two-story brick house that would've fit into the Pennington's two plus times. Robert helped me to the front door and I rang the doorbell. "Where's *your* key?" he teased.

"I don't have one. I usually have my garage door opener, but it's in my car." I nudged him in the side and giggled. Mom opened the door and welcomed us in. Dad joined. There was the usual flurry of greetings as I hugged my parents. "Mom, Dad, this is my boyfriend, Robert Pennington. Robert, this is Dora and James Davies."

They shook hands and exchanged pleasantries. Mom looked at my foot and her only comment was, "Nice fashion statement," as she turned to lead us to the family room. We sat and visited for a while before Mom stood and offered to make some snacks. I volunteered to help her, figuring this would give my father and Robert time to become more acquainted.

From the kitchen I saw the two of them having a serious conversation. I had no clue as to what they were talking about, but whatever it was, they both had a vested interest in it. We were almost finished with the food when I motioned to her to hold up. "They're talking about something and I don't want to interrupt." Mom looked into the den and slowed down, keeping an eye on the two men.

Whatever they were discussing ended as they both stood up with broad smiles on their faces and a handshake. Mom and I looked at each other apprehensively. She took the handshake as her cue to announce, "Snacks anyone?" She gracefully moved into the family room with a tray of food.

Mom was so much the homemaker and seemed out of place in her jeans. She should've been wearing a crisp, starched, collared dress, fitted at the waist with a full skirt covered by an apron. She acted like a mother I'd seen on a rerun of a '50's TV show.

We all made ourselves comfortable around the coffee table. I sat next to Robert on the couch. Mom and Dad sat across from us. Now it was mom's turn to ask twenty questions. She fired them off in rapid succession and, to my amazement, Robert kept right up with her as he politely answered.

In a well-timed pause, Robert stood up and turned toward my parents, taking in a deep breath. "Mr. and Mrs. Davies, I know this is all happening rather quickly, but I'm hoping this will prove to your daughter how much I love her and want to be with her forever. I'd like to ask you for her hand in marriage."

My mother looked at me, big eyes questioning. Mom was about to ask something when my father calmly reached over placing his hand on hers as a request for her to remain quiet. She sat back in her chair as we looked at each other. From my father's reaction to Robert's request, I now understood what their conversation was about.

My father sat back in his chair. "You know my answer." Robert looked toward my mother. She was just staring at him. Dad's hand was still on hers. "The young man asked me politely a few minutes ago. There wasn't time to talk it over with you." He smiled at her. "So what do you think?"

Mom looked at me. I'm sure she could tell how anxious I was. She already knew how I felt. Full of anticipation, I bit my lower lip as I stared at her. She looked up at Robert. "Young man, the subject of you has dominated most of our phone calls. I know marrying you would make my daughter very happy. So, you have my permission."

Robert then turned toward me and pulled something out of his pocket. He took my left hand and knelt on one knee. I tingled from the gentleness of his touch and from what I was hoping he would ask next. "Belinda Davies, I love you with all my heart and promise to love you forever. Will you marry me?"

I started to cry tears of joy and didn't hesitate to give my answer. "Yes...yes, I'll marry you!"

He slid a ring onto my finger. "This was my great-grandmother's engagement ring." It had three diamonds. The center stone was larger than the two side stones. The setting was fourteen-carat white gold. "My grandmother and my mother also wore it as their engagement ring. All who have worn it have been happily married. They thought of it as a good luck charm. Mom wanted me to give it to you."

Lifting my hand, I looked at the jewels placed on my finger. "I love it." I wrapped my arms around his neck and kissed him. Gazing into his eyes, I felt my heart bursting with love.

"Did I get it right this time? To your satisfaction?" I gave him a puzzled look. "Our first date?"

I laughed remembering the scene I made at the restaurant when I questioned how Robert had asked me to marry him. "Yes, it was perfect."

My father interrupted our little walk down memory lane. "We only request one thing—that you graduate from college before you get married. You need to finish your education. Robert gave me his word when we talked. Can you give me yours?"

"Dad, I promise I'll finish." That was a commitment I intended to keep.

"He's a senior. You're a junior. He's graduating," Mom pointed out.

"He'll be working on his master's for the next two years, starting this summer." I glanced at Robert, looking for his acknowledgement. "We'll only be apart during the summer and I'll go visit him as often as I can."

Robert sat down next to me. "Sir, I promise she'll graduate."

"Young man, I'm holding you to that promise, and you better keep her happy." My father glanced at my mother for approval.

Robert stood up and extended his hand to my father. "Sir, I'll do the best I can to ensure both." My father stood and returned the handshake. I knew he was impressed with Robert. He had manners and was respectful.

"You'll have to excuse me, but I need to head back home to visit with my parents." He turned to me. "I'll pick you up at 7:30."

"Oh, Mom, Dad. Robert and I are going to dinner with his parents tonight, if you don't mind. Maybe we could have lunch here tomorrow so we can talk more." This was my attempt to make sure both sets of parents had equal time. I knew my parents would be expecting that and, in light of Robert's surprise proposal, they would want more time to visit with him as well. My mother was excited over the prospect of having a small luncheon. She loved having company.

"Okay, 7:30 is fine." I started to stand to see him to the door.

"You just stay seated and off that foot. I'll see you in a little while. Mr. and Mrs. Davies, it was very nice to meet you." Robert headed for the front door with dad following.

He saw Robert out and returned. He shoved his hands in his pockets as he paced back and forth, thinking. I grew up with my father's pacing habit, his ritual when something concerned him. "He seems like a nice guy, but aren't you two rushing this? You've only known him for—what—about a month?"

"Mom, Dad, the first time I saw him, I knew I had to meet him. The first time he touched me, I felt this overwhelming connection to him. I knew I had to date him…to get to know him…and the first time he kissed me…" I briefly closed my eyes, remembering the kiss. "I knew *he was the one*. I'm in love with him."

My mother had been fairly quiet to this point. "Alright, we just want you to be sure…to be happy. Honey, I don't want you making any mistakes."

"I'm not. I've never been more positive about anything in my life."

We visited until it was time for me to get ready. I was dressed and waiting by 7:30. The bell rang and I limped to the door. Robert stepped in and swept me up into his arms. "What are you doing answering the door?"

"My parents are busy and I was the closest."

"Are you ready to go?"

"Yes." I called out to my parents to let them know I was leaving.

At the restaurant, he walked next to me with his hand at my waist as I hobbled in. He was getting better at staying beside me, instead of a few steps in front. We attracted some attention as we entered at a snail's pace, moving to his parents' table.

His mom got up and came around the table to us. "Let me see it!" She looked elated, reaching for my hand. I showed her the ring on my finger. She was smiling radiantly. "Do you like it?"

"Yes, I love it. It's exactly what I would've picked." I really meant it.

Before we sat down, she hugged each of us. "So, when is the wedding?" She was thrilled and smiling as she looked first at Robert, then me.

"I told my parents we'd wait until I graduate."

"Oh…well, that's okay. That will give us a year to plan a big spectacular wedding. There's so much that we'll need to do. I can start a guest list. I'll need your mother's phone number so we can coordinate."

Big spectacular wedding?! With a panicked expression, I looked at Robert. He saw the pleading in my eyes and interrupted his mother. "Mom. Belinda and I haven't discussed wedding plans yet. We just got engaged. We don't know what we want. There's plenty of time to decide and we'll give you all the notice you need." I discreetly reached under the table and gave Robert a gentle "thank you" squeeze on his thigh. Grinning, he placed his hand over mine to comfort me, but it did a little more than that.

Over our meal, we were engaged in conversation when a silver-haired man approached our table. "Please excuse my intrusion, but I couldn't help noticing what an attractive couple you are." He was looking at me. "I noticed others admiring you two as you walked in. I'm Frank Johnson. I own a modeling agency. I'm always looking for fresh new faces for advertisements and commercials. If you think you'd be interested, here is my business card." He handed it to me. "You could earn some extra money. Again, please excuse me for interrupting your meal." He left for his table without waiting for a response.

We all looked at each other amazed at what had just occurred. Robert's father told him it wouldn't be a good idea, since he'd eventually be running their company and a seemingly innocent ad could tarnish the company's image.

"I'm not interested. I think he was mainly interested in you." Robert was looking at me.

I was chuckling to myself as a mental picture of Robert, the future head of the Pennington Financial Firm, could've been plastered across a billboard in nothing but men's briefs. A second thought filtered into my head that caused sheer horror. What if I had to actually model? I imagined myself walking down a runway and falling flat on my butt to the laughter of the audience, just like what happened in the modeling class. I shook my head. "I'm not interested. I don't have time for that now." My first impulse was to toss the card on the table and leave it. Instead, for some reason I put it in my wallet.

My ankle was starting to remind me of its existence. I leaned over to Robert and asked if he could take me home. I knew a pain pill and elevating my leg would relieve my growing agony. We said goodbye to his parents. On our way out of the restaurant, Mr. Johnson nodded and made a "call me" sign with his left hand. I just smiled knowing that would never happen.

I was so excited about being engaged, I could hardly sleep. I knew morning would be coming soon, but without him next to me, I tossed and turned all night. Light was starting to appear through the curtains. I pulled myself from the bed to clean up and dress, then made my way downstairs to have breakfast with my parents. As I reached mid-stairs the aroma from the kitchen hit me full force. Mom was at the stove cooking my favorite, pancakes.

"Good morning. Did you have fun last night? Orange juice or coffee?" She started with her rapid fire as she flipped a pancake.

"Both." Mom had a habit of asking too many question at once. This made it difficult to answer everything, but it did have its good points. I could select what I wanted to answer then go on to the next set of questions. I sat at the table across from my dad, who had his nose stuck in the newspaper. As long as I could remember, this is how I saw my father every Sunday morning. Mom brought me the orange juice and coffee, followed by my plate of pancakes. "Mom, come sit down. I have something to ask the two of you." To my surprise, my father dropped the newspaper from in front of him as Mom sat down.

"Can I go to summer school and take a class to lighten my fall schedule?"

Mom crossed her hands in front of her on the table and looked at me. "Don't you mean so you can be with him?" She knew me too well.

There was no good reason to be dishonest. "For both reasons."

"We didn't budget for summer school. It won't hurt you to be away from him for a few months." Dad scooped up a bite of his pancakes, then picked up the newspaper and leaned back, giving it a quick jerk to make it rustle. I grew up knowing that usually meant he'd had enough talking for now.

That didn't stop me from trying. "I can find a job to pay for my rent and food. You'd only have to pay for the class." I had to be there with Robert. I was afraid I'd lose him if I wasn't.

"We'll think about it and let you know." Dad's nose was buried in his newspaper. I knew pressing my father would only make him more determined, so I dropped the subject for now. Mom's pancakes were the best in Texas and this was one thing I missed about not living here on a regular basis.

After breakfast, I gathered some things I wanted to take back with me. I had to limit my choices—Robert's car could only hold so much. I was moping around my room, trying to kill some time. Mom knocked at the door and asked if she could come in. She sat on the edge of the bed. She has always been in my corner when I was troubled. I could talk to her when there was no one else to turn to in high school. She was my cheerleader when nobody else would cheer for me. She loved me with a mother's love, a kind that is given unconditionally. "You really love this boy, Belinda?"

I looked up and sat next to her. "I feel complete with him. It's like I found a missing part of me. Mom, I don't want to be away from him."

She smiled in that familiar way that comforted me so many times as a child. She took my hand, patting it. "Oh young love, how I remember…." She shifted her weight to face me. "If he really loves you, he'll wait for you."

I looked at her with a straight face. "*Mommm*, how cliché." We both burst out laughing. She knew how to get a good laugh out of me. My mood changed. I felt a little less depressed.

"Honey, I'll see what I can do. I'll talk to your father."

With a big smile plastered on my face, I hugged her neck. "Thank you. I love you."

"I can't promise anything, but I'll do what I can." I tightened my hug at the news of the sketchy promise. "Okay, enough. You need to come downstairs and help me with lunch. Don't you want to show him you're a good cook?"

"Nooo! Then he'll expect me to cook all the time. What he doesn't know won't hurt him."

Mom flashed a smile as she patted me on the back. "Good job. I taught you well, never let them know everything." We burst out laughing as we headed downstairs.

Robert arrived promptly at 12:30. He stepped in scrutinizing the room to make sure we were alone. With a lunge, he swept me up in his arms and gave me a stirring open mouth kiss. My eyes widened with longing, but I knew a kiss like this was pushing our limits. He nuzzled my hair. "All this touchy feely stuff is driving me nuts. I can't wait till tonight." I threw my head back and giggled.

Lunch was going very well. Dad and Robert were talking about a variety of subjects. He seemed to know instinctively what my father's interests were and hit on most of them.

Robert asked for another slice of the spinach quiche I had made. "This is very good, Mrs. Davies. I'd like to have this recipe."

"Oh, do you cook, Robert?" Mom looked innocently at him, taking a sip of juice.

"I dabble." He stuffed another man-size bite in as he glanced over at me.

"Well, Belinda made this, so I'm sure she can share the recipe with you." She smirked at me.

My eyes grew wide as I glared back. She knew I didn't want him to know I cooked. She was bantering with me. It was her favorite sport. I have to admit, I liked to return the teasing right back to her. "Mommm!" I squealed at her. She knew I was onto her. She just smiled at me as if to say, *What did I do?*

Robert turned to me with a surprised look on his face. "Well, you've been keeping secrets from me."

I looked him straight in the eye. "Just because I don't cook, doesn't mean I can't. Besides, why should I if I can get other people to do it for me."

Robert paused, and then exploded into laughter. "I'll get you back for this one, I promise."

Mom and dad looked puzzled. I waved my hand in dismissal. "Inside joke and thanks, *Mom*." I exaggerated my wide-eyed look at her.

Robert made a good impression on my parents. He knew how to talk to people and seemed to be interested in what they had to say. He made people feel like they were special, a feeling I was all too familiar with.

***

Admiring my ring, I held my hand out so that the rays of sunlight coming through the windshield made it sparkle. I was glowing and couldn't have been happier with the way my life was turning out. Robert glanced over at me for a second. "Do you still like your ring?"

"Definitely—it's perfect."

Robert reached for my hand and kissed it. I took a deep breath, enjoying his touch when I noticed a concerned look on his face. "What's wrong?"

He took a few moments before answering. "I have this gut feeling I'm going to lose you, that you're going to leave me. Promise me you won't run away, that you'll confront me if something bothers you."

"Robert, I'm in love with you. I'll never leave you. You're worried about losing me. Well, I'm also worried about losing you." I held his hand next to my cheek then kissed his palm. It seemed as good a time as any to tell him about my conversation with my parents concerning summer school and not wanting to be away from him.

He frowned, then stroked my cheek. "We'll work something out."

We arrived at the apartment and I sat on the couch while he went for our luggage. Returning, he headed into the kitchen. Without saying a word, he disappeared into the bedroom carrying two glasses of wine. He quickly came back and scooped me up into his arms. "We need to celebrate our engagement." He kissed along my jawline and down my neck. My back arched as impulses fired up my spine. I gasped and pulled him closer as my lips found his. He groaned and his muscles tensed. Our responses intensified as we reached the bed. We celebrated our engagement by showing each other our love in the most passionate way.

"I love you so much." I snuggled up to him.

"I love you more." He held me tight.

***

Robert insisted on carrying me to class despite my continued protest. "I don't think you need to carry me anymore. My ankle doesn't feel sore."

"You're too slow with that boot on." He darted around campus in his usual manner. His pace remained the same, with or without me in his arms. He raced into the Fine Arts building and up the stairs, then into my class room. After scanning the room, he located Abbey and put me down in the seat next to her. "Stay right here until I get back."

"Yes, Master." I liked feeling his arms around me, squeezing me tight. Even though the need was no longer there, I didn't insist he stop. He bent down and kissed me tenderly on the head as he stroked my hair ever so lightly. We found this display of affection seemed to block the pulsing sensations we felt when we touched each other's skin. Robert stood and winked. He was walking out when he turned to Abbey. "Keep her out of trouble. I have a lot invested in her."

"Oh, I always take care of her." Abbey turned to me. I was settling in, preparing for note-taking during class. I flashed my hand in front of her, but she didn't notice anything. So again, this time more exaggerated, I paused and waved my hand in front of her face.

"Belinda! You're engaged?" Her eyes looked as though they were going to pop out of her head. She was smiling, bouncing in her seat. Abbey clutched my hand and stared at the perfect diamonds that constituted Robert's latest symbol of our love.

"Uh-huh." I rested my head on her shoulder so we both could admire the perfect ring sitting on my finger.

"Tell me all about it. When? Where?" Just as she asked her question, the professor started his lecture. Abbey's expression of excitement diminished to disappointment as she realized my answer would have to wait.

The minute the professor finished the lecture, Abbey snapped her head toward me. "Okay, start talking."

So I started from the beginning, telling her about our perfect weekend and how Robert's mother gave him the ring. And then I described how he asked my father for my hand in marriage. I finished with the scene when he popped the question down on one knee.

Abbey hung on every word with her usual enthusiastic nature. "So, when is the wedding?"

"I told my parents we'd wait until after I graduate."

Abbey looked concerned. "Isn't Robert graduating? What are you going to do with him gone?"

After explaining Robert's plan to start working on his master's degree this summer, I described the plot to deceive my parents about my future. I didn't want to tell Abbey that I was worried what would happen if Robert and I were separated. I wanted to believe I could trust him, but Robert being at school without me wouldn't work. After all, I did catch him kissing another girl. Yes, I forgave him, but I hadn't forgotten. Then, there was Lora and her motives. I wouldn't put anything past her. If Lora decided to go to summer school because he'd be here, no telling how far she would go to get him back, or get back at me.

Abbey tapped my shoulder and brought my attention back to her. She took me by surprise with her next question. "Are you and Robert going to the Delt spring formal?"

"What formal? He hasn't mentioned it. When is it?"

"It's in two weeks." Abbey looked like she'd let a cat out of the bag.

I did my best to act like nothing was wrong. "I'll have to ask him. Are you and Garrett going?"

"Yep. I was hoping you and Robert had planned on it too." She had a disappointed expression on her face. Abbey couldn't hide her emotions—she wore them on her sleeve.

After class, Robert, with his signature smile flashing, arrived to retrieve me. "Hey ladies." He reached over and kissed me.

***

With the day over, our drive home was quiet. I wondered if I should inquire about the formal. I had to ask about it since he wasn't saying anything. "What's this I hear about a spring formal in two weeks?"

"Ah. I forgot about that."

I wanted to attend the formal on Robert's arm. "Sooo, are we…"

"Do you want to go?"

"Of course I do, silly. I'll have to call mom and ask her to send me a dress. It might need to be altered, but I'm sure she can handle that as well."

"Then it's settled. We'll go to the formal."

The next few days passed rapidly. My life with Robert couldn't have been more perfect. My ankle was improving with exercise. I even surprised Robert with a few home-cooked meals. On one occasion when he was coming in late from class, I had a romantic dinner planned. Timing his entrance perfectly, I smiled and walked out of the kitchen wearing nothing but a bib apron, carrying our plates of food. "Dinner is served." He must have liked my outfit—dinner was microwaved much later that night.

CHAPTER 16

ON FRIDAY, I was able to officially walk around by myself. My ankle was in pretty good shape and the boot was gone. Since my Education class was dismissed a few minutes early, I decided to surprise Robert by meeting him as he came out of class. It was a beautiful sunny day as I ambled along thinking about how wonderful my life was turning out. I felt like the luckiest girl in the world—engaged to the man of my dreams.

As I rounded the corner, coming in view of the front of the building, I saw Robert and Lora standing under a tree—kissing. Coming closer, I had trouble registering what I was witnessing. Shock filled my body as I froze and my heart seemed to stop beating. Her arms were wrapped around his neck and his at her waist. Oh my God! Not again. I felt nauseous. Tears flooded my eyes and streamed down my cheeks. *Confront him*, he had told me. So, picking up my pace, I raced over. I grabbed Lora's arm and ripped her off of him. And then I spun around to face Robert and slapped him across the face so hard my hand went numb as I screamed, "I trusted you! Liar! Cheater!" Holding his cheek, he stood frozen and seemed stunned.

"Monster" reared her head, charging out of her lair. I turned and ran. I was sobbing—my tears blinding me. I heard Garrett yell, "Belinda, watch out!" A well-placed hand reached out and yanked me back just before I was about to run in front of an oncoming car. Garrett lifted me up into his arms and carried me away.

"Garrett, put me down!" I demanded, crying, shoving against his chest.

"No, I'm not gonna let you run away again. You're too upset. You almost got hit by a car. You're coming home with me. I saw them too." His tone was distressed as he trudged to his car with me in his arms.

At his apartment, we sat on his couch while tears formed flowing streams down my cheeks. He didn't say anything. He just put his arm around my shoulders and let me sob.

My cell phone played Robert's tone. Scowling, I sat up and retrieved it from my purse then turned it off. Garrett's cell rang. "Don't answer it," I spat out, staring into his face. "I don't want to talk to him." I felt as if my insides had just been ripped out and my heart had Robert's foot on it.

Garrett shrugged his shoulders, and didn't answer the call. He attempted to wipe my tears away with his fingers. "Belinda, you need to talk to him. Find out what that was about."

"No! They were locked in each other's arms and he wasn't pushing her away. I can't trust him. I'm an idiot for thinking that I wouldn't end up like his other girlfriends."

"No you're not. I know he loves you very much." Garrett's cell rang again. This time he turned it off and then slid his arm down around my waist, comforting me while I cried. I fell asleep in his arms. The motion of him carrying me to the bedroom stirred me from my sleep. Aware he had left the room, I heard him talking to someone on his cell. "Yes, I have her at my place....No, leave her here...she's asleep....She almost got hit by a car for chrissake....What were you thinking, kissing Lora?...No, I won't let you in....No Robert, let her calm down....I'll try to get her to talk to you later."

Turning over into a fetal position, I felt confident Garrett would keep Robert away from me for now. I was emotionally exhausted and depressed. Sleep came, but it was fitful and plagued with disturbing dreams. I tossed and turned the whole time.

When I awoke, I was startled by my surroundings at first until the vision of the confrontation with Robert and its aftermath engulfed my memory. I didn't want to think about it or cry anymore. I stumbled into the living area where Garrett was sitting on the couch, and noticed light coming in the window. "What day is it? Is it still Friday?"

"No, it's Saturday. I just let you sleep." He walked over and hugged me.

It felt good having someone with me when I felt so dreadful. I cast my eyes up to his face. "Why couldn't it have been you that I fell in love with?"

"I wish it had been." He placed his hand on my head, hugging me again.

We both knew we'd be nothing but friends. Our relationship was sealed when I started seeing Robert. Garrett would always have a place in my heart and my life, especially if he and Abbey were together.

"You hungry?"

"Yeah, a little."

Garrett started walking toward the open kitchen area of his apartment. "How about some scrambled eggs and toast?"

"Okay." Moving to a stool at the counter, I rested my head on my arms as I watched Garrett whip together breakfast. As he cooked we talked, avoiding the subject of Robert.

The meal was just what I needed. "Thanks, that was delicious. And thanks for being there yesterday and letting me stay here. I really appreciate all you've done for me."

"Anytime. It would've devastated Robert if something had happened to you. Not to mention how I'd feel." He reached over and took my hands in his. "You mean a lot to everyone."

"I don't think he really cares. I'm just another one of his many girlfriends. If he cared, he wouldn't have kissed Lora."

He looked at me with a shocked expression. "Belinda, you're wrong. You're all he talks about. How he can't imagine living without you. You need to talk to him. He's been calling all morning."

"I can't!" Robert's foot was still grinding away at my heart, pressing so hard the pain was almost unbearable.

We sat on the couch and I lay down with my head on his lap. He stroked my hair, comforting me. It was very evident that my reaction to Garrett was so different from Robert. When Garrett touched me, it was soft and tender, but no excitement. With Robert, it was stimulating—always triggering a ravenous urge to kiss, that would make every inch of my body feel like it was on fire and he was what I needed to satisfy the burning. The more he kissed me, the more I needed him. Our love was different from anything I had ever experienced. There was a sensitivity I felt with Robert. He made me feel as if nothing could hurt me, until he did. Garrett continued to stroke my hair and I fell asleep, finally finding relief from my aching heart.

I woke up about 4:20. Garrett had fallen asleep as well. I tried to get up without disturbing him, but failed. "Sorry, I tried not to wake you. I guess I should go home. Would you drive me?"

Garrett yawned and stretched. "To his place?"

"No. My place."

At my front door, I hugged him. "Thanks for caring."

"If you need anything, just call me." Garrett spun around and left.

Abbey must have heard us pull into the driveway because she was waiting at the top of the stairs. "I've been so worried about you. Garrett told me what happened. I wanted to come over there, but he said you needed some time to calm down. Jeez Belinda, I'm so glad Garrett was there. You need to control your 'Monster.' You could've been seriously injured this time," she chided and then hugged me. "Have you talked to Robert yet?"

Shaking my head, I began to take off my engagement ring when Abbey placed her hands around mine, stopping me. "Belinda, don't go making any hasty decisions. You need to hear his side of the story. Maybe Lora surprised him again." She was staring into my eyes, tightening her hold on my hands.

"He didn't look surprised to me. It looked like he was enjoying himself. But, I sure surprised him." I slid my hands from hers and fingered the ring, but didn't take it off. I plopped on my bed and sat with my legs crossed, Indian style, facing her.

"What do you mean?" Abbey joined me with a bounce.

"I slapped him across the face so hard he probably still has my hand print on his cheek. He told me to confront him next time something upset me...so I did." Tears were welling up in my eyes and starting to trickle down my cheeks. "Abbey, what am I going to do? I can't keep going through this. It hurts too much."

She put her hand on my shoulder and gave me the most understanding look before she pulled me close and hugged me. "I know you don't want to hear this, but you need to talk to him. Let him explain. You know Lora hates you." Her arms felt so good around me—comforting.

"I can't, not today. Maybe tomorrow." Now I could feel the tears running down my face. It felt good to be held, but I'm sure I was soaking Abbey's neck. I pulled away and scanned the room for a box of tissues. Reaching for it, I bumped my purse, knocking it over. My cell phone fell out onto the bed. Abbey and I looked at it, then each other.

"Go ahead—check it."

There were a lot of voice and text messages from Robert. They all said it was just a misunderstanding and to please let him explain. My cell started singing. "It's him." I turned it back off. Abbey didn't question my action.

I looked over at her. "I'm hungry. Are you? But, I don't want to go out and risk running into *him*."

"We could just order our usual—pizza would be okay with me."

"That's fine. Would you order it? I'm going to take a long, soaking bath." I imagined I was a sight. I hadn't bathed for over a day—or changed clothes.

"Sure, I'll let you know when it's here."

The bathtub, a real soaking type, was an antique claw-footed tub—one benefit of living in an old house. I lay covered with Cherry Blossom bubbles trying not to see a repeat of the kiss that was seared into my mind, but finally gave up. I just finished putting on my pajamas when Abbey called through the door that our pizza had arrived. But that wasn't all that was at the front door. Robert was here.

"Belinda, he wants to talk to you. Go downstairs and talk."

I wasn't ready to face him yet. So, I walked out of the bathroom straight to our front window. I opened it and yelled, "Robert, go away! I don't want to talk to you right now! Go!"

"Belinda, please let me…" I slammed the window closed and walked away. A few minutes later, I heard squealing wheels as he left.

Abbey and I sat quietly on my bed and ate our pizza until she broke the silence. "If you want to talk about it, I'll listen. Maybe I can help you through this." Her cell rang. She rolled her eyes. "Of all times for this thing to ring." She picked it up. "Hi….She seems to be doing okay….We're eating right now….He is?…She'll be glad to hear that….Yes, I agree. I'll see you tomorrow. Good night." She didn't hesitate to give me an explanation of the conversation. "It was Garrett checking on you. He said Robert was coming over to his place and that he's really upset that you won't talk to him."

"Were you supposed to go out with Garrett tonight?"

"Yeah, but we agreed I need to stay with you." She took another bite of her slice of pizza.

I let out a sigh of relief. "Thanks, Abbey."

"Let's make this a girls' night in. We need to do something fun." Abbey walked to the closet. She brought out a big bottle of wine and some paper cups. Holding them up for me to see, she sashayed back toward her bed. "This should help. And some singing. You game?"

"Sure, pop the cork." I had a big smile as I sprang from the bed and walked to the CD player. Looking through the discs, I selected one and started the music.

"It's more a twist off," she joked as the cap was rotated off the bottle. She poured us each a cup of White Zinfandel. "I have another one of these if we run out."

We sang and danced to several songs while keeping our cups filled. I began to relax as my thoughts of Robert faded.

Abbey and I were in full swing with our makeshift karaoke when our landlady came upstairs and peeked into the room. "Hey girls, you're being a little noisy."

"Sorry, Mrs. Hughes." Abbey pointed to me. "Fiancé problems."

"Oh. Are you alright dear?" Mrs. Hughes' expression was that of a caring grandmother.

"I'll be fine. I'm drowning my woes." I held my cup out toward her. "We have another cup. Would you like to join us?"

A huge smile of acceptance spread across her face as she walked into the room. "Sure, I'd like that." Mrs. Hughes went over to an upholstered wingback chair. She paused then gently ran her hand along the top, smiling like she had a pleasant memory. She sat in it and rested her head against the back. "Mr. Hughes and I had our fair share of problems in the beginning. But, we hung in there and worked them out. We were happily married for forty-two years. If you love each other, you can work it out." She took a sip of wine from the cup I handed her. "Which one of you has the good voice?"

"That's her." Abbey pointed to me.

"Continue singing...I'll just sit here and listen. Both of you seem to be having such a good time."

Abbey put on another CD. The show continued as we pretended to be pop stars, jumping around with air guitars and singing. With two bottles of wine under our belts, we were having so much fun and making a lot of noise.

Exhausted and tipsy, we had collapsed to the floor when we heard a commotion coming from the frat house next door—loud voices—engines revving up—wheels squealing. Mrs. Hughes walked over to our front window and looked out. "Doesn't your boyfriend drive a little blue sports car?"

"Yes, why?" Feeling light headed, I weaved my way toward her.

"It's parked out front. He must be next door. Most likely he wants you to know he's near," she said smugly.

I peeked out the window. "Yep. That's it. He sure is upset. Huh, out partying." *The asshat*!

Mrs. Hughes looked at me with a devilish grin that put a glint in her eyes. "When I was upset with my Sam, I used to pull playful pranks to get back at him."

She had my attention. "Like what?" I was game for anything.

"One time, I stuffed his car with crumpled newspaper during the night. I waited until he fell asleep, and then struck. I watched the next morning as he cleaned up the mess. He didn't come back into the house—he would've been late for work." She smiled and chuckled. "I just happen to have a recycle bin full of papers." Her face was even more mischievous when she looked at me with one brow lifted.

"I'm in," Abbey chimed in, looking toward us from her reclining position on the floor.

"Okay, let's do it." I knew how much he loved that car. It would be like I was attacking him physically without causing any real damage. "He should be home, not out partying."

Mrs. Hughes told us to go to the back porch and she would be there in a few minutes. When she arrived, she had two extra-large garbage bags. "Just loosely crumple the newspapers and put'em in these bags. Fill them full. It won't take much for that little car." Her grin widened, like she was having the most fun she'd had in a long time.

I went inside and peeped out the front window. His car was still out front. The party next door sounded like it was in full swing. So, we decided to go for it. Abbey and I hauled the two full bags to the front yard and crept out to his car, while Mrs. Hughes stood guard peering through the hedge at the house next door. Luckily, the car was unlocked. We did our deed quickly and ran back inside.

Mrs. Hughes joined us. "Are you going to stay up and watch?"

"I am, if I can stay awake."

"Me too. This is exciting!" Abbey was jumping up and down with excitement. *Way too much energy.*

"Well, I'm off to bed. Thank you girls for a wonderful evening. Good night." She shuffled toward her bedroom. "Let me know how this turns out. Keep the noise down," Mrs. Hughes warned in a playful voice at her bedroom door. Just before it closed, I heard her chuckle.

Abbey and I dashed upstairs and turned off the lights. We lay across my bed on our stomachs with our heads propped up on our palms, watching out the sheer lace curtain-covered window. The street light made it easy for us to see his car. Abbey spoke first. "Do you think he'll suspect us?"

"I doubt it. He'll probably think it was the pledges."

Silence fell over the room. It was odd Abbey didn't have anything to say, but the quiet was short lived. "Are you going to talk to him tomorrow?"

"I don't know, maybe." I thought about it for a few seconds. "No, I don't think so. He must not be too upset, since he's partying."

"You let your 'Monster' out again. You should've stayed there and really confronted him. Asked him what that kiss was all about? Then told the bitch to keep her hands off." Abbey never took her eyes off me, appearing intent on my hearing her out. "Running doesn't solve anything—it could have put you in the hospital or even the morgue. He'd blame himself. You wouldn't want him to live with that, would you?"

"No. I panic and run without even thinking about it." Fear shot across my face. "I'm afraid of losing him."

"Belinda, he hasn't left you. It's you who keeps leaving him."

Dumbfounded, I realized she was right.

The party went on longer than we could've imagined. Lying still on the bed and feeling the effects of the wine proved to be too much. We fell asleep.

It was about seven a.m. when Abbey and I were awakened by someone yelling, "Dammit! Who did this?" Looking at each other, we smiled, then immediately turned to the window. The lace curtains offered the perfect protection from peering eyes that might look up from outside.

We peeped out the window as Robert stomped around the hedge to the house next door. A few minutes later, he and Brian walked back to his car with a big garbage bag. Robert opened the passenger door and started pulling out the paper, handing it to him. Brian said something glancing toward our house. Robert stopped and glared right at the window. His piercing eyes made my heart jump. I swear he looked right at me. He stared for a few seconds then returned to the paper removal. When they finished, Robert drove off and Brian, with the bags, returned next door.

Abbey and I rolled onto our backs, laughing our heads off. I wondered what other ideas Mrs. Hughes had. It seemed we could learn a lot from her.

This was the first time I'd ever seen Robert look like a mess, not Mr. Perfect. His clothes were all wrinkled and his shirt tail was hanging out. His hair was sticking up all over his head, but he was still gorgeous and I knew I loved him despite everything that had happened.

Sunday I isolated myself and planned on missing school on Monday morning. I knew Robert would be outside my first class. I didn't want a scene, so avoiding one would be the easiest thing. I just had to decide when I'd have the strength to talk with him. That was going to be something I had to do if I would have any peace of mind.

Abbey left to buy us breakfast, but first she was going to walk over to Robert's place and pick up my car. When she returned she told me she talked to Garrett. "He wants us to come over for dinner. Will you go?"

"I guess. I have to eat and his place is more private than a restaurant. There'd be less of a chance of running into Robert."

Sipping her coffee, Abbey suddenly flung her hand over her mouth when sputtered coughs erupted. She regained her composure quickly. "It went down the wrong pipe. I'm okay."

Abbey stayed with me the rest of the day. We talked and laughed about Robert's reaction to our stunt. It felt good to laugh. I temporarily forgot how bad I was hurting inside.

The afternoon was rather lazy with us lying on our beds watching old reruns. I found it difficult to concentrate. My mind kept drifting back to Robert. I really did miss him, but not his actions. Why couldn't he stay away from Lora? Maybe she confronted him. Too many questions were in my head with no answers. During a 50's sitcom I had seen for the umpteenth time, I dropped off to sleep....

I shot up in bed, sitting straight up. I looked over at Abbey and asked how long I had been asleep. Abbey had an alarmed look on her face. "About two hours. Are you okay? You look like you've seen a ghost?"

My hair was sticking to my sweaty forehead. "I had a horrible dream." Terrified, I stared at Abbey. "We were all at a party. It was a formal affair. I was there with Garrett and you. Robert came later...he didn't know who I was." I looked at Abbey, distressed. "I don't know what I would do if I lost him. I love him so much. I couldn't live without him. Abbey, I wouldn't want to either." Tears were streaming down my face. She came over and wrapped her arms around me as I cried on her shoulder. "The dream seemed so real."

I had difficulty concentrating on the TV shows after I calmed down. My mind would wander off and the fear of not having Robert in my life terrified me. The rational part of me warned to be cautious and think about my decision, but the emotional aspect overrode the practical. I was almost ready to forgive him rather than live without him. Relief came when we left to go to Garrett's. My mind would have something to do other than think about Robert.

When we arrived, Garrett was busy in the kitchen finishing up preparing our dinner. We were filling our plates when someone entered the front door. I looked around the corner into the living area and there stood Robert. Feeling betrayed, I yelled at Garrett, "*Why?*" Enraged, I pointed at Robert. "*Why* did you invite him?"

Garrett snapped me a sheepish look. "This was his idea so he could explain to you what happened and I agreed."

I slammed my plate of food on the counter and headed for the front door. Robert moved over and blocked me from leaving. He seized my arm as I reached for the door knob. "Belinda, listen to me!"

I jerked away. "I don't want to hear your excuses." Ducking under his arm, I lunged for the knob again.

He grasped me around the waist and tossed me over his shoulder, then headed for the bedroom. "Garrett, do you mind?"

"No, not at all. Abbey and I will make sure she doesn't get out if she escapes from you."

I pounded on his back yelling, "Put. Me. Down!" He just swatted me on the butt and ignored me. I looked at Abbey. "How could you do this to me?"

"Because I love you."

Robert kicked the door closed and tossed me on the bed. With the speed of a leopard, he straddled me, pinning me down by the wrists. I struggled to get loose when he started kissing my neck. He knew what to do to get his way. I was betrayed by my fiancé, friends, and now my body. I could feel myself giving in to his advances. With every kiss, I lost more control. When I could no longer fight my impulses, I found my lips searching for his and remembered how much I loved him.

In an instant, he pulled back. Our eyes met and locked. "Belinda, we need to talk, okay? If I let you go will you give me a chance to explain." His breathing was heavy as he sucked in air.

It took me a few minutes for my breathing to settle down. "I'll listen if you'll get off of me." He agreed and released me.

"I know you won't believe me, but it's all just another big misunderstanding. I don't want to lose you."

"You're right I don't believe you, it's always a misunderstanding. An excuse to justify your behav...."

He put his hand over my mouth. "Belinda...please, let me finish. Lora heard we were engaged and wanted to talk to me. She sounded really upset when she called, so I agreed to meet her. We were talking when she threw herself at me. That's when you arrived." Raising his hand to his cheek, he rubbed it. "Man you dazed me for a few seconds with that slap and then you were gone. I was about to run after you when Lora grabbed me and was all over me again. By the time I got her off, she was crying hysterically and I didn't want to just walk away."

I jerked my head out from under his hand and snapped, "You'd rather console her than me?"

"No, no. There was so much going on I didn't know what to do first. Besides, I thought you'd be in class and wouldn't find out about us meeting." A blank stare of realization came over his face before he lowered his head shaking it slightly, knowing he'd just stuck his foot in his mouth with that remark.

"Oh! So you think it's okay when I'm not around and won't know! How long have you been sneaking around with Lora?"

"Belinda, I haven't been. I'm with you every free minute!"

"Except when I'm in class and won't find out." I started pulling my engagement ring off. "I wish I'd never met you."

His eyes were full of hurt after my last jab. He placed his hands on mine to stop me. I attempted to pull away from him, but he wouldn't let go. "I swear I haven't. I wouldn't do that to you. Angel...I'm not prepared to live without you. I love you."

His face was sad and remorseful, but it was his pleading eyes that touched my soul. And then the thought of my dream from earlier in the afternoon flooded my mind. The pain of not having my love in my life felt so real. I never wanted to experience anything like that again. Somehow we'd have to overcome this. I loved him, yet I was mad he couldn't own up to his part in this whole fiasco. So now, I had to decide to forgive or leave. I felt conflicted. Just then he leaned down and gently kissed my neck. Despite my rational judgment, I instantly decided to stay and murmured, "Let's go home." I added, "I will never go through this again." I stared at him waiting for his reply.

"*Never.*"

We walked out of the bedroom and explained to Abbey and Garrett that we wouldn't be staying for dinner.

Robert pulled out of the parking lot and headed toward his place. "I had a small problem this morning." He cocked his head in my direction. "My car was stuffed full of newspaper. I questioned several of the pledges. No one knew anything about it. Do you?" He gave me a little nudge in the ribs.

"Nope, can't say that I do. Besides, do you really think the pledges would tell you? Anyway it serves you right. You should have been home crying your eyes out last night instead of partying."

"Guys respond differently to being upset. It was a good way to blow off some steam."

"Well, I'm sure the car stuffing will remain a mystery." Now I was being sarcastic. I would never give him the satisfaction of knowing Abbey and I were responsible. Moving my foot, I heard a piece of paper crunch. I picked it up. "Look, you left one."

"Yeah, I know. I thought I'd keep it. There's an address label on it." He reached over and tapped it with his finger.

"You've already seen it?" I was frozen waiting for his answer.

"BUSTED," passed over his lips followed by a snicker.

With an exaggerated motion, I crumpled it up and reached out the window, then opened my hand, letting the wind do with it as it may. I never took my eyes off of Robert, and could tell he enjoyed my display.

He had a light playful look on his face and finished the scene saying, "Drama Queen." I had a feeling I was going to pay for my prank tonight.

I barely had time to walk in the door when Robert turned and wrapped his arms around me. I gasped at his spontaneous touch. Every muscle in my body tensed with excitement as he held me. He studied my face, not saying a word. With a slow deliberate motion his lips found mine. The kiss intensified into a burst of passion. His hands reached into my hair, pulling me close. I could hardly breathe from the surge of euphoria as I reached for the buttons on his shirt. His lips traveled down my neck through heavy breaths as we peeled off each other's clothes. We never made it to the bed.

CHAPTER 17

I WOKE UP to Robert studying me with a half-grin curving his mouth. "Good Morning. You look like the cat that ate the canary. Why?"

"I'm so grateful to have you back in my bed. I missed you being wrapped around me. I didn't sleep very well with you gone. Saturday night the alcohol helped, or should I say caused me to pass out on your neighbors' couch."

Turning on my side, I slid over next to him and wrapped myself around him, laying my head on his shoulder. "Like this?" I asked in sexy voice.

"Yes, and I missed holding you tight to me. Like this." He gave me a squeeze, sending me into a twitter.

"And did you miss this?" I ran my fingers over his chest, down his abs to his navel and back up, while kissing down his neck.

"Yes, I missed that," he purred, enjoying my touch. Gently, he rolled me off of him and turned onto his side facing me. "We need to keep our wits about us. I think we need to stay here this morning and do some more talking." This was serious. Never in the past had he let us cut class.

I motioned toward him with my palm up. "Okay...you first." I was very interested to hear what he was going to say.

Robert propped himself up on his elbow and peered down at me, fixing his eyes on mine. "Garrett told me you were almost hit by a car, but he caught you just in time. What if Garrett hadn't been there?" A frown furrowed his brow. "Angel, please don't ever run off like that again. We were lucky Garrett was there to stop you....I'm so sorry. If I'd lost you, I don't know what I would've done."

I was surprised by his apology and display of emotion. It made him seem less perfect. Yet it caused a primal response in me to feel empathy for him. I found myself wanting to protect him. Reaching over, I ran my hand across his cheek. "I'm sorry I ran, but when I saw you kissing her, you looked like you were enjoying it. I thought my fears had become reality again."

He held me at bay, his eyes still locked on mine. "Belinda, I've *never* asked another girl to marry me and I've *never* said I love you to anyone but *you*. Why do you keep running away?"

"I guess to avoid the pain of losing you." Tears were now building up in my eyes.

He winced. "Talk to me. Tell me when something is bothering you."

"Okay." I swallowed hard. "You act like kissing other girls is no big deal. I have no desire to kiss anyone but you." I looked at his lips then back into his blue eyes. "I don't understand why you do."

He stalled before he answered. "Angel, when I kiss you that's different. The thing we have...that connection, makes me want only you. The others mean nothing to me."

Shocked, I sat up and glared at him. "The others! This is the whole point of everything that's happened." I was starting to get upset and angry all over again. I was curt with my response. "It hurts me when you flirt and kiss other girls. It's like you're not really in love with me."

Looking exasperated, he scoffed, "Of course I'm in love with you!"

"Then how can you kiss them? I don't understand!" I could feel my anger rising. If I hadn't been naked, my urge to run might have overpowered me. But I stayed, fighting the very essence of my self-preservation. I was managing to keep my "Monster" under control for the first time in my life. Closing my eyes, I took a deep breath, and allowed myself a few seconds to calm down. Robert must've figured out what I was doing. He said nothing and gave me the time I needed.

"That's just what I've always done....I'll stop." Now his tone was more subdued. He pulled me back to his side and kissed my forehead. "I don't want to hurt you. I *love* you. I'll make a deal with you. I'll stop kissing other girls if you'll trust me and stop running every time something upsets you. Do we have a deal?" He held out his hand to seal it with a shake.

I didn't offer my hand. I needed more of a commitment. "Okay, you should be able to control your behavior, but what if a girl tries to kiss you? What then?"

He took a deep breath and thought for a few seconds. He let me go and sat up in bed, raising his right hand. "Belinda Davies, I swear I will discourage any females from kissing me." He looked down at me with sincere, thoughtful eyes.

I believed him. "Okay, you have a deal." I extended my hand, he took it and we shook on the agreement.

After pulling his hand from mine, he positioned himself on top of me, nestling between my legs. He straightened his arms on either side of my head, propping himself up, then studied my lips. "Just so you know, the only kisses I thoroughly enjoy are yours, and I'm dying for one now." He lowered himself until his lips were crushing against mine and all was forgiven. All I wanted was to be one with him.

We spent the morning expressing our love in the most affectionate way. This time it was different, more intense as we affirmed our connection. The full force of our feelings for each other flowed through us. Our minds and bodies reveled in the passion we displayed.

In the afternoon, we decided we should attend our classes. It was a beautiful sunny day, so we walked to the campus. In silence, enjoying our moments together, we meandered with an arm wrapped around each other. Almost there, he slowed down his pace. "I've been seriously thinking about something."

I looked up at him. "What?"

"I think I have a summer solution, if you're game?" He stopped walking and turned toward me.

"What?" I was willing to do anything to be with him.

With a big smile on his face, he suggested, "Let's get married right after my graduation ceremony."

I popped my eyes wide open in astonishment. I never expected that as a solution from him.

"My parents will be here. Just invite your parents to come to your fiancé's graduation. Afterward, we'll surprise them by driving to the Justice of the Peace, and tell them we're getting married. Then you can stay here with me and if you want a break, forget about summer school. Your parents won't have to pay for rent and food, and my parents won't mind—the rent will be the same and the food bill won't go up that much. All your parents will have to pay for is your fall school tuition."

"Are you sure?" I was still in shock, frozen where I stood.

"*Absolutely.* I'm in love with you and I want you living with me as my wife." Cupping my shoulders, he asked, "So, is it yes or no?"

I didn't need to think about his proposal. "Yes!" I was ecstatic as I drew him closer, planting my lips on his. My senses heightened, but he pulled way.

"Later." He smiled. "Let's keep this to ourselves right now." Agreeing, we continued to walk hand in hand to my class. "I'll meet you in the Cave after class."

Going to class was a waste of time. I didn't hear a word the professor droned. My mind kept thinking I'd be Mrs. Robert Pennington, his wife, in less than a month. We would be together this summer and forever. When class ended, I rushed to meet him. He arrived at the Cave the same time I did.

"You're absolutely glowing."

"I'm so excited!"

He smiled. "Well, calm down or the guys are going to suspect something is going on."

"Okay." I tried to contain my emotions, but it was so hard. I just wanted to yell out for the whole world to hear, *I'm going to be Mrs. Robert Pennington*! Instead, I calmly walked into the Cave to the Delt area with Robert.

A few brothers were there talking about an upcoming baseball game. Brian looked over at Robert. "Are you ready for the game today?"

Robert's brows pulled together. "That's today?" He grimaced. "I forgot."

"Yeah, we're playing the Kappa Psi's at 4:30." He looked at his watch. "In about an hour."

Robert looked at me. "The team needs me. You want to go?"

"Sure, I wouldn't miss it for anything. I like watching you play."

***

The crowd gathered on their respective team's side of home plate. Just before the game was about to begin, I gave Robert a kiss and retreated to my position on the sidelines that put me in his line of sight.

The game started right on time. The Delts were up first—they'd won the coin toss. Robert came to the plate first. He missed the first pitch. "STRRRIKE!" the umpire screamed. Now Robert looked determined. He kept his eye on the pitcher. His bat met its target full on. The ball went soaring to right field. Robert flung the bat to the side and took off running. I loved to watch him run. He had the grace and ease of a gazelle. His long legs stretched with each stride bringing him closer to first base. He rounded first and slid into second base. "SAFE!" yelled the umpire. Robert stood up and looked at me with a big grin on his face. My heart melted.

Paul was up next and made two strikes. The third pitch met its mark, a grounder through the hole into left field. Robert took off with the crack of the bat, leapt deftly over the ball as it skidded toward left field, and scored easily. Paul made it to first. The Delt crowd went crazy.

The next three batters were retired. The Delts were up one to nothing in the bottom of the first. Now it was the Kappa Psi's turn. Robert ran onto the field, positioned himself at third base and awaited their first batter. The leadoff batter hit a drive into the right-centerfield gap and was able to make it to second base. Now the tension was mounting. Robert was set and watching home plate. Then for some reason, and I can't imagine what possessed him, he stood up a bit and turned his head to look at me just as the batter clobbered the ball. It shot like a bullet toward Robert and ricocheted off the ground, smacking his left shoulder, knocking him to the ground.

I screamed, "Robert!" and ran onto the field. By the time I arrived, other team members were checking on him as a crowd began to circle around. He was lying there holding his shoulder, wincing in pain.

I was over him in a flash. "Robert, Baby, are you alright?" I'd never been so scared in my life. If he hadn't stood up a little, the ball could've hit him in the head and caused a more serious injury. Now I truly knew what he went through when I ran from him. The fear of losing someone you love was scary.

"My shoulder is killing me." He was clutching it. His teeth were clenched from the pain.

Garrett appeared next to me. "Robert, do you think you can stand up? I'll give you a hand."

"I think so." Robert released his shoulder and extended his hand to him, but immediately grabbed his shoulder after he struggled to stand.

"Belinda, I think we need to take him to the emergency room."

"I don't have a car."

"We'll go in mine."

I wrapped my arm around Robert's waist as we walked. The hospital wasn't that far, but the ride was uncomfortable for him. I could tell he was in pain—he clutched his arm close to his body, flinching every time the car hit a bump.

The emergency room was busy. We had to sit and wait awhile. Robert called his parents and explained what happened. His mother's first reaction was to drive to the school, but Robert talked her into waiting until the final diagnosis was obtained.

Soon after Robert hung up, he was called to be examined. His shoulder was checked out by the doctor and then x-rayed. There were no broken bones, just badly bruised. He gave Robert a prescription for the pain with instructions to keep the sling on for a few days. He was to return to an orthopedic specialist for a follow up as soon as possible.

Garrett dropped us off at the apartment. "Call if you need anything."

I helped Robert get comfortable on the couch and began to help him out of his t-shirt. He seemed to enjoy me undressing him, until it came to the left shoulder. I could tell the pain was too much even though he was trying to tough it out. "I have an idea." I went to the kitchen and retrieved a pair of scissors. Walking back with a bit of a swing to my hips, I snapped the scissors open and closed, then sat next to him. "I hope you can live without this one."

He nodded and smiled. I began at the bottom of the shirt and with each snip I licked my top lip or bit my lower lip, making it more seductive, adding to Robert's enjoyment of what was a painful situation. When I reached the top, the garment slipped off easily. "It's too late to cook us something to eat. I'll order something in. Is that okay with you?" I went to the kitchen to prepare an ice pack. His instructions from the hospital included ice on the shoulder for at least twenty-four hours.

"That's fine. Come make the call over here when you're done." He motioned for me to return to his side.

Once the ice pack was ready, I sat next to him. I had it wrapped in a towel and motioned for him to lean back. I brushed my lips over his bruised, soon-to-be-discolored and swollen shoulder, feeling his warm skin twitch. After placing the pack over it, I made the call and ordered our food.

He grabbed my hand and pressed his lips to my palm. When I shivered, he grinned. "I'm glad you're here, but you may not get much sleep. I'll probably be pretty restless." He glanced at his shoulder.

"I don't care. You took care of me. Now it's my turn." I turned sideways on the couch and leaned over, brushing my lips against his. I closed my eyes and tensed up to control the sensations.

He frowned. "Don't do that."

"I had to. You're in no condition. Tonight, it's my turn to just hold you while we sleep."

"That'll be nice." With his head resting against the couch, his eyes fixed on my face.

"You had me so scared today. Why did you turn and look at me?" I gently placed my hand on the ice pack and looked him in the eyes. We exchanged a long glance.

"I just lost my concentration. I was thinking about you becoming my wife." He leaned his head over and kissed the back of my hand.

"You need to pay more attention when you're playing. Thank goodness you stood up a little or it could have hit you in the head. Your brain would've been scrambled." He chuckled and smiled at my description. I stared into his eyes, trying to make him take me seriously. "That's not funny. I like your brain the way it is. It loves me." I laid my head on his good shoulder. We sat in silence until our food arrived.

When we finished eating, he took a pain pill. We knew it wouldn't be too long before it took effect. I helped him shower and get into bed. Curling up next to him with my arms around him, I held him all night.

CHAPTER 18

WHEN TUESDAY MORNING came, I found myself alone in bed. I sat up immediately scanning the room and called out, "Robert?" I was concerned that he had snuck out to class while I was asleep.

He poked his head out of the bathroom. "Good morning." Walking into the bedroom, he was trying to put on his shirt, grimacing with every attempt.

"Where do you think you're going?" I climbed out of bed, naked, and walked toward him.

Looking me over, he smiled. "Nice outfit....Ah, I'm going to class. I have a project due Thursday that needs to be worked on. I can't expect my partner to finish it. It's a major grade." He flinched again still trying to put on his shirt.

"Is this for your three o'clock class?"

"Yes."

"And doesn't Garrett have the same morning classes as you do?"

"Yes, why?"

"Then, you're not going anywhere this morning." I swatted his hand away and carefully removed the shirt. His shoulder looked painful—the bruise was black, blue, and purple with a little yellow streaked through it. The sight of it made me remember how close the ball came to his head. I frowned at the thought of what could have been a potentially dangerous outcome. "Where's the sling?" He pointed to the dresser, smiling, enjoying the attention. I reached for it and placed it on the arm.

He saw the face I made and looked at his shoulder. "Pretty bad, huh?"

"Yeah, and that could have been your head. Now get back in bed!" I ordered pointing to it.

"Belinda, I need to go."

"*No.* Call Garrett and tell him you're staying here this morning. Ask if you can get a copy of his notes later. I'll call Abbey and do the same. I'll make sure you attend your afternoon class." I wasn't about to let him go anywhere.

He needed to rest, take a pain pill, and ice his shoulder. He agreed. While he made his phone call, I refilled the ice pack and we both crawled back into bed. I made my call then curled up around him and we fell asleep.

A couple of hours later I woke up before Robert. I quietly crawled out of bed so I wouldn't disturb him. Throwing on my robe, I headed for the kitchen to make some breakfast. I put on a pot of coffee, scrambled some eggs, and made a few pieces of toast. The smell of the coffee must have awakened him because he appeared in the kitchen just as I was finishing up.

Robert stood there with his eyes closed, a smile on his face, and took in a deep breath. "Smells delicious. I'm starving." He walked to the cabinet and pulled out two mugs. "Can I pour you a cup?"

"Sure. Thanks, Baby." I finished putting the eggs and toast on our plates and carried them to the table. We picked up our mugs and touched them together causing a slight clinking sound. He leaned his head over to mine, closed his eyes and smiled. In unison we said, "I love you."

After eating, we retreated back to bed where we spent the rest of the time cuddling and watching TV. I made sure the shoulder stayed iced and the sling remained on his arm.

Robert was doing pretty well as long as he kept the sling in place. I dropped him off at his class, with the promise he would call if he had any problems walking to the Cave afterwards. As planned, Robert met me at the Delt tables. He explained he had to meet with his project partner. He didn't know how long it would take, but he promised to call me for a ride home.

I headed to his place and settled on the couch, attempting to study, but fell asleep. I awoke to an apartment that wasn't quite dark. The light that came in from the windows confused me. I didn't know how long I'd been asleep. It took me a few minutes to determine it wasn't morning. I reached over to the lamp next to the couch and turned it on. The clock said 6:20. I started to reread the chapter, but it again had the same effect. I woke up about 7:45…no call from Robert. I washed my face, brushed my teeth and my hair expecting a call at any time. Eight o'clock, no Robert. My imagination started to go where it shouldn't. What was he doing? Who was he with?

I crawled into bed and reached for his pillow, pulling it to me. Taking a deep breath, I caught a faint familiar scent of Robert. I nuzzled my nose deeper into the pillow, taking another breath, as I closed my eyes and fell asleep.

I awoke to his lips kissing mine, making me quiver. I threw my arms up around his neck and pulled him to me as my heart started racing. He grimaced and pulled away. "Be careful."

"Oh, did I hurt you?"

"I'll be okay."

To show my annoyance, I expressed my remark with a rising inflection. "I thought you were going to call me."

"Sorry, I should have, but I got a ride home. Are you hungry?"

"Yes, I'm famished." I was still annoyed, but my hunger was in overdrive.

"We stopped and I picked up lasagna and salads." He extended his hand and helped me out of bed.

As we walked to the kitchen, I looked over at him. "Do you need to work on your project anymore tonight?" I was curious to know if he'd be able to stay home for the rest of the evening. I wanted to make sure he didn't push himself too much for a while until the shoulder had a chance to heal.

"No, but I do have to meet with my partner tomorrow afternoon—it's due Thursday. I can't let her do the rest of the work," he casually mentioned, attempting to minimize the gender of his partner.

"Her?"

"Yes, my partner is a she, Erin Pennison. The professor decided who would work together. He just went down the list pairing everyone up." He paused and could see the look of concern on my face. "Angel, I had no choice."

"Okay."

As he poured us each a glass of wine, I dished out the lasagna and salads. We ate and cleaned up the kitchen with hardly a word spoken. He kept looking over at me, but didn't say anything.

After filling an ice pack, I walked into the living room and turned on the TV. He walked to the couch and sat next to me. I placed the pack on his shoulder then laid my head in his lap. He started running his fingers down through my hair as I surfed the channels. Finding nothing of interest, I rolled over onto my back and stared into his blue eyes that were focused on me.

"What are you thinking about? You're so quiet." His eyes peered deep into mine. "Are you upset with me?"

"No, I'm not upset. I'm just thinking about what I should do tomorrow." I knew I needed to keep myself busy or my mind would drive me crazy thinking about Robert and Erin being together. Staying in the apartment alone wasn't a good idea. "I'll go home and visit with Abbey. I miss talking to her. I think that's what I need to do, go home." I was quiet again as I thought through my plan. I didn't want to tell him it bothered me he had a female partner.

"I want to make sure you're alright and not overdoing it." He assured me he was fine as long as he kept the arm immobilized. "I'll come by and pick you up when you're finished. I worry about you when you don't call." I sat up next to him. "Promise you'll call when you finish?"

"I promise. It won't take long. We're almost finished." He pulled me closer to him and kissed the side of my head. I laid my head against his good shoulder while he held me tight. He looked at me with adoring eyes. "You're so beautiful. I see how other guys look at you. It makes me proud you're mine." He brushed his lips over the top of my head. "You have this air about you when you do that strut of yours. Guys notice, but you don't respond to them." He had a curious look on his face.

"I responded to you. Once that happened, no one else had a chance."

"Why me?" He looked puzzled.

"Because when I saw your face the first time, you left me breathless and my heart started racing. I felt drawn to you—like there was some kind of connection between us. I'd never experienced anything like that before." I paused to take a breath. Once I started talking I couldn't stop. "I rode around that day trying to find you again. And then when you touched me—the sensations—I couldn't get you out of my mind. I just wanted to be with you."

Robert sat and listened. "I was so upset when I found out that Garrett was also a Delt and your best friend. When you and Lora showed up to play pool, I wanted to crawl in a hole. And when you called to cancel our date—my heart felt crushed. All of those feelings were new to me," I confided, letting my emotions gush forward. "And that first kiss? I didn't want it to end. I couldn't believe how my body responded to you—the feelings that rushed through me. I attacked you. I was *so* embarrassed." I closed my eyes remembering that encounter. "Once I saw you, I didn't notice other guys. Only you existed."

Robert looked serious, but surprised as I explained. He smiled and opened the flood gates to his soul. "That first time I saw you, I couldn't take my eyes off you. You were mesmerizing, and my heart started pounding. You stole my heart with your shy smile." He looked at me and tightened his hold on my shoulder in an affectionate way. "I asked around if anyone knew who you were, but no one did. I was concerned that maybe you were just a weekend visitor and I'd never meet you. When I saw you strutting around at the Spring Carnival, I knew fate had given me a second chance. So, I had you arrested. Your reaction to my touch had me concerned at first. I thought you didn't like it."

I interrupted. "Oh no, it startled me. I wasn't expecting that feeling or my reaction. Nothing like that ever happened before."

He grinned and nodded in agreement. "I could feel this…this type of…the only way I can describe it is a pleasant…pulsating sensation. It instantly made me aware of how attracted I was to you." He smiled. "And then when we danced, I could feel your heart pounding and your sensual touch. What an arousing feeling that was and still is." He kissed me on the side of my head and I could feel his breath on my hair. "When I saw you with Garrett, my heart just seemed to stop beating. I knew I couldn't date you if he was. Canceling our date was the hardest thing I've ever had to do.

"That first kiss, I'll never forget. It was like nothing I've ever experienced before. The sensation I felt when our lips met was intensified by a hundred times. I had to pull away before I lost control. I was so glad you ran into the house." He took a deep breath and looked down at me making sure he had my attention as he stressed his next explanation in a hushed tone. "I was so close to attacking you. I've never forced myself on any girl before, but that night I wanted you so bad. The feelings were overwhelming. If you hadn't left I wouldn't have been able to stop."

I sat forward. My sudden movement stopped him from talking. I placed my lips close to his ear. "You wouldn't have forced yourself on me. I left because I knew I wouldn't be able to stop."

He held me just a little tighter with his cheek resting against my head. "Remember when you said you'd never give it up to any guy? I thought, 'Oh god, she would have to be a virgin.'" He smiled sheepishly and shook his head. "I knew I was going to have to be on my best behavior if I wanted to keep you around. It was *so hard* to not take advantage of you." He paused for a moment, leaning his head back against the couch, and closed his eyes. When they opened, they were sensual. "The night I pinned you, I couldn't believe it when you said you wanted me to be your first. Remember, I kept asking if you were sure, but in my mind I kept saying, 'please don't change your mind.'" He chuckled and that brought a smile to my face. "That was the best night I've ever had, and each time just keeps getting better. Never have I experienced such pleasure. I firmly believe we're meant to be together."

I was touched by his words. This was the most he had told me about his feelings the entire time we had been seeing each other. I don't think I ever felt closer to another human being than I did at that moment. Mindful of my connection to him, I now knew he had one to me. He was right. We were attached at a different level than two people usually are. I couldn't explain why. I didn't want to either. All I knew was I loved him with all my heart.

"When we danced that first time, you muttered something about 'lost in the moment.' What did you mean by that?" I was curious.

His cheeks flushed pink before he bent his head over, shaking it. "I was imagining what it would be like to kiss you—to have you naked in bed next to me."

"Oh?" I was a little shocked at his fantasy revelation.

He gazed into my eyes. "I'm glad we're having this talk. It's nice knowing what you're feeling."

"Me too. I love you so much. Please don't ever leave me."

"Angel, I'll never leave you. I *am* in love with you. It'll be you who'll leave me, I'm afraid." He stared with a pained expression at me.

I wrapped my arms around his neck and pulled him close. "Please don't think like that." My eyes moistened as I remembered the dream I had where Robert didn't know who I was. The thought made me cry more as I looked up through my now tear-soaked lashes.

"Angel, it's okay." He gave me a slight squeeze before pulling away and looking straight into my eyes. "But you need to work on something for me. I have to know you trust me." I nodded. His eyes held mine for what seemed like an endless moment. "I love you and I don't want anyone else. You are the best thing that's ever happened to me." He wiped the tears from my face. "Graduation is close. Let's go apply for our marriage license next Wednesday after class. We can also ask about making arrangements with a Justice of the Peace."

"Okay." I sniffled through my smile and hugged him. He pulled back. Seeking my lips, he kissed me. In a flash, the zingy spinal feeling raced up my back—my eyes closed and I inhaled a deep breath, pausing its release. Robert's chest expanded as his hand caressed my hair. When I opened my eyes he was studying me intensely. His respiration quickened. With a sudden plunge of his hand behind my head, our lips made contact. As gently as possible, I straddled him on the couch.

CHAPTER 19

ON WEDNESDAY, I accompanied Robert to his follow-up appointment with the orthopedic doctor. As expected, the shoulder was only bruised. There would be no more baseball for Robert as a participant—he would unfortunately only be a spectator for the remainder of the season. Robert was encouraged to start moving the joint as much as possible. To prevent the shoulder from freezing up, he was given a series of exercises. The doctor felt, because Robert was so young, he wouldn't require physical therapy as long as he followed the instructions and exercised. The sling would only be necessary if he needed to give his arm a rest. He was instructed to make a follow-up appointment in three weeks.

***

Sitting in the Cave with Abbey and Garrett, I leaned over and nudged Robert. "When are you supposed to meet Erin?"

He looked at his watch. "In about twenty minutes."

I wasn't happy Robert would be spending time with Erin again, but I didn't want to let him know. I turned toward Abbey. "Abbey, I'm going home with you this afternoon. Robert has to work on a project. I'll treat you to a pizza." I raised my eyebrows encouragingly. "Oh, by the way, I forgot to tell you we're going to the Spring Formal too." Abbey's face lit up with the news. "Mom is sending my dress to the house. Would you watch for it and let me know when it comes?" With my mind now on Saturday evening, I hoped my mother had worked her alteration magic on my dress so it would keep Robert thinking only of me as I dazzled him. "I hope it fits. Mom is altering the top. I pray it comes by tomorrow so I'll have Friday to shop for one if it doesn't look right."

"Maybe it's there now."

"I need to get going. I'll call when I'm ready to be picked up." Robert kissed me on the top of the head and left.

I looked at Garrett. "Do you want to eat some pizza with us?"

"Sure. We can go to my place to eat first. Then I can study, avoiding the girl talk." Abbey poked him. Startled, he stiffened and protested as he gave her a stern look. "What's that for?"

"It's because you're such a guy." She reached over and gave him a sweet peck on the lips.

Garrett remained motionless for a few seconds, letting out a long sigh. "Do you think Robert would let you and Abbey stay together the night of the formal?" I gave him a puzzled look. Groveling, he further explained. "Um, could you do it for Abbey?"

I finally figured out what he was asking. "I don't know. You'll have to ask him." I hoped Robert would object to that arrangement.

Driving in the direction of Garrett's apartment, I suggested we go by the house and see if my dress had arrived. Abbey's excitement heightened because she was such a clothes hound. The thought of the dress arriving thrilled me. Garrett on the other hand didn't seem to share our enthusiasm, but he agreed to go along to pacify us. I guess the sooner we resolved the dress issue, the faster we would order the pizza and that was Garrett's main priority.

When we arrived, Abbey and I sighed. There was no package at the front door. Garrett encouraged us to keep going and head over to his place. Abbey put her hand on his chest. "Hold on, buddy. Belinda, go inside to see if Mrs. Hughes brought it in. We'll wait here."

"Okay." I parked the car, ran inside and looked around the living room. The package was lying on the couch. I grabbed it. As I walked back to the car, I thought how silly it was for us to go over to Garrett's, order pizza, and then come back before I could try on the dress. I knew we weren't supposed to have boys upstairs—this was at the top of Mrs. Hughes' rule list—but I couldn't wait to try it on. "Let's stay here and sneak Garrett upstairs." Abbey eyes widened. She was game. Garrett on the other hand needed some convincing. He was worried about what Mrs. Hughes would do if he was caught. I was able to coax him into going along with my plan when I said, "The worst thing that could happen is we get kicked out. Then, Abbey would have to move in with you and I'd have to make it official that I was living with Robert."

He looked at Abbey, smiled, and without a hint of hesitation answered. "I'm in."

Abbey looked shocked and just whined, "Belinda!" She shifted her eyes toward the box in my hands. "So how do we do this?"

"I'll go in first. Mrs. Hughes wasn't in there before, but she may have come in while we were talking. If the coast is clear," I pointed at Garrett, "you run up stairs." We all walked toward the porch keeping our eyes open for any sign of our landlady. Garrett and Abbey waited by the side of the door. I opened it and peered around the living room. No one was there. I motioned for him to go in. "Walk softly, but hurry." And then, Abbey and I strolled up the stairs like nothing happened.

We ordered the pizza and while we waited for it to be delivered, I tore open the box. I was anxious to see my mother's handiwork. Praying she followed my instructions, I dug into the package and pulled out the long, flowing, pale blue, chiffon dress. First I examined the top. My mother hadn't failed me. Her alteration was to my exact specification. I held it up to me. "It looks nice. I hope it fits." I took the dress and laid it on my bed, then methodically hand pressed the wrinkles out before returning to Abbey and Garrett in our sitting room.

Garrett looked at me. "Try it on."

"Okay, but I have to get some things together first. The dress doesn't go on until we've eaten. No pizza on my dress." Disappearing into the huge closet, I began to rummage through what was left of my clothes, gathering more apparel to take to Robert's place. At this pace, my side would soon be empty. It would be easier and cheaper to just move in with him, but I had to keep up the facade for my parents' sake and mine. Mom might understand, but my father would never forgive me. So, I still lived with Abbey until graduation, when I would become Mrs. Robert Pennington. I liked the way that sounded. I'd just finished pulling out a pair of silver heels to wear with my dress when I heard Abbey announce, "Pizza."

I emerged from the closet with my belongings and placed everything on the bed. Abbey and Garrett started without me, so I had some catching up to do.

After we ate, I cleaned up every bit of pizza I could and retrieved the gown from the bed. Vanishing into the bathroom, I put on the dress and silver heels. I pulled the sides of my hair up on the top of my head and fastened them with an elastic band. I wanted to be as close to the total effect as I could. Once satisfied, I walked into the room. "Well, what do you think?" I twirled around so they could obtain a view of the back.

Garrett stared with his mouth hanging wide open. Words finally emerged. "You look stunning. Robert is going to love that dress on you."

"Does it really look alright? It's not too revealing is it? Mom must've forgotten I filled out last summer." I was a bit concerned too much of my breasts were exposed.

"No, it's perfect. You look gorgeous in it," Abbey assured me.

"NO...NO...it looks just fine from where I'm sitting. I'd like to get a picture of Robert's face when he sees you in it." Garrett was still staring.

Abbey elbowed him in the ribs. Garrett responded with a puzzled look. "What?"

Abbey looked at Garrett and smiled, then reached for him, cupping her hands on either side of his face as she stretched over and gave him a slow, passionate kiss. When she pulled back, her face was full of adoration for him. Garrett just gazed at her with the most loving eyes as she warned, "Have fun looking, but remember hands off. She's taken…and so are you."

He just smiled. "Yes Babe." They were so right for each other.

Abbey turned her attention to me. "Wear your hair like you have it. I have some long, dangling rhinestone earrings that would be perfect."

Garrett's ogling of my dress was interrupted when the sound of my cell phone alerted me that Robert was calling. I answered. "Hi. You ready?"

"Yep, we just finished. I'll be at the Admin in ten minutes."

"Okay, I'll need a few more minutes than that. I'm trying on my dress."

"Your formal?"

"Yes, they say it looks fine."

"They?"

"Um…Garrett is here too."

"Are you at Garrett's?" Robert asked.

"No, we're at my place."

"So we're going back to your place after you pick me up?"

"No, you can't come up." I rolled my eyes.

"Why?"

"Robert! After I pick you up, we're going home. Okay? I'll be there shortly."

Garrett and Abbey caught the gist of my conversation. "So, he wants to come up too." Garrett laughed. "Well, now I have to get out of here. Can you drop me off at my place after my escape?"

"Sure, but we need to pick up Robert first." I headed for the bathroom to undress. "You two better say your goodbyes while I'm changing. I'm leaving as soon as I'm finished and packed up."

Not wanting to walk in on them unannounced, I knocked on the bathroom door and said I was coming out. They were still in each other's arms. I don't know why I knocked—it didn't make any difference. As far as they were concerned I wasn't even there. They were lost in each other.

Carefully, I hung the dress on my almost-empty side of the closet then finished gathering what I was taking with me. I walked over to them, but they were still entwined in their loving embrace. They never came up for air and I wondered, if left alone, how long they would remain in an upright position. It was very clear how they felt about each other. They were both great people, good friends, and deserved to be as happy as Robert and I were. To get their attention I cleared my throat in a loud manner. "Garrett, I'm leaving now, are you ready? I'll see you tomorrow, Abbey." Chuckling, I gave her a quick wave goodbye as Garrett and I made our way quietly down the stairs and safely out the door.

We swung by the Administration building to pick up Robert. I spotted him standing on the curb talking to a blonde with a very short, almost pixie-like haircut. As I pulled up, I caught a glimpse of her face before she turned and walked away, not allowing for an introduction. Robert opened the front door and motioned with his head for Garrett to vacate the front seat. He knew what Robert wanted—that he was expecting to ride shotgun. Garrett climbed in back. "Was that Erin?" I nodded in her direction as Robert climbed in.

"Yeah." He closed the door and immediately turned his attention to Garrett. "You got to go upstairs?" Robert was frowning. "Is there anything I should know?"

Sensing Robert's jealousy of missing out on seeing my dress and room, Garrett apparently decided to rub salt in the wound. "Yep, Belinda modeled her dress and DAMN! Wait till you see her in it."

"Really?!....When can I see it?" Robert shot an unsmiling glance in my direction. I couldn't tell if he was grumpy because he was in pain or jealous because he was left out of our escapade.

"Saturday." I tried to change the subject. "Did you finish your project?"

"Yes, it's finished." Without stopping to take a breath, he started again. "Why Saturday? I'd like to see it sooner, like tonight." He was staring at me, still not very happy.

I didn't answer him. I just tsked. We arrived at Garrett's apartment. As he was exiting the car, I turned around and gave him a stern look. He just laughed knowing he had opened a can of worms. "See you later, Robert."

Robert wasted no time starting in on the dress again. He wanted to drive back to my place so I could pick it up. I put my foot down and told him he needed to wait, but he wouldn't let up. I didn't want to argue so I changed my tactics and used a more seductive tone. "Baby, I want you to get the whole effect. I want my hair and makeup perfect as well." My finish was a pouty face and a fingering of his shirt collar. "Garrett only saw half the picture. I want you to see all of it." Robert just rolled his eyes. He seemed to relax and accept my reasoning. He winced. Trying to reposition himself, he laid his head against the headrest and closed his eyes. Now I knew he was uncomfortable and most likely in pain.

At the apartment, I helped make him comfortable on the couch. I still had to ask about our sleeping arrangements at the formal and figured if he was in less pain, his mood might be better. "Baby, Garrett is going to ask you if it would be alright for me to stay with Abbey Saturday night and you two share a room. She's not into sleeping with him yet."

A frown furrowed Robert's forehead. "I'll talk to him." He paused. "So, he gets to see you in your dress, but I have to wait, and now I'm supposed to sleep with him as well?" His look told me how screwed up the situation sounded. "That's not fair."

"Yep, something for you to look forward to. You and Garrett should have fun together, at *night*." I giggled and gave him a quick peck on the cheek. "It's been a long, busy day. I'm exhausted." I yawned. "You relax on the couch. I'm going to take a quick shower. When I'm finished, I'll come help you."

Our interaction was completed by Robert planting a quick, well-placed slap on my rump. "You're too bad," he teased, but I could tell he saw the humor in our conversation. His wit was one of the many things I loved about him.

After my shower, I gathered up everything he needed for his and took it to the bathroom. Robert had fallen asleep. I fingered his hair and was admiring his face when he opened his eyes slightly. "Do you want to forget the shower?" He looked so comfortable and relaxed.

Forcing his eyes open, he looked around. "No, I need to get some heat on this shoulder."

I helped him up and he put his arm around me as if he needed assistance walking. He had walked all over campus without me, but now he was unsteady. I didn't mind. I liked feeling needed by him. He sat on the shower bench where I helped him undress. I was about to leave when he pulled me close with his good arm. "I need someone to wash my back," he said, with wishful eyes.

I just studied him and thought about what he was requesting before answering. "No, you need to let the water run on your shoulder. We don't need any of our acrobatics causing another injury to either of us." He gave me a slight look of disappointment as he released me. Just before closing the shower door, I gave him a sweet kiss on the top of his head. "I'll wait up. Let me know if you need help dressing." Somehow I knew he would, even though he was capable of handling the process himself. He always seemed to enjoy me dressing and undressing him, and I liked it too.

CHAPTER 20

WITH EVERY PASSING day my excitement grew and I couldn't wait for Saturday evening to arrive. My first fraternity formal! Robert made occasional comments about missing out on the first dress viewing. To make sure he didn't see the dress, I kept it at my place. He would see me in it when I was ready. I wanted the vision to be complete.

By the time Saturday afternoon arrived, I had packed and repacked my suitcase several times making sure I had everything needed. That morning I picked up my dress and hid it from Robert's view in a garment bag. I was so excited, but Robert didn't share my sentiments. He had agreed to let me and Abbey stay together. So we were staying in one room, and Garrett and Robert were staying in the adjoining room. Robert had hoped for different arrangements, but was being very gracious to accommodate Abbey's needs.

The formal was being held at a hotel in Dallas. Abbey and Garrett were already there in the lobby waiting for us. After our check-in process, we rode to our floor where we separated to our respective rooms—the girls in one and the boys in the other. Abbey immediately busied herself unpacking and spreading her stuff all over the vanity area. She staked her claim to the bed closest to the door.

I was busy unpacking when there was a knock on the door that connected the two rooms. We unlocked our side and there stood the guys eager to enter, but I stopped them by standing with one hand on the door jamb and the other on the door. "Yes, may I help you?" I motioned to Abbey to put the dresses in the closet for safekeeping, away from peering eyes.

"We came to see your dress, Belinda," Garrett sneered for Robert's benefit. Robert looked at him, with a frown, not amused. Garrett was snickering at his reaction. Confident Abbey had secured our dresses, I broke the tension between the two by grabbing Robert's arm and pulling him into the room. Garrett was left standing in the adjourning room as I attempted to close the door. *"Hey."* He stopped the door from completely closing with his hand and pushed his way in. "So, what's the plan? We have a few hours before we need to be downstairs. Anyone for some pool time?"

Abbey and I looked at him in disbelief. "Garrett, are you out of your mind? It's going to take Belinda and me a few hours to get ready, Sweetie."

"So what are we supposed to do while we're waiting?" Garrett pointed to Robert and himself.

Abbey offered no solution to their plight. All she did was shrug her shoulders. I had a suggestion, if Robert was willing. "You could go to the pool. The exercise and water would help your shoulder." Then a thought came to me. There might be bikini clad co-eds there to distract our guys and offer Robert an abundance of sympathy. But after contemplating the situation, my bet was that every girl attending the formal would be busy doing the same thing we were—getting ready. I was pretty sure the pool area would be filled with guys all banned from their rooms.

We all decided to go for drinks in the bar before the dance, then Abbey and I gave the guys a time to pick us up. Once everything was resolved, they were pushed out the door with strict instructions to leave us alone. "You two stay out of trouble," I teased, closing the door.

Abbey and I primped for about two hours, doing everything from head to toes. My hair was worn with the front and sides pulled up on top and the back hanging down in curls. I wore Abbey's rhinestone earrings and a simple diamond drop necklace. My gown had an empire waist and was strapless with a sweetheart-cut bodice. The extra fabric in the center under the bustline added some fullness causing the body of the skirt to flow when I walked. Silver heels completed the effect, making me feel like a princess.

I was sitting at the desk putting on the final touches of makeup when Abbey walked out of the bathroom area. I turned to face her. "You look beautiful. Turn around." She made a few complete turns as her dress swirled around her. "Perfect." She stood there moving her hands down the sides of her dress, smoothing it. Abbey wore her hair hanging down and slightly curled under. Her dress was a beautiful, aqua, chiffon, off-the-shoulders gown with a fitted waist and an A-line skirt. There were no embellishments of any type. Around her neck was a strand of pearls, and she had matching earrings. She was simply elegant.

"So do you. Robert's eyes will pop out of his head." Smiling, Abbey motioned for me to join her by the adjoining door.

"You ready for the guys?" I gave the bodice one final tug.

"I think so." She was anxious to see how Garrett responded to her. I gave her arm a slight squeeze to assure her that she looked absolutely beautiful, then knocked on the adjoining door. "Are you two decent?"

"Come on in." Robert had a slight tone of disgust in his voice.

Before opening the door, I turned to Abbey. "You sure this dress doesn't show too much? I feel self-conscious."

"No! You look gorgeous and sexy." She raised her eyebrows repeatedly while smiling. "You go first. I want to see Robert's face."

"Sexy is the part I'm uncomfortable with. That's not me." Adjusting the bodice again, I took one last look in the full-length mirror on the door.

Abbey put her chin on my shoulder. "Maybe not the old you, but the new you, yes."

I opened the door and walked in with Abbey following. Robert was standing in front of the window looking out. As he turned, his mouth fell open and his eyes grew wide. Garrett took the opportunity to snap a picture of him. He knew Robert's expression would fade and wanted to capture it.

I stood there and gazed at Robert. "Do I look okay?" I twirled around waiting for his response.

Robert said nothing. His eyes just wandered over me from head to toe, making me feel more self-conscious as they stopped at my bodice. Finally he spoke. "You look absolutely...*gorgeous.*"

I told him he looked very handsome in his tux. And he was breathtaking. The tuxedo fit him perfectly. It accentuated his broad shoulders and narrow hips. For a rental, I couldn't believe how well it fit. He looked like a million bucks. I could've just stayed in the room, peeling it off one layer at a time. My trance was broken when Abbey asked me to take a picture of Garrett and her.

Robert glanced at Abbey. "Wow, you look awesome." He looked at Garrett. "We'll have the two hottest babes in the whole place."

Garrett pulled out the desk chair and sat in it. He asked Abbey and me to stand on either side and give him a kiss on his cheeks. We obliged, stroking his ego while Robert snapped the picture. Next there were the individual pictures, more couples, and triples, all of which Garrett or Robert photo-bombed whenever they could.

Robert walked over and stood in front of me. "Can I hug and kiss you?"

"Of course you can." I reached out for him. He carefully hugged me. The kiss, though, was very passionate and long. Quivering and starting to react, I ran my hands up the back of his neck and locked my fingers in his hair to pull him close, fantasizing about removing those layers of clothes. My back arched...I adhered myself to him. I felt my heart race as his tongue waltzed around mine.

If Garrett hadn't interrupted, we may have never seen the outside of the hotel room. "Okay you two, let's go." Garrett tugged Robert away from me.

"Hey, I was enjoying that," Robert protested.

"I know, and to tell you the truth, so was I." Garrett smirked.

My eyes widened at Garrett's remark, somewhat embarrassed because Robert and I would always forget who and what was around us when we kissed. From the corner of my eye, I could see Abbey coming over to fetch Garrett. "Sweetie, leave them alone."

Garrett, now feeling playful as ever, turned and swept Abbey into his arms dipping her down, placing a long passionate kiss on her lips. She went limp for a few seconds, and then wrapped her arms around his neck as she responded enthusiastically. He stood her upright without interrupting their exciting moment. After several short, sweet kisses, he stopped as Abbey stood there mesmerized with her eyes closed. Garrett turned to Robert and me and gloated, "Now we're even." Abbey was back in reality when she gave Garrett a love tap on the arm. He adoringly smiled from ear to ear at her, and then at us with a different, impish expression. Abbey just looked at him with an admiring smile.

Robert turned his head to Garrett, then me. "And I have to stay with him tonight?" His piercing eyes went back to Garrett. Robert then whipped his eyes to Abbey with a questioning look on his face. Abbey stood there and said nothing, but I could tell the wheels in her head were working overtime trying to decide if this would be the night for Garrett and her.

"Maybe we'll let you have these rooms and we'll get another one." My ears perked up when I heard Robert's comment. However, that wouldn't happen. I was sure the hotel was full. So our fate was sealed. We would be apart tonight and that idea didn't appeal to me at all. I took a deep breath to clear my head, hoping Abbey would make the right decision for all of us. Robert held his arm out to me.

I took it and slipped my key card into his pocket. He noticed—I winked and smiled stepping into the elevator. "Just in case."

When the doors opened, the lobby was bustling with ladies and men of all ages, dressed in formal attire. The lobby lights had been dimmed to accommodate the dignified atmosphere. We headed in the direction of the bar. It was situated in the back of the lobby behind two huge doors with leaded glass panel inserts. As we walked in, I soon became very aware all eyes were looking at us, the two very attractive couples who just entered. "I love that dress and color on you. You look so exquisite. And sexy," Robert whispered in my ear, as he gave the top half of my dress a rapid glance.

"You're pretty hot yourself. How did you get a tux that fits you so well?"

"You have one tailored for you."

I should have figured it out, that he owned a tailored tuxedo.

When we reached the bar there were frat brothers with their dates, parents of frat brothers, and alumni gathered around. We drank and mingled until it was time for the dinner to start. When the time arrived, the head waiter announced that the ballroom was open for seating.

The room was very impressive. The lights were dimmed to enhance the mood. On each table was a floral arrangement that was about three feet tall. The column vase was filled with flowers that spiked upward from the top, giving the arrangements a grander look. The height allowed for some of the longer stems to weep down, softening the place setting on each table. There was a ring of votive candles around each vase adding to the ambiance. The round tables were scattered about the periphery of the dance floor in a horseshoe shape.

We wandered around, socializing as we looked for our assigned table. It was near the dance area, not far from the band. After seating Abbey and me, the guys left for more drinks. While they were gone, I was tempted to ask Abbey if she'd mind if Robert and I stayed together, taking one of the rooms. I wanted so badly to be with him. As we talked, there didn't seem to be a right moment to ask her before Robert and Garrett returned. They arrived, drinks in hand, just as our meals were being served. My chance to ask for the room instantly slipped away.

Robert leaned very close to my ear. "Angel, I'd like to tell Abbey and Garrett about our wedding plans and invite them. Is that okay?" He pulled away and waited for a response. I smiled as I looked at Abbey. I couldn't imagine her not being there on the most important day of my life. Returning my gaze to Robert, I gave him a nod of approval.

He faced the only other people currently seated at our table. "Abbey, Garrett, we have something we'd like to share with you, but you have to promise to keep it under wraps."

Abbey looked at me with a look of sudden awareness. I wondered if she figured out what the secret was. I placed my hand on Robert's arm, getting his attention so he wouldn't say anything just yet. I knew Abbey's usual excited reaction to the news would give it away. "Abbey, you have to promise you'll sit quietly after you hear what Robert has to say."

Abbey and Garrett looked at each other then both simultaneously blurted out, "I promise." I looked at Abbey sternly to get another commitment that she'd control herself. "Okay, okay. I promise that too. Now what is it?" She leaned forward on the table closer to Robert.

"Belinda and I are getting married after graduation." He turned and smiled at me before returning to them. "We'd like for you to be there, with our parents. They don't know yet. We're surprising them. Will you come?"

Abbey's eyes doubled in size as she placed her hand over her mouth to control herself. It worked. She lowered her hand. "I wouldn't miss it for the world." She reached across the table for my hand. Gently squeezing it, Abbey smiled as her eyes filled with happiness for me.

"You know I'm here for you, bro." Garrett had a smile as wide as Texas across his face. "You two are meant for each other. But why are you keeping it a secret?"

"We can't invite everyone, just immediate family and you. We don't have time to plan a big wedding. I want Belinda here with me this summer and the only way to accomplish that is to marry her."

"Belinda, just stay at school and live together. You're doing it now," Garrett pointed out.

A look of concern came over Robert's face. "Her parents wouldn't approve of that. They don't know about us being together all the time. We want to keep it that way until we're married." He looked my way and gave me a nudge so I knew he was thinking about my situation. "Her father wouldn't stand for us just living together and I don't want to give him anything else to be angry at me for. It's bad enough we're planning to be married so soon." Garrett nodded his head with understanding.

After we finished eating, Robert scanned the room. "Please excuse us. I'm going to show her off." He took my hand and led me out into the room. We walked around and mingled with all of his friends. People were looking at us as we made our way through the crowd. This made me feel more self-conscious. I felt I was bubbling out of the top of my dress and had to fight the urge to tug on it. I knew fussing with it would attract more attention, so I kept both of my hands on Robert's arm to control my impulses.

Soft music filled the air and people began to dance. "Can I have this dance?" Robert reached for my hand.

"I'd love to."

Robert was such a good dancer. With his lead, we glided around the dance floor. I felt myself float with every turn we made. Lost in his clear blue eyes, I was unaware of anything or anybody around us. It was just he and I, alone as time seemed to stop. His eyes never left mine.

We were in our moment when the band started playing my favorite song, "Forever in My Mind." With my head leaning against his shoulder and my eyes closed, I quietly sang the words to him. They just poured out of me.

Dear love, my only sweet true love
You've captured my lonely heart
My destiny is with you, love
I pray we shall never part

Our fate has been forever sealed
I'm bound by your gentle touch.
By a true love that is so real
I love you so very much.

My eyes met yours and I was lost
You found your way into my heart
We fell in love despite all cost
But shattered fate kept us apart

No matter where this life takes me
You're always there in my dreams
Each night I sleep, it's you I see
Loving me in all the scenes

To gaze upon your loving smile
With soft eyes of sparkling blue
That guide me down the chapel aisle
As I give my heart to you

My eyes met yours and I was lost
You found your way into my heart
We fell in love despite all cost
But shattered fate kept us apart

Forever 'til the end of time
We will be what makes love bind
As our world was in perfect rhyme
You're forever in my mind

When the song ended, I kissed Robert on his neck and laid my head back against his chest keeping my eyes closed. I savored the moment until I heard applause. Still enveloped in his arms, I looked around as people were facing us. "Why are they doing that?" I nestled closer into his chest.

He never let his grip on me loosen as he looked at me with a slight smile on his face. "I didn't know you could sing. That was beautiful. Everyone was looking around trying to figure out where the singing was coming from."

"They could hear me?" Now I was embarrassed again. "I thought I was singing only for you. I didn't mean for everyone to hear." Feeling my face warm from blushing, I buried it in his chest. "The words have a lot of meaning for me."

"You were quiet at first. I even had trouble hearing you, but as you got into the song, you sang louder with more feeling." Robert had an admiring look on his face as he studied me. "It was beautiful and I think everyone was enjoying it. They were trying to dance near us to hear you." He sounded proud.

Glancing around the crowd, I nodded, saying, "Thank you," for the unwanted attention I had brought upon myself. I reached for Robert's arm that never faltered from my waist and whispered in his ear, "Get me out of here." Without saying a word, Robert led me back to the table for a much-needed break and more wine.

The dance floor was filled with partygoers whose attention was back on themselves and off of me. We joined in and danced the night away—never sitting down. We took occasional breaks at the bar where Robert kept my wine glass filled. I was feeling no pain. Abbey and Garrett also enjoyed themselves dancing and he made sure to keep her wine glass filled as well. I was praying Abbey wasn't going to be my roommate tonight. All this wine was making me feel amorous and all I could think about was loving Robert until morning would creep in to disturb our bliss.

Robert kept staring at me with those intoxicating blue eyes. We managed to maintain minimal contact. I was grateful for that. With the amount of wine I'd had, one kiss would have sent me over the top. I wouldn't have cared where we were or who was around as my reactions took over. Up to now, I had managed to keep my dignity and act like a lady. I wanted it to stay that way. Robert helped out all night. He was the perfect gentleman who maintained my honor.

Robert gave Garrett and Abbey a look of exasperation. Taking a deep breath, he glided us toward the dancing couple and demanded, "Okay you two, I have to be with Belinda tonight. Do I need to get another room?"

Abbey looked embarrassed. "No, I'll stay with him." She flung her arms around Garrett's neck and kissed him. They were doing a lot of that lately. I knew he would be in for the ride of his life tonight trying to maintain *his* virtue.

"Thank you, Abbey." Robert wasted no time as he took hold of my hand and led me out of the ballroom to the elevator. As soon as the doors closed, he embraced me and crushed his lips against mine. I returned his kiss with a feverish one. I wanted him and he wanted me. When the elevator doors opened, he took my hand and we ran to our room while he undid his tie and unbuttoned his vest. He reached into his pocket, pulled out my key card, swiped and opened the door without skipping a beat.

I discovered that wine wildly enhances my passion. My reactions to Robert's advances were more intense. As we inched our way to the bed, Robert grabbed my hair pulling my head back as he kissed every exposed area of my neck and breasts. Blood rushed in my ears as my heart accelerated. Full of desire, I pulled back and tore at his tux, attempting to remove what was left as fast as I could. I felt the zipper slide down my back, dropping my dress to the floor. His hand grasped the back of my head as his mouth collided with mine in a hot, endless kiss. With his other arm wrapped around me melding our warm bodies as one, we toppled over onto the soft sheets. We didn't take the time to find a foil packet because we were like wildcats—our bodies entwined, writhing, groping, devouring…This was not making love, it was raw SEX. We couldn't seem to get enough of each other. With exhaustion finally consuming us, we collapsed.

Beads of sweat trickled down his chest as he rolled over on his back and. pulled me close. "Oh my god! That was incredible!" He gazed at me with crazed eyes, in between his gasping breaths. "I am never…using a condom…again!"

He pressed his lips against my shoulder in a quick kiss. "I keep thinking about you in that dress—you looked so sexy. I get aroused just thinking about it." He rolled over on top of me and started kissing my cheek, my neck, everywhere. My senses came alive and to my surprise, Robert was ready to start all over again, but this time we made warm, gentle love. Our newfound sensuality was wonderful. It was driving us crazy as we made love again, and again, and again….

CHAPTER 21

A KNOCK ON the adjoining door awoke us Sunday morning. "Hey you two, I need my stuff." It was Abbey.

I was still half asleep, wrapped over Robert's side. He pulled the covers over my head, making sure no part of me was exposed. "Okay, you can come in," Robert called out. Pulling the sheet from my head as they entered, I wondered if Abbey's night was as wonderful as mine. I couldn't wait till we were alone to pry her for all the details like she relentlessly did to me.

Abbey and Garrett walked in and came over close to the bed. She took a seat on it, bouncing up and down as she settled in. "Belinda, everyone was talking about how gorgeous you looked in that dress."

"Really? I think the top is a little too revealing."

Robert and Garrett chimed in in unison. "No it's not—it's perfect." They looked at each other and smirked.

I rolled my eyes. "Sheesh! Typical males—sex on the brain."

"I want to see you in it again." Robert flashed me an irresistible smile.

"Later, Tiger. Right now I think we need to call room service for breakfast." I became aware of the pain in my head as I repositioned, sitting up carefully so I wouldn't expose myself. "And something for a headache."

Abbey was fiddling with something gold hanging around her neck. It took my eyes a few seconds to focus. "Abbey, come here." She scooted closer. "Move your hand." She complied with a grin on her face. "You're wearing a Delt drop!" I forgot about my throbbing head as my attention was now on her newest acquisition.

"He gave it to me when we came back to the room." She was all excited. If she and I had been alone, we would've been jumping up and down squealing, but the only thing between me and immodesty was the sheet. I was determined Garrett was not going to get a peek at my lady parts.

Garrett had a half-grin. "Yeah, I don't want to share her anymore."

"Congratulations Bro." Robert flashed a thumbs up to Garrett. I leaned over and gave Abbey a kiss on the cheek.

"Hey, we're getting ready to check out. Robert, I packed your things in your duffel. You need to hurry if you're checking out by eleven."

"We're staying for a while longer." He rocked a brow. "Just bring my stuff in here, if you don't mind." Robert was bare-chested with the sheet draped across his lap, the only barrier between him and exposure.

Garrett disappeared from Abbey's side, then reappeared with the duffel in hand. "Well, I guess we'll let you get back to...." Garrett's voice trailed off in a knowing smile. Abbey blushed and nudged him as he placed his arm around her to escort her out of the room.

On his way back from locking the door, Robert picked up my dress. "Put it on." He had a naughty look on his face, standing there with the dress offering the only form of cover for his perfect naked body.

I slipped the dress over my head then turned for him to zip it. Slowly, I faced him with my hands to my side fidgeting with my dress. His voice was low and his lustful eyes were focused on the bodice. "Don't move." His fingers feathered across the top of the fabric that outlined my breasts. My breathing quickened causing them to heave. With the gentlest touch he softly caressed my left breast. Electricity shot through me as I threw my head back, clenching fistfuls of dress fabric in each hand. His lips brushed my skin as he kissed down my neck, to my shoulder, to my chest, each breast, and up the other side, all the while his hands moving and exploring. With a slow even motion, he opened the zipper and the dress slipped, puddling on the floor. I threw my arms around his neck as he gripped me close causing our heated bodies to rub against one another. Our lips searched until they pressed against each other's. We fell back on the mattress as our emotions exploded into the perfect rhythm of our love.

When three o'clock rolled around, we decided we should leave. The man behind the checkout counter said, "You're that young lady in the pale blue gown last night. Everyone was commenting about how lovely you looked. Ahhh, I see you're engaged." He smiled at Robert. "You're a lucky man, sir."

"Yes I am." Robert was beaming as he glanced at me.

"Your charge is for one night. I'll put it on your credit card." I noticed his name tag indicated he was the manager.

Robert corrected him. "But we stayed past the check-out time. Shouldn't it be for two nights?"

"No, don't worry about it." He smiled and went about his business.

Robert reached into his pocket and pulled out a folded $100 dollar bill. He slipped it across the counter to the man. "Thank you very much." My curiosity was piqued by the way Robert acted. Had he done this before? I wondered. Robert told me he'd bring the car up to the front door. I was to wait for him at the counter.

"How long have you been engaged?" The manager never stopped typing on his computer.

"Two weeks." I assumed he was trying to make small talk.

He looked up. "Have you set a wedding date?"

I glanced around the room to make sure none of Robert's frat brothers were close by and then whispered, "In two weeks with just our immediate families." I was probably offering too much information, but he seemed genuinely interested.

"Well, I hope you have a long and happy life together."

"Thank you very much." Just then Robert drove up.

"Let me help you with your bags." He escorted me outside and placed the luggage in the very small trunk space. Robert emerged from the driver side. "Roadster. Nice car, sir." Robert acknowledged him with a nod and started to walk around to my side of the car. The manager held up his hand. "No sir, allow me." He graciously bowed as I got seated. "Come stay with us again."

"Thank you." I smiled as he closed the door.

We were on our way home, flying down the highway with the top down. It was a beautiful, warm, sunny afternoon. "I'm glad we decided to go. I had a great time. Did you?" I excitedly looked at Robert.

"Do you even need to ask?" He flashed a grin. "Best Spring Formal *ever*."

"*Best* ever? Did you have sex with your other dates?" He didn't respond. "Eewww!" I contorted my face in disgust.

He caught a glimpse of my expression. "What's wrong?"

I was frantic. "You've had sex with so many other girls! How many? Did I just have sex with the Student Directory?" That hadn't dawned on me before.

"Belinda, calm down. I don't know. You're the only one that matters now. Let's leave the past in the past. Okay?" He changed the subject. "Abbey and Garrett getting dropped sure was a big surprise. I'm his best friend and I didn't see that coming."

Staring out my side of the car, more or less in a trance, I kept silent.

"Angel...Angel...Belinda..." He nudged my arm.

"What?"

"Please leave the past in the past." He reached over and squeezed my hand.

"I'm okay. I was just remembering last night. That wild, crazy sex...did you enjoy it? Which do you prefer?"

"I prefer making love to you, but if you want wild, crazy sex, we can do that too." Robert shot me a ravenous grin.

"Typical." I looked at him and just laughed, but could feel "Monster" twitch her tail, wondering just how many more girls there were before me.

With a thump, Robert let the luggage drop on the living room floor. The sound startled me, but not as much as feeling Robert grab my waist before he flung me up over his shoulder and carried me to the bed. He tossed me down and straddled me, pulling his t-shirt off with a mischievous look. "Well, which do you want first? Make love?" His eyes went sultry. "Or wild, crazy sex?" His eyes went back to mischievous. He started tickling me, making me squirm and laugh so hard I could hardly breathe. "Well, which is it?"

"I love you, even if you *have* had sex with hundreds of girls."

He lifted his head, and with a furrowed brow, his hypnotic eyes stared down into mine. "Hundreds?"

"What—thousands?" I giggled.

He chuckled. "Way too low, more like millions." Now he was in a full blown laugh which took him a few seconds to recover from. He looked down at me. "I'm yours and you're mine. I can't wait 'til you're Mrs. Robert Pennington. You know, we could probably get married this week."

I considered his proposition. "No, we need to wait." Just then my stomach growled loud enough for both of us to hear. "I'm hungry, are you?"

"Yeah, for wild, crazy sex!" he teased with a naughty look in his eyes.

I poked at him. "I'm craving pizza."

"*Craving?*" He gave me a curious look and became very serious. "Are you trying to tell me something?"

I waved my hands. "Oh no! Wrong word. I'm hungry for pizza."

He smiled, looking relieved, and then something brought a bigger smile to his face. "You sure you're not up for some wilder, crazy sex?" I pushed him off of me and got up. Walking toward the bedroom door, I gave him a stern look. He heaved a sigh. "Just checking. I'll order our usual."

My full stomach magnified my exhaustion. "I'm going to shower."

"Can I join you?"

"Sure, but no funny business." I grinned as I shook my finger at him, thinking this shower was going to last longer than planned. But, it didn't. We were both pretty tired from the weekend's escapades. In bed, I curled up to his side and relived the formal—the way I was treated, and how this guy lying next to me made me feel. I was a princess living in a fairytale.

CHAPTER 22

IN TWO WEEKS, finals and school would be over, Robert would have graduated, and I'd be Mrs. Robert Pennington. So much was happening in such a short time. I was on cloud nine, but what would my parents say when I called them. Would they come to Robert's graduation? Would they let me marry him? If not, what would we do? On my way to meet Robert in the Cave, I was walking along lost in my thoughts when Matt startled me. He ran up beside me just outside of the Student Center and took hold of my arm. "I heard something I want to check out." He reached for my hand and looked at the ring. "I guess it's true, you're engaged to him. So, you are in love?"

He was gripping my hand a little too tightly. I pulled it loose and turned to face him. "Yes, I love him."

The usual sparkle in his eyes faded and he looked sad. "Well...I hope you'll be happy together."

Robert walked up and put his arm around my shoulders, giving me a slight tug to him. "What's going on?"

Matt reached out to shake Robert's hand. "Congratulations, you're a very lucky man." Robert hesitated and looked at me. He cocked his head and let out a small huff. Even though Robert didn't like Matt, he was too much of a gentleman to make a scene. So he graciously reached out and took Matt's hand in return. "Thank you."

Matt half smiled. "I wish you all the happiness in the world." He turned and slowly walked away. That's when I realized my relationship with him was over.

Robert didn't question the encounter with Matt. Instead, he politely changed the subject. "Have you talked to your parents yet about coming to my graduation?"

"No, I need to do it soon. I'll call tonight when we're at home." We continued toward the Cave.

"What if they won't come? Will you go through with the plan?" He looked concerned and very serious. Sitting down at one of the Delt tables, we continued our conversation.

"*Yes, absolutely.* If they say they can't come, I'll tell them they're going to miss me getting married. That'll make them come, but they'd try to talk me out of it. 'You're too young. It's too soon. You haven't finished school yet.'" I glanced down. "They think I need some time away from you." I was now more downhearted and my voice reflected that.

"I don't want to cause problems between you and your parents. Maybe this isn't a good idea." Robert paused and seemed to be thinking to himself before he started talking again. "Will you miss not having a big wedding?" He turned to me, very anxious. "We never discussed that. I don't even know if that was something you wanted."

My heart jumped. All I could do was think about how sweet this guy was and how much I loved him. "I wouldn't mind a big wedding, but it isn't something I've dreamed about. Hell, for a long time I wondered if I'd even *get* married. I'm more concerned about my parents."

I was making myself upset. The notion of our plan backfiring and all the problems that could arise started to fill my head with one thought after another coming so fast. Tears were starting to well up in my eyes. Ashamed and on the verge of a full-blown meltdown, I hid my face in my hands. "I need to go to class." An overpowering urge to run came over me. I stood and rushed out as "Monster" raised her ugly head.

"Belinda…." He caught up and grabbed me from behind, around the waist. I was weeping, almost sobbing. He tried to console me with a hug as he placed his chin on my shoulder. "Everything will work out. Let's think positive." He turned me toward him and gave me a gentle squeeze. "Look, after everything's over, we can plan to renew our vows and have a proper wedding."

His arms around me made everything feel alright and melted away my fears, forcing "Monster" back into her lair. "Okay, I'll see you after class."

Robert wiped my tears away and kissed me on the lips. Immediately, exhilaration filled me as I responded by kissing him back.

I was about to put both my arms around his neck when he broke the kiss and took a step back. "I'll see you after class."

***

Sitting on the couch, I stared at my cell phone. Robert sat next to me with his arm around my shoulders. He encouraged me to confront the situation. My conversation only lasted a few minutes, but Mom agreed she and Dad would attend Robert's graduation since they'd be here to move me home. I was rather surprised, but Robert was right. Making the call and confronting my fear wasn't as bad as I thought.

"See, that wasn't so hard. We can meet at the apartment after graduation. We'll introduce our parents to each other and tell them we're taking them out to eat, but instead head for the Justice of the Peace." He had constructed the perfect plan. "Okay, now let's go celebrate. What are you hungry for?"

"What do you want?"

Robert sat upright and had the strangest expression on his face. "Do you have to ask? What am I *ALWAYS* hungry for?" Now he was in a full-blown smile, waiting for me to say something.

"Okay, Mexican. You know I'll *always* choose that." I grinned. He looked at me and said nothing. I was obviously missing something. A light bulb went on in my head and I closed my eyes. "Wild, crazy sex." When I opened them to look at him, he appeared satisfied that he had made his point. "Later, Cowboy. First we eat Mexican food."

***

The next day we were sitting in the Cave talking to Abbey and Garrett after our Tuesday classes. "Have you talked your parents into coming to his graduation yet?" I gave Abbey a quick explanation of the phone call to my mother and how we would pull off our deception using packed suitcases to let my parents think I was moving back home.

Robert interrupted when he leaned in close to my ear. "We have something we need to do now."

I looked at him puzzled. "What?" I couldn't think of anything.

"We need to ask Garrett and Abbey about standing up for us at the ceremony." Now I felt stupid. I hadn't asked my best friend to be my maid of honor yet.

I looked at Abbey. "There's something I need to ask you. You promise not to jump up and down and get all crazy on me?" Now Abbey was the one with the puzzled look on her face, but she gave me a nod yes. I made sure to keep my voice low. "Would you be my maid of honor?"

Abbey's eyes became misty. "I'd be honored." I reached for her hands and held on while Robert asked Garrett to be his best man. I could feel Abbey's bubble level start to increase, but my grip on her helped keep it under control.

Robert looked back at me. "There's still one more thing we need to do." He smiled and held up his left hand, inconspicuously rubbing his thumb against his ring finger. "Our wedding rings."

"Oh. That slipped my mind too."

"Do you want to start looking today?"

I nodded.

When we arrived at Downtown Jewelers, the salesman greeted us as we entered the store. "Can I help you?"

Robert acknowledged him with a nod. "Yes sir, we're interested in looking at your wedding bands."

"Right this way." The man led us to a glass display case containing the wedding rings. "Do you see anything you're interested in?"

I pointed to a tray of rings and looked at Robert. "I like these simple, thin, white gold bands. Do you?"

"I think I like these wider ones better." The man handed Robert one and he slid it onto my finger.

Joy filled me as I breathed, "I do." I held my hand out in front of me. The lights in the shop above the cases made my engagement ring sparkle. It was magnificent. The wider band balanced more with the diamonds in the engagement ring. "I like this one too. What kind of band do you want?"

Robert looked at me. "One like yours, but a little wider." The salesman showed us some plain men's bands, handing me one. I took it from him and slipped it onto Robert's finger. "I do," he reciprocated then half grinned. "I like this one. It's perfect."

Robert handed the rings to the man. "We'll take these two bands."

On our way home, I had the ring boxes open, staring down at them. "I promise I'll never take my ring off. 'Til death do us part." I was very serious, looking at the bands that would bind our love forever.

"'Til death do us part." He glanced over at me. "There is nothing going to stop us."

"Oh...yes there is."

He wrinkled his brow. "What?"

"I don't have a dress to wear. Do you want to shop with me?" Oddly, Robert jumped at the chance to help pick out the dress.

Inside the dress boutique, I glanced around at the dresses displayed on racks. Everything looked expensive, but that was okay because this dress had to be special and surely they had what I needed. I grabbed Robert by the hand and led him over to a saleslady who asked, "Can I help you?"

"I'm looking for a nice dress that I can be married in."

"I have a few that would work perfectly. I'll be right back." She reappeared and showed me three pretty dresses and one suit that were shades of white to cream, and then led me to a dressing room.

Robert sat outside my dressing room door. I modeled each one for him and he was adamant with his opinions. He liked the cream-colored strapless silk dress with a short straight skirt and matching short-sleeved bolero jacket. Robert pulled out his credit card. "We'll take this one."

I tried to grab the card, but he grasped my arm and shook his head. "Robert, you've given me enough."

"What, an engagement ring?" He looked perplexed.

Now facing him, I placed my hand on his shoulder. "You gave me you, that's enough."

Looking into my eyes, he said in a loving tone, "Angel, you've given me more—you gave me you, your love, happiness, understanding. I could go on and on. Let me do this for you, please."

I rubbed my hand on his shoulder in a slow motion. "Okay, if it'll make you happy….I love you."

"I love you more," he murmured back. "I saw something at the jewelers that will go perfect with the dress. It'll be a surprise for you on our wedding day. You shop around for anything you want. I'll be right back."

"Robert, n…." He put his finger over my mouth. Not saying a word, he let his eyes speak for him. His message was loud and clear. I gave up my protest.

The saleslady tried to be discreet giving Robert and me some space. When he was gone she approached me. "What else would you like to look for?"

"There isn't anything I need."

"Have you thought about what you'd wear on your wedding night?" I shook my head. She left for the back room and came back with a sexy, little, sheer, pale blue teddy. "Wear this for him." She smiled, draping it across the counter.

I felt the fabric of the minimal excuse for sleepwear. "This is his favorite color on me." It was next to nothing and so see-through. I held it up against me. Just looking at it made my cheeks burn. It would be fun to watch his face when I walk out in it. I verified the size. The saleslady had guessed correctly. "Okay, I'll take it." I handed her my credit card.

After paying for my purchase, I was browsing around the store flipping through the racks with my back to the door when a familiar sexy voice spoke in my ear. "Well, did you buy something?"

"I did." I turned toward him and glanced at the saleslady. "We think you'll like it." He had a confused look on his face. "But I don't need anything, except you," I taunted as I strutted by him walking my fingers across his chest, and then turned looking seductively over my shoulder at him.

***

It was finally Wednesday afternoon. We were on our way to entering a new phase of our lives, taking another step to becoming Mr. and Mrs. Robert

Pennington. The county courthouse was a few blocks from the campus, right in the middle of the town square. For a small town, it was an impressive building. It was small by bigger city standards, but it offered everything the citizens of the county needed to conduct their civic business.

Our destination was the County Clerk's office to apply for our marriage license. An elderly lady behind the counter helped us fill out the application and went through the steps necessary to obtain our requested document. We asked her how we'd go about making arrangements with a Justice of the Peace. "Come here any day, Monday through Friday, we'll work you in."

"You're closed on the weekend?" Robert asked. We looked at each other, worried, knowing we had a problem since graduation would take place on a Saturday.

The lady noticed our reaction. "What day are you looking at?"

"A week from this Saturday." There was a slight nervous twinge to Robert's voice.

Her lips pursed, then she suggested we should make our wedding more memorable. She very openly suggested we marry in a chapel. "No matter how small your wedding is, a chapel makes it feel special." She finalized her speech with a sweet grandma smile. "My husband is a minister and he would be glad to marry you." She handed us a card with his name and phone number.

We were examining the card when Robert looked at her. "If we decide to change the day and use the Justice of the Peace, what do we need to do?" The clerk answered all of his questions. He scanned the card again, and then lifted it up as we were leaving. "Thank you for the information."

Climbing into the car, I wondered why there always had to be a complication. Our only chance would be to go for a chapel wedding. "A chapel would be nicer than a courtroom or judge's office. It would feel more like a wedding."

"I agree. I'll call when we get back." Robert gave my hand a squeeze as we sped back to the apartment.

Robert had a long discussion with Reverend Matthews, making all the arrangements. The reverend's wife would play the organ for us. "Just a second, let me find out." Robert turned to me. "We have a few songs we can choose from." He gave me the titles and we made our decisions. He returned to the phone and confirmed the melodies to be played. All we had to do now was be at the chapel by four.

CHAPTER 23

I HAD TO wait about a week and a half for the surprise Robert bought me. I thought waiting would be torturous, but the time flew by. We both had to finish projects and papers and cram for finals. Robert had to prepare for graduation and summer school. We hardly saw each other and were grateful when the school year ended.

After our finals, all the things I wanted were packed and most were moved into my official new home—our apartment. We hid them in his closet so our parents wouldn't suspect anything when they came to visit. I packed the remaining items and had them ready to go home with Mom and Dad.

***

It was eight o'clock in the morning. For once, I awoke before Robert. I was restless all night and slept lightly. I turned toward Robert, trying not to disturb him. Unlike me, he was sound asleep. His hair was tousled, but even as he slept, he looked perfect. Excitement was racing through me. I would be married to him today. My exhilaration was disturbed by my thoughts of everything I had to do before my parents arrived. I tried to slip out of bed, but it didn't work. My Mister Wonderful woke up and pulled me back to him. "Where are you sneaking off to?"

"I need to shower and dress so I can be at my place when my parents arrive. I'm not sure when they'll be there."

"Can you believe that in a few hours you'll be Mrs. Robert Pennington?" He was beaming, and then his expression became solemn. "I hope our parents will be happy for us....Call'em to see when they'll be here."

Picking up my phone, I called Mom and learned they were about an hour and a-half away. When I looked at Robert, there was a look of disappointment on his face. There would only be enough time for me to get ready and have a quick breakfast. "I hope everything goes as planned."

"Don't fret—if we have to, we'll elope. Nothing is going to keep us apart."

His mood was determined, but his touch was gentle as he stroked my hair. "I have your surprise for you."

He opened the drawer of the nightstand, pulled out a small, black velvet box, and handed it to me. Taking it in my hand, I softly fingered the fabric. I looked up at him and smiled. Slowly, I opened the little box. In it was a double heart necklace. Two diamond studded hearts linked together. He had our initials engraved on the back, his initials on one heart and mine on the other. I admired the gift lovingly. "Oh, it's beautiful! Thank you." I hugged and kissed him. My senses were ignited, so I squirmed away. "Not until after we're married."

He let out a long breath. "So now you go all virginal on me?"

I giggled. "You know what I mean, silly. When you get your wedding gift tonight, we'll see who's going virginal," I teased as I headed into the bathroom.

Robert went to the kitchen and prepared our staple breakfast of blueberry bagels and coffee. When I entered the room in my wedding dress, a huge smile flashed across his face. "You look gorgeous."

"Thank you." I handed him my new necklace. "Put it on me." Turning my back to him, I lifted my hair away from my neck. He secured it, then took hold of my shoulders and pivoted me around. With tender lips, he pressed his against mine. I pulled away when I began feeling all tingly inside. "Not until after we're married." He grimaced, but complied. I carefully scarfed down my breakfast, and then prepared to head to my place. Robert came along to move some boxes that were going to the apartment and to have his first tour of my soon-to-be-vacated room.

Abbey was up and dressed when we arrived. She gushed about how beautiful I looked in my wedding dress and I returned the compliment before we hugged. Garrett, like Robert, was a senior in Business Management, so he was graduating at the same ceremony. "So you finally made it up here." Abbey snickered. Robert flashed a grin at her and responded with a snort.

I gave him the nickel tour of my humble dwelling. "See, you haven't missed much."

He quickly scanned the place, appearing satisfied. "Angel, I'm going to head back to get ready and wait for my parents." He kissed me and then picked up the two remaining boxes before he left.

Looking at Abbey and around our room, I had a wave of sadness come over me. This would be the last time she and I would be together as roommates. "Abbey, are you staying here this summer or are you going home?"

"I'm moving in with Garrett. We're taking the summer off to enjoy ourselves before he starts grad school in the fall."

I looked at her shocked. "Things are going that well?"

Abbey nodded her head slowly. "Yep. Belinda, I think he's the one."

In our usual giddy manner, I hugged her. "I'm so happy for you! We really need to talk more. Abbey, I'm sorry I wasn't around very much. I haven't been the best roommate."

"Yes you have. Remember, I was also out a lot with Brent and Garrett. However, I did miss talking to you—discussing our dates…stuffing cars." We laughed then sat in silence for a few seconds. "He sure seems anxious to marry you."

This whole affair mystified me as well. Often I would run the events of the past few weeks through my mind. Everything had moved so fast. I would ask myself if I was doing what he wanted so I could keep him, or did I really want to get married as well? The only answer I always came up with was *yes*. I loved him with all my heart. "It still puzzles me. Why me? I hope he truly loves me." I paused and looked at Abbey. "We have to keep in touch more."

"We will. Remember, we're sisters."

***

My parents and I found seating near the stage. I anxiously sat waiting for Robert's name to be announced. As he walked across the stage the audience broke into a loud roar of applause. Robert played on the attention as he was presented his diploma. I was jumping up and down with excitement. He scanned the crowd and found me. Our eyes locked as he mouthed, *I love you.*

The two-hour ceremony ended and we headed for our apartment. Robert and his parents were already there when we arrived about three o'clock. He handled the introductions of our parents. Sandra jumped right in with her remarks. "We just love your daughter. We can't wait for her to become part of our family. We're so happy Robert found her."

Everyone made themselves comfortable in the living room. The moms sat on the couch and were engaged in planning the wedding. Robert looked at me and then his watch. "Belinda and I are taking you out to eat. We need to go before the graduation crowds arrive. You can continue getting aquatinted at the restaurant." We left with Robert driving his parents in their car and I followed in mine with my parents aboard.

To keep myself calm, I told my mom about the reaction to the dress she altered. I knew if I kept the small talk going, I could contain myself, and maybe my parents wouldn't suspect anything.

When we arrived at the chapel there were a lot of cars parked around.

"Are we eating at a church?" My mom was looking around bewildered.

"No, Robert and I have a surprise for you." *Please don't get upset.* We started walking toward Robert and his parents. They were smiling and I hoped it was because they approved of our plan.

I motioned to Robert to stay where he was. When I stopped walking, my parents turned toward me with their backs to Robert and his parents. I needed to talk to them with no one else around. "Mom, Dad…Robert and I want to be together this summer and from now on. So we made arrangements to be married today. Reverend Matthews is waiting inside." I tilted my head toward the church.

Dad frowned, stiffened and folded his arms across his chest. "Don't you think you're rushing into this? You're too young."

"She's as old as I was when we were married," Mom reminded him, placing her hand on his arm. She was standing behind his shoulder and flashed me a wink. I knew that she was in my corner.

"I love him. I want to be with him."

Dad relaxed and let out a huff. "Okay, if it makes you happy." He struggled to display a half-smile.

I reached over and hugged him. "Thank you, I love you."

We joined Robert and his parents who were waiting patiently. There was handshaking and congratulations from both sides. I could tell my father wasn't sure about this wedding. He was doing his best to act cordial. As Robert and I walked arm-in-arm toward the chapel, the crowded parking lot made me wonder what was going on. "Why there are so many cars here. I hope something didn't get messed up with the minister's schedule." I squeezed Robert's arm and gasped. "What if he forgot?!"

He attempted to ease my concern. "Maybe there's some church function going on in another room."

We walked into the foyer, surprised to see Abbey, Garrett, and Brian standing there apparently waiting for us. Abbey was dressed in a light blue polished cotton dress trimmed in white. The center door that led to the chapel was open. We could see that it was full of frat brothers and their dates. There were two white rose floral arrangements on either side of the opened doors. Blue bows and ribbons were tied on each pew. A white runner was rolled out and led to an arch where the minister stood at the front of the chapel. Two more white rose floral arrangements were placed on either side of the arch. Robert and I were astounded at the sight presented before us.

"How did you find out?" Robert asked Brian.

"Oh, a little bird told us. We all wanted to share this special occasion with you." It was apparent Brian wasn't going to tell us just how he found out.

I looked at Abbey. "Why didn't you say something to me?"

"And spoil the surprise?" She was glowing. "I have a bouquet for you. Cheryl made all the floral arrangements, and she and Russell are having a reception for you this evening at eight." She handed me a bouquet of white roses, light blue ribbons, and baby's breath. "I hope you don't mind, but after all, I'm your maid of honor and Garrett is your best man. We're supposed to help with the planning." She shrugged her shoulders. "In this case, we did most of it."

My eyes started filling with tears. Abbey was such a good friend. I was so lucky, I thought, as she handed me a tissue. Drying my eyes, I turned to my father. "Dad, will you walk me down the aisle?" He smiled and extended his elbow to me. I linked my arm in his.

Brian escorted our mothers and Robert's father to the front pew. Robert and Garrett walked up the right aisle to stand with the minister. Abbey started down the center aisle. My father and I positioned ourselves between the doors. Almost like magic, the minister's wife started to play my favorite song, "Forever on My Mind." When I heard it, my heart skipped a beat and I looked at Robert. His gaze was intense and full of love. At that moment, I stepped onto the white runner and walked toward my love, to become Mrs. Robert Pennington.

The ceremony was perfect. We exchanged our vows and placed our wedding rings on each other's fingers followed by the words, "I do." I could hardly wait for the minister to say, "I now pronounce you husband and wife. You may kiss your bride." The kiss was…well, he had to peel me off of him. It was a kiss he'll never forget.

After the ceremony everyone was congratulating us and saying they'd see us at the reception. The chapel quickly cleared out and became quietly reverent. There was a small group of us left standing in the foyer. "You have to stay for the reception." Our parents agreed. Robert called the hotel downtown and made two reservations.

I turned toward Abbey and Garrett. "Come eat with us. Our treat." With her usual enthusiasm, Abbey latched onto Garrett's arm, nodding her head with a Cheshire grin, accepting our invitation.

As we exited the chapel, I was flabbergasted. All the attendees of the ceremony were lined alongside the pathway, armed with bottles of liquid bubbles. Robert and I were encased in thousands of tiny bubbles as we walked down the stairs as Mr. and Mrs. Pennington to our beautiful BMW Roadster, decorated with white paper carnations, streamers, and cans tied to the rear bumper. A sign, almost as big as the car, stretched across the trunk announcing Just Married in big bold letters. We wondered how the car found its way to the chapel. No matter who we asked, no one knew or would admit to anything. The decorated car was a nice touch to a perfect day.

***

The front yard of the Hinds' residence gave off a romantic glow. The driveway was lined on both sides with candle-lit white paper bags, marking a path that led all the guests to the back of the house. There were two huge white bows on either side of the six-foot gate. Two of Robert's frat brothers were posing as sentries, stopping us from going in. One brother slipped behind the gate as the other stood outside and visited with us. Finally it opened. Robert took my arm and we were escorted to the back of the house. Robert's elusive frat brother announced, "May I present to you, Mr. and Mrs. Robert Pennington!" All the guests stood up and clapped. The frat brothers were making so much noise with their animal sounds and screaming cheers, it was almost deafening. Robert motioned for everyone to calm down and be seated. This took a few attempts, but finally he was able to talk. "Belinda and I would like to thank everyone for this wonderful surprise. We didn't expect any of this. So, from the bottom of our hearts, thank you."

While Robert was talking, I had a chance to look around and almost cried. Cheryl had transformed her backyard into a wonderland. The yard was strung with hundreds of twinkle lights. Floating candles and white balloons drifted over the pool surface. The flickering flames between the bobbing balloons gave them an effervescent appearance. The atmosphere had a mystical effect.

The tables were adorned with white floor-length tablecloths covered with pale blue toppers. On each table was a hurricane-covered candle with white flowers and ribbons encircling the glass shade. The front table held punch, petite sandwiches, and other assorted snacks surrounding the feature piece, an all-white wedding cake scattered with small, pale blue flowers.

People started congratulating us as we made our way around the yard greeting and thanking everyone individually. Our host and hostess were last. "Cheryl, I can't believe you did this for us. Thank you so very much. I just love it." As I threw my arms around her neck and gave her a big hug, tears welled up in my eyes.

"Yes, thanks so much," Robert agreed as he shook Russell's hand.

"Your brothers chipped in and helped. They wanted to share in this special moment. They think you're a lucky guy." Cheryl still had me clinging to her. She returned my affection with an embrace. "And so do we."

"I know. I'm extremely lucky that she loves me."

I let loose of Cheryl. Robert put his arms around my waist, resting his chin on my shoulder as he kissed my cheek.

"I'm the lucky one." Looking out the corner of my eye, I cocked my head and flashed him a smile.

The rest of the night was spent socializing and drinking until it was time to cut the cake. I got very close to Robert and whispered, "If that cake goes anywhere but my mouth, you're on the couch and your surprise will never be seen." I smiled ever so sweetly at him. He knew I meant business. With our hands on the knife, we sliced the cake, retrieving the first piece. We fed each other a bite, which neatly met its mark, then drank a sip of wine with our arms linked as a toast was made to us by Russell.

The first dance of the night was ours. Robert took me in his arms and we glided around the pool like we were on air. My body moved with his. I couldn't and didn't want to restrain the shivery feeling inside. He smiled. When the song ended, he kissed me so passionately my knees buckled. His tight hold kept me from falling and making a fool of myself.

Robert only let me go because of all the hooting and hollering from the frat brothers. I remember something about us "getting a room" being shouted from the crowd. I felt embarrassed at our display, especially in front of our parents. Robert didn't seem bothered at all. He just chuckled and went on.

The next song, Robert danced with his mother and I with my father. When he took me in his arms and started dancing, he stiffened his body. At first I thought, *Oh no, here we go again.* And then I realized he was trying to hold back the tears. When the dance was over I leaned close to him. "I love you." With this simple statement, my father attempted to wipe his eyes as discreetly as he could while we walked hand-in-hand toward Mom.

Robert danced next with my mother and I with his father. I liked Mr. Pennington for what he told Robert the first time I met him. He thought I was a *keeper*. His opinion meant a lot to me. Since our first meeting, I'd had the opportunity to talk with him a few more times on the phone. He made me feel welcome and part of his family. I felt accepted and that I belonged, even more than with my own parents. It wasn't because of the money or the fact the house was so big. There was something else, but I couldn't quite put my finger on it.

Everyone was enjoying themselves—visiting, eating, and dancing. It was around eleven when I prepared to throw the bouquet. Cheryl made the announcement that all the single girls should gather around the patio steps. On the count of three, with my back to the crowd, I threw it in Abbey's direction. When I turned back to see if I'd been successful, Abbey was jumping up and down with it in her hands.

The reception was winding down as the guests started to dwindle. We told our parents we'd see them in the morning for breakfast before they started their trip home. Finding our host and hostess, we thanked them again before turning my beautiful wedding day into a wonderful memory.

When we arrived at my official new home, Robert whisked me off my feet and carried me across the threshold. "Welcome home, Mrs. Pennington." There was a glint in his eyes. They sparkled as he smiled more than I had ever noticed before. His pace seemed more confident as he walked straight for our bedroom. Placing me on the bed, he gently lay on top of me.

"Mr. and Mrs. Robert Pennington." I was elated and glowing. I wrapped my arms around his neck and kissed him. Zing! I didn't want to stop, but I stiffened in an attempt to restrain myself. "I'm going to get cleaned up and ready for bed."

He jerked his head up. "Can I join you?" I smiled and agreed, then took his hand and led him into the bathroom.

The shower lasted a lot longer than I planned. I didn't want my hair all wet, but how could I say no to Robert? My original plan was to occupy the bathroom by myself to prepare for his surprise. Now he'd have to wait.

I towel dried my hair as much as I could while I waited for him to finish. When I tried to kick him out, he put up a fight as he attempted to persuade me to come to bed with him. "I don't care if your hair is wet." Pulling me in the direction of the door, I latched onto the sink and wouldn't let go.

He was ruining everything. The more he pulled, the more I dug in my heels. He started to reach for me to pick me up. I screamed, "NO!" He stopped and looked shocked. "Robert, please. You're ruining your surprise." He let go of my hand and with a devilish grin on his face, he pointed to the bedroom with me pushing him out of the bathroom. Securing the lock, I blow dried my hair and parted it on the left side, letting it hang partially over my face. Opening the cabinet door, I pulled out the teddy and three-inch heels I hid there the night before and slipped them on.

Studying myself in the full-length mirror on the back of the door, I felt self-conscious looking through the veil of pale blue fabric that barely covered my form. After practicing a few seductive poses, I placed my hand on the doorknob and took a deep breath. I opened the door and struck my pose in the doorway.

Robert was lying in bed with one light on next to it. When I opened the door, he swung his head in my direction. His jaw dropped at the sight of me and his eyes filled with lust. "You are so hot!" He admired the view for a few more seconds. "Thank you, it's the perfect gift." He crawled across the bed and sat on the edge closest to me. Taking hold of my waist, he tugged me to him and rubbed his cheek against my abdomen and then showered it with kisses. My hands dove into his hair and over his tense shoulders. Our breathing became irregular and panting. He reached up and caressed my breasts then pulled at the thin straps of the teddy. I hummed as my body moved beneath his wandering hands. My desire for him grew with every pass. With lust in his eyes, he looked up at me and extended his hand. "Mrs. Pennington." My heart almost leapt from my chest as he pulled me down to him, and we made love as husband and wife for the first time.

***

Good morning, Mrs. Pennington." As usual, he woke up before me. Robert was the type of person who hit the ground running in the morning. I was the lingering type and could take hours before my blood pumped enough to entice me to become vertical. Getting to class on time was my main motivation for moving, but the school year was over. My plan now was to wake up every morning when I wanted. My biggest obstacle would be convincing Robert that I needed my beauty sleep.

I rolled over to face him, wearing my best smile. "Good morning, Mr. Pennington." Reaching up, I put my arms around his neck and pulled him to me, giving him a big hug. His touch incited the same zeal as always. "Do we have to get up now?" I wanted to feel his magnificent body next to me.

"If we're going to meet our parents for breakfast we do, but I'd like a rain check, Mrs. Pennington."

Releasing my hold, he stood up to leave but I grabbed his hand to stop him. "I don't know if I can wait until tonight. What time is it anyway?"

"About seven." He had a playful look on his face. "I know." He pointed his finger straight up like he had a brilliant idea. "Let's take another shower." He reached down and scooped me into his arms. He flashed a slight grin, then kissed me on the nose. "To the shower with you!" Throwing my head back, I laughed as Robert tried to get us through the bathroom door without any major injuries.

There on the shower bench was a single rose. Still in his arms, I looked at my wonderful husband. "When did you have time?"

He puffed his chest, apparently proud of himself. "After I left your apartment with the boxes." Ever so tenderly my lips met his, igniting our passion. The shower was long and wonderful. I was glad I didn't have to wait until the evening to be with him again.

We were late arriving at the hotel after our morning distractions. Our parents were waiting for us in the lobby. "Here come the newlyweds, finally." Robert's mom pointed at her watch, tapping it. She knew full well why we were tardy.

Everyone was chatting while we walked to the hotel restaurant. We were waiting for our food when Sandra said, "Your mother and I thought it would be a great idea if we could do a reception for you later this summer. We could have it at our house. This way all our family and friends could come wish you well." Robert and I looked at each other and, with a nod of agreement, we told our parents we'd be more than happy to have another party. "That's great. Now don't worry. We both know you'll be busy with summer school. Dora and I have agreed we'll do everything. All you'll have to do is show up."

The meal was enjoyable and blended into our mothers' first planning meeting for the reception. Colors were decided, food choices, and yes, even the wedding cake was planned. Mom looked like she was enjoying herself. She loved parties and, more so, planning them. She just never had much occasion to do anything like that when I was growing up. I never had any birthday parties like other kids. Mine were small family affairs. So this would be fun for Mom. I was glad I could do this for her. After about the umpteenth cup of coffee, it was time to say our goodbyes and see our parents off.

"Well, I think our parents got along great," Robert said as we were leaving, walking to the car.

"I think our moms will have fun planning the reception. They'll probably be spending lots of time together coordinating it. Look what they did at one breakfast." My concern rose as I thought of what the expense of hosting a lavish reception could do to my parents financially. I surely wasn't in a position to help. "I just hope your mom doesn't make it too expensive. Remember, we come from a different tax bracket."

"I'll talk to her and remind her of that. Give her a little credit. She may have champagne taste, but she knows how to party on a beer budget."

He changed the subject to what we needed to accomplish the rest of the day. "We have to pick up what's left at your place and figure out where to put it. Then there is the matter of the love mobile. I have to clean up my car." He grimaced and wrinkled his nose at the thought. "It's worse than the paper stuffing incident." He half smiled and became serious. "I hope the guys used stuff that won't hurt the paint."

"Oooh. I forgot about that." I couldn't stifle a smile, remembering the wonderful surprise of the decorated car. Now he had the mess to clean up, and the tissue paper carnations would've become wet from the nightly dew causing them to stick to the surface of the roadster. The plan, for now, was to go pick up his car and then proceed to my old place. Robert and I would go next door to our neighbors' to clean the car. They had a nice driveway with a handy hose and everything Robert would need to restore his vehicle to its former glory. An added benefit was the possibility of talking some of the masterminds of the decorating detail into helping with the cleanup. After finishing, we'd pack the rest of my things into our cars for their final destination.

I wasn't looking forward to the tasks of washing the car and moving. A good nap was the only thing I wanted. We hadn't fallen asleep until about four a.m., but for now, closing my eyes would have to wait. Before summer school, we would have two glorious weeks together to do all the sleeping we wanted.

I drove my car, following behind the love mobile. As we pulled into the driveway, several of his frat brothers were sitting on the porch. It looked like their curiosity had been piqued by the noise of the cans hitting pavement. It amused me to watch Robert endure the relentless teasing of his friends as he walked past them into the house to retrieve the needed cleaning supplies.

The car cleaning went as planned. Several of Robert's brothers took pity on us, pitching in. The flowers made a mess. They fell apart into millions of little pieces. I had the job of rinsing the car to remove every one. It was boring work and I was already tired from the lack of sleep.

Hosing off the car on the passenger side, I could no longer control myself. Robert was on the driver's side soaping down the door. I waited for just the right moment. He stood up and I struck, spraying every part of him I could. He was attempting to dodge the water spray when he threw the rag on the ground and ran around the car lunging at me. I knew I was a goner. I turned squealing, running into the yard to give myself some distance, then spun around and let him have it. He tucked his shoulders in like he was protecting a football as he made a calculated charge for me. His well-planned tackle took me to the ground. I was still spraying him as he knocked the hose from my hand.

With lightning speed he was off me and armed with the hose. I looked in horror at him standing there, preparing to spray me. I lifted my hands in front of my face in a feeble attempt to protect myself. I shouted, "Robert, you wouldn't dare!"

He mouthed, *Payback,* as he raised his eyebrows and began his devilish task of revenge. Rolling from side to side, I tried desperately to avoid the cold stinging water. I got up and ran toward the porch and the possible protection of my neighbors. They were no help. They scattered like roaches, thinking of their own self-preservation. I was helpless as Robert trapped me in the corner of the porch. As he approached, closer and closer, his face was menacing. He raised his weapon as I crouched waiting for the impact.

To my delight, the scattered brothers picked the hose up off the grass and gave it a good tug, yanking it out of Robert's hand. Robert was now defenseless and they were laughing hysterically at him. As he looked at his brothers, I made my escape to the lawn. Robert was fast on my heels. He caught up to me, bringing me to the ground. We rolled around as I fought to get free. I gave in when he had me pinned by my wrists, straddling me. I looked up into the mud-streaked face of my husband of less than one day. He was panting as hard as I was. We both burst out laughing. Robert bent down and kissed me on the lips. With my adrenaline pumping so fast, I didn't have my usual response to his touch. That was a good thing. We had work to finish and the front yard of some frat brother's house was not the place to become amorous. He stood up and offered me his hand. I accepted and in a flash I was on my feet. Looking me over, he shook his head. "You're a mess." I had mud everywhere with leaves and twigs stuck in my hair.

I laughed. "You're no better."

He contemplated the situation. "I can finish the car. You go next door and clean up. I'll shower here and borrow some clothes from someone. When I'm finished, I'll come over." That plan was music to my ears. I could hurry through my clean up, then relax on my old bed one more time. As I was about to walk around the hedge between the two houses, a cheer arose from the group gathered on the porch. I turned and saw Robert. He had taken off his shirt and was wiping his face with it. He turned and flashed me his signature smile. My heart stopped as I had to remind myself—he was my husband.

When we arrived back at our apartment, we unloaded the boxes into the living room. "Where are we going to put these?" I looked around our meager square footage. Robert shrugged. There was only a small empty corner in our bedroom. "I guess we'll have to stack them in here until we go to my parents."

"We can move to a larger apartment."

"No, I like this one. It's cozy and I have a lot of good memories here. This is my first home with you." I wanted this part of my life to stay around as long as possible. We were happy here. Although our lives were busy, the apartment offered us a place of privacy. It was a place to close out the world.

"A lot of wonderful memories," he added beaming.

CHAPTER 24

THE NEXT TWO weeks were spent being newlyweds. First we took a quick trip to Sugar Land to visit our parents, and then we stayed home relaxing, watching TV, cooking together, and more bed time when the notion struck either of us. Of course, it struck Robert the most. Making love to him felt more special being married, knowing he would be mine forever. Nothing could have been better than being with him as his wife and lover. The days passed quickly being loved and pampered by him. I made the most of every minute of each day, knowing that when summer school started, class would take him away from me.

Summer school began without me. We agreed, if we both took a summer school class, we would be too busy with no time to be newlyweds. So, I took a break from studying to relax and just be a little homemaker. We were tired of eating out and after the visit to our parents, we started cooking together more. I was truly surprised how well his mother taught him to prepare his favorite meals. He told me his mom felt every man should be able to eat right and he was no exception.

Our plan didn't work out like we'd expected. We forgot to take into account that his class was on the graduate level and crammed into a shorter-than-usual time span. He spent most of the time studying, working on reports and projects after class. In the evenings and on weekends he was with his study group. At first, he always managed to arrange his schedule so we could be together, but that changed causing us to spend time apart.

So for now we treasured whatever time we had. On one rare evening he was able to get home early. Thrilled we'd have a whole night, we cooked then relaxed in the living room, sipping wine. I lay across his lap and looked up at his perfect profile.

He didn't look at me, but fixed his eyes, staring across the room. "Are you happy, Mrs. Pennington? Any regrets?"

I was stunned by his question. "I couldn't be happier. No regrets at all. I got what I wanted…to be with you. Why did you ask me that?"

He looked down at me. "You didn't get to wear a beautiful wedding gown and have a fancy wedding to invite all your friends and relatives to. Did I rush you into this marriage?"

Delaying my answer, I watched him as his face grew more serious. He was thinking too much about something that wasn't worth the effort. "No, I wanted this as much as you did. And those things don't matter to me, only you do."

He softly rubbed my arm. "I'll make this up to you. When we graduate next year, I'll take you on a long babymoon wherever you want to go."

I shot up, stunned. "What babymoon? Are you planning a family without asking me? Don't you think I might have some ideas as to when I'd like to have a child?"

Surprised by my questions, he spat out, "Hell no! I wouldn't plan something like that without your input, but it is something to think about. And we could have lots of fun trying." His eyes lit up as he stroked my face asking his next question. "Did you just stand up for yourself and confront me?"

Somewhat taken aback by his question, I gave it some thought then looked him in the eye, beaming. "Yes I did and I'm damn proud of it."

***

The July Fourth weekend was quickly approaching, and Cheryl and Russell were having another swim party, but this one was also to introduce Russell's nephew, Declan, to all the Delts. He was going to start his master's program in the fall. Robert thought he'd be able to take some time off from studying to accompany me. If not, he had made arrangements for me to go with Abbey and Garrett.

Our best friends had moved into the same house we lived in. Their apartment was located behind ours. Abbey and I had access to each other daily and I always enjoyed her company. Since neither of us was attending classes, we spent lots of time talking about cooking, apartment décor, and, of course, clothes—Abbey's favorite.

***

The day of the July Fourth party, Robert informed me that he couldn't go. He had to meet with his study group to work on a project that was due on Tuesday. I'd be going with Abbey and Garrett as the third wheel.

With my head nestled against his chest, Robert cupped my chin and lifted my face to his. He kissed me very softly and then with more intensity, sparking a response. I attempted to wrap myself around him, but he stopped me. "I wish I could go with you. I don't like you going by yourself."

I raised an eyebrow and smirked. "I'm not going by myself. Remember, you arranged a chaperone."

"Yeah, but you're going to be there without me."

"I'll be okay—don't worry." I was trying to reassure him. "I'm an adult. I can take care of myself."

"Okay. Well, I'll try to be home by nine so we can have some time alone." He winked and gave me a half-grin, then picked up his backpack and keys. He nodded his head as a further goodbye, and walked out the door.

***

As Abbey, Garrett and I walked into the Hinds' backyard, I noticed a new guy who reminded me a lot of Robert. He wasn't as tall, but very handsome, with dark brown hair, nice build, and captivating green eyes. He caught my glance and winked. I returned the flirt with a half-smile and a nod. Garrett stopped to talk to some of his brothers while Abbey and I went to claim three of the lounge chairs that were scattered around the pool. After stripping down to my bathing suit, I sashayed to the deep end and dove in. I swam the length of it and back. The new guy was now sitting on the edge with his legs dangling in the water, a few feet from where I came up.

"Seems like you're the only girl here who doesn't care if she's wet. Hey, I'm Declan Hinds." He extended his hand to me. "and you are?"

"Married." I heard a gruff recognizable voice coming toward me.

"Oh, Garrett. This is Declan Hinds, Russell's nephew."

"You two are married?" Declan looked disappointed as his hand retreated back to the edge of the pool.

"No, she's married to a Delt brother, Robert Pennington." Garrett looked like a pit bull, frowning at me and Declan.

"Okay, she came with you and that other girl." Declan appeared to be trying to figure out the pecking order.

"My husband is studying today. So I'm here with my chaperone." I pointed at Garrett.

"And you are?" Declan asked again as I was climbing out of the pool and sat next to him.

"Belinda Pennington." This time I extended my hand. I turned toward Garrett and glared, warning him to keep his distance.

Declan glanced at him before he shook my hand. "Your husband's a lucky guy. I don't think I would've let you come alone."

Garrett was still frowning. "She's not alone. I'm watching over her," he added in an abrupt, harsh tone.

"Chill out Garrett, he's just being friendly." I scowled at him. "Can't I be sociable toward a new brother? Just go tend to Abbey. I'll be fine." I was trying my hardest to remove Garrett from the scene.

"He's my pit bull." I shot daggers back at Garrett's menacing glare. Garrett didn't look very happy. He walked far enough away to not be too bothersome, but I noticed him look my way every now and then. I frowned at him each time I saw him keeping tabs on me.

Declan gazed at me with his fascinating green eyes. "How long have you been married?" I found myself staring into them unable to look away. For a few minutes, I felt as if I was looking at Robert. If it weren't for the different eye color and that he was shorter, they could have been twins.

"Oh, ah...," I came out of my trance, "...a month and a half, we tied the knot after his graduation."

He smiled like he knew what he was doing with his eyes. "Have you been dating all through college?"

"No, we just met the first of April." I looked at the water to avoid his eyes. I didn't want to be distracted again.

"Man that was quick!"

"Yeah, kind of love at first sight." I was playing in the water with my feet making whirlpools when I stopped and looked at him. "Where are you from?"

"Dallas, and you?"

"Sugar Land. It's southwest of Houston."

Russell announced that the grilled hamburgers and hot dogs were ready. "Shall we?" Declan helped me up, then slid his hand across the small of my back causing a spontaneous shiver. My back arched slightly, surprising me, but his tough was different, not like Robert's. It wasn't sexually arousing. "Did I shock you?"

It was just my luck that Robert decided to make an unexpected appearance. As he walked toward me, I could tell he noticed my reaction by the questioning look on his face. His eyebrows were knitted together and his mouth was drawn. "No. I just had a chill." I kept my eyes on my husband.

Robert snatched me away from Declan, pulling me to him. I managed to stay upright from his rough tug and snapped my arm out of his grasp. Now I was embarrassed. I looked around to see if anyone else noticed him acting like an ass. Everyone seemed busy partying.

My voice was soft and muted when I glared into his eyes. "I'm glad you came. Did you finish your project?" I was trying very hard not to draw any attention to us. It was very evident to me that Robert was not a happy camper. It was bad enough that Declan witnessed our unpleasant exchange.

"No. Garrett called me." His words were low, deliberate, sharp and direct.

I stepped back and looked at him. "Why?" I quickly looked around for Garrett. Now I was pissed.

He leaned toward me pressing his cheek firmly to mine as he whispered in a stern tone pronouncing his words very clearly. "He just thought I *needed* to be here." Slowly he pulled away brushing his cheek against mine, exciting my senses before his soft lips caught the corner of my mouth, knowing full well what that would do.

My heart beat rapidly and I had trouble keeping my breathing under control, but I was still angry. I snapped my head toward him whispering in my own stern manner. "So, I'm not allowed to talk to guys?"

Robert didn't say anything for a few seconds, but never took his squinted eyes off me. I felt like my skin was being cut by his glare. His next move surprised me. I saw his eyes change and soften a bit as he gave a quick glance in Declan's direction. "This must be Russell's nephew." Declan had moved away a discreet distance. Robert reached out to shake his hand, stretching to invite him closer to us. "Hey, I'm Robert Pennington." The asshat's voice was now friendly.

"Declan Hinds." Stepping closer, he reached over to take Robert's hand, never taking his eyes off of Robert's, nor letting go of his hand. "You have a very nice wife. I've been enjoying her company." The two just stood there for a few more seconds not saying anything, still in a hand grip.

"Thanks." He broke the stare-down with Declan and released his hand. "Excuse us for a minute. I need to talk to her." He placed his hand in the middle of my back and guided me to the front yard. "What was that? You reacted to his touch." Concern shown in his eyes, but his voice was calmer.

"No, it was just a chill from him sliding his hand across my lower back. It wasn't like when you touch me. But, it did surprise me." Now I was getting worried. I had been spending less and less free time with Robert. The time I had now was being marred by my reaction to Declan's touch. I wanted to cry, but held it in. "Don't worry. I'm not interested in him." I desperately wanted to change the subject with my next feeble attempt. "Can you stay?"

"I need to go back." He didn't look at me as he answered in a solemn voice. When he did look, he appeared surprised. "You're still reacting. Why?"

"Because you kissed me and you've been touching me." He didn't say anything, but stared at me. I had never seen him like this before. Looking him in the eyes, I tenderly pressed my hand against his chest and hoped I would get the answer I wanted when I asked my next question. "Can we go to your car?"

"*NO!* I have to get back." He looked at me, almost despondent. "Did his touch start this?"

"No. You did when you touched my cheek and kissed the corner of my mouth. Remember?" He nodded. "I want to try something. Stroke your hand across my lower back." When he did, it caused a hot rush up my spine that mixed with the sensations I was already experiencing—I gasped and trembled. I lunged for him, but he reached out and stopped me. This unexpected action cut me like a knife. I just stood there staring as I examined Robert. It was like he was a different person—someone I didn't like.

His darkened eyes locked on mine. "Hmmm. Interesting. So, you're extra sensitive there."

Still feeling aroused, I took some deep breaths to calm myself. "Robert stay with me."

"I need to go back, but I don't want to leave you here around him." Now his possessive nature was showing.

"I'll be alright. At least eat before you go." Gazing into his eyes which seemed to have lost their glint of blue, I lovingly ran my hand down the side of his face. Wrong move. It just prolonged my physical need for him, but to ease his mind, I breathed, "Robert…Baby, I love you."

He half grinned and stared into my eyes as though he were trying to believe me, then looked away. "I have to go. They're waiting for me. I'll see you later tonight." As he started to turn to leave, I reached up and tried to hug him. He scowled and stepped back away from me. "*Belinda*, you'll get me all wet." His sudden outburst was sharp, biting.

I froze where I stood. I couldn't believe how he was acting. The coldness in his voice was like a dagger through my heart. "Geez! It's just water. You'd be dry before you get back there." I glared at him. "Just go back to your group," I angrily said, then turned and hurried away.

"Belinda…."

"Just go!" I waved my arm motioning him to leave. Fighting back the tears, I ran back to the pool area. This was a side of Robert I hoped I'd never see again. I missed the loving, caring person who usually couldn't keep his hands off me, and prayed I'd find him when we arrived home.

After picking up some food, I sat next to Abbey. Garrett was sitting by my best friend. "Where's Robert?" Garrett was looking all around.

"He had to go back to his study group." I pursed my lips trying very hard not to tell him off.

"Just hang around with us." Abbey leaned over and butted heads with me. She had no clue as to the events that just transpired.

I leaned around her and punched Garrett in the arm. "Why did you call him? You just created a bigger problem."

"Ouch!" Scowling, he grabbed hold of his arm. "I didn't like the way that guy was looking at you. What problem did I create?" He seemed confused by my remark.

Too upset to explain, I just spat out a quick reply. "Oh, never mind!"

Declan walked over and sat next to me. "Where's your husband?" He was scanning the area with very cautious eyes.

"His study group. He had to go back."

Garrett was frowning at me. I scowled back at him and stuck out my tongue.

Several couples started dancing after Cheryl put on some music. Declan reached for my hand. "C'mon, let's dance."

"Wait a minute." I put on my shorts and jacket, trying to avoid him touching my back since I was in enough trouble already. We danced to several slow songs and talked. I also danced with Brian, Paul, Garrett, and some of the other brothers. As I danced with Garrett, I scolded him. "Are you going to tell Robert I danced with Declan? Oh, and don't forget Brian, Paul, and you." I said it as sarcastically as I could. I wanted him to get the point. "It really wasn't a big deal, you know. I was having fun and you were ruining it." I quit dancing and strutted away not giving him a chance to reply. As I was walking by Brian, I overheard him say he was leaving. "Brian, I heard you say you were leaving. Can you give me a ride home?"

"Sure, I'll wait for you out front."

"Thanks, I'll be right there." I looked around and found Abbey lounging by the pool. "I'm leaving. Brian is taking me home."

Abbey looked at me and sat up. "Why?"

"Do you need to ask?" I pointed my head toward Garrett.

"Oh, sorry. I guess he's being overprotective. Do you want me to talk to him, tell him to back off?"

"No, that's not necessary. I'm ready to go. See you later." I turned, heading for the front yard to meet Brian.

On the way I saw Declan. As luck would have it, he was in clear sight of Garrett. So, when I approached him, Garrett was watching. I politely shook Declan's hand. "Thank you. I had a great time."

"Me too. Hope to see you around." He smiled and focused his green eyes on mine.

Taking in his gaze, I noticed they didn't have the same effect on me as Robert's. As I walked away, I could feel Garrett glaring at me. I turned around and glared back. With a bounce, I flipped my hair as I turned heading for Brian, making sure my signature sashay walk was in full swing.

The apartment was empty, but that was good. I was still upset with Robert for treating me the way he did. He hurt my feelings. Trying to avoid thinking about it anymore, I took a long hot shower to relax and crawled into an empty bed. I just lay there staring at the ceiling, running the disturbing events over and over through my mind. It was one a.m. according to the clock when I heard the click of the front door closing. I was tired and didn't want to talk, so I rolled onto my stomach with my head resting on my forearm and pretended to be asleep.

Robert quietly crept into the room and began to strip. I peeked over my arm and saw him pull his shirt off over his head exposing his well-formed silhouette. He discarded it on the floor. The sound of the zipper and the rustle of him removing his jeans thrilled me but I was still angry with him and continued pretending I was asleep.

He slipped into bed and tried to pull me over to his side, but I pulled away, turning my back to him. He rolled over next to me and put his hand on my arm, but I just shook it off.

"Belinda." I didn't answer. "Belinda." I ignored him.

Before he rolled over away from me, I heard him murmur, "I do love you, Angel."

I do love you??? What was that about? Was he trying to convince me or himself? All I wanted was to hear him say was *I'm sorry*, but those words never passed his lips.

I finally dozed off. That was the first time I wasn't in his arms when we went to sleep. I didn't like it. Sometime during the night, I awoke and rolled over, curling up over his side, laying my head on his shoulder. His arms wrapped around me and I whispered, "I do love you, too."

CHAPTER 25

THERE WAS A slight movement of the bed as he got up. "Where are you going?" I reached out for him. "Come back—it's Sunday." I knew I should still be mad at him, but I just couldn't. So for now, I was resolved to form a truce with him. Not wanting to waste time fighting, I rationalized that if I tried to keep the peace, all would work out. He wasn't around enough, so what time I did have had to be the best. "What time is it?"

He was standing next to the bed, looking down at me. "It's seven o'clock. I have to meet with the group. Hopefully, we'll finish today."

"Can't you come back to bed?" Giving him a pouty look, I squirmed seductively under the sheet, trying to have my way. That was all it took. He flashed that irresistible smile, rolled his eyes, and jumped back into bed. He lightly ran his fingers across my lower back, sending a surge of electricity up my spine. He had a newfound power over me and was using it. I loved every splendid second!

***

"I'm sorry I upset you. The pressure from my class is really stressing me out. I didn't mean to take it out on you. I'll try to come home early." He sounded very sincere as he rose and headed to the bathroom to shower. I jumped out of bed and joined him, prolonging his stay.

After he left, I crawled back into bed and slept as long as I could to make the day shorter. When I couldn't sleep any longer, my time was spent cleaning the whole apartment, doing some laundry, watching TV, and making us lasagna for dinner.

Robert's promise was short lived. I wound up eating by myself and crawled into an empty bed. About two in the morning, I woke up and found him asleep on the couch with an open book lying across his chest. On the coffee table was a single rose, but no card. Knowing what it meant, I placed it in the vase that was sitting on a small mirror, now a permanent fixture on the kitchen table. Fetching a blanket, I covered him the best I could without waking him and kissed his forehead. I went back to bed feeling a little more loved by his simple gesture of taking the time out of his busy day to pick up a rose.

Morning came and I was alone in the apartment. After dressing, I walked to the campus and went straight to the Cave, hoping to see Robert. He wasn't there, but Declan was so I sat and talked to him for a while until Garrett came in. I didn't want to talk to him, so I excused myself and left. As I passed by, I snubbed him and kept walking.

Again, the rest of the day was spent by myself. I ate some leftover lasagna and later went to bed alone. Once more, I found Robert asleep on the couch. This was becoming our routine and I didn't like it.

We needed to talk, so I called the next day. At first he said he was busy and couldn't talk—he'd call me back later, but no call was returned. Over the next several days, I tried calling but all of them went to voice mail—with no return calls. I even tried texting. His response was either "can't talk now," or no reply. I was confused and felt abandoned.

***

Thursday after lunch, I was tired of being alone. Normally Abbey would be a good source of companionship, but she had decided to take a trip to see her parents. So I headed for the Cave on the off chance I might see Robert or anyone else to hang out with. Walking in, I saw Declan. He smiled and waved me over. We sat and talked like we had almost every day that week. Wanting to do something different, I took a chance. "How would you like a tour of the campus and town."

His eyes lit up. "Sure, I'm game."

We walked to the student parking lot and looked up and down the rows until I found Robert's car. Declan's eyes grew wider as I opened the door and looked at him. "Get in." I put the top down and drove off, and gave him a quick tour of the campus pointing out the different buildings before heading out of town. Taking the winding road to the top of the hill, I parked facing the view of the town below. "This is 'Make Out Ridge.' At night it's so beautiful with all the campus and town lights reaching up to the stars." I glanced over at him. "You need to see it at night sometime."

"You'll have to bring me whenever you can." He flashed his hypnotic eyes at me.

"You need to stop doing that."

"Doing what?" He looked innocently at me.

I rolled my eyes and smiled. "You know."

He knew the power he had over females and was utilizing his best asset to charm me. He just smirked and chuckled, then did it again.

I glared at him because he knew what I was talking about. For now, I'd just let him think he had some spellbinding power with those eyes of his.

Driving down the main street, I gave Declan the nickel tour of the few shops that made up the hub of the town. On our way back to campus, we stopped for some sodas. Pulling into the campus parking lot, I parked in a different spot and left the two empty cups in the car, hoping to entice a reaction from Robert.

"Thanks for the tour. I look forward to seeing the night lights with you," he joked, grinning at me.

I smiled back. "You're very welcome. See you around." Lowering my head, I slowly shook it as I walked away. There was no way I'd be the one to take him to 'Make Out Ridge' at night. That task would be left to some unmarried college co-ed.

Once more, the apartment was empty. Again, I ate alone, then sat around, which allowed my mind to formulate hideous scenarios about Robert's absence. The walls began closing in on me. So at about nine o'clock, I called Declan. "Hey, this is Belinda. Do you want to see the lights with me *now*?"

"Sure. But what about you-know-who?"

I didn't respond to his question. "Meet me out front of your house. I'll pick you up in ten minutes. Watch for a silver CRV."

He was waiting when I arrived. Opening the door, he was about to say something when I glared at him. He hesitated a second and raised an eyebrow, then slid into the seat, giving me a nod before he closed the door. We drove in silence toward 'Make Out Ridge.' Almost there, Declan broke the ice. "Is everything okay? You seem upset."

Trying to concentrate on my driving up the dark winding road, I just answered his question briefly. "I'm fine. I wanted to get out of the apartment."

"Where's Robert?" Declan sounded concerned.

I didn't think I should discuss my problems with him, but I decided to open up a little. It would be nice to talk to someone. The pitch in my voice dropped. "He's busy with the study group. I hardly see him anymore." I kept my eyes on the road in front of me. Declan didn't comment. He just sat quietly.

When we arrived, we were the only car on top of the hill. We sat on the hood leaning back against the windshield. "Isn't it beautiful and so peaceful here? I just love to look at the stars," I breathed. The coolness of the night air and stillness of the surroundings put me at ease.

"Beautiful indeed."

I looked over at him. He was staring at me. "Thanks, but not me. Look at the stars. The whole area looks like twinkling lights."

"I'd rather gaze at you." His voice was soft, almost a whisper. I elbowed him. "I probably shouldn't say this, but I wish you weren't married. I'd like to have had a chance to date you. I really enjoy being with you."

"I've enjoyed your company too." He leaned over to kiss me, but I backed away. "I can't do that. I can't cheat on Robert no matter how much of a dick I think he is right now."

Declan was on his elbow looking down at me. "You know, no one needs to study all the time, especially when he has a beautiful wife at home waiting for him. Have you seen this study group—who's in it?"

I stared at the stars for a moment trying to organize my thoughts. *Cheating? Is that what he's been up to all these nights?* A gripping feeling in my chest turned to agony as I focused back on Declan's face. "Do you think he's cheating on me? Have you heard something? Tell me!" I begged, staring at him, holding back my budding tears.

"No, I haven't heard anything, except that he *was* a ladies' man."

I started thinking about what Declan just said. At first I just passed off Robert's mood and absence as being due to the stress and complexity of the class. Declan planted a seed that now had me wondering if something else was going on. Had some girl caught his attention or was he growing tired of me?

Trying to shake the doubts from my head, I confided in him. "I need to trust him. When I don't I get hurt—mentally and physically." I was becoming more upset. Tears were now flowing from the outer corners of my eyes into my hair. I had promised Robert I'd trust him. We made a pact and shook hands on it. I couldn't go back on my promise to him.

"Why are you putting up with this?"

"Because I love him," I sniffled in a pitiful voice.

"Then give him an ultimatum. Let him know you don't like being alone all the time, that he has to find some time for you."

I spoke through the sniffles, tears trailing down my cheeks. "I can't do that. I don't want to add to the pressure he's under."

He locked his eyes on mine. "Belinda, do you want to be with someone who doesn't want to be with you? You deserve to be happy."

As a wave of panic overcame me, I looked away. I'd be hysterical in a minute if I didn't get my mind on something else. "Okay. Let's change the subject. Now look at the stars."

He uttered a sigh and jumped off the car hood. Great, now I had three guys mad at me—Robert, Garrett and Declan. I heard the passenger door open then slam shut. He came back and handed me a tissue. I smirked at myself for my silly thought, as he jumped back to his previous position. "Now dry those eyes. We have some serious stargazing to do." We spent the next hour picking out constellations and visualizing funny pictures in the stars. I hadn't laughed so much in a long time. It helped put me in a better mood.

Pointing out a constellation, I caught a glimpse of my wrist watch. "Jeez! It's almost midnight. I need to go home. Thanks for coming with me. I had a great time."

"Me too. Thanks for inviting me. I'm available any time you want to come back." He flashed me a big grin.

When I arrived home, Robert's car was parked out front. *Oh shit*! He would decide to come home early tonight. Entering the apartment, I saw him sitting on the couch watching TV. He ignored me.

Warily, I smiled and said in an upbeat tone, "Hey! What are you doing home?"

With emotionless eyes, he looked up from the TV at me. "I thought I'd spend some time with you."

"Oh, I didn't know. You should've called." Now I was being sarcastic as I locked the door.

"I did. We decided to stop around nine." He was upset.

"I didn't hear my cell." I dug around in my purse. "It's not in here. Call my number." He reached for his phone and complied with my request. The music came from the kitchen. I picked it up from the counter, put it in my purse, and returned to the living room. "I forgot to put it back in my purse. I left around then."

"Where did you go?" I noticed his brows were drawn together as he glanced at me.

"I got bored, so I went to see the lights."

Now he was glaring at me. "By yourself?"

Oooh, I'm in trouble now. "No, I told Declan about the lights. So I called him to see if he wanted to see them. I didn't want to go by myself. It was so beautiful tonight. I wish you could have seen it."

"For three hours?" he spat out.

"No, about two hours. We talked and also looked for constellations. He's a real nice guy and he's been a good friend. We talk every day in the Cave. Oh! By the way, I borrowed your car today to give him a tour of the campus and town."

"Is there something going on that you need to tell me?" He was scowling.

"*What?* How *dare* you ask me that? I could ask you the same." I tromped into the bedroom, dug my sleep t-shirt out of the dresser drawer, and went into the bathroom to shower. I locked the door. After toweling off, I put on the t-shirt, the same one I had borrowed the first time I slept in the apartment. I kept it and cut the neck hole bigger so it wouldn't choke me. Now too big, it hung off one shoulder, and just barely covered my butt.

Robert was stewing on the couch as I walked in front of him to the kitchen to get my romance novel. To reach the book, I leaned across the table, showing just enough of my bare bottom. In a flash he was off the couch. He grabbed me around the waist from behind and held me tight as he kissed my neck. I moaned as I leaned back into his chest with my head against his shoulder. Turning, I ran my hands up the back of his neck and laced my fingers in his hair, pulling his head down to mine. Planting my lips firmly on his, our kiss excited me to my depths. He returned the emotion with enthusiasm. His hand slid up the bottom of the t-shirt and headed straight for the small of my back. It arched as he tugged me closer. He picked me up and I wrapped my legs around his waist. Our reactions took over. The results were explosive.

Fulfilled, I wrapped myself over his side, entwining my legs with his, and held him tight as I prepared to go to sleep. "I love you…and I miss you."

"It'll be over soon." He squeezed me to him.

When morning came, he was gone again.

Each day I went to the Cave hoping to see Robert. Instead, I talked to Declan until he left for Dallas. The fraternity brothers would ask where Robert was. I didn't know, so I lied. "Studying," became my usual answer. It was becoming embarrassing, so to avoid the awkward questions I quit going. I spent nearly all of my time in the apartment. For all I knew, I was the last one to find out Robert was busy with someone else.

One day I waited outside his building to talk to him—he never came out. I went to the parking lot—his car wasn't there.

Lonely days and nights turned into weeks. The only time I saw him was at two or three a.m., when he was asleep on the couch. There was always an open book nearby. Was he really studying or just faking? Each night I curled up in a ball and cried myself to sleep. Why was he doing this to me? Why weren't we talking about whatever the problem was? I tried calling and texting with no response. I even woke him up one night and asked him what was wrong. He just said everything was fine. I asked if he still loved me. He took in a deep breath and exhaled loudly as if he were upset. "Of course." That night he came to bed, but he insisted he was exhausted and told me to go to sleep. That upset me and I started crying. He spooned me with his arm over my waist. I laced my fingers through his and hugged his hand over my aching heart as I tried to stop crying. His response was cold. "Belinda, nothing is wrong. Just go to sleep."

Belinda? What happened to Angel? What happened to my warm and loving husband? raced through my mind as I tried to fall asleep.

In the morning I tried to talk to him, but again I was told there's nothing wrong. "I'm just under a lot of pressure, and stressed out. Don't worry. Please don't add to my stress," was his final answer as he walked out leaving me alone.

I put those thoughts out of my head and just endured the heartache, convincing myself that everything would return to normal when summer school was over. *But what about the fall semester?* The thought that this could continue made me shudder.

The next morning was more of the same—no Robert. I forced myself out of bed and walked to the kitchen for a cup of coffee. There on the counter was a single rose lying in front of my empty vase. There was no card.

I studied it, trying to decide what to do. As I saw it, I had two choices. I could pick it up and put it in water then dry it, or I could just leave it there. A single red rose is the symbol of love. I wasn't feeling very loved, so I decided to leave it. That afternoon I found it in the vase on the table. He evidentially came home while I was out. "Huh! He cares more about the rose than he does me."

CHAPTER 26

IT HAD BEEN weeks since Robert had kissed me, made love to me, or even had a conversation with me. I felt deserted. It was the last day of summer school—finals. I decided to surprise Robert, hoping I could talk him into having dinner, a kind of finals celebration. So, I drove to campus to wait for him by his car. After driving up and down the aisles of the parking lot, I finally located it. I found the closest spot and pulled in. As I approached his car from the front passenger side, I noticed movement and stopped. Squinting my eyes, I froze as my brain tried to make sense out of what I was watching through the windshield of my husband's car. He was in there, but not alone. His study partner, Erin, was cradled in his arms. Her arms were wrapped around his neck and he was caressing her back. They were kissing. He was so involved in what he was doing, he didn't even notice me standing there. I didn't know whether to confront them or run. *Screw our deal*! *Why confront him*? There wasn't any acceptable reason for what I was seeing. Watching the long kiss made me want to puke. (I should have on his beloved car.) I turned and ran to my car and sped out of the parking lot toward home with tears of disbelief flowing down my cheeks.

I tossed my purse on the table and headed into the bedroom to pull out my suitcases. After emptying my two dresser drawers of clothes into one of them, I packed everything I wanted from the closet in the other. I left my wedding dress and the pale blue teddy lying on the bedroom floor where I threw them. Tears were streaming down my face the whole time. He needed to know why I left, so I decided to leave him a letter. Unnerved, I shuffled through his desk draws for a sheet of paper and wrote…

Robert,

How could you do this to me? I saw what you did, so you know why I'm gone. Now I know why you've been avoiding me these past <u>weeks</u>. You've hurt *me so badly. I feel as though a part of me has died. Was I just another one of your many conquests? I thought you loved me. Is it time to move on to the next challenge? I see now the rumors about you were true. I just never wanted to believe them.*

What I saw you and Erin doing in your car was not an accident or my misunderstanding this time. There's no reason that can justify what I saw. You were so engrossed in the kiss that you didn't even notice me standing a few feet away watching. From the first day I saw you, I knew you were the one for me—that we'd be together forever. But I don't see that anymore. My heart will always ache for you, but now at least it won't suffer through the daggers of pain that you inflict with your cheating. It's hard to imagine my life without you, but I don't trust you now. You promised me you wouldn't do it anymore and you did. So what do I do? I'm in pain with you and without you. I need time to think and heal without any influence from you. I feel abandoned and betrayed. Oh God! I love you so much, but you're ripping my heart out, piece by piece.

You know why I'm not confronting you about this—my willpower, that you have control over.

Always,

Belinda

When I finished I placed it on the coffee table and went back to packing. The whole time my life with him was going through my mind. I went back to the letter and wrote…

PS—Remember what I told you in the beginning? I can do what you do!!! Well I can and will!!!

I let the pen fall next to the paper and took the packed suitcases to the car. Still reliving our short life together, I returned to the paper…

PPS—Do you recall your gut feeling that I was going to leave you? Maybe that was your subconscious warning you that you'd cause me to leave if you didn't change your ways. Something to think about!

I got up to make sure I had everything I needed then decided to write one more thing before leaving…

PPPS—Keep the engagement ring. It belongs in your family. It wasn't good luck for us after all.

I left the tear-stained letter on the coffee table with my engagement ring and double-heart necklace lying on top. I kept my wedding ring on. I had never taken it off and promised I never would—*'til death do us part*. It had never entered my mind that our marriage could end in divorce.

Giving the apartment one last check, I saw my treasure box and retrieved it from the end table. With it tucked under my arm, I stood in the middle of the living room looking around. The memories of better times flooded my head. I started to doubt myself. Was I making the right move? I shook the thought off.

Now it was time to say goodbye, but I'd always have the good memories. I'd never forget the times when Robert swept me off my feet and took me to the bedroom. And there were the long night talks lying next to him, wrapped in his arms. I don't think I ever felt so safe and protected. Hearing his voice always drew me into whatever he said.

No, I would always have the good memories. Unfortunately, there were also the bad ones. Those would be harder for me to recover from. At this point, it didn't matter who was at fault, Robert or me. I still would have the bad ones and all the feelings that went with them, making me a victim of my own shattered fate.

For now it was time to leave. Walking toward the door, I reached for my purse on the kitchen table. I snatched up the handles not slowing my pace, and with one swift movement, dragged the purse across the table. I heard the crash of breaking glass. Turning, I saw my precious vase and mirror smashed on the floor with the rose lying on top. The scene before me compounded my already bruised emotions as I stared down at the mess. While attempting to pick up the rose, I accidently dropped my treasure box of dried rose petals. My tokens of his love spilled everywhere over the broken glass. My first instinct was to pick up my valued memories. I bent down to reach for the petals, then stopped myself as I realized they no longer held any meaning. Leaving them where they lay, I stood and turned for the door.

After opening it, I hesitated, taking one last look around. I stepped into the entryway, shutting the door on my life with Robert. Opening the outer door of the building, I stepped into the sunlight. My cell rang as I stood on the porch. It was Abbey. I was too upset to talk to her, so I ignored it.

I didn't know where to go. Home was out of the question. If Robert looked for me that would be the first place he'd check. I didn't want him bothering my parents or them having to lie about where I was. It would be best not to tell anyone of my whereabouts. As I drove past the campus toward Houston, I saw, in my rear view mirror, a blue roadster pull out and head in the direction of our apartment. I again questioned my decision to leave, but there was *NO* acceptable excuse for what I watched today. This was the right decision. I left my love and my life behind.

Though I wasn't in any condition to be driving, I had to leave town. The drive to Houston seemed to take forever. It gave me too much time for my mind to keep playing the car scene over and over again. I used almost a whole box of tissues to wipe away my tears. When I arrived within the city limits, the rush hour traffic was very heavy, so I pulled into the first nice-looking motel and checked in. I was starving because I hadn't eaten since breakfast. I noticed a restaurant next door and walk over there. After ordering, I decided to check my voice and text messages. Abbey was the first to call. "Belinda, where are you? Call me." The second call was also from her. "Belinda, are you okay? Why aren't you answering your cell? Call me." The third call was again from her. "Belinda, I knocked on your apartment door. Answer your cell. I'm getting worried about you. I'm going to the Cave to find Robert." The fourth call was from HIM. "Belinda, where are you? Call me." There was one text message. It was from him: "R U OK? Call me."

I sent Abbey a text: Im OK. Saw him kissing Erin in his car. Made me sick. Why doing this—why abandon me? WISH I WERE DEAD—HURTS SO BAD. Will text later, if can.

I turned my cell off.

As I ate, I kept questioning whether or not I should've stayed and talked to him. Leaving was the right decision, I concluded. Paying for my meal, I ran across a business card in my wallet. It was the one the gentleman gave me at the Mexican restaurant in Sugar Land—Johnson's Modeling Agency. Studying the card, I realized it could be the answer to another problem I was facing—the need to support myself. Maybe I could model. How hard could it be? Just pose in front of a camera. Surely I could do that as long as I didn't have to walk a runway. I decided to call the number in the morning to make an appointment. After returning to my room, I felt more lonely and upset. My mind kept reviewing the kiss. I tried to watch some TV, but that didn't help, so I dug my cell out of my purse and called Abbey.

"Oh! Hi Mom!" Abbey answered in her normal tone.

"No, it's Belinda."

"Hold on Mom, I'm having bad reception. Let me go outside." I heard a door slam. "Belinda, sorry about that. I figured you didn't want to talk to Robert, since you haven't been taking his calls. Garrett and I are at your apartment again with him. Garrett is really mad at him for what he did to you, but he is also worried about him. He has never seen Robert this despondent before. Are you alright? Your text had us worried."

"I'm fine. I didn't mean to upset you, but I was hoping you'd show it to Robert."

"I sat with Garrett and Robert in the Cave after their finals. I asked Robert where you were, and said that I hadn't been able to reach you. He said he didn't know. He tried calling you. When you didn't answer, he said something like, 'Oh crap,' and ran out. On our way home we decided to check on you two. Robert was sitting on the couch with your letter in one hand and your engagement ring and necklace clutched in his other one. Glass and rose petals were scattered on the floor. He was very upset, but also angry. He said you promised you wouldn't run away again, but you did. You packed and left. Your text came while I was there. I showed it to Garrett and Robert. Both of them are very worried about you. I was so mad, I punched him on the arm as hard as I could and told him he's a self-centered, spoiled SOB, and that I couldn't stand being in the same room with him. I walked out. Garrett came home a little later."

"Well, what excuse did he give Garrett for what he did?" I was curious to hear if this was somehow entirely my fault, as usual.

"He said Robert wouldn't talk about it. I guess he's feeling guilty."

"I guess I know now why he was coming in at two or three every morning. He was spending all of his time with his study partner, Erin. Abbey, he was thoroughly into that kiss. He hasn't kissed me like that in weeks or even touched me in any way. One day everything was perfect, the next day I was alone. I was married, but had no husband." Tears began rolling down my face.

"Why didn't you say anything to me?"

"Robert doesn't like me airing our dirty laundry with other people. So I kept quiet to avoid making the situation worse." I was starting to sob and my voice was cracking. "I've missed him so much, but I guess he's found a replacement."

"You said he was coming home at two or three in the morning. Is that all?" Her voice conveyed concern about what I'd been going through.

"Abbey! He came home after I'd already gone to sleep. I'd wake up and find him asleep on the couch. Then he'd be gone in the morning before I woke up. I went to the Cave time after time, hoping to see him, but no Robert, so I quit going. I felt like an idiot sitting there without him, not knowing where he was when his brothers asked. I never saw him so we could talk. His cell always went to voice mail and he quit returning my calls. I don't understand what happened." My voice was quavering through my sobs.

"Where are you? Can I come see you? We can talk." Abbey sounded really upset.

"I'm not telling anyone where I am right now. I'll let you know later after I find a job and settle somewhere."

"So, you're not coming back to school?" Her voice broke.

"No, too many bad memories and definitely not with him there. Tell Garrett not to be too mad at him. He is his best friend. I just should've known better than to get involved with someone like him. You're lucky. You have a really decent guy you can trust. I need to go."

"I'll tell him. I love you." She added, "Please stay in touch."

"I will. Good-bye." Looking at my phone, I imagined Abbey telling Robert about our phone call and wondered if he would be sadder because he was losing me or because he was caught again. I guess none of that mattered at this point. I was alone for the past several weeks and alone now, something I was used to. Having grown up that way, if I had to, I could do it again.

I was exhausted mentally and physically from the most horrible day I'd ever had. But I still held a small glimmer of hope that we could work things out in the future. For now, I needed to find out who I was and if I could live without him.

After a quick shower, I crawled into my empty bed. Sleeping was difficult until I curled up around a spare pillow. It wasn't warm like Robert, but it filled the void.

CHAPTER 27

MY FIRST TASK upon awakening was job hunting.

"Johnson's Modeling Agency, may I help you?" A nice, older-sounding lady answered.

"Yes please, I'd like to make an appointment with Mr. Johnson. Does he by any chance have an opening today?" I was ready to start my new life in some direction.

"Yes, he's available at two. Will that work for you?"

"That'll be fine."

"And your name please."

"Belinda Pen...ah. I mean Davies. Belinda Davies." *Why use my married name if it might change*?

"Belinda Davies, see you at two."

"Thank you."

No sooner had I ended my call, Robert's ring played. There were enough reminders of him in my head, so he was bumped back down to the standard ringtone before I turned it off.

It was nine a.m. and there was much to do before my appointment. I studied myself in the mirror, almost fainting at what I saw. My eyes were red and puffy from all the crying yesterday and my hair resembled a rat's nest after my restless night. I decided to shower again and wash my hair. When that was done, I finished dressing, putting on my best jeans, a red blouse, and my espadrilles. I needed to do something about my puffy eyes. I remembered hearing about applying cold compresses to reduce puffiness, so I went down the hall to the ice machine and scooped out a few pieces. After wrapping the ice in a damp wash cloth, I relaxed on the bed, and placed it over my eyelids. The ice stayed there as long as I could stand the stinging cold. My eyes had improved a little when I examined them again. Luckily a bit of concealer, some eye shadow, and mascara made my eyes appear better, but not quite normal.

I had about two hours to find the Johnson's Modeling Agency. I wasn't familiar with that area of Houston or how long it might take to get there, so I typed the address into the GPS app of my cell. The agency was located across town. Not wanting to be late, I decided I'd better be on my way because in Houston, being stuck in traffic was the one thing you could count on.

For once in the past twenty-four hours, luck was on my side. I saw a branch of the bank where Robert and I had our savings account. I stopped and withdrew two thousand dollars. It would be enough for me to live on for a few weeks and Robert probably wouldn't notice the money missing right away.

I pulled up in front of the agency about twenty minutes early. Since there was some time to kill, I sent Abbey a text message: Wish me luck. Going for job interview.

After a few minutes, she texted: Good luck. Doing what?

I texted: Secret, tell u later if works out.

The agency was located in an old remodeled house in Bellaire, a town surrounded by Houston. All the houses on the street had been converted into businesses. An attractive middle-aged lady sitting at a desk looked up when I entered. "May I help you?"

I walked over and stood in front of her desk. "I'm Belinda Davies. I have an appointment at two."

"One moment, please." She left the room for a few seconds and then returned. "You can go in now." She pointed the way. I had expected to have to wait while some phone call or something else was attended to before I'd be allowed my scheduled audience, but to my surprise that wasn't the case.

"Thank you." I entered the door she directed me to.

Without looking up at me, Mr. Johnson motioned to a chair across from his desk. "Have a seat." He looked up and addressed me from behind his big wooden desk that was covered with photos of models and papers he had been going over. "What can I do for you, young lady?"

"My name is Belinda. Do you remember me?" His eyes examined me. "A few months ago at a Mexican restaurant in Sugar Land, you gave me your business card. You told me if I wanted to make some money to come see you."

"Oh yes! You and a young man. I remember now."

"I found your business card in my wallet when I arrived in Houston and thought I'd give you a call." I was trying not to sound too desperate, but I didn't think I would be good waitress material and finding a job that would pay the bills could take weeks. I might have been able to make another withdrawal from the joint account, but it was logical that at some point the well would go dry.

"When you arrived in Houston? Where are you from?" He looked puzzled as he stroked his chin.

"I'm from Sugar Land, but I've been away at college."

Mr. Johnson's eyes wandered over me, stopping at my left hand resting on the arm of my chair. He gave me a curious look. "Is that a wedding band? Are you married to that young man?"

I hesitated, wondering if I should be honest. I decided honesty was still the best policy. "Yes, but I've left him for personal reasons." Tears started to well up in my eyes at the very thought of Robert. I did everything I could to hold them back, but to no avail.

Mr. Johnson must have noticed them. He changed the subject. "I think I can find some work for you, but first, where are you staying?"

I speculated he could see how desperate I was. "I still have to work that out."

"I think I know of a nice place you can live. It's with a woman who's an ex-model. Now she rents out rooms to young ladies. I could take you there and if you like it, you can make the arrangements with Mrs. Foster." I nodded in approval.   He picked up his phone and dialed a number. "Adele, Frank Johnson....How are you doing?...Oh, good to hear that....I'm doing fine, thank you. Do you have a room available?...You do? Great. I have a young lady I'd like to put in your care. Can I bring her over now?...Okay....Thanks." He hung up. "I think you'll like it there."

"Thank you very much." I was floored. If this whole thing worked out, I'd be okay.

"Let's get you over to her place. I'll ride with you and walk back. Now, you need to stop crying so your eyes won't be red and puffy. We need to put together a portfolio of photos of you. Come see me as soon as you can so we can start."

I took a deep breath. "Alright, no more tears."

The house was just around the corner from his business. Mrs. Foster was waiting for us at the front door. She was an attractive white-haired lady who had retained a shapely figure. "Adele Foster, this is Belinda..." He turned toward me. "I don't remember your last name."

"Belinda Davies. I'll be using my maiden name."

"Ms. Davies wants to be a model. I think she has a lot of potential." He glanced at me, then looked back at Mrs. Foster. "Can you help her?"

"She has all the qualities needed to be one," she agreed, studying me. "I'll help her settle in if she likes the room." Mr. Johnson left, reminding me to come see him as soon as I was ready.

The house was a white two-story—very similar in layout to the house I had lived in with Abbey at college. She led me upstairs to a good-sized room. It was furnished with antique cherry furniture, lace curtains and a chenille bedspread. It was dated, but very warm and inviting. "Rent is eight hundred a month and that includes breakfast and dinner. My only rules are no loud music and male guests stay downstairs." She stood quietly as I roamed around, occasionally touching the furnishings. "Will this do?" I scanned the room quickly once again and gave her a nod, sealing my status as her tenant.

I unloaded my car and was unpacking when Mrs. Foster came in. "If there is anything you need, let me know. By the way, I can help with those eyes." She had a grandmotherly quality about her as she waited for my reply.

Pausing from my task, I looked at her. "I must look a mess. Can we start now?" I was thinking the sooner the better.

"Sure. Go take off your makeup, then lie down and relax. I'll be right back." I followed her directions, but the bed was so comfortable I dozed off.

"I'm back," she announced, waking me up. "Keep your eyes closed. I'm going to lay chilled steeped chamomile tea bags over them. Just relax and leave 'em on for a while. We may need to do this several times. I'll be back in a bit."

Right now my eyes hurt from the swollen lids. The cool sensation of the tea bags felt soothing. Unfortunately they did little to distract my thoughts. I wondered what was going on at college. Was he missing me? Why did he do this to me? I thought our marriage would last forever. I missed him so much, but I had to stop thinking about him or I'd cry again. How long was she expecting me to lay here? I finally heard footsteps coming up the creaky wooden stairway and down the hall to my room.

"Okay sweetie. I think that's long enough for now." She removed the teabags and looked at my eyes. "Yes, that helped some. We'll do it again in a few hours."

I walked to the dresser mirror to inspect the progress. "You're right. It did help. Maybe they'll look normal tomorrow so we can start on the photos."

"Maybe so. I'll leave you now to relax." I lay down, settling my head into the soft pillow and fell back into a much-needed sleep.

A knock at my door woke me up. "Are you ready for your next treatment?"

"Sure."

Mrs. Foster placed the teabags on my closed eyes. "I'll be back in about twenty minutes."

I wasn't sleepy and lying still for that long was like putting my mind on a treadmill. It ran full speed as thoughts raced through it. I wondered why

Abbey had to ask him where I was. Wasn't he concerned about me or where I was? Maybe I should have confronted him and asked why he was treating me this way. But that kiss! There was no excuse for that...I guess he grew tired of me. *Oh, stop thinking about him or you're going to drive yourself crazy!*

I was never so relieved to hear footsteps coming across the old wooden floor. Mrs. Foster returned and removed the teabags. "Oh yes, they look much better. I think one more treatment will do it." She sounded positive and proud of her accomplishment.

"After dinner or at bedtime?"

"Bedtime. Just lay here and relax. I'll let you know when dinner's ready."

Thinking I'd check my cell for any missed calls, I took it out of my purse and turned it on. It started ringing. It was Robert. I wasn't ready to talk to him, so I let the call go to voice mail. After waiting a few minutes, I checked my text messages. There was one from him: Im sorry, please call.

I listened to his voice mail. "Angel, I'm sorry. Please call me. We need to talk." Hearing Robert's voice made me want to cry. *No crying.* I had made the right decision to leave. I turned my cell off and tried to go to sleep and succeeded.

"Belinda. Belinda—dinner's ready." Mrs. Foster shook my shoulder to awaken me.

I opened my eyes and yawned. "Okay. Thanks, I'll be down shortly."

Mrs. Foster and I chatted while we ate her delicious meat loaf and creamy mashed potatoes. "Where are you from?"

"Sugar Land, but the last three years I've been away at college."

She pointed at the ring on my left hand. "Is that a wedding band?"

I looked at my ring and nodded. "Yes ma'am...I'm married." The feeling of sadness deepened a bit with the reminder.

"I hope you don't think I'm being nosy, but why do you want to use your maiden name." She had a curious expression on her face as a forkful of food was scooped up.

"I just think it would be simpler if we divorce. I wouldn't have to change my modeling name and explain why. I'd still be Davies." I took a quick bite of meat loaf, anticipating another question.

"*If* you divorce?" She took a sip of water.

I managed to swallow my food. "Yes, *if*. I don't know what I want to do or what he wants. I love him, but I can't trust him. It all happened so fast. We met in April and were married after his graduation in May. All his idea."

She looked shocked. "My goodness! That was quick. He must really love you."

"I thought so, but I kept catching him kissing other girls." I hesitated and glanced at my food. "He always says it's just a misunderstanding on my part." I looked at Mrs. Foster. "I wouldn't mind a hug or a quick peck on the cheek, but definitely not like this last kiss in his car that I witnessed. It made me feel nauseated. I need to stop talking about this or I'm going to start crying." I took a deep breath to hold back the tears. "Let's talk about you. Mr. Johnson said you used to be a model. Did you like it?"

She reached out, clutched my hand and smiled to let me know she understood my situation. "Yes, I was a model. I walked the runways all over the world for several years. It was a lot of fun. But, I gave it all up when I married. We met on one of my trips back from New York. Between his traveling and mine, we didn't have a lot of time to spend together. So I quit and we saw the world together. It was wonderful....I lost him about three years ago. I miss him, but having young ladies live here helps. I enjoy the company."

"How did you meet Mr. Johnson?"

"He's such a dear gentleman. I put a <u>Rooms for Rent</u> sign in my front yard and he stopped by to inquire about it. He said he sometimes needs a place for a model to stay, and this is close to his office. I've had several stay here. Sometimes they stop by and visit when they're in town. They're all sweet young ladies." She smiled at me.

We finished eating and I helped her clean up the kitchen. With the last plate put away and the counters wiped down, Mrs. Foster turned to me. "Now you go relax and I'll bring the teabags up in about an hour or so." She motioned with the wave of her hand for me to leave the kitchen.

I was bored just lying on my bed. I wanted to talk to someone, so I called Abbey again.

"Belinda, I'm so glad you called. Are you alright?"

"Yes, just lonely, although I should be used to that feeling. Where are you? I hear a lot of voices in the background?"

"I'm with Garrett at the frat house."

Out of curiosity I asked, "Is Robert there?"

"Yes, they're outside and Garrett's reading him the riot act. Do you want to talk to him?"

I spat out, "*NO*, definitely *NOT*." I heard Robert's voice in the background. "Is that Belinda—let me talk to her!" Abbey snapped at him. "She doesn't want to talk to you." The phone went dead. A few seconds later my cell rang. My heart skipped a beat—it was Robert. I turned my cell off and waited about five minutes and then turned it back on. There were two new messages. The last one was from Abbey saying he's gone and to call back. The prior one was a text from him: Miss u, love u, please call.

I texted: U didnt miss me b4. U love me? U sure have strange way of showing it.

I called Abbey back.

"Belinda, sorry about the hang up. He was trying to grab my cell. Garrett wants to say hi. Do you want to talk to him?"

"Sure."

"Belinda I'm so sorry. I wish I'd never talked you into going out with him. Although, I guess it would've happened eventually. Look, I'm mad at him too, but I think you two need to talk. He's really upset. He wants to explain."

"*EXPLAIN what*? That it's just my misunderstanding again? Garrett, he hasn't kissed or touched me in about a month. What was I supposed to think when I saw him making out with that girl in his car? He needs to take responsibility for his actions. He's married. If he still wants to play around, then I want a divorce. I can't live this way. It hurts too much." I was upset and could feel the tears threatening. *Don't cry! Don't cry!*

"I noticed you left your engagement ring and necklace. Where's your wedding ring?"

"I still have it on. I promised to never take it off, and I won't until a divorce is finalized, if that happens. I don't want a divorce. I love him so much, but he needs to change and I don't know if he can." *Don't cry! Don't cry!*

"You should've talked to Abbey or me. Maybe we could've helped. He might have listened to me." Garrett sounded distressed.

"I was afraid he'd get upset with me for talking about it, then that would've made matters worse."

"Belinda, I know he loves and misses you. I've never seen him cry before, but this has him so upset, tears were welling up in his eyes while we were talking. He doesn't want to lose you. I can't believe I'm telling you this, but…give him another chance."

"Not yet, I need some time away to decide what's best for me."

"Are you coming back to school?"

"No, I'm getting a job. I already have someone helping me."

"Doing what?"

"I'll tell you later, if it happens. Do me a favor. Tell him to read my letter again. I meant every word."

There was a knock on my door. Mrs. Foster said that the teabags were ready. I told Garrett I needed to go and to tell Abbey I'd keep in touch. Mrs. Foster came in and repeated the process. "I'll be back to remove them."

***

When morning arrived, I jumped up and headed for the mirror. Great, my eyes looked normal—no redness, no puffiness. I decided to call Mr. Johnson. "Hi. Mr. Johnson. This is Belinda. My eyes look fine now. When can we take the photos?" I was excited to begin my new life and forget the past for now. I needed to be happy again—somehow.

"You seem to be in better spirits today…and rather eager." He chuckled.

"Yes, I want to start my new life as soon as possible."

"Well, let me call the photographer to see when his next available time is. I'll call you right back."

A few minutes later my cell rang. "Hello."

"Belinda, please don't hang up, I need to talk to you."

"Robert," I sighed. "I don't have time to talk right now. I'm expecting a very important call. Sorry." I disconnected his call. His voice made me tremble. I closed my eyes as a wave of excitement came over me at the thought of him. Even just the sound of his voice made me want to forget everything that had happened so I could be with him. If I talked with him now, I'd be lost forever. I needed to be strong and stand my ground. He had no right to do what he did, but hearing his voice made me realize I still loved him.

My cell rang again. I read the name this time before I answered. It was Mr. Johnson. "Hello, when does he have time for me?"

He chuckled. "Today. We need to be there about three. Wear your best jeans, a form fitting sweater, and high heels. Leave your hair down, but bring whatever you need to change the style. I'll pick you up around 2:30."

I ran downstairs for breakfast, and to talk to Mrs. Foster about what to expect at the photo shoot. "We're taking my photos today. Do you have any advice for me?"

"Just be happy. Then your smile will look natural, not forced. Do you know who the photographer is? I hear Kyer Saunders is the best."

"Mr. Johnson didn't say. Will the photographer help me with the poses? I have no idea what I'm doing. This is all new to me."

"Tell him this is your first shoot and you need help. He should work with you, if he's a good one." Mrs. Foster's tone was confident, putting me at ease.

I took a shower and washed my hair so it would be dry in time. When I returned to my room, my cell was ringing. Robert again. I wished he'd leave me alone for a while. There was no way I could talk to him now and be happy for my photo session, so I let the call go to my voice mail.

It was almost 2:30. I was ready to go and very nervous when Mr. Johnson arrived. On our way I asked, "Who's the photographer you're using?"

"Kyer Saunders. He's the best around."

"Oh good! Mrs. Foster said he'd help me."

The studio wasn't far from the boarding house. Mr. Johnson said he was going to drop me off and to call him when I was finished. He had something else he needed to do.

The studio was located in another old remodeled home in the area. When I entered the office, a young lady looked up from the front desk. "Can I help you?"

"Yes, I'm Belinda Davies. I have an appointment at three with Mr. Saunders. Mr. Johnson sent me."

"Have a seat please. I'll let him know you're here." She left the room and returned shortly. "He'll be right with you."

I thanked her and waited. Looking around the room at the framed photos of beautiful models, I wondered if I really looked like them.

"Belinda?" My thoughts were interrupted when a short gentleman with ash blonde hair entered the room. "I'm Kyer." He reached out and shook my hand. "Come with me." I followed him into his studio. "Turn around slowly. Let me look at you." My nerves were doing a number on me, but I did as he requested while he propped his chin in his hand and studied me. "I think you'll make a terrific model." I informed him that I brought what I needed to change my hair style. "Okay...I understand this is your first time to pose."

"Yes sir, I have no idea what to do. I heard you're the best and that you'll help me."

"Don't worry. We'll get some great shots."

We spent two hours taking pictures in a variety of poses. It was exhausting, but fun. Kyer was very patient and I learned a lot. When he finished, he pulled the photos up on his computer and we analyzed each one. That was very helpful. He put my ten best shots on a flash drive for Mr. Johnson to view. "I think you have some good photographs here. Tell Mr. Johnson I'll make prints for him. He can pick them up tomorrow."

When we returned to the office, Mr. Johnson put the flash drive in his laptop to view the photos. "These are terrific. For a first timer, you did great." His voice was full of enthusiasm. "There's a new jeans manufacturing company looking for a model for their ads and commercials. I don't know if they've picked someone yet, but I'm going to email these to them first thing in the morning." He had a huge smile on his face. "You look terrific in jeans."

"What's the company's name?"

"Every Body Jeans Manufacturing Company," he answered, as he studied each photo.

"Interesting name....If we're finished, I'm heading home. Hopefully, I haven't missed dinner. I'm starving. See you tomorrow."

The next morning, I checked my voice mail to see if Mr. Johnson called. No messages or missed calls, except for the one yesterday morning from Robert. I hurriedly dressed. After breakfast, I rushed out the door to Mr. Johnson's office. He was in the process of sending an email with my photos when I arrived. "Hopefully, we'll hear something soon." He crossed two fingers and grinned.

"Do you need any help around here?" I was hoping he had something to keep me busy.

"No, but I'll let you know as soon as I hear something. It probably won't be until Monday or Tuesday."

"Okay." I left, trying to figure out what to do with all my spare time. I thought I'd go for a drive and maybe visit my parents. I needed to see them and explain what was going on.

It didn't take long to drive from Bellaire to my parents' house, but I should've called—no one was home. I drove around and inadvertently found myself in very familiar surroundings. I was in the Penningtons' neighborhood. I'd only been to their house two times, so I wasn't sure where it was. Whatever possessed me to start looking for my in-laws house, I'll never know. I drove all around, finally seeing a house that looked like theirs. As I approached, I saw a blue roadster parked in the circular drive with someone sitting in it. *Oh shit*! It was Robert and he saw me. I zoomed on by. I looked in my rear view mirror and saw he was closing in on me. Speeding up, I made several turns, but he managed to stay on my tail. I put distance between us when he was stopped by a red light. With some other fancy maneuvering through adjacent neighborhoods, I lost him and headed straight for the safety of Mrs. Foster's. Having been so close to Robert, even just for a minute, made the emotional part of me wish he'd caught up. The practical, more logical side told me to stay away. I was so conflicted, but I knew logic would win because it had to if I was to pull through this.

Now in my new sanctuary, I figured he called, so I checked my voice mail. He did. "Why didn't you stop? Why did you drive by here? Please call. We need to talk. I love you."

I texted: Went 2 parents. Not home. Found myself looking for ur parents home. Not ready 2face u. No will power.

Robert: Sorry to put you thru this. Let me explain. Come back. Please.

Me: Cant. Need time 2 heal & forgive. No excuse for what I saw.
             Why r u at parents?
Robert: So sorry. Please forgive me. I dont want to lose you. Give me
             another chance. Moving back. No school w/o you.

My judgment was being tested. Now I wasn't sure if leaving was right. One thing I did know—I needed time to think without being influenced by our physical connection to each other. I looked back at my phone and turned it off as the smells from the kitchen made my mouth water. It was almost time for dinner, so I headed downstairs. Mrs. Foster was setting pot roast on the table as I slid into my chair. "It smells delicious. I'm starving."

We ate and chatted about the day. "Did you spend all day at Mr. Johnson's office?" Mrs. Foster seemed truly interested as she cut her meat.

"No, he didn't need me. So, I went for a drive and found myself driving by my in-laws house. Just my luck, my husband was there and saw me. He tried to follow me, but I lost him."

"Why did you go there?" Mrs. Foster had a puzzled look on her face as she took a bite of meat.

"I don't know. I was going to visit my parents, but they weren't home. Before I knew it, I was driving through their neighborhood." I was shaking my head. "My mother and father-in-law are very nice people. I feel close to them. Maybe I was looking for some help figuring all this out."

"Do you think, maybe, subconsciously you were hoping to see him?"

"You think so? But I didn't know he was in Sugar Land. Maybe so. I feel like a part of me is missing." Looking down, I played with my food.

"If you feel this bad, you should go see him or at least call him. Try to work out your problems."

"I can't. If I do, I'll just forgive him and nothing would've changed. Then, I'll feel worse if he continues his behavior. He needs to realize I'm not going to put up with his kissing other girls and who-knows-what else. Can a player…I guess you'd use the term playboy, change his ways?" I was almost in tears.

She placed her hand over mine and looked me in the eyes. "If he truly loves you, he can do anything." Her hand was the first human contact I'd had since I left school and it felt good. I was glad I decided to take refuge with Mrs. Foster.

Sunday was a do-nothing day. I slept late and just relaxed around the house. After a while, boredom allowed my mind to start thinking about Robert. So, to keep myself busy, I volunteered to help Mrs. Foster clean the house. About halfway through, I decided I should try to contact my parents and let them know what was going on. I didn't want to talk to my father. It would be hard for me to admit defeat to him. Besides, I'd have to break the news about me leaving school and was confident that would send him over the edge. Hopefully, Mom would answer. I knew I could get more sympathy from her. "I'll be back shortly. I'm going upstairs to make a call."

"Are you calling your husband?"

"No, I need to let my parents know what's going on. This will be almost as hard as talking to him right now." I was very conflicted about this. I ran upstairs and retrieved my cell from my purse. After taking a deep breath, I called my parents' house.

"Hello." Thank goodness it was Mom.

"Hi, Mom. How are you and Dad doing?"

"We're fine. How are you and Robert?"

"Ah…well, that's what I'm calling about.…We've separated." I waited for her reaction to this startling development. There was only stunned silence on the other end.

"*What?* You two were so much in love. What happened?"

"We've just had a few disagreements, so I moved out." I didn't want to give her all the details and have them hate Robert.

"Moved out? Where are you?" Mom sounded concerned and upset.

"I left school. I'm living in Houston at a boarding house with a nice elderly lady. She's like a grandmother to me. So Mom, I'll be fine."

"Come home until you go back to school."

"I can't. He'll find me there. I'm not going back to school, at least not now. Maybe next year."

"He doesn't know where you are?"

"No, he doesn't, and I don't want him to. That's why I'm not telling you where I'm living. Then you won't have to lie for me if he calls. I have enough money to live on for now and I'm waiting to hear about a job."

"Doing what?" Her voice sounded surprised.

"I'll tell you later if I get it. It should pay very well."

There was a short pause. "Is it serious enough that you'll be getting a divorce?"

"I don't know what's going to happen. I just need some time away from him so I can think. I still love him." With tears threatening to fill my eyes, my voice became a little shaky. "Don't worry about me. I'm going to be alright. I'll try to visit as soon as I can. I don't want to risk running into him right now."

"Well, keep in touch. If you need anything, just call us. You know we'll help anyway we can."

"Love you, Mom. Will you tell Dad about this for me? I don't think I can face him." I hated the thought of letting him down.

"Don't worry about him. You just get your life straightened out. Sweetie, I'm here for you."

"I know. You always are. Love you. Bye." That went better than expected. I was so lucky I had my parents and a good friend like Abbey. With their support I'd be fine someday, but would I ever really be happy without Robert?

Relieved that the call was taken care of, I ran back downstairs to continue helping Mrs. Foster. "Well, how did it go?"

"Fine, but my mom is more understanding and easier to talk to than my dad. I just gave her the basics, not all the details." I looked around. "Is there anything else I can do?"

"No, unless you want to help me with dinner."

Afterwards, we spent the rest of the evening watching a movie and eating popcorn, a girls' night in. It made me think of Abbey.

***

The repeated sound of a melody filled my ears, awakening me. My phone was ringing. "Hello, Mr. Johnson. Any word yet?"

"No, not yet, but I could use your help today. Can you come to the office?"

"Sure, in about an hour, okay?"

"That's fine."

I arrived at his office as agreed. "What do you need me to do?" I was bored stiff and willing to help, since he was helping me.

"Joan has to leave at one. I'd appreciate you filling in for her. She'll show you what to do," Mr. J explained, as we stood by his receptionist's desk.

Joan went through the steps. It seemed easy. All I had to do was answer the phone and take messages. Piece of cake.

There were enough calls coming in to keep me busy and my mind occupied. Before I knew it, it was almost five, time to leave, when I took the last call for the day. "Johnson's Modeling Agency."

"Mr. Johnson, please. This is Jayne Carter with Every Body Jeans Manufacturing Company."

My heart sputtered. "One moment please." Eagerly, I placed the call on hold then sprinted into his office. "It's them. Ms. Carter wants to talk to you."

Mr. J looked happy and anxious to take the call. He gave me a knowing wink that seemed to say "you're in," and invited me to eavesdrop on his side of the call. I heard, "It's narrowed down to one, but not announced yet. Okay....You liked her photos. Great...thanks for giving her a chance....Okay,

Wednesday at three. See you then." He had a big grin on his face and held up his thumb. He jumped up and gave me a hug. "We've got our foot in their door. They want to meet you this Wednesday in Atlanta."

"Really? The day after tomorrow?" I couldn't believe how quickly everything was moving along. I had just left school last Wednesday, and this Wednesday I was going for my first modeling job interview. All of a sudden, I was shaking all over.

Mr. J saw the panic in my eyes. "Are you alright?"

"I don't know what to do!"

"Don't worry. I'll be with you. You need to have self-confidence and act like you know what you're doing. They'll ask some questions and probably have you do some poses. Do the ones Kyer recommended and remember—it's all about the jeans. They'll also want you to demonstrate your runway walk."

"Runway? You mean I might have to walk down runways?" I had assumed this job would only involve photography. How naïve of me. Bile rose in my throat as a panicky feeling took over.

"You can do this. I have confidence in you. Now, let's see your walk."

"Okay, I have two." Remembering my modeling class fiasco, I dug deep to concentrate. I showed him my straight walk—one foot crossed over in front of my other foot, and my sassy sashay—same walk, but more hip emphasis.

"They both look good, but I like your sassy strut best. It draws attention to the jeans. Show them both." He winked. "Okay, go home and tell Mrs. Foster. Ask her for some pointers. She's been through this many times. Stay home tomorrow and sleep and relax because Wednesday will be hectic. I want you looking your best, and *No Worrying.* Now go, I have airline reservations to make. I'll call you tomorrow."

I took off my high heels and ran to the boarding house. I was so excited and couldn't wait to tell Mrs. Foster. She was setting food on the table as I came flying through the door. "Guess what! I'm going on my first interview Wednesday with a new jeans manufacturing company in Atlanta. I'm so nervous!"

"Don't worry. There's nothing to be concerned about. Just take some deep breaths before you walk in very self-confident. Jeans look great on you. So strut in like you're trying to sell the jeans to them and you'll do fine. I hope you don't have to move there if you get the job. I'd miss your company." Mrs. Foster appeared sad and sounded glum.

"I don't want to move there. I want to stay here. Surely they won't need me every day. I could fly there when they do." I hesitated and thought about what I just said then added, "I hope." Like so many other things in my life, I didn't have time to worry about a detail like that right now. What I needed was sleep. So, after dinner, with the last dish washed and the kitchen tidied up, I headed for the stairs. "I'm going to go relax and turn in early. I hope I can sleep."

"I'll bring you some chamomile tea a little later. That should help."

When I reached my room, I turned my cell on to check my messages. There was one voice mail from Abbey asking me to call. One text from Robert: Do u live in Sugar Land?

I texted: No.

I called Abbey. I had to tell her what was going on.

"Belinda, I'm so glad you called back. I have some good news. Robert is moving to Sugar Land. So now you can come back. We can be roommates again. I miss you." She was elated.

"Abbey, I don't think Garrett would like me taking his place. Thanks for thinking of me....Wednesday, I'm flying out of state to my first job interview."

"Out of state! Doing what?" Abbey suddenly sounded sad.

"You have to promise not to tell anyone, not even Garrett. If I get the job, everyone will find out soon enough."

"I promise, not a word."

"A modeling job with a new jeans manufacturing company. They liked my photos and want to meet me."

"How did this happen?"

"The weekend I was engaged, we were eating at a Mexican restaurant in Sugar Land when a man gave me his business card. He said if I wanted to make some money posing for advertisements to give him a call. So I did. He had some photos taken of me and emailed them to this company. They liked my pictures. I'm so excited, but nervous, too. I've never modeled before. My agent is helping me."

"Your agent! You already have an agent?"

"Yeah, the man who gave me his card runs a modeling agency. Now remember, not a word. And I know Robert is moving home. I saw him."

"You saw him? Did you talk to him?"

"No." I told her what happened.

"What are you going to do?"

"I don't know. He needs to see what it feels like to be left hanging and not know what I'm doing. And that car scene with Erin. That was no misunderstanding. One big difference though—I miss him now—he didn't miss me then—he was preoccupied with his new friend. Anyway, I won't have time for him right now if I land the job."

"Garrett's been talking to him. He says Robert is really hurt and worried that he's lost you.   Something about a gut feeling he's had that you know about."

"Yeah, he told me he had a feeling he was going to lose me.   Well, his actions made that happen.   Now he wants to explain, but I told him in the letter there's no reason that can justify what I saw.   I don't ever want to feel that pain again.   I gave him my heart, and he just stomped it into the ground.   I've got to stop talking about him or I'm going to start crying.   I can't cry.   I have to look my very best on Wednesday."

"You're still in love with him aren't you?"

Her question made me pause as my emotions took control.   "Yes."   I could feel a wave of despair creeping over me when I snapped at Abbey.   "Let's change the subject or I'm going to hang up.   How are you and Garrett doing?"

"Do you really want to know?   It's not going to upset you?"

"Yeah, I really want to know."   I wanted to talk about anything that didn't involve Robert.

"It's great.   He's so nice and loving.   He'd do anything for me."   She paused.   "You know he still cares and worries about you."

"As a friend.   He's great and I know he'll never hurt you.   Well, I need to let you go.   I hear my landlady coming.   She's bringing me some chamomile tea to help me sleep.   I'll keep you informed.   Miss you."

"Miss you, too," Abbey said as Mrs. Foster set the tea on the nightstand.   I nodded.   She smiled and left.

My cell indicated that I had a new text.

Robert:	Do u live n Houston?
Me:	Yes
Robert:	Where? Need 2 see you.
Me:	NO
Robert:	Please, Im begging you.
Me:	No, going out of state.
Robert:	Why?
Me:	Job interview.
Robert:	What?
Me:	Not telling.
Robert:	Move out of state?
Me:	Hope not.
Robert:	Please don't.
Me:	Got 2 go. Good nite.
Robert:	Truly do love U miss U.

I couldn't continue. It was making me emotional, so I turned my cell off. I sipped the tea and slowly began to relax until I couldn't keep my eyes open. Falling fast asleep, my thoughts of Robert drifted away.

Mr. Johnson called in the morning to tell me our flight would leave at 9:30 a.m. and he'd pick me up at seven. He instructed me to pack for several days and be prepared for any scenario. As the call ended, a nervous twinge settled in my stomach. Crap, I had so much to do.

Later in the day, I scanned the room trying to decide what to do first. Denim jeans were a staple, so I pulled out two pair from the bottom drawer, one stone-washed and one indigo. Tackling the closet, I frantically flipped the hangers shuffling through my knit tees and blouses pulling out the ones that best complemented my complexion and shape. I again glanced around the room and my eyes paused on the top dresser draw, *underwear!* I dug out my best panties and bras and tossed them on the bed. Doubting my selections, I paced around. The slight queasy feeling that lingered in the pit of my stomach began to erupt into a gut-wrenching panic. This interview was a chance of a life time and I knew I needed to be perfect, but I wasn't sure I could pull it off.

Before going to bed, I packed enough clothes for a week, including my bathing suit and formal. My suitcase was crammed full.

Mrs. Foster continued her nightly ritual of providing warm chamomile tea to relax me. Her simple remedy worked like a charm. I slept well.

CHAPTER 28

***

SEVEN A.M. CAME too quickly. As I was leaving the house, Mrs. Foster placed a small spray bottle of liquid in my hand. "Honey, take this with you. It's a mixture I used while I traveled. Planes can dry your skin. Just a quick spritz now and then will do wonders to keep you looking fresh." I gladly took her gift and promised to use it. Her little tricks worked and I had come to trust her.

I was so nervous, the flight seemed like it took less than an hour. After we checked into our hotel suites, there were only a few minutes for me to unpack before meeting Mr. J at the elevator. We were having lunch in the hotel restaurant, then I'd come back to my room to prepare for my interview. I was excited about this opportunity and at the same time looking forward to this ordeal being over.

There was a knock at my door. "Are you ready for lunch?"

"Be right there."

***

A very handsome young man was in the elevator when we walked in. I saw him give me a quick once-over as the doors opened. He was standing there with his hands crossed in front of him. His chest seemed to puff more after his brief glance, as if he was attempting to look more attractive than he already was. When he expanded his chest, he looked as if he was standing at attention. I flashed a smile at him in acknowledgement. Again, there was the once-over as I turned to face forward. His reflection in the elevator doors gave him away as he paid more attention to my backside before he positioned himself closer to me, smiling. "Ay," he uttered, full of confidence.

I continued to watch his reflection and returned the greeting. "Hey."

We exited on the main floor and headed for the restaurant. The man from the elevator followed behind, but was met by the hostess and seated first. He said something to her as he glanced in our direction. My curiosity was piqued, but my questions were answered when the hostess led us to our table. I was about to sit down when a waiter pulled a chair out for me in the direct line of sight of MR. ELEVATOR.

Every time I looked up, MR. ELEVATOR smiled at me. Then he winked. Oh my God! He was flirting. I felt flushed and sure my face was turning red. To hide, I gave my head the customary jerk to flip my hair in front of the side of my face. This enabled me to peer through and watch in a less obvious manner.

"What's wrong? You're turning red." Mr. J appeared bewildered.

"MR. ELEVATOR just winked. He's flirting." Now my hand was up at my forehead with my elbow resting on the table, shielding my face as much as possible.

"Well, if I was his age and single, I'd be flirting with you, too. You're the prettiest woman in here." He had a big grin on his face that made me smile.

When we finished eating, Mr. J went to the bar for a drink and I headed for my room. The elevator arrived and I walked in. As the doors were closing, a hand stopped them. It was MR. ELEVATOR. He entered with a swagger, and then resumed his military-like pose.

"You here for business or pleasure?" He gave me the once-over again.

"Business—job interview. And you?" It seemed as if I was being stalked, but I felt free to scrutinize him as well, starting at his feet and ending with his head. He seemed to enjoy the returned attention and gave me a wide grin when my inspection reached his face.

"Both—meeting some people for business and pleasure." He looked at my hand. "I see you're wearing a wedding band. Was that man you were with your husband?"

"No, he's my agent," I said very insistently.

He pointed to my left hand. "But, you're married?"

"Aren't you getting a little personal for a stranger? Why do you want to know?" My curiosity was piqued.

The elevator stopped on my floor and he held the door open. "Oh...ah. Sorry. I'm Jonathan Morse. I wanted to ask you out for a drink this evening, if you were available."

"Ummm...I'm Belinda Pe...ah, Davies. I'm married, but separated, if you must know."

"Sooo...would you join me this evening?" A huge grin of perfect, pearly white teeth appeared as the pressure of Jonathan's hand prevented the repeated attempts of the elevator doors to close.

"I guess so, but only here in the hotel." Why not? Robert was seeing Erin.

"That's fine." With brows drawn together, he gave me yet another once-over. "He's your *agent*? Let me guess—model or actress? Probably model."

"Aspiring model. This is my first job interview."

"Well, good luck! Then, I'll see you at seven. What's your room number?"

"I'll meet you in the bar. Bye." Walking toward my room, I glanced back and noticed he was watching.

"I'm just making sure you get to your room alright. I'm a gentleman." He was smiling ear to ear, still fighting the elevator doors, now with his back against it and the buzzer blaring.

Looking him squarely in the face and with an air of authority, I questioned him. "How do you know this is my room?" I waved him on to let the elevator doors close. His expression was priceless as his image disappeared behind them.

Once I was sure Mr. Morse had left, I opened my door. Great! I wouldn't be alone this evening. Now my focus shifted as I hurried to prepare for my interview. Needing Mr. J's opinion, I walked toward his room. He was exiting the elevator. "Mr. Johnson." He stopped and turned. "Do I look alright?" I pivoted around.

His face lit up. "Perfect. They'd be crazy not to pick you. I'll meet you here in fifteen minutes."

I went back to my room. Being so nervous, all I did was pace back and forth until my cell rang. I forgot I changed Robert's ringtone and answered without checking the display. "Belinda, don't hang up." My heart skipped a beat and the pain of my decision to leave emerged with the sound of his voice. "I just wanted to tell you good luck with your interview."

I hesitated. I was already nervous and didn't need to become more upset talking to him.

"Hello? Belinda, are you there?"

His voice snapped me out of my thoughts. "Yeah, I'm here. Thanks. I'm so nervous, I feel like I'm going to faint. I have to go. Call me later. Bye."

As I pulled the phone from my ear I could hear his voice. "Angel, no! Wait! Don't hang up!" I took a moment then realized I'd only start crying. My heart was broken with and without him. It was a no-win situation. My finger hovered over the end call button. I could still hear his voice pleading for me to talk with him, then I hit the button and closed my eyes, fighting back the tears.

I was heading out my door when my cell rang again. Instinctively, I answered it. "Angel, it's me again. Just checking to make sure you're not passed out on the floor."

I chuckled at his statement, but it still wasn't a good idea to talk to him right now. "Thanks for checking. I'm fine, but I still can't talk, really." My next response came as a surprise to me. Impulsively, I blurted out, "I'll call after the interview. Love you." When I heard the words my heart stopped. There was no response from the other end. "I Gotta go."

Mr. J was waiting for me at the elevator. "You ready to get this over with?"

"Definitely." My mind was still on the phone call with Robert. I was encouraging him with my response, giving him hope and myself as well. But was it false hope?

Mr. J and I walked to the building next door. He told the receptionist we have an appointment with Ms. Carter. She buzzed in and announced our arrival, then sent us up to the ninth floor. There, a lady asked us to be seated. "Ms. Carter will see you in a few minutes."

I was keyed up and couldn't sit still. I was wringing my hands, looking around the waiting room, when I felt the gentle touch of a hand over mine. It was unexpected and so comforting, my fidgeting stopped. I looked over at Mr. J. He was looking at me with a slight warm smile and a subtle glint in his eyes. I hadn't realized how much I missed the ability to touch another person almost at will. Since I left school, Mr. J's touch was the second human contact I'd had. Beginning to physically relax, I felt my tension magically dissipate. Mr. J must have felt my muscles relaxing. "You'll do fine. I want you to continue to relax. I'm here for you. Now take a few deep breaths. Okay, straighten your back, look straight forward, and when we go in, walk with all the confidence you can muster." I followed his instructions and he never removed his hand from mine the whole time we were in the waiting room. His simple gesture helped me stay relaxed. Finally, Ms. Carter's secretary asked us to come in. I strutted in with self-confidence—head held high.

There was a handsome middle-aged man in the office. He was seated in a wingback chair near the window. As we walked in, Ms. Carter rose from behind her desk to greet us. She was a very well-dressed executive type, wearing a tailored crisp, white blouse and a black pencil skirt. Her dark hair was meticulously styled in a short bob with bangs. She was definitely a power dresser. "Thank you for coming. This is Steven Burton, the owner and founder of Every Body Jeans Manufacturing Company, and I'm Jayne Carter, head of advertising.

"Thank you for inviting us. This is Belinda Davies, and I'm her agent, Frank Johnson."

Ms. Carter motioned for Mr. Johnson to sit in the other wingback before she turned her attention to me. She circled, checking me out. "First, we need to see you in our jeans. What size do you wear? A six, I'm guessing?"

"Yes ma'am." This lady made me feel uneasy with the way she was looking me over.

She pulled a pair out of a pile of jeans on her credenza and handed them to me. Pointing to a door, she told me to go change.

They were stretch jeans and felt great on. After a few practice poses that accentuated my ass, I felt confident that the jeans and I were a good match. I strutted back into the room.

"Turn around so we can see how they fit." Ms. Carter was studying me.

I pivoted slowly. She walked over and pulled my sweater up to see the waist. "She wears them well—perfect. How do they feel?" Ms. Carter tugged at the jeans.

The way I was being groped by this strange woman came as a surprise to me, but everyone else acted as if this was a normal procedure, so I played along. "They're very comfortable. They fit well, not too tight, and just right through the crotch. They're long enough and best of all—they're not *butt crack jeans*." Everyone smiled and chuckled. "I think you have a winner. I'd buy a pair. I live in jeans—that's all I wear."

"Let's see your walk. Walk away from us and back." Ms. Carter motioned waving her hand.

"I have two—straight and sassy. This is my straight strut." I demonstrated it. "This is my sassy sashay." Again I showed them.

Ms. Carter and Mr. Burton raised their eyebrows at each other. Ms. Carter had an approving look on her face. She walked over to Mr. Burton's chair and stood next to it facing me. "What do you think, Steven?"

Mr. Burton leaned forward with his head cocked. "Do the sassy again."

This time I emphasized the strut and hip action.

Mr. Burton was nodding. "I really like your sassy walk. It draws attention to the jeans. That's what we want the public to see."

"Can I make a suggestion?" I walked over to Mr. Burton and turned, striking a pose that pushed my right hip up and out. Peering over my shoulder, I pointed to the right hip pocket. "Stitch 'Sassy' across the top of the right pocket on some of the jeans in the style I'd be wearing. Then some girls can be sassy gals too, and do the sassy sashay, if they want to. Ahhh, I mean the style the model you pick would be wearing." I flushed at my faux pas and glanced at the floor.

The three of them were looking at each other smiling when I looked up. Ms. Carter and Mr. Johnson were watching Mr. Burton. His brow creased. "I like it, but why the right pocket?"

Breaking the pose, I turned to face him. "Um, right pocket—right jeans. I'm not sure—right sounds 'right.'"

Mr. Burton grinned and gave me a big nod of approval. "Okay, I like the idea. Have you ever thought about going into advertising, young lady? Jayne, (he addressed Ms. Carter by her first name) you should think about hiring her."

She smirked and changed the subject. "Would you be willing to cut your hair? It's a distraction."

"No, I can make it shorter looking." I flipped my head over and finger combed my hair all up on top of my head and secured it with a small scrunchy from my wrist. I arranged it into a shoulder-length pageboy style, then into a ponytail. "Or I can French braid…"

Mr. Burton interrupted. "You can do a lot with long hair. I don't think it would cause a problem. In fact, I like it."

Ms. Carter crossed her arms over her chest. "Have you modeled before?"

I hesitated and looked at Mr. Johnson. When he nodded, I took it as a sign to tell the truth. "No, but my photographer said I'm a quick learner."

"Do some poses for us." I did several that Mr. Saunders recommended and a few I had practiced on my own.

Mr. Burton turned toward Ms. Carter. "I like her. I think she'll sell a lot of jeans for us."

"I agree."

I sassy sashayed toward them, stopped and posed with one hand on my hip. "Be a Sassy Gal." I spun around and sashayed away.

"I think we just saw our first commercial. I liked that. Belinda, you have the job, if you want it." Mr. Burton's confirmation was music to my ears.

"Thank you, sir!" I was so excited to be employed. Walking over to shake Mr. Burton's hand, I remembered what city I was in. I stopped and turned to Ms. Carter. "Excuse me. I want the job, but I have two things I need to talk to you about first. Do I have to live in Atlanta? Can I stay in Houston and fly here when you need me? I like where I'm living."

Mr. Burton answered. "We won't need you every day, so I don't see that being a problem. Mr. Johnson, have the details delivered to my legal department so we can prepare a contract as soon as possible. I want this project started right away."

I interrupted the men's interchange when I spoke to Ms. Carter. "Also, I don't want there to be any secrets. I need to tell you that I'm married, but separated. I'm using my maiden name. That way if I get a divorce I won't have to change my professional name. I can hide my wedding band, if you don't want it showing."

Mr. Burton chimed in again. "Being married isn't a problem. Our jeans are for everybody—young and old, single and married. But thank you for your honesty. I find it refreshing."

"Okay. Yes, I want the job. Thank you very much. I'll do my very best."

"Then, welcome to our family." He walked over to shake my hand.

I took hold of it with confidence. "When can I start?"

Ms. Carter answered as she walked behind her desk. "You seem eager, but not until after we have a signed contract. Now you're part of the fashion world and nothing is done until it's in writing. Mr. Johnson will take care of that. We need to start preparing ads and commercials, and prepping you for the fashion show. My department can start working on those layouts. As soon as all the legal paperwork is in place, we'll be good to go."

"I'm very excited. I can't wait to start, but what's this about a fashion show?" The words almost stuck in my dry throat. "Monster" stirred as panic was settling in.

"We're doing a fashion show in New York City with Mr. Burton's designer friend, Jessica Loren Deats – Fashion Designs by JLDeats. It will be good exposure for the jeans. We have two and a half weeks to prepare you for the runway. Can you stay here 'til after the show?"

"Yes, but I didn't bring enough clothes to stay that long."

"Don't worry about that. I'll give you a company credit card so you can buy what you need. I'll also give you some more of our jeans. It'll be good advertising—you walking around in the stores with them on."

"That'll work."

"Well then, be in my office about nine tomorrow morning." Ms. Carter made herself comfortable in her large, leather desk chair. "Mr. Johnson, I'll have the papers for the salary advance ready in the morning, so get me a signed contract as soon as possible."

"I'll start on that right away. It was nice meeting both of you." Mr. Johnson and Ms. Carter shook hands. Facing Mr. Burton, he repeated the gesture. "I'm looking forward to doing business with you."

"No…thank *you*, Mr. Johnson. I think we have a winner here." Mr. Burton looked at me, nodding his head in my direction.

Mr. Johnson acknowledged his gesture, then turned and walked toward me by the door of the office. I leaned closer to him. "Do you need me anymore? Remember the MR. ELEVATOR. His name is Jonathan Morse and he invited me for drinks tonight.

Ms. Carter looked up from behind her desk, surprised. "I'm sorry, did you say you're meeting Jonathan Morse?"

"Yes, why? Is that going to be a problem?"

Her face changed to a puzzled look. "Don't you know who he is?"

"What do you mean? Is he someone special?"

Ms. Carter smiled, shaking her head. "So...you don't know? Well, I'll let him tell you. Have fun, but be careful."

"Tell me. Be careful of *what*?" Now my curiosity was heightened. What was I getting myself into?

"No, you'll find out soon enough." She smiled, raising an eyebrow. "Go have fun."

I returned to my hotel with the feeling I was in for a big, big surprise.

Jeez, this hotel elevator is slow. Is it ever going to get here? When the doors finally opened, there stood Jonathan. "Oh! Hey." I was shocked to see him.

"Well, how did your interview go?" He flashed his pearly whites at me as he stepped out to finish our conversation.

"I got it. I can't believe it. I'm on my way to my room to call my best friend."

"Congratulations! I had a feeling you'd get it. I think you look terrific in jeans." He raised an eyebrow, then stretched his neck to give my backside the once-over. "Do you want to start celebrating early? Join me for dinner?" Jonathan extended his hand to me.

"Sure, I'd like that. I'll call Abbey later." I paused for a moment surveying his hand and then took hold of it.

Curious about what Ms. Carter said, I started our conversation after being seated at our table. "What line of work are you in?"

He leaned forward crossing his arms on the table. He looked befuddled, almost hurt, as his eyes studied me. "You've never seen or heard of me before?"

"No, should I?" He didn't look familiar. I was being honest. He looked at me like I'd been living in a cave all my life.

He cocked his head. "Do you watch movies?"

"Not much, I've spent my last three years in college going to class and studying every day. I didn't have much free time." I was confused by his question. What difference did it make if I watched movies?

"O...kay." He pursed his lips before continuing. "I'm an actor. We're getting ready to start filming a movie here next week. I have the lead part."

"Ohhh. You're a movie star? Sorry, I didn't know." Leaning forward, I rested my crossed arms on the table.

"That's alright. In fact, it's kind of nice meeting someone who doesn't know. Less baggage. Why did you pick modeling?" He leaned in closer, giving me the impression he was interested in what I had to say.

I sat back in my chair and explained. "Mr. Johnson, my agent, saw me at a restaurant and gave me his business card. I ran across it in my wallet on my way to Houston the day I left my husband. I needed a job, so I went to see him. This all happened last Wednesday and Thursday." I shook my head in disbelief. "Everything is happening so fast."

He looked shocked. "Seven days. That's quick to land a major modeling job. Your agent must be good."

Leaning forward, I murmured, "Where are you from? You have a slight accent."

"Canada. I take it you're from Texas. I like that cute drawl."

"You're good, I am. My parents moved from Houston to Sugar Land when I started high school. How did you become an actor?"

"I took drama in high school and joined the drama club. I was in a few school plays. Then I landed parts in some plays in a local theater. The owner told me I should try my luck in L.A. So, I moved there, found an agent and here I am, in demand. Can I ask you a personal question?" He looked determined to find something out.

"I guess, but I won't guarantee I'll answer it."

"What happened? Why did you leave him?"

His question took me aback because it was so personal, yet I needed to talk to somebody who had nothing to do with the whole mess. Abbey was great, but she was biased. Jonathan had no vested interest in the outcome of my drama at this point, so I took a chance. "I really don't know what happened. We met in April and were married after his graduation in May. Up until the Fourth of July weekend, everything was wonderful. Then about a week later, he just kinda' left me." Jonathan's face told me he didn't understand my last statement, so I gave him a bit more information. "He was busy with school and almost stopped coming home, except to sleep. Then on the day of finals, I saw him making out with a girl in his car." I had to look away to fight back the tears and gain some composure. "After watching them, I ran home, packed, and left. The rest is history."

He frowned, shaking his head. "He's crazy."

"No, he's a campus player who can't give up his old ways." My tone was depressed as I replied in a soft voice.

"Are you going to divorce him?" We exchanged a brief glance.

I took a sip of my wine. "I don't know. I still love him and miss him very much. He's called and texted. He keeps apologizing and says he wants to explain what happened. But one look at his face, one touch, one kiss, and I'd forgive him for anything and he'd just keep doing it." I stared at my wine glass as I fingered the rim then looked back at Jonathan. "He says he doesn't want to lose me and misses me....I just can't face him yet. He needs to realize that I'm not going to put up with his escapades anymore. He'll just have to live without my reactions for a while."

Jonathan zoned in on two of my terms. "What do you mean 'one touch' and 'reactions'?" He wore a quizzical expression.

I stared at him. Another personal question I decided to answer. "We have this physical connection. When he touches me, it's beyond exciting and when he kisses me, it's explosive. This feeling that runs up my spine makes me go nuts, quivering....There are no words to describe how wonderful it is when we're together." I couldn't believe I was telling all this to a stranger.

He frowned, shaking his head in disbelief. "He's crazy, no *stupid,* to have it all and throw it away."

"I don't see a ring. Sooo, why aren't you married? You seem like you'd be a good catch for some lucky lady."

"I just haven't met the right one...until now...and she would be married." He smiled and winked.

I let out a loud breath. "I don't know what I want to do with my big mess of a life. I have too much baggage."

"We can at least be friends, can't we? At least until you figure out your mess." He reached over and placed his hand on mine.

I looked at his hand, but made no attempt to move it. If this were Robert, I'd have experienced a very different sensation, but he was Jonathan and offering something I needed—friendship. "I could use a friend right now."

A grin came across his face. "I'm invited to a party tomorrow evening. It's in this hotel by the pool. Would you like to go?" Needing something to keep my mind off of Robert and figuring a party would be a nice diversion, I accepted.

"I need to turn in early. I have to be at work by nine. Thank you very much for dinner and listening to me. Talking about it helped. You're a good shrink." I winked at him.

He charged our meals to his room, then walked me to the elevator. We were in the elevator when he started up the conversation. "Thank you. I really enjoyed your company. Now, will you give me your room number?"

"603."

We stepped off the elevator and he escorted me to my room. Stopping at my door, I turned to face him. He pointed to the lock. "Now swipe it so I know this is your room." I clutched the card in my hand and shook my head. Then he did something that was totally unexpected. He took me in his arms and kissed me. Great kiss, so I went along with it and enjoyed it, letting it last as long as he wanted. I justified my action because now I could do what Robert did, but Jonathan's kiss was nowhere in the same league as Robert's.

He frowned. "No quiver?"

"Sorry, but I really enjoyed it." I ran my hands up the back of his neck and into his soft brown hair, and pulled him to me. I kissed him. His response was more vigorous than I expected. I ended it because I couldn't go beyond that. Without saying anything, I reached behind me, swiped my card and opened the door with an audible click. I slipped out of his arms and waved goodbye.

As I started to close the door, he put his hand up to stop it. "He is *definitely* crazy." He took me in with his hazel eyes and nodded as he left.

CHAPTER 29

WITH CONTRACTS SIGNED, the next day brought a new experience. They were photographing me with Sam, a male model. He was nice looking, but Jonathan and Robert were a lot more handsome, in my opinion. They took several photos of us in different poses. It was fun. Ms. Carter informed me that tomorrow I'd be practicing on a runway.

The day was flying by faster than I'd realized. During my afternoon break, I remembered that I hadn't called Abbey and Robert back. Before leaving the studio, I told the aide I'd be in my dressing room. To my surprise, I was assigned a plushy furnished room to apply my makeup, change clothes, or go to when I felt the need for privacy. It was my own little oasis away from the hustle of the studio.

I tried to contact Abbey, but she didn't answer, so I left a message that I got the job and I'd call back later. My cell indicated a voice mail. It was from Robert. I listened to it. "Did you get the job? Call me, Angel."

Hearing him call me Angel made my heart feel heavy. I contemplated my next move. Should I return the call or should I ignore it? I did say I'd call him last night and I hadn't. I was busy having dinner with another man. As I paced back and forth, I nervously studied my cell phone then hit the number two.

"Angel." His voice was soothing and made my spine react.

"Hey. I'm sorry I didn't call last night. I had a dinner to go to." I was being half-honest and figured if he ever found out, I could say I told him.

"Well…did you get the job?"

"I signed the final contract this morning. Today was my first day."

There was silence. Neither one of us said anything until he broke the void. "What kind of job, if you don't mind me asking?" He was being extremely polite and not pushing for answers.

"Something you told me I could do very easily."

"Well, are you going to tell me?" I heard a somber tone in his voice.

"I'm modeling. I signed a contract with a jeans company." I waited for his response, letting him lead the conversation, then answered his question offering as little information as possible.

There was a long, awkward pause. "Will you be moving out of state?" Robert's voice was hushed with a distinct quaver.

"No, but I'll have to travel." More silence.

"When can I see you?"

"You'll see me in commercials and ads in a few weeks."

He took a deep breath. "You know that's not what I mean."

"I have a very busy schedule for the next few weeks and I'll be gone a lot."

"I could fly to meet you anywhere."

Hesitating, I thought about his proposal. I'd love to be in his arms again, to feel the warmth of his body next to me, to make love to him, but I had to be strong. If I gave in, I was afraid I wouldn't learn how to set limits with him. He knew what it would take to make me give in. Keeping a distance between us prevented him from physically touching me so I could maintain some semblance of control. I needed this time to learn who I was and to heal my heart. I finally answered. "No, that wouldn't be a good idea. I still need time."

The next question caught me off guard. "Do you still love me?"

Without hesitation my answer flowed out. "Yes."

"So, I still have a chance?" There was a tone of uncertainty.

"I have to go now." By this time I was fighting back the tears. I didn't want to cry, but it was so hard not to.

"Belinda?"

"What?"

"You know you're breaking my heart."

My breath stopped as a pain so strong hit me just below my breast bone. "You *did* break mine." I ended the call and dropped my cell to the floor. Collapsing into a chair, I cradled my head as I wept.

There was a knock on my dressing room door. "I'll be right out. I just need a few more minutes." I went to the dressing table and looked at my reflection. I was so torn. Closing my eyes, I cleared my mind, pushing Robert back as far as I could. I had a job to do. I returned to the mirror, dried my eyes and went to work repairing the damage to my makeup. With one last glance, I was ready to go back to work.

We finished early, so I headed back to the hotel to take a nap. I was on the verge of falling asleep when my cell rang. "Hey Abbey," I yawned.

"Congratulations, I'll bet you're thrilled. I wish I were there so we could celebrate." Her tone was high pitched and full of excitement.

"Me, too, but I did celebrate last night and you'll never guess who with."

"Who? Robert?" She trailed the last part of his name in a higher pitch.

"No silly—Jonathan Morse."

Abbey went silent, which was unusual. Her tone changed. It was more cautious. "*The* Jonathan Morse—the movie star?"

"So you know who he is?" I was surprised, because like me, she hadn't been to very many movies in the past few years. "I didn't."

"Of course I do! How did you meet him?"

From Abbey's response to Jonathan's name, she sounded impressed. "He's staying in this hotel." I gave her the rundown on how we met and the dinner that followed. "He's a really nice guy and good looking. He invited me to a party tonight." I waited for her next comment.

"You're so lucky. He's really popular. The tabloids call him a player."

"Oh great, that's just what I need, another player. Is there a sign on my back saying, 'Wanted! All Players'? Why are they attracted to me?"

"Look in the mirror. You could have any man you wanted, if you were that sort of girl. You don't use your looks like other pretty girls because you don't see yourself that way. But Belinda, you could if you chose to." I was speechless. Abbey was right. I could use my looks to get what I wanted, but that's not who I was nor did I want to be. "Where's the party going to be?"

"The hotel swimming pool. I have to let you go now. I need to take a nap. I worked most of the day. I'm a little tired."

"Oh! You started working today?"

"Yeah, they want commercials and ads out to the public as soon as possible. It was fun, but tiring. Oh! I found out that I'm going to be in a fashion show in New York in two and a half weeks. I'm nervous about that. My luck I'll probably fall and embarrass myself. Well, I gotta go." I was about ready to say goodbye when Robert entered my mind. "Abbey, you have to promise me you won't say anything to Robert about my dinner last night. I don't want him taking anything the wrong way."

"Okay, I'll keep my mouth shut."

"You swear, Abbey?"

"I swear."

"Thanks, I have to go. I'll call you later." Resuming my nap, I wrapped myself around a pillow and imagined it was Robert as sleep fell upon me.

At six, I woke up to dress for my date. Having a limited wardrobe, I wore my usual—jeans, a blue blouse, and my mules. I was ready just before there was a knock on the door. With my hand on the knob, I paused. Was I cheating? Dismissing the thought, I opened the door for my date. "Hey."

The producer, Vincent Morrison, had reserved the pool area and had the party catered for the evening so the cast members for Jonathan's next film could become acquainted. He was a likable man, gracious and very down-to-earth. At the party, I danced with several men as Jonathan busied himself flirting with other ladies. The party was a good filler for the night and I enjoyed Jonathan's company when he was around.

It was getting late and I needed to retire for the evening. I had an early morning planned at the studio. I hunted down Jonathan to tell him I was leaving, but he insisted on walking me to my room.

I leaned against my suite door with my key card in my hand. "Thanks for another great evening."

"I'm glad you had fun. By the way, I have an extra ticket for a charity benefit I have to attend tomorrow night. Would you come as my guest? Mr. Morrison's wife can't attend and he didn't want to waste the ticket. He asked if I knew someone who would like to go." He positioned his forearm above his head, propping it against the door and leaned in closer. "I think he had you in mind." His pearly whites flashed into a full blown smile.

I giggled. "Is it formal?"

"Black tie all the way, Baby."

As we were talking, a group of people walked by. We both instinctively stopped talking until they passed. I looked at Jonathan and motioned. "Come in. We don't need to be discussing this in the hallway." He stepped inside, walking straight to the couch. The interruption gave me more time to think about his invitation. "I would love to go." We made ourselves comfortable on the couch and he was about to kiss me when my cell rang. He grimaced. I rummaged through my purse and retrieved it. "It's Robert, my husband. Should I answer?"

"Can't he wait a little longer?" He threw his hands in the air, looking frustrated. "I can't get a break!"

"I'll call him later. I'm still uneasy about talking to him. I wish he'd stop calling me so I can think without him affecting me. He wants another chance."

Jonathan put his arm around my shoulders and took my chin in his hand. Staring into my eyes, his voice was serious. "I'm not encouraging you to go back to him, but if you don't give him another chance, you'll always wonder if you made a mistake."

"He can wait a little longer for my decision. I need more time."

"Thatta girl."

"I need to cut this evening short. I have an early morning meeting with Ms. Carter."

"Shhh! No more talking. You're wasting time." He pulled me across his lap and his lips found their way to mine. The kiss...I didn't want it to end. It felt so nice to have his warm, strong arms around me and to feel wanted. I wasn't cheating—this was payback. Jonathan's hands started to wander too much, attempting to move to the next level, but I stopped him. Kissing was as far as I was willing to go. He grunted in frustration. "I have to be in LA Saturday. But, I'll be back Tuesday. How about giving me your cell phone number so I can keep in touch?"

I ignored his request for my number, but a small wave of sadness came over me. Jonathan was the only person I knew in Atlanta. "I'll still be here. They want me to stay until after the fashion show in New York. It's in two and a half weeks. Oh! I didn't tell you about that. I have to walk a runway in New York City. Then I guess it's back to Houston. How long will you be filming here?"

"I'm not sure."

I moved from his lap and sat next to him. "I'm going to miss you."

"I'm going to miss you, too. Well, I guess I'd better go." I walked him to the door. "I'll come to your room around 6:30 tomorrow to pick you up."

"If you don't mind, let's meet in the lobby." He didn't question my decision, but nodded in approval. Before leaving, he gave me a sweet kiss on the cheek, sighed, and left.

I was putting on my favorite t-shirt when my cell rang. "Hey, Abbey."

"Belinda, can you talk?"

"Sure, Jonathan left a little while ago. I'm just getting ready for bed."

"Well, how was the party?" From the pitch of her voice, I pictured Abbey sitting on the edge of her bed waiting for any details I was willing to offer up.

The next thirty minutes were spent going over the events of the evening. Abbey, as usual, wanted to hear everything, but I selectively kept my slightly intimate contact with Jonathan to myself. "We've been spending quite a bit of time together, and I'll probably be seeing him more."

Abbey's voice became very low. "Belinda, what about Robert?"

"Jonathan is just a friend. Robert—I've talked to him. Jonathan thinks I should give Robert another chance." My mood became more somber as I thought about Robert. "I do miss him, but I'm still hurting. Abbey, if I go anywhere near him I'll give in. I need to learn to be stronger, to stand up for myself around him." I let out a deep breath. "I have to be sure I can trust him. Without that, nothing will change."

"Are you going to give him another chance?"

"Probably, but later. Don't tell him."

"Garrett says Robert's lonely and misses you terribly." Abbey became quiet and I didn't say anything. Suddenly she changed the subject. "I almost forgot! You're invited to the Delt homecoming party. It's the third weekend in September. All the brothers want to see you."

"Is he going to be there?"

"I don't know. Would that be a problem?"

"Could be if I'm not ready to see him. Besides, I don't know if I'll be free that weekend. I'll have to let you know closer to that time. I have to go, it's late. I have an early meeting tomorrow morning, and then we're filming another commercial. I'll try to call you later."

So much had happened today, keeping me busy. As glad as I was to have things to keep my mind off Robert, now I was alone and he was back in my thoughts.

***

Ms. Carter had invited me to take a look at my new layout for one of the magazines. It was very early in the morning and the building was almost empty. When I entered the outer office, the secretary wasn't in. The door to Ms. Carter's inner office was open. I tapped on the door and peeked inside. She was sitting at her large, modern wood-and-glass desk, looking at several photos that were spread out across the top. Ms. Carter looked up over her black-rimmed glasses. "Hi Belinda. Your photos for the magazine ads are really good. Come look."

I stood next to her as she, in a methodical way, handed me photos, one by one. She paused in between to allow me enough time to study each picture. I had never thought of myself as pretty, but the woman I analyzed in these pictures was me, and I was beautiful.

After seeing the ad layout, my increased self-confidence made doing the commercial more fun. Mr. Burton requested I show off the jeans the same way I did at my interview. I sashayed toward the camera, posed, and said, "Be a Sassy Gal—wear jeans by Every Body Jeans Manufacturing Company" in a sexy voice, then turned and sashayed away. We shot several takes consuming most of the day. I asked when the first commercial would be on TV and was told they would start airing in about a week. The jeans would be in the stores around the same time. Soon everybody would know—my secret would be out.

When we wrapped up the commercial, Ms. Carter took me to a large room with a stage that T'ed out into a runway. She instructed me to go up there behind the curtain on the left. I was to sashay out across the stage to where it met the runway, do a pose, then walk down the runway to the end, and pose again. On the way back to the stage, I was to stop at the T, turn and pose then exit to the right. She told me not to look down during the show, but to keep my eyes above the heads of the people in the audience and look to the back of the room. After watching me rehearse this routine a few times, she left for her office and I continued to practice. It seemed easy, but there weren't any people watching. The thought of hundreds of eyes on me made me cringe.

The more I thought about it, the more concerned I became. I decided I needed a friend at the fashion show with me for support. I wanted Abbey there. She always helped me with my self-confidence issues and this would give us a chance to visit. After I finished practicing, I called her.

"Hey, Belinda. What's going on?"

"I have something I'd like to ask you."

"What?"

"Would you like to go with me to New York to that fashion show I told you about? I could use your support. It's the first weekend of September."

Abbey didn't respond at first. Then in a loud, almost deafening shriek, she cried out, "AAAH! SHUT THE FRONT DOOR! Yes! Yes! I'd love to go!"

I held the phone about six inches away from my ear until I was sure it was safe to resume our conversation. "I'm really nervous about walking down that runway. I keep visualizing myself falling on my butt."

"Don't worry, you'll do fine. But, how would I get to New York? How can I even get to an airport?"

"I was thinking maybe Garrett could take you to Houston. I'll fly both of you to New York. Do you think he'd mind doing that?"

"He better not! I'm sure he wouldn't want to pass up a chance to see you and all those models."

"I'll try to reserve a room for you two in the hotel."

"No, no. I want to stay with you so we can visit. We can have a girls' night in. Oh, but where would Garrett sleep?"

"I'll have a suite, so he could sleep on the couch...on second thought, I'll try to reserve you a room. He doesn't need to be uncomfortable."

"No, don't bother. The two airline tickets will cost you enough. You don't need to pay for a room too. He won't mind sleeping on the couch."

"Don't worry about the cost. I'm being paid very well. Talk to Garrett and let me know ASAP, so I can make the airline reservations."

"I'll call you tomorrow. I can't believe I'm going to New York! I won't be able to sleep from now until then."

I chuckled at her. "Okay. Bye." My fear of embarrassing myself on the runway calmed, knowing I'd have my best friend in the audience.

CHAPTER 30

AS SOON AS we were finished for the day, I rushed back to my hotel room to dress for the benefit. There wasn't a lot of time, so I showered with my hair crammed into a shower cap. I put on my little bit of make-up, curled my hair, and dressed in the same gown I had worn to the Delt formal. At 6:30 I stepped from the elevator into the hotel lobby. Mr. Morrison saw me first. His eyes widened and his mouth dropped open. Jonathan must have seen his reaction because he turned and looked. The same expression soon covered his face as I walked over to them. "Gentlemen."

Mr. Morrison stuttered, "You look absolutely ravishing."

Jonathan didn't respond for some time. He just stood there. His eyes slowly softened, becoming seductive as they roamed my body. "You are the most beautiful woman I've ever seen. I love that dress on you." With a slight shake of his head, a smile spread across his face before he winked.

The corners of my mouth slowly turned upward producing a shy smile.

"Shall we go?" Jonathan extended his elbow, so I linked my arm in his. Mr. Morrison did the same. I was escorted out to our limo by two very handsome men. When we walked out the door, camera flashes began bursting everywhere.

"I can't see. What's going on?" I lowered my head to shield my eyes.

"It's the paparazzi." Jonathan was right behind me guiding me through the car door before he did an about face and posed for the cameras.

In the safety of the shiny black limo, I had a chance to recover from the barrage of lights. "So some of these pictures could be in newspapers and magazines?"

"Probably in tomorrow's tabloids and maybe on TV. Paparazzi follow Jonathan everywhere he goes."

Oh no! What was Robert going to think? What would the tabloids say? And I certainly would need to call my parents in the morning.

When we arrived, I walked arm-in-arm between the two of them up the stairs of the massive Gothic stone structure. Camera flashes were everywhere, blinding me. As soon as we walked through the doors, they stopped. It was a relief to be able to see normally again. "Why aren't they following us?"

"Oh, they're not allowed. This is a safe zone, so to speak. Only authorized pictures are allowed beyond this point." Jonathan looked around, scoping out the crowd in the foyer.

We entered a huge grand ballroom that had the most enormous crystal chandelier I'd ever seen. Large round tables with floor length black linen tablecloths surrounded a spacious dance area. Each table was decorated with a huge floral arrangement and candles. There were crystal goblets, silver plate chargers, white linen napkins, and fancy silverware at each place setting. In the dim light, the room looked elegant.

Our names were on place cards perched in silver holders sitting on the chargers. I was Mrs. Morrison for the evening, so I was seated next to him. Jonathan found his place next to me. We hadn't been seated very long when the ballroom came alive with waiters dressed in white jackets dashing from one table to the next. They started off the meal by pouring ladles of cream soup into china bowls for the first course. Four more courses followed with the last being a luscious rich dessert. The wine flowed freely at the hint of a half-full glass.

Shortly after indulging ourselves, Mr. Morrison excused himself and disappeared, off socializing. Jonathan extended his hand to me. "Come on. I'm going to show you how to work a room." Jonathan flashed that bright smile as he looked over the attendees and focused on his planned target. "Let's go." He led me to a group of young people gathered across the dance floor. We managed to cover the entire room, meeting and greeting all of Jonathan's associates. Mr. Morrison was now sitting alone at the table. I excused myself and went over to join him.

The orchestra started playing my favorite song and people began filling the dance floor. I looked across the room and saw a band of white teeth rushing toward me. "May I have this dance?" Before I could say anything he twirled me onto the floor. Listening to the rhythm of the song, I laid my head against the hollow of his shoulder, closed my eyes, and began singing softly. He bent his head down closer, resting his cheek on my head.

When the song was over, I opened my eyes and saw a lot of people with smiling faces staring at us.

"That was beautiful." He hugged me. "You sang it like it has a lot of meaning to you."

"It does." I looked up through my lashes at him. "I hope I didn't embarrass you." Feeling my cheeks getting warm, I knew I was blushing.

"No, not at all. It was beautiful." He was studying my face, but I tried to avoid his gaze. "Are you blushing?" My hands went to my cheeks to hide the increased redness. He wasn't making this any better. He gave me a huge grin, picked me up around the waist and we spun around. When he put me down he remarked, "You're so cute."

We resumed dancing to a few more songs. As the music faded, the crackle of a microphone turned the dancer's attention to the stage. Sporting a wide smile, a man holding a mike made an announcement. "An anonymous donor has offered to contribute ten thousand dollars to our cause." The crowd started clapping. "Only if..." The crowd started clapping louder. The announcer raised his hands to quiet the audience. "Only if the young lady who was singing would share her song on stage with everyone. So Miss, if you're still out there, we could use the money." He started scanning the room for anyone coming forward.

I froze, panic-stricken. "Is he talking about me? I can't get up in front of all these people and sing. My mind will go blank." I trembled.

"You can do it. Just take some deep breaths and close your eyes. Imagine you're singing for just us again. It's for ten thousand dollars. Charity!"

"You have to come with me." I was clinging to his arm. There was no way I was going up on the stage by myself. As we made our way there, people noticed our movement. The applause started slowly and increased in intensity as Jonathan led me up the stairs to the stage. As he wrapped his arms around my waist, I took the microphone and made an announcement in a quavering voice. "I've never done this before, but I'll try."

The orchestra played, but I missed my cue. Closing my eyes, I took a deep breath, and exhaled. They started again—I began to sing, softly at first. I was surprised the spotlight on me blacked out the audience. I couldn't see anything past the end of the stage. Becoming more relaxed, I put my soul into my performance with, *"Dear love, my only sweet true love. You've captured my lonely heart."* About the second verse, Jonathan released me and stepped away. With more confidence, I gave it my all until I finished with, *"As our world is in perfect rhyme. You're forever in my mind."* The spotlight dimmed and I saw everyone stand and applaud. It was an amazing feeling. I graciously dropped my head.

Jonathan rushed in, taking me up in his arms and planted a very passionate kiss on my lips. From the corner of my eye, I could see flashes everywhere. I had unknowingly put myself in a compromising position. What if these were in the tabloids and Robert saw them? I ended the kiss and rushed off the stage with Jonathan close behind.

Everyone complimented me as we made our way back. People even came to our table. To help give me more space so I could calm down from my panic attack, Jonathan towed me back out onto the dance floor. We danced to several songs. He and Mr. Morrison were my alternating dance partners for the rest of the evening. I had a great time, except for my stint on the stage.

As with all fairytales, there must be an ending. It was time to leave and we headed for our hotel. "Thank you both very much. It was an evening I'll never forget." In the hotel elevator, I extended my hand to Mr. Morrison expecting a handshake.

"I also had a great time. Thank you." He took hold of my hand and kissed it.

When we arrived at my floor, Jonathan and I exited the elevator. He turned back and addressed Mr. Morrison. "Good night, Vincent. See you tomorrow." Mr. Morrison just waved as the doors closed.

Jonathan walked me to my room. "Thank you for a wonderful evening." After unlocking my door, I held it open a few inches. He evidently didn't want the evening to end because he took the liberty of pushing it open as he escorted me in. He clutched my face between his hands pulling it up to his and kissed me ardently. Not wanting the kiss to end, I wrapped my arms around his neck to hold him close. I shivered inside at the thought of what *could* happen, *would* happen if this were Robert. I ended the kiss.

"You look so sexy in that dress. Stay with me tonight." His lustful eyes were peering down, deep into mine. They made me feel all tingly.

"I can't. I can't cheat on my husband like that. It's bad enough that we're kissing, but that's what he did. I told Robert, 'I can do what you do.'"

He looked upset. "Okay, I understand. But I feel we have a connection."

"I like you, but if the roles were reversed, how would you feel if I slept with him?"

He didn't like what I said. He was frowning. "I wouldn't like it, but I'd never desert you. So this situation wouldn't have happened."

"That's what you think now, but you're a player just like Robert. Life was wonderful one day, and the next—nothing. I don't know what happened." I could feel my eyes begin to moisten.

"Did you ask him why he was treating you that way?" Jonathan wiped away an escaping tear.

"I tried, but after that kiss I saw in his car…I left. I couldn't bear any more pain." Tears began to trickle down my cheeks.

Jonathan and I sat on the couch. "He wants to talk to you, so talk. Get him to answer your questions."

"I'm tired of all his excuses. He knows he could have any girl he wants, so why me?" I laid my head on his shoulder, tears flowing.

Jonathan hugged me tight to him. "He saw how special you are, just like I have. You're beautiful inside and out."

"Thank you, but I'm not special. I'm just an ordinary girl from Texas."

"Belinda, you need to build up your self-confidence. You could have any guy you want. Look, you captured the heart of a campus player and married him. He still wants you. Hell, I want you and I don't say that to just any girl." I could tell he was trying to cheer me up.

"But he was never around. It felt like he abandoned me. And let's not forget I caught him cheating."

"That wasn't your fault. It was his. Something must have freaked him out—maybe that everything happened so fast. I don't know, but I'm sure you didn't do anything to cause that. Look, he misses you and wants another chance. Let him explain." He squeezed me a little harder and kissed my forehead. "I can't believe I'm not looking out for my own best interest and I'm telling you to talk to him. I'm an idiot." He shook his head. "Look, it's getting late, but first we need to exchange phone numbers."

We entered each other's number into our cell phones. "I'll try to come see you in the morning before I leave. Do you want me to get you anything?"

I shook my head. "There is something I've been meaning to ask you."

"What?"

"Would you like to go to the fashion show with me? I could use all the support I can get. I'm really nervous about walking down that runway. My best friends, Abbey and Garrett, are coming. I can introduce you to them. Abbey would love to meet you."

"I'd love to be there for you, but I don't know what my filming schedule will be. If I can, I'll be there."

"Thanks." I walked him to the door.

"Good night." He placed his hands on either side of my head and kissed my forehead. "You'll get through this. You're stronger than you think. You'll make the right decision and everything will fall into place." He gave me a wink and left.

After I got ready for bed, I turned my cell on to check my messages. I had two. Abbey left a voice mail to call, then I listened to Robert's. "Angel, please come back, I miss you terribly." Before responding to him, I had to think if our relationship would even work. I had a decision to make.

I now had a job that required traveling to who knew where, and Robert would have to stay in Sugar Land to work for his father. No matter how I looked at my possible chaotic schedule, there would be little time for Robert and me to be a couple, let alone see each other. Maybe it would be better to just let things be, to let him go. It wouldn't be fair for him to expect me to give up my plans for him, just as I shouldn't expect him to do the same for me.

There was still the issue of Erin and the kiss. Was he ready to change like he said? He told me that before, but he strayed. If I ended our relationship, it would end the pain I endured as a result of his cheating, but I'd be giving up the strong connection I had with him. Was I willing to let him go and take the chance I'd be able to find another man I'd be as close to? I could sense a void in my heart when we were apart. Leaving after witnessing the kiss was the hardest decision I'd ever made, but I hoped we'd eventually work things out. I knew I still loved him, but could I actually leave him for good? It wouldn't be fair to continue to lead him on, to give him false hope. I knew I was making the right decision as I picked up the phone to send him a text.

Me: Need to tell u something. Been thinking. Dont see how we can b together. Me out of state & traveling. U in sugar land. Don't want to keep u hanging on. Get on w/your life & b happy.

Robert responded immediately: NO Angel. Cant b happy w/o u. Not just ur decision. Mine too. Will never leave. Will follow u anywhere. Can find way to make this work.   No more texts.☹☹☹ Talk only. ☺☺☺ Won't let go. Im your pit bull now!

Me: How? So complicated. Confused. Frustrated.

Robert: Doesnt matter. We love each other. Belong together.

Me: Heart hurts. Mind hurts. Still need time.

Robert: Talk ONLY!!!

Me: Ok. Tomorrow.

Ending the text, I lay back on the bed, staring at the ceiling for a while. My heart was more settled. I now had some hope Robert and I would find our way to happier times. Sleep came quicker than it had for days—I wasn't crying.

CHAPTER 31

SATURDAY MORNING CAME with a knock on my door. My first thought was to stay in bed and ignore it. I was tired and needed more sleep. It was only eight o'clock and I had hung the "Do Not Disturb" sign on the knob the night before. Rolling over, I covered my head with a pillow. KNOCK! KNOCK! KNOCK! It was louder than before. Whoever was at the door couldn't read. Upset by the intrusion, I threw my pillow across the room. I found my robe and staggered to the door. I was about to twist the doorknob and open it, when I remembered the paparazzi from the night before. What if one of them found out what room I was in and was waiting for me to open the door, ready to snap a picture? I scrutinized the doorknob, my robe, and then my reflection in the mirror on the wall. Whoever was on the other side of the door would be shocked. My hair was a mess and I was only covered by a thigh-length wrap-around robe. KNOCK! KNOCK! KNOCK! The noise startled me and I jumped. Looking through the peephole, I saw Jonathan with his fist raised, prepared to knock again. My timing was perfect, opening the door before he could make contact. He almost fell into the room as I giggled.

After Jonathan regained his footing, he produced a smile wider than the Pacific Ocean. "Good morning gor…geous." He hesitated, looking me over. "You're a mess! Like the robe though." He reached out into the hall and pulled in a cart, the kind room service would use. "Ready for breakfast?" He was just too energetic for this early in the morning. He reminded me of Abbey. I followed him into the living room and sat on the couch. Reaching under the tablecloth covering the cart, he pulled out a stack of tabloid papers. "Have you seen any of these yet?" He was too excited. "And look at this!" He reached for the TV remote and turned it on, flipping through the channels until he found what he was looking for—a show that reports on celebrity gossip. Right in front of me was a clip of Jonathan kissing me and I was being referred to as "Jonathan Morse's new mystery girlfriend."

My mouth popped open as I edged to the end of the couch. Jonathan handed me the tabloids. I glanced over the pictures that pass for newsworthy information. He had all the pages turned and folded back to the images of him and me. "How could this happen?!" I shouted in total shock. "I thought no one was supposed to take any pictures. I thought it was a safe place from this sort of thing!"

"Isn't it great? We're going to get so much mileage from this!" Jonathan was too full of exuberance.

I looked at him mystified. "Am I to understand you're happy about these?" I stood up, crushing and shaking the papers in my hand.

He threw his hands up. "Whoa! Whoa! Hang on princess. Of course I'm happy about them. We made the news. Any time you can be in the public eye, it's a good day."

"Jonathan, my parents don't know anything about this. What about Robert? How do you think he'll react?" Robert was all I could think about. I had such hopes that we had a chance and now that could all be gone. I sank back on the couch trying to make sense of everything and figure out how I was going to explain away this new drama in my life.

Jonathan came down from his tabloid high long enough to see my reaction was the total opposite of his. "You don't understand what's going on, do you?" He was more solemn as he sat next to me. "Okay, last night was a real advantage for both of us. I thought you understood that."

I glared at him with squinted eyes. I couldn't believe what he was saying. "Are you telling me, you were just using me to get publicity? What about it being a paparazzi-free zone?"

Now Jonathan was very serious and concerned. "Well, yeah. Whenever I'm out I look for every opportunity to get into the papers. Last night was no exception. And the benefit was a paparazzi-free zone. Anything like that is supposed to be, but there's always some underpaid worker with a cell phone trying to make an extra buck." He was so matter-of-fact about the whole incident. "Why are you so upset?"

I looked at him dumbfounded. "You used me." I was hurt and still confused by all of this.

"Okay. Yes, I did use you. That's just part of this whole lifestyle."

"How could you? And what about all this?" I motioned with my hands to encompass our situation. "Are you going to tell the tabloids about everything we've talked about as well?" I looked away in disgust.

"Hell no! What we have here is private. What we say to each other is for us only, but when you go past that door, all bets are off. That's the way it works and you better start learning that really fast." He was direct and to the point. "So you better get on that phone when I leave and tell everyone who means anything to you that what they see is not necessarily true. Once your butt gets plastered all over the place, you'll be fair game for anyone with a camera." He stopped and just stared at me with warm, gentle eyes. "Look, let's keep it simple. Once you become a celebrity, you have to be very protective of your privacy. You have to make very sure, *very sure* you can trust the person you tell anything to."

Crossing my arms in front of me, I looked him straight in the eye. "Can I trust you?"

He readjusted his position. "Whatever we talk about in private is between us. Whatever we do or say out there is an open book."

I thought about what he said for a few seconds. "How will I be able to learn all this?" I knew he was right. Once the ad campaign went public, so would I and my life. I didn't need this right now. There were other problems I needed to deal with. I just never gave this any thought. It all had sounded so simple—get a job, make some money, and live my life. Boy, was I learning it didn't work that way. I felt like I had been kicked in the stomach. It would take hours on the phone trying to talk my way out of this mess. I was glad I didn't have a lot of people in my life that I was very close to.

Jonathan interrupted my concentration by placing his arm around my shoulders. "I'm sorry. I've been doing this for so long, I just take it for granted. Call your family and tell them we're just friends and nothing more. Call Robert and tell him I would be glad to talk with him if he wants." He was trying to soften the mood and I appreciated his effort, but it didn't help much. "Look, I have to leave in about thirty minutes. Do you want to eat?" He pointed to the cart of food he brought with him. My appetite wasn't that great after this morning's events, but I figured I'd better eat something. After all, he went to all this trouble.

After Jonathan left, I went to the bedroom and picked up my cell phone. I sat on the side of the bed just staring at the little device like it was alien to me. Considering who I'd phone first, I made a mental list according to whose call would take the longest. Mom and Dad first, then Abbey, and then Robert. Robert's call would be the hardest one of all to make. I pressed number four to speed dial my parents, praying that my mother would answer.

"Hello."

"Hi Mom."

"Belinda, how nice to hear from you. Are you alright? Did you get the job?"

It was twenty questions time. I had to slow her down so I could go through everything about the job, Robert, and the tabloids. Our conversation lasted over an hour. Robert hadn't contacted them about our separation and she hadn't seen or heard anything about Jonathan and me, so it made the situations easier to discuss. She assured me nothing that could be reported would ever taint her opinion of me. In fact, talking to her helped me put some things into perspective. Mom pointed out that I had blown some of the recent events out of proportion. She helped me look at the reality of the situation and not what could happen. She reminded me to step back and look at every situation as if I were not part of it, then study it before acting on it. I told her about the latest text from Robert and how the tabloids were going to ruin everything. She encouraged me to call him and fill him in on everything that was happening and to keep him in the loop. "Honey, I know you were mad at him, but too much is happening to you with this job. You have to talk to him every day to let him know what you've been doing. Let him hear it from you first. Then when you're ready to see him, it'll be easy."

We said our goodbyes and I was on to my next call, Abbey. This one would be easier now. I was glad I called Mom first. I felt more grounded. Abbey would want every sordid detail like she always did, but I'd be able to put her off with a shorter call if she knew I needed to call Robert.

"Belinda, what do you think you're doing?" she spat out.

I knew exactly what she meant. "You saw the pictures?"

"They're spreading like wildfire around here. Everyone is talking about you. After all, you just left last week."

We continued our conversation and covered most of the bases. She had no idea if Robert had seen or heard anything about the pictures. I was hoping to get more information from her, anticipating Garrett had talked with him. Abbey also told me that they could go to New York with me. I told her we'd work out the details later. My next call wasn't going to be as easy as I had wished.

Taking a deep breath, I pressed the number two on my phone. It rang and went right to voice mail. *Oh shit*! He saw the tabloids. He always answered immediately. Now I was getting nervous. "Robert, call me." All I could do now was wait.

I lay back on the bed holding my cell phone, wishing it would ring. Fifteen minutes went by, and then thirty minutes. No call. This wasn't like Robert. I called again and left another message. "Please," I emphasized. "Call me." What if he never took another one of my calls? I hadn't been taking his. He was probably paying me back.

I decided to text: Left voice message. No return call☹.

Now all I could do was wait again.

After an hour passed by, I was getting panicky. I decided to call Abbey back to see if they could reach him.

"Hi. Did you talk to him?" I could tell from Abbey's voice she was worried.

"No. He's not taking my calls or replying to my texts. Usually I receive an immediate answer. Do you think he saw those pictures and he's mad at me?"

"I don't know. Could be."

"Would you ask Garrett to call him to see if he answers?" If Robert took his call, that meant he was upset with me.

"Okay, I'll see." I heard Abbey say, "Sweetie, would you give Robert a ring to see if he'll answer? He's not taking Belinda's calls."

"Okay, give me a minute," I heard Garrett say in a muffled tone.

"He's calling now." She paused. "Is he answering?" she asked Garrett. The conversation turned back to me. "He's shaking his head no. Maybe he's out, or busy, or his phone could be run down. I'd take that as a good sign. Just keep trying."

"Okay. Tell Garrett thanks for me. I'll keep trying. I'll call you later."

Deciding to wait awhile to see if he'd call me back, I got up and showered, dried my hair and dressed to go out for a late lunch. I wasn't very hungry. There were butterflies filling my stomach from worrying about Robert.

The day was overcast and as dreary as my mood when I left the hotel. There was a small bakery a short distance down the street. They had just what I wanted—blueberry bagels with cream cheese and coffee. I didn't eat much of the breakfast that Jonathan served me. I was too upset from the thought of Robert's reaction to the tabloids. Hanging around with Jonathan wasn't a good idea, but he was my friend, and being in the news would continue to happen once my ads and commercials became public. Robert would just have to understand that. I decided from now on there would be no more physical contact in public, except with Robert.

As I made my way back to the hotel, I was lost in my thoughts of him, wishing he'd return my calls. I was interrupted by the sound of my cell phone. Frantically, I dug around in my purse looking for it, hoping the call was him. But no such luck. It was Jonathan.

"Hey, Jonathan. Are you getting everything done?"

"Well, it looks like it's going to be late Monday before I can come back. I have to run by the studio that morning. Are you alright?"

"Yeah, I'm okay." I faked trying to sound in a good mood.

"Have you talked to everyone yet?"

"No, Robert's the only one left. I haven't been able to reach him. He's not responding to my messages. I hope it's not because he saw the photos."

"Belinda, I'm sorry. I shouldn't have kissed you like that in front of everyone. I hope I didn't hurt your chances with your husband. Again, I'd be glad to explain to him."

"Thanks, but I think I need to explain to him that you and I are just friends. He can't complain. He kissed Erin…no, he *made out* with her in his car." I corrected my comment, as the picture of them flashed in my mind. I flinched and shook my head to rid myself of that tormenting image. "I'm going to let you go and try texting him."

"Okay, call if you need to talk."

Back in my suite, I decided I'd waited long enough to hear from Robert, so I sent another text.

Me: Why aren't u responding to my calls? Are you okay?
           Something wrong?
He texted immediately: Is there?
Me: Dont know.
Robert: So what Im looking at is ok?

Oh shit! He was looking at the pictures now. My explanation needed to be in a call.

He answered on the first ring.

"Robert, please let me explain." There was nervousness and excitement in my voice. I was scared stiff this wouldn't go well.

"I'm listening." His tone came across as cold and calculating.

I was taken aback for a second by his voice, then attempted to recover with my next words. "We're just friends, that's all."

"Looks pretty intimate for a friend," he snapped back.

Now I got mad. "Hey, bud, what I had to watch was pretty intimate-looking! PAYBACK, remember. Except you weren't here watching my kiss like I was there watching you making out with Erin. So, what about Erin?"

"What about her?"

"Your fling with her? Is it over?" I used a sharp tone to make my point.

"What? You thought I was having a fling? No, I wasn't." He tsked.

"What about all those days and late nights?"

"I was with the study group. There were five of us. Three guys and two girls. We were studying and working on class assignments. I swear nothing was going on. I'll give you their names and numbers—you can call them."

"Then what about that kiss in your car?" I demanded incredulously.

"That happened only once. She followed me to my car and…."

"No, No, No! I don't want to hear it. I don't want that image in my mind, too. I see you kissing her every time I close my eyes now. I don't want a complete picture. Anyway, I've had my payback with Jonathan. But he kissed me for publicity. I didn't know he was going to do that. He saw a chance to make the papers so he took it. He thought I knew that's how it's done." I inhaled deeply before continuing with my explanation. "I was having fun that night for a change. Someone said they'd donate ten thousand dollars if I would sing my favorite song. There was no way I was going up on stage by myself—I dragged him along. When I finished singing, he just planted that kiss on me."

"So you went to that benefit with him?"

I explained how the plans for the evening unfolded and emphasized I was accompanied by Mr. Morrison and Jonathan. "When they asked me to sing, I'd been dancing with Jonathan. If I'd been with Mr. Morrison, he would've been on the stage with me." I waited to see if Robert would say anything. I was nervous and trying to explain everything like Jonathan suggested. So when there was silence from Robert's end, I continued, hoping not to hang myself with my words. "Robert, I promise. Jonathan and I are just friends. Nothing has happened. You can't believe everything in the tabloids. When my ads and commercials debut, I'll be fair game for the paparazzi. You'll have to trust me. Can you live with that?"

To my shock, Robert answered me in a calm and affectionate voice. "Angel, I need to be with you. Let me come to you. Where in Atlanta?"

"No, I'm not ready to see you yet and my schedule is very busy right now. Remember how busy you were in school? You didn't have time for me." I hesitated for him to respond. Nothing, so I continued. "I wouldn't have time for you. You'd just be sitting in the hotel alone all day. That wouldn't be fair for either of us." Still, nothing from Robert. "Okay, you know as well as I do, if we're intimate, we wouldn't leave the hotel for days."

Finally he spoke up. "I'm sorry. I can't change the past, but you're making some good points, and congratulations you've managed to confront me again. I agree with you about our intimacy."

"I can't change what happened either." I paused, proud of myself that I told him how I felt. "So where do we go from here?"

"Let's keep the lines of communication open. Talk frequently. We'll do this your way if it helps you tell me how you feel. I think this is what our relationship was lacking. I always made all the decisions….I have an idea. Would you be willing to meet me at the Delt homecoming party? If you can take some time off, we could find someplace secluded to go so we could be alone. That would take care of the intimacy issue. I'm not giving up on us."

My pulse was racing from his answer. It was just what I was wishing for. At least now I had hope. "Okay, I'll see what I can do about the time off and yes, I think we should talk every day. There will be all kinds of changes in the next few weeks and I want you to know about them before they happen whenever possible." Feeling antsy, I found myself pacing. "A friend of mine, who knows a lot about the paparazzi, told me I need to tell you everything, to explain what's going on, and to keep our lives private."

"Sounds like a good friend. Tell *him* thank you and that I look forward to meeting him in the near future."

I was relieved he understood, or at least was trying to. Our conversation continued for several hours. We made a commitment to talk every evening after we were both finished with work. Thank God for unlimited cell minutes. I fell asleep with Robert still on the phone. The last words I remember hearing were, "Angel, I love you."

Sunday, Robert had a golf date scheduled with his dad, so I had to wait to talk to him. Time was creeping by and with every minute the butterflies in the pit of my stomach increased as my anticipation grew. To pass the time, I took a walk. On my way back to the hotel my cell chirped that I had a text message.

Robert: Golf boring. Like being w/dad. Love you. Talk tonight. ☺☺☺
Me: ☺☺☺

Before I could return to the home page, my phone chirped that I had a response.

Robert: Glad to hear from you. Miss you.
Me: Not playing golf?
Robert: Not my turn. Playing with 3 others. In cart thinking about you.
Me: Same here. Teach me to play golf.
Robert: Have to b in same city.
Me: SMARTASS. Be patient!
Robert: Im too good to you. My turn. Love you.
Me: Love you too!

I lavished in the thought of seeing Robert and being with him. I missed his irresistible touch and my insatiable response to it.

Robert was on my mind as I opened the door to my room. I couldn't open it fast enough, fumbling in my purse for my phone to call him. The conversation was short. He was just finishing up with golf and would be heading home to call me, he figured in about an hour. With my phone in my hand, I made myself comfortable on the bed and tried to relax. My fluttering butterflies were telling me it was close to the time Robert assured he'd call. I couldn't wait any longer, so I called.

We spent the rest of the evening chatting. I told him about my decision to have limited contact with male counterparts at any time. He seemed to appreciate that decision more than anything else we talked about.

Robert's mood shifted, becoming more playful. "What are you wearing?"

I played along and answered in a soft, sexy voice. "Nothing, I'm naked."

There was dead silence.

"Robert?"

"One second, I'm picturing that."

I jumped in. "I suppose you just got out of the shower and only have a towel wrapped around you."

There was a pause. "As a matter of fact, I did just get out of the shower when you called and I've been naked this whole time."

My heart jumped at the memory of his well-formed body and how much I missed being touched by him. The memories were overwhelming and I started thinking, maybe he could get his father's corporate jet and be here in a few hours. He could leave in the morning and be back to work a little late. Lost in my fantasy, I heard, "Belinda?"

"I'm here."

"You know I could be there in a few hours and back by morning."

Did he just read my mind? I couldn't answer him immediately. I had to get a grip. "Very tempting, but I don't think that would be a good idea. I have to be up early and look like I slept. Somehow I don't think we would get much rest." I was biting my tongue because I wanted him here so badly. "We have to change the subject."

"Why?"

"Robert, change the subject or I'll hang up!" My voice was firm so he'd get the point. After a short pause, he complied with my wishes. We started talking about his work and things that were different from what he learned in school. He liked what he was doing, but was very busy. He felt confident that once he learned the ropes and the menial details of the office routine, he'd be in more control. For now, the job seemed to be controlling him.

When the call ended, the image of Robert's body haunted my mind. It kept me up most of the night. To feel his warm body next to mine was what I needed to sleep. It may have been easier having him fly here.

CHAPTER 32

OVER THE NEXT two weeks there were more photo shoots and we taped another commercial. Each day I practiced with diligence on the runway, rehearsing my poses and walking in the stiletto pumps supplied by Fashion Designs by JLDeats. I was starting to feel a little more confident. The ads and commercials hit the media at the same time. My face and butt were now everywhere.

Jonathan had returned from LA as planned. He checked his schedule and found out he'd be filming the weekend of the fashion show. At least Abbey and Garret would be there. I still didn't think it was the right time to see Robert. Besides, when we did get together, there would be no stopping us. We would end up locking ourselves away for days as we became reacquainted.

Having Robert more involved in my life made me realize how important he was to me. As promised, no matter what was going on, we talked every night. That was our time to be together, if only over the phone. We'd go over our day and were always there for each other. We talked about our careers and started making work decisions based on how it would affect our lives as a couple. I found having him in my life made my performance at work have more purpose. I had a new self-confidence that showed in every aspect of my life.

One evening he seemed distracted and his tone was off compared to previous evening calls. "What's bothering you? You sound upset."

There was a brief silence from the other end before he began explaining. "I made a very bad business decision for one of my clients. It's nothing that can't be repaired, but Dad and the client aren't too happy. Dad had to step in to fix the mess. So you can imagine I'm not feeling real proud of myself at this point." There was a pause in his conversation. "I'll be alright. To tell the truth, I'm feeling a bit stupid right now."

"You're far from stupid. Everyone makes mistakes." This was the first time I'd ever heard him say anything about himself that was less than perfect.

Now that we were telling each other about everything, I decided to bring up the fashion show. It didn't feel right keeping it from him. At first I wasn't sure my broken heart was ready to be with him, but now I wanted him there to share the experience with me. "The first weekend of September I'll be flying to New York to be in a fashion show."

Immediately he cut in. "Can I come watch you?"

"Of course you can, I'd love for you to be there. But we may not get to spend much time together. I'll be very busy before the show, and afterwards I don't know what will be going on. I may be expected to fly back to Atlanta that evening with Ms. Carter. I just can't make any commitment right now." Not knowing how much time I'd have with Robert was killing me. I wanted my first time back with him to be special. With my hectic schedule, I was afraid we would only have a few stolen moments. I tried to lift my downtrodden mood by giving Robert what I thought would be good news. "Abbey and Garrett will be coming to the show. You could hang around with them. They're flying in at noon on Saturday."

"You invited them before me?" He sounded wounded.

"Sorry, but we weren't talking when I asked them to come." Feeling bad that I waited so long to tell him, I knew I had put my foot in my mouth again.

"Correction, I was trying to talk to you. You weren't talking to me," he quickly reminded me.

"I stand corrected. Surely we'll be hanging around there for a little while after the show. Then all four of us can visit some. I really miss y'all."

"Angel, I can fly you back to Atlanta. Remember, corporate jet. Talk to Ms. Carter and see what you can work out. Ask her if you can have the week off after the show. I'd like to spend some time with you....You know we'd need at least a week to do some catching up."

"Okay, I like the way that sounds. Baby, I'll see what I can do from this end and let you know."

"I'll be waiting for that call. Hope it works out."

All arrangements for Abbey and Garrett to attend the fashion show were finalized. I managed to reserve a room in the same hotel I was in and their airline reservations were made. I even arranged for limo service to make sure they had transportation to the hotel and show.

Robert's and my plan to take time after the show fell through. After talking with Ms. Carter, she informed me I would be needed back in Atlanta on Monday. The preliminary market testing and sales of the jeans were showing strong numbers. If the show increased the sales, as expected, another commercial would be needed and they wanted the taping to start without delay.

"I have some good news and some bad news. Which do you want first?" This was my greeting to my husband during our nightly call, a week before our planned rendezvous at the fashion show.

He was quiet, but I gave him time to decide what he wanted to hear first. "Okay, hit me with the bad news first." It tore my heart apart to tell Robert we only had one day to be together. "Okay, I'll take whatever I can have right now. I'll bring the jet and fly in on Saturday. We can go to dinner with Abbey and Garrett. Right after the dinner we can fly back to Atlanta." He was disappointed, but understood how busy I was. "Now what's the good news?"

"Are you sitting down?"

"Uh, yeah. What else would I be doing?"

"Come on Robert, play along." I was trying very hard to change the mood. Our failed plans were depressing both of us.

"Okay. I'm sitting down."

"I have the whole week off after the Delt homecoming party. I told Mr. Johnson to make the arrangements with Ms. Carter so that I wouldn't be available for the week. I told him I wouldn't take any calls from them and as far as I was concerned, they didn't exist. Mr. Johnson told me today everything was set. Do you think you can arrange for some time off that week? If you can't, I can stay with your parents and at least we could have the nights together...."

I would have kept talking if Robert's laughter hadn't interrupted me. "Whoa, Angel. Come up for air. I already made plans to be off at least two extra days, but I'm sure I can take the week off as well." He sounded more upbeat. "At least something is working for us."

It was good to hear Robert sound less gloomy. The rest of our conversation was more uplifting as we made plans for our week together in Texas.

***

The Thursday night before the fashion show, Robert called. "Hey Baby. How was your day?" I was always glad to hear from him. We would be seeing each other in two days and couldn't wait for Saturday to arrive.

"I'm not going to be able to come to New York."

Budding tears were forming in my eyes from his bad news. "Why?"

"Remember the bad business decision I told you I made? Well, I have to meet with that client this weekend before he goes out of the country Sunday afternoon. He's my account and Dad thinks I need to meet with him to rebuild our rapport. I have to fly to Chicago Saturday and I don't know how long it will take to win him over. I'm so sorry. I was really looking forward to this weekend."

"Me too. Robert, promise me nothing will interfere with our plans to meet at the Delt homecoming party."

"I'll do everything I can to not let you down again."

Friday morning, Ms. Carter and I were off to New York in the company jet. That afternoon we met with Ms. Deats, the designer of the blouses I was to model in the fashion show. She went over my role. I'd be third in the line-up of ten models. She told me that I'd have a lady to dress me and that my changes would be easy since I only had three different tops, three color-coordinated pairs of shoes, and accessories. Her fashions were contemporary, so she also wanted her models to match. Hired cosmeticians and beauticians would be applying our make-up and styling our hair. She wanted my hair pulled up in a knotted ponytail on top of and a little to one side of my head. Ms. Deats didn't want anything covering up the clothes.

After our meeting, Ms. Carter took me to the room where the show would be held. She wanted me to practice walking down that runway to get a feel for it in heels. The room was spacious with a countless number of chairs. When I walked up on the stage, my stomach kinked as I peered down what seemed an endless runway. I took some deep breaths then proceeded to rehearse my walk and poses several times until Ms. Carter seemed satisfied. "We should head to the hotel to eat dinner and get you to bed early. Tomorrow is going to be an extremely busy day and you need lots of rest. You have to look perfect. You'll be representing us and Fashion Designs by JLDeats."

The first thing I did when I arrived in my room was check my cell phone for missed messages. Robert had called earlier and left a message to call.

"Hi Angel. How was your day?"

"It was okay, but it would've been better if you were here."

"You don't know how much I wish I was there, holding you, kissing you." He heaved a loud sigh. "I miss you so much….So, you were telling me about your day."

I filled him in with all the details. "My stomach is doing flip-flops right now. I keep seeing myself falling on my butt and everyone laughing at me." My lack of self-confidence was coming out in force.

"Don't worry. Angel, you'll do fine. If you can get up in front of the people at the benefit and sing, you can do this."

"But I wasn't up on the stage by myself. Jonathan was my support."

"Then pretend. Visualize me standing at the end of the runway, waiting with open arms."

"If I do that, I'd be running to you and would probably fall off the end because you wouldn't be there to stop me." I giggled at the thought.

He was chuckling at my comment. "Angel, I know you can do this. I have faith in you."

"Thanks. When are you leaving for Chicago?"

"Tomorrow morning about eight. I have a lunch meeting scheduled at a restaurant near the airport."

"I hope everything works out okay for you. Show him your charismatic personality. You can talk anyone into anything."

He snorted. I could imagine him rolling his eyes and shaking his head. "Now, who's encouraging who? Thanks. I think everything will work out just fine."

"Well, I hate to do this, but I need to go to sleep. I can't look tired tomorrow. I wish you could be here."

"Me too, Angel."

"I'm going to curl up around the spare pillow and pretend it's you, so I can sleep. Good night. Love you."

"Good night. Love you too." His voice resonated pure affection.

Saturday morning was hectic. Upon arriving at the convention center, I was met by Ms. Deats' assistant and taken to a large open area room sectioned off by racks of clothes. There were a number of young and older ladies (I assumed they were models and their dressers) standing around looking through the racks and talking. I was shown my dressing area and introduced to Lorraine, my dresser. She was an attractive lady, probably in her late thirties, and very nice. Next, she took me to a beautician and left while I waited for my turn. He already knew how my hair was supposed to be styled. It didn't take him long to do my knotted ponytail. While I was with the hairstylist, I received a text from Abbey telling me that they were at the hotel. I texted back that I'd see them after the show. Next, I was off to the cosmetician, where I had to wait again. She applied all kinds of stuff to my face. I had never worn so much makeup in my life, especially eye makeup. I almost didn't recognize myself. Finally, I was sent back to Lorraine to relax for about thirty minutes until it was time to put on my first outfit and get in line.

That morning, I had awakened with some knots in my stomach, but now it was worse. I was becoming a nervous wreck. My butterflies were bombarding my stomach walls. With me wringing my hands and fidgeting, I guess Lorraine could tell I was uptight. She massaged my neck and shoulders, and told me to take some deep breaths and try to clear my mind. She said to think of something pleasant. I thought of Robert and how he used to gently rock me in his arms. I started to sway ever so slightly, side to side, and calmed down.

It was finally time to start dressing, kicking up the calm butterflies. I was wearing black SASSY jeans on each walk. Lorraine helped me put on the brightly-colored abstract-print, butterfly-sleeved blouse that came just to my waistline, my coordinating jewelry, and red stiletto pumps. This was my favorite outfit of the three. I stood in line, number three, and waited eagerly to complete this first walk.

Ms. Deats' part of the show began with her introduction and then the peppy music started. The first model began her walk down the runway—when halfway back, the next model followed. During her walk, she tripped, but managed to stay upright. I heard a mixture of gasps and laughter. My agitated butterflies were now frantic. A shudder raced through me. *Oh please don't let that happen to me.* When she was halfway back, I took a deep breath and strutted out. I posed and then sassy sashayed down the runway with my arms held out from my sides so that the butterfly sleeves fluttered behind me. I kept my eyes above the heads in the audience, looking to the back of the room. When I reached the end of the runway, I did another pose and then turned, whipping my ponytail around, looked back over my shoulder and forward again, and then repeated my strut back to the stage. I turned and posed and then walked off behind the curtain. On my way back I saw Abbey, Garrett, and Jonathan sitting in the front row of seats. As I passed by, I half grinned to acknowledge them.

Rushing back to Lorraine, I started removing my blouse. She met me with my next outfit and started assisting me. This blouse was an oddly shaped wraparound in an abstract design of black and white with accents of hot pink. Again, I had coordinating jewelry and hot pink stiletto pumps. Once changed, I returned to the line a few minutes before it was time to make my second walk. This time as I headed down the runway, I saw what appeared to be a tall male figure enter the back of the room. The bright lights of the runway hampered my view. It was too dark and he was too far away to see any features. I thought of Robert, but it couldn't be him. He was in Chicago. I concentrated on the figure as he moved to the center of the room—facing the end of the runway. Watching him took my mind off the walk and helped to slightly calm my nerves. During my pose, I strained to see him, but couldn't. I spun around and headed back up the runway completing my routine.

For my third run, I wore a dressier accordion-pleated royal-blue blouse, jewelry and royal-blue patent stilettos. I sashayed out, posed and headed down the runway looking at the tall, dark figure. Concentrating on him made my walk easier. I didn't feel uptight. On my way back, I thought, *Thank you, whoever you are.* My part was over. The only thing left was the grand finale parade of models. I waited in my area until that time came, then got in line. As the parade made its way around the runway, I nodded at the dark figure of a man and it appeared that he nodded back.

Ms. Carter met me in the back behind the curtain. Her smile was a mile wide. "You looked *great* out there. Our jeans and your sassy walk are going to bring us a lot of customers. Cha-ching! And lots of money. We had several buyers already contact us about orders right after your first walk." She was glowing with excitement. "Go enjoy yourself with your friends. We won't be leaving until tomorrow around noon. Have fun. You've earned it."

"Thanks. It was much more fun and easier than I thought it would be. See you tomorrow." I headed for my dressing area. Lorraine helped me change back into my jeans and blouse. I thanked her for her help, then rushed out to where my friends were. I thought if the mysterious man was still there, I'd go thank him, but I got sidetracked. Before I could do anything, Jonathan had me around the waist, swung me around, and then planted a kiss, drawing a scowl from Garrett. I pulled away. "Ah. Have you met my friends, Abbey and Garrett?"

"Yes, this one." He pointed at Abbey. "She recognized me and introduced herself. She said you two are best friends."

I hugged Abbey and Garrett. "I've missed you two."

"We've missed you too." Abbey flashed her engagement ring in my face. She looked so happy, and so did Garrett.

I took her hand in mine and looked at her ring. "Abbey, it's beautiful. I'm so happy for you. I can tell you're in love. You're glowing."

She hugged Garrett. "I couldn't be happier." She looked around. "Is Robert here?"

"No, that fell through. He had a last minute meeting with a client."

Jonathan reached down to his chair, picked up a bouquet of long-stemmed red roses, and handed them to me.

"Thank you! They're beautiful. I thought you said you couldn't come. What happened?" I had this strange feeling, like someone was watching me. As Jonathan replied, I looked to the back of the room just as the tall dark figure turned and walked out the door. I had to find out who this mysterious person was. "Excuse me for a minute." I shoved the roses back at Jonathan and took off running for the door the man left through. When I reached the lobby, it was still fairly crowded. On my tiptoes, I craned my neck to look above people's heads to see where he'd gone. I managed to spot the back of a man's head with dark hair, leaving the building. I rushed to catch up, but by the time I arrived outside I lost him. Scanning around, I even checked inside taxis, but he was nowhere in sight. I would've liked to thank him for being my rock.

Disappointed, I walked back through the lobby which had almost cleared. Reaching the door to the stage area, I noticed a single red rose on the floor. I picked it up and stared at it. Was that Robert I saw? That didn't make sense. He would've made sure I knew he was here. So I dismissed the idea and went back to my friends, leaving the rose on a chair.

"Sorry about that. I thought I saw someone I knew, but I guess not." I reached for the roses. "You were explaining how you got to come."

"Are you okay?" Jonathan looked concerned.

I nodded. "I'm fine."

Jonathan proceeded to explain his presence. "Mr. Morrison asked where you were. I told him you were in New York for your first fashion show. He asked why I wasn't there supporting you. I reminded him I was filming according to his schedule. He ordered me to get my butt to New York. So, I caught the first flight here." Jonathan had a way of explaining the simplest situation using his facial expressions to emphasize his words.

I smiled. "Thank you for your support. Remind me to thank Mr. Morrison later."

We all decided to go out and celebrate. The exit doors were surrounded by paparazzi wanting pictures of Jonathan. Every time a door opened all that could be seen were camera flashes. I turned to Garrett and Abbey and warned them of what was about to happen. "Head straight for the limo. Don't stop. It's going to be a zoo out there." We all exited together and aimed for Jonathan's limo. Paparazzi were everywhere, but we managed to make it unscathed.

"Holy smokes! Does that happen all the time?" Abbey's head was bobbing around, looking at the rapid explosions of light from the cameras.

Jonathan closed his eyes and shook his head letting out a long deep breath. "Yeah, all the time. These pictures will be in the gossip rags tomorrow."

Abbey's eyes got big. "Belinda, I want one of those, especially if I'm in one of the pictures with him." She pointed at Jonathan and smiled.

Garrett gave her a sour look. She glared back. "What? It's not every day you meet a popular movie star and are in a picture with him." She snapped her head toward Jonathan. "Would you sign it for me?"

"I'd be glad to. But I think Ms. SASSY over here may have something to do with this as well. You need to get her autograph, too."

I looked at Jonathan, amazed by his disclosure. "Why me? I'm nobody."

He hung his head and laughed in a low snicker. "Who's butt and face is everywhere, Missy? Don't you think we'd be newsworthy for the paid-for-hire photographers?" He gestured with his thumb connecting us as a couple.

I scowled, popping him on the arm. "It's not true!"

"Go with it. Remember we talked about this. Play it up and have fun. Otherwise, you'll go nuts." Heeding his words, I remembered our earlier conversation. I was going to need lots of practice when it came to the tabloids, but for now, I was going to enjoy my friends.

The rest of the evening was wonderful. We all enjoyed visiting at dinner. Back at the hotel, Abbey insisted on staying with me for a girls' night in to catch up on everything that had been going on in our lives. All the rooms were booked in the hotel. Garrett decided to retire for the night, but before he did, he offered Jonathan the extra bed in their room. Jonathan gladly accepted. This arrangement allowed Abbey and me to have our time together, while assuring Garrett that Jonathan would be safe from Abbey's clutches.

Robert was etched in the back of my mind. We had agreed to skip our nightly call because of our busy schedules, but he crept into my thoughts constantly.

Sunday morning the men joined us for breakfast in my room. Abbey was beside herself to be spending all this time with Jonathan. She was starstruck and looking at him like a puppy. Jonathan seemed to get off on her attention and played right into her infatuation. Garrett on the other hand was not that amused. "Oh, when will I get a chance like this again?" she scolded Garrett, who by then had no choice but to accept her harmless flirtations with another man.

It was like pulling teeth to get Abbey away from Jonathan. Finally, she had to relent in order to get to the airport on time. Once again, we all made a beeline from the hotel entrance to the limo, dodging the sea of cameras.

The first stop was Garrett's and Abbey's terminal. There weren't any cameras as I exited the limo with them and said goodbye to my dearest friends. The next stop was the chartered plane terminal where the corporate jet was waiting. Ms. Carter was thrilled when I asked if Jonathan could fly back to Atlanta with us. She was older, but still enjoyed eye candy, and Jonathan was surely that.

***

Dusk was approaching, and I was anxious to talk with Robert. I wondered if he had a hard time winning the client back into his confidence. I decided to send him a text.

Me: Can u talk? Miss u.

He responded immediately: At SL airport. Will call when home. Miss you. Love you.

Me: Love you too. Cant wait to talk to u.

I put on my favorite t-shirt and crawled into bed, lying there holding my cell expecting his call. I answered on the first ring. "Hi, I missed you." I gave him a kiss over the phone. He returned it. Chills ran up my spine as I imagined what it would feel like.

"Belinda, are you there?"

"Sorry, I was just imagining that kiss—how it would feel. I miss them and my reaction."

"Me too, Angel."

"How was your meeting? Was it successful?"

He chuckled. "Slow down. You sure are wound up. Is this twenty questions?"

"I'm just excited to hear your voice. Continue." I loved listening to him talk.

"I think the meeting was sort of successful. He's an older client and I sensed he'd prefer Dad to handle his account. I assured him he had nothing to worry about. I'll probably have to meet with him a few more times." He paused and cleared his throat. "So, tell me about the fashion show."

"I was a nervous wreck at first. But after I completed the first walk, the second one seemed easier. I didn't need to imagine you standing at the end of the runway. There was a tall, dark figure standing in the back of the room. I just focused on him, pretending he was you. You have to be there next time, okay?"

"I'll try. So, who was that tall dark figure?"

"I don't know."

Robert was quiet before his next question. "What happened after the show? What did you and Abbey and Garrett do?"

"Jonathan showed up, so we all went out to eat and visit. Abbey and Garrett got to experience the chaos of the paparazzi." I chuckled. "She didn't care. She was thrilled to meet Jonathan. I think Garrett was a little jealous the way she was flirting with him." I gave a brief description of the impromptu sleeping arrangements. "She showed me her engagement ring. They're so happy and very much in love."

"Sounds like you had a great time without me."

"Robert, it was nice, but *nothing* could replace your being there."

After talking for a couple of hours, Robert suggested that we plug in our cells and put them on speaker. Later during our conversation, I snuggled with a pillow and fell asleep. It was one of our phone sleepovers and the closest thing

I had to being with him all night. In the morning, I'd wake up to the sound of his voice. "Belinda, are you still there. Angel, it's time to wake up." We'd have breakfast, get ready and dress, then hang up when it was time for work. Such would be our lives until we could meet in Texas in two long weeks.

***

The fashion show had been a huge success. There were going to be more commercials and ads of me posing for the two companies. The details of the contracts were being ironed out. Mr. Johnson explained I had to be present and available during the negotiations. In short, I was the signature model for Every Body Jeans Manufacturing Company with an exclusive side contract with Fashion Designs by JLDeats. Once an agreement was reached, my life would become extremely busy in a short time.

As promised, Robert and I talked every night and sometimes slept together via phone. Our relationship was more solid than it had ever been. I was learning so much and my self-confidence was much stronger. Now coming into my own, I no longer felt pressured about our relationship, but saw myself on a more equal basis with Robert. He was still *My Mister Wonderful*, but his responses to me were different. He was more open about how he felt about decisions and surprisingly, I opened up to him. This was a new approach— mutual participation. It was working very well and it was marvelous.

CHAPTER 33

ROBERT HAD PLANNED to pick me up at the airport and drive us to the fraternity homecoming party. But, a last minute business meeting changed our plans. He didn't know how long it would last, so he suggested I should go without him. I made him promise to meet me there.

Saturday morning I flew into Hobby Airport, then caught a taxi to Mrs. Foster's boarding house for my car and headed for the college. After checking into our room about two hours before the party, I began preparing—wanting to look sexy and perfect for Robert. I wore a pair of my SASSY jeans and a pale blue, deep V-neck sweater. I left my hair down, parted on the side, the way he liked it.

I was ready, but it was too soon to leave. Wanting to hear his voice, I lay on the bed and thought about calling him, but knew it might interrupt his meeting and cause a delay in his arrival. My anxiety level was as high as it had ever been. It seemed like years since I was able to feel Robert. I closed my eyes and imagined his strong protective arms around me. Just thinking about him made me a nervous wreck, so I decided to leave early and drive around the campus before heading for the party.

As I drove down the long driveway to the frat house, I reminisced about all the good times we'd spent there. It made me wish he'd be standing with open arms in the doorway. I missed him.

On the front porch, I took a deep breath and knocked before entering. Immediately several of the brothers yelled, "Belinda, the *SASSY GAL* is here!" They rushed over to hug me. I was surrounded by people all talking at once. It was a regular mob scene, but I was getting used to this and learning to handle it.

I was managing the group when Abbey and Garrett arrived shortly after me. Excusing myself from the remaining frat brothers, I hurried over to hug them. "Good to see you again. We need to make sure we keep getting together like this. You still okay?"

"We're doing great. I love living with him." Abbey whipped her head around. "Where's Robert?"

"Another last-minute business meeting. He said he'd be here as soon as he can. I hope it's not too late. I can't wait to see him."

Garrett interrupted our conversation by placing his arm around his soon-to-be wife and my best friend. "Why are you always with that Morse guy? Everywhere I look, I see you and him on the front page of the tabloids and magazines." He grimaced for my benefit, but gave Abbey a scowl of disgust, attempting to make his point.

"Like I explained at the fashion show, we're just friends. Don't believe those tabloids. They're just assumptions, not true. Besides, Robert knows all about my relationship with Jonathan and understands." I poked Garrett on his chest with my finger. "So butt out, buddy." I smirked at him.

My eyes roamed about the room. Something on the wall next to the front door caught my attention. I grabbed the first brother who was walking by and pointed at a large poster of one of my SASSY advertisements. "Where did you get that?"

"Brian liked that ad and had it enlarged. He wrote DELT above SASSY." Paul handed me a black marker. "Would you sign it?"

"Sure." I wrote, *Love you all, Belinda.*

Music started playing. Paul grasped my hand and led me into the gyrating crowd. We were on our third dance when I saw Declan walk in alone and survey the room. When he recognized me, he rushed right over and politely asked to cut in. Paul stepped back. With a gigantic smile on his face, he pulled me close and gave me a big hug. "I was disappointed when I got back to school and found out that you'd left." He took a step back, just far enough to look me over. "Sooo, now you're a model and dating movie stars. I like those commercials. You're perfect for that jeans company." He gave me a nod of approval. He took my hand, and with a snap, I was back against him dancing.

"Thanks, I've enjoyed my new occupation so far. But I miss everyone here. It's lonely in Atlanta, and Jonathan Morse is only a good friend who has helped me through it."

"Sooo. What about your husband? Are you getting a divorce?" He glanced around the room. "I don't see him here."

"No divorce. We're getting back together. He's going to meet me here tonight." I noticed a hint of disappointment on his face before he responded back to me.

"That's good. I'm glad you're happy." He hugged me as the song ended.

In silence, we stood on the dance floor. He was looking down. I was about to thank him and move on when another song came on. He lifted his head displaying a massive grin. "Would you like to dance again?"

Holding his hand out for me, I took it. "Sure." It was a fast song and I worked off some tension with my moves, thinking about Robert.

When the song ended, Garrett walked over to us and asked if we'd be interested in a game of pool. He winked at me and I knew exactly what he was thinking. So I played along. I impishly smiled at Declan. "Do you play pool?"

"Yes, but it's been awhile."

I turned toward Garrett making sure my hair shielded my face from Declan before I winked. "You're on."

Garrett racked up the balls, then handed Declan a cue stick, and told him to break. He sank three balls. Garrett sank three. Now it was my turn. Taking small deliberate steps around the table, I contemplated my best shot. I sank one, then six more and had two balls left. I was setting up my next strike when I heard, "You better watch out for her. She's a pool shark." My concentration was broken by the voice.

I froze. My heart started to race. Standing on my tiptoes, I looked around and caught a glimpse of Robert moving across the back of the room. I dropped my cue stick and pushed my way through the crowd, rushing toward him. When I broke through, I was beaming with excitement at the thought of seeing him, gazing into his hypnotic, clear blue eyes, and feeling his touch. My smile put a smile on his gorgeous face and a glint in his eyes. Leaping into his outstretched arms, I wrapped my arms around his neck and my legs around his waist, almost knocking us both over. I planted a kiss on his waiting lips. I didn't just quiver, a feeling I'd missed, I trembled all over as I tightened my wrap around him. I was lost in him and the moment.

He returned the feelings by squeezing me tight to him. We kissed each other fast and frequently, with short and long kisses. Robert reached for my hair. We might never have stopped if it wasn't for the chanting of the other partygoers. It started out low and whispered then rose to an ear splitting shout, "Get a room!" It was repeated over and over.

We both looked around, somewhat embarrassed. Robert may have been more cavalier about what had just happened, but we hadn't seen each other in months. We were on the verge of losing control.

"Damn you feel good! I've missed you so much." Tightening his grip, he carried me to the back porch and set me down. "We need to talk." With my hand in his, he led me out into the starlit night. "It will be quieter, more private out here." We walked across the yard to a wooden bench sitting under a large oak tree. There on the bench was my treasure box, a single red rose lying across the top. Attached to the rose was a note with little hand drawn hearts that read, ***To Our New Beginning!***

In astonishment, I gazed at his face. He just shrugged his shoulders with that appealing smile across his face. I sat on the bench clutching my gifts as tears flowed. He gently wiped away the droplets. "Why are you crying?" His brows drew together over his warm eyes as he sat next to me.

"I'm just so glad to see you. I've missed you so much." I pulled myself across his lap, then wrapped an arm around the back of his neck and laid my head against his shoulder. He wound his arms around me. I felt at home in his arms again. "This is where I want to be—where I'm supposed to be—with you....And I've realized I don't want to be without you. I gave you my heart and you still have it. A little trampled on, but I still love you. I don't want to live without you in my life."

He hugged me tight to him and kissed my forehead as I experienced a faint shiver. "Me either. I'm so sorry I made you feel unwanted. It wasn't your fault. It was all mine. Can you ever forgive me?" He paused and stared into my eyes before he continued talking. "I don't know what came over me. I've loved you from the first moment I saw you. It took me by surprise. I liked the way my life was—carefree. But I couldn't stop thinking about you—wanting you. Then I let that class take me away from you. The stress really affected me. The group was relying on me to get them through it. But it cost me you. And then there was Declan. I always saw you with him in the Cave."

I cut in. "I went there to see you, but you weren't there. So I talked to him."

"The two empty cups in my car?"

"I did that to get your attention. You came home that night," I reminded him. "I was desperate to see you. I felt I was losing you." I sighed. "I was so lonely and confused. I didn't know what I did to drive you away."

Robert rested his head against mine. "I'm sorry I let that class come between us. And then seeing you with Declan...I started wondering if I'd rushed you into marriage."

With both arms wrapped around his neck, I pulled my body close to his. "I only wanted to be with you and still do. I'm in love with you—only you. My insecurities kept screwing everything up. Why do you put up with me?" I closed my eyes waiting for his response.

He lifted my chin so that he could look me in the eyes. "Because, I'm in love with you." He kissed me long and deep. When I quivered, he pulled away and grinned. "I missed that." He leaned his head against mine. "I'm so glad to be away from here." He sounded relieved.

"All the temptations?"

"No, I wasn't tempted. I had you. Because of all the problems it caused for us." He hugged me tight to him and buried his face in my hair. He raised his head. "I've worked out a solution so we can be together."

I turned and stared at him. "How?"

Gazing into my eyes, he explained his plan. "Dad is hiring Garrett when he graduates to help run the business when I'm out of town with you. I can work with Garrett via cell phone and the internet."

"I don't want to take you from your obligations. Your parents are counting on you."

"This will work. They would do anything to help us get back together. Angel, every time I saw your picture in the tabloids, the magazines, even your commercials, I looked for your wedding band. Seeing it still on your finger gave me hope." He held up his left hand to show me his ring. "My wedding band has never left my finger either. And neither has this." He pulled on a chain around his neck, lifting out my engagement ring. "It has been hanging close to my heart ever since you left. Angel, I will always want you. Never doubt my love for you."

"I will always want you, too. But, you deserted me at school."

"We deserted each other."

"I thought I had lost you. Especially after watching you make out with Erin. I don't even want to think about it now." I closed my eyes, trying to erase that unpleasant image from my mind.

"I now know how you felt seeing me kissing Erin. I swear these lips will never again touch anyone's but yours." He gave me a sincere look.

"What?" I was shocked.

"I saw Jonathan kiss you at the fashion show. I...I didn't like it."

"How?"

Before he continued his explanation, I felt him tighten his arms around me as he rested his head against mine. "I was there. I came to the fashion show. I was your tall dark figure in the back of the room."

"So that was you? Why didn't you tell me?"

"After the show, I noticed Abbey and Garrett and was headed their way when I saw your tabloid friend next to them. I stopped when you appeared and he swung you around then kissed you. You looked so happy. Then he handed you that bouquet of roses. I didn't want to interfere. I wasn't supposed to be there, so I left." He shrugged his shoulders looking sad. "But seeing how you looked with him, it tore me up."

"Robert, I asked him a while back, before I asked you. He told me he couldn't come. I didn't know he was going to show up. He surprised me. That seat next to Abbey and Garrett was yours. I wanted you there, not him....Look who misunderstood and left this time." I kissed his neck. "I sensed the guy in the back of the room was watching me. I saw him leave and chased after him to see who he was, but I lost him. I wanted to thank him for helping me make it through the fashion show. I felt relaxed on the runway looking at him." I combed my fingers through his hair as my eyes roamed his face, settling on his eyes. I smiled. "I should've known it was you, but I couldn't see any features because of the lighting and distance."

"When you nodded, I wondered if you recognized me. But you made no attempt to head my way. Instead, you headed for Abbey, Garrett, and him."

A thought came to me. "You dropped the rose I found?"

"I saw the roses he gave you, so I just dropped it and left." He sounded jealous and hurt. "You know he wants you."

"I know, but I don't want him and he knows it. He'll have to live with that fact...and so will you." I gazed at him. "I gave *you* my heart." I kissed Robert on the cheek and changed the subject. That was enough about Jonathan. "How were you able to be there? What about your meeting?" He resisted the change and attempted to keep the conversation on Jonathan. Placing my finger on his lips and in a slow motion, I shook my head. "No more about Jonathan."

"Okay...Mr. Reynolds, my client, asked me about you, my wife. I told him you were in New York in your first fashion show. He told me to go be with you—that we could have this meeting later, on Sunday or when he returned from his trip. I wanted to surprise you. That's why I didn't let you know I was coming. It didn't dawn on me that Jonathan would be there. I guess I shouldn't have let that bother me."

"You're right, it shouldn't have." I delayed my next response long enough to let the point sink in. "Look, I'm sorry your surprise was messed up. I wish you would've confronted me, and then we could've spent that time together. To tell the truth, I'm kind of mad at myself." Robert looked at me with interest. "I was going to head straight for the back of the room after the show to see who the dark figure was, but I let myself get sidetracked and missed you." I looked at him perplexed. "Why didn't you tell me on the phone?"

He took a deep breath before he started his explanation. "I wanted to tell you, but I didn't want to upset you. I didn't want anything to interfere with our reunion. Besides, this was something that needed to be said in person. I needed to see your reactions and feel them." He gripped me tighter. "I know now, because of how you feel, you still love me." His fabulous eyes concentrated on mine.

I tightened my hold around his neck pulling him close to my lips, longing for his kiss. Knowing what it would do to both of us, I couldn't wait any longer. I crushed my lips to his, and shuddered.

Responding to my reactions, he gently placed his hands on my shoulders and pulled me from his lips. Our breathing was heavy. "Let's go. We can continue this at the hotel. I've missed holding you at night...and loving you." He was gazing into my eyes.

"Okay. But wouldn't it be rude if we left now?"

He was pulling me behind him as he walked across the yard when he stopped dead in his tracks. "Who cares!" I looked at him, surprised. I only had a brief moment before he picked me up in his arms. He continued his pace, like a man driven, bypassing the house as he headed for the cars. "You can call Abbey later to fill her in. For the next few days you'll have other things to keep you busy."

In the hotel elevator, he kissed me with such ardor that I trembled and my legs gave out under me. Thank goodness he was holding me tight as I went limp in his arms. When we reached our floor, he picked me up and carried me to our room. I somehow managed to unlock and open the door. We almost didn't make it to the bed. Clothes miraculously disappeared in seconds as our hands explored each other's body. Our kisses were wild as we fulfilled our desires. The night was spectacular, making up for lost time.

Six thirty Sunday morning I awoke before Robert. Seeking to surprise him, I decided to go for our favorite coffee and bagels from the bakery. I thought I'd be able to make it back before he woke up. I was ready to go, then decided I should leave a note. I wrote, *Back soon, Love Belinda.*

I drove straight to the bakery and bought two coffees and four blueberry bagels, his favorites. Having accomplished my mission, I drove to the intersection. The traffic light was red and seemed to take forever to change. I was sure Robert would be up by now. When the light turned green, I drove into the intersection, only to hear squealing tires, a blaring horn and the shifting of gears. Looking out the passenger window in the direction of the sound, everything seemed to be moving in slow motion as I watched the grill of a semi come closer to my car, just before it collided with me. Like a ragdoll, I felt my body being whipped about before slamming into the driver's side door. A searing pain shot though my body as my head smashed the glass and my arm melded into the door. There was a sharp pain on the side of my head followed by something warm running down my face. The horrifying sound of crushing metal filled the air as everything around me went black.

CHAPTER 34

I KNEW MY eyes were open, but the light was so bright I couldn't see anything. The light hurt. So I closed them again. I tried to lift my arms to rub my eyes, but they wouldn't move.

I heard a faint voice in the distance. "She's waking up!" Moments later, a different voice, much louder than the first, kept repeating my name. "Belinda! Belinda!" I heard the louder voice again. "Go get the doctor." This is when I realized I was in a hospital.

I must've blacked out. This time, when I opened my eyes, the light was much dimmer. With limited eye movement, I looked around, observing more of my surroundings. I could see a clock on the wall across from my bed. It read four o'clock, but was that morning or afternoon? I couldn't see any windows. I tried to move my head, but I couldn't. Why couldn't I move? I tried to call out for help—nothing came out of my mouth. I heard a voice, a familiar one—it was my mother. She leaned into my field of vision and told me not to try to move, the doctor was on his way. I could feel her lift my hand and hold it. With all the strength I could gather, I managed to stroke her hand with one finger. Tears began to run down her face. I wanted to tell her I was okay and everything would be fine, but I couldn't talk to her. I wanted to ask her where Robert was. I needed to know he understood I was alive. Surely someone called him to let him know I was in the hospital. I again drifted out of consciousness.

I opened my eyes to the same dim light. This time the clock said six. There was no way of knowing if it was morning, evening, or what day it was. Hearing whispering nearby, I tried to turn my head and I did. So I turned it in the other direction, just to see if I could. I did! I tried to lift my arms. This time I could move my hands a little bit. They felt heavy, as if they weren't part of my body.

Two men approached my bed. One stood on either side of me. The one with the white coat introduced himself. "Hello Belinda, I'm Dr. Shane Covington, your neurologist. This is Dr. Martin Rosen, your psychologist." *Psychologist?* Why did I need a psychologist? I understood a neurologist but...this didn't make sense. Dr. Covington continued. "We have you under sedation. That's why you're having difficulty moving or talking right now. As we wake you up, you'll have many questions. Things may be confusing at first, so that's why Dr. Rosen is here. He'll help answer all your questions and readjust." *Readjust to what?* I wanted answers now—not a few days from now. I somehow managed to grab the wrist of the doctor in the white coat. He looked surprised. His eyes widened as he looked down at my grip. I could feel his hand cover mine. His eyes softened. "Okay, this is enough for now. The nurse is going to give you something to put you back to sleep. The next time you wake up, we should be able to talk."

Wanting him to understand I needed to stay awake, I moved my head side to side. I tightened my grip on his wrist. From the far reaches of some unknown place, I heard a sound resonate in an almost animalistic tone. It was guttural, a growl. I realized the sound was my voice. I was screaming "No!" I wanted to see Robert.

The sedative Dr. Covington gave me did the trick. I slept. This time when I opened my eyes, the clock read ten. There were no electric lights on, yet the left side of the room was illuminated. Turning my head toward it, I could see a window. It was sunlight. Okay, it was ten o'clock in the morning. I didn't know how long I'd been asleep.

I faintly remembered my mother and, I think, Dr. Covington talking about me during one of the times I was supposed to be sleeping. He was explaining something to her. I didn't understand what he was saying. I was confused. I tried to move my arms, but all that moved were my hands. So, I tried my toes and was able to wiggle them. Then I fell back asleep.

Now the clock said seven. There was light from the window, so I knew it was daylight but not what day it was or how long I had been out this time. I tried to lift my arms. I raised them off the bed, but not enough to see them. They felt so heavy, as if they were made of lead. A nurse approached my bed. "Relax. Things will start coming back." She opened each eye and checked it with a small flashlight. The light hurt my eyes. She told me the date, month, and year. I tried to talk to her. The only thing that came out was mumbled syllables. What was going on? I should be waking up. Why was I being drugged? Sleep overcame me again.

My mind was very foggy. As I looked around the room, the memory of being in a hospital came to me. This time the light was bright from the ceiling fixture. I closed my eyes and did a mental check of what I knew. I was in the hospital. I couldn't talk. I was having trouble moving.

I opened my eyes again. The bright light hurt. I lifted my hands to shield my face. To my surprise, I could move. It felt good, but when I took my hands away, I caught a glimpse of my arms. These *couldn't* be my arms. They were pale and horribly thin. They had very little muscle mass. My arms were well-shaped and strong. They had more color than these. Yet these foreign arms were attached to my shoulders. I could move them at will. My mounting horror was interrupted when the door opened and the two men came into my room, followed by a nurse. The one who called himself Dr. Covington had a concerned look on his face. I guess he could see the horror on mine. He rushed over to the bed and took my hands, cradling them. Something was terribly wrong. My eyes started to fill with tears.

"Okay, we're going to start from the beginning." He sat on the side of the bed. "Can you talk?"

I opened my mouth and to my surprise words came out. "Yes...Yes I can." I looked over at Dr. Rosen. He was writing in a notebook.

"Dr. Rosen is just taking notes for this session. He'll be doing that frequently....What do you remember last?"

Struggling to form the words, I answered. "I...got...up...left a note...for Robert." It was all I could get out because I fell back asleep again.

The next time I awoke, my mother was standing beside my bed. "What happened to me? Where's Robert?" That was all the energy I had before I drifted away.

"Belinda, wake up." I heard a male voice that sounded like Robert. *Finally!* I could feel myself become elated with the thought, but something wasn't right. It wasn't Robert's voice. I opened my eyes and there stood the two white-coated men. "Belinda, we need to talk." I fought to focus as I woke up. "Okay, I need you to tell me the last thing you remember."

Struggling, I answered. "I was with Robert. I left him a note that I was running an errand and would be right back. I was driving to our favorite bakery to pick up breakfast. Blueberry bagels are Robert's favorite." The memory of Robert sleeping came back and made me smile. I was getting lost in my thoughts of him.

Dr. Covington interrupted. "What happened next?"

I snapped my gaze back to his face and became more serious. "I paid and headed back, but when I drove into the intersection, a big truck seemed to come out of nowhere." I paused with the memory that filled my head. "It hit me."

"Where were you?"

"At college." I looked over at Dr. Rosen who was writing everything that was being said. He made me uncomfortable, so I looked back at Dr. Covington. "Does Robert know I'm alright? Why isn't he here with me?" My mind started jumping to conclusions.

Dr. Covington's gaze intensified as he asked his question. "Belinda…Who is Robert?"

Waiting for my response, Dr. Rosen stopped writing in his notebook. He didn't look at me. He simply lifted the pen from the pad. "Robert is my husband." With my answer, Dr. Rosen again began to write in his notebook. What did I say that had him so interested?

"Can we talk about something else right now?"

"No!" I scowled at him. "What is more important than my husband knowing I'm okay?"

Dr. Covington didn't respond. He simply changed the subject. "What year did you graduate from college?"

His question baffled me. "I didn't finish. I became a model." Dr. Covington looked very surprised.

My horrible thin arm came into view. I reached out with my other arm, in the same condition, to touch the first. I looked at the doctor. "What happened to my arms?" I stretched them out in front of me as far as my strength would allow. "This doesn't happen in a week." I looked at him as my eyes flooded with tears.

He glanced at Dr. Rosen who had stopped writing. Turning his attention back to me, he took a deep breath before starting. "You had a car accident. You were hit by a semi, but it didn't happen last week…it happened six months ago. Belinda, you've been in a coma for six months. That's why you're so thin. You haven't been using your muscles. They atrophy without use."

There was silence. I didn't know what to say as I studied my arms. Running my fingers over my face, I could feel my cheekbones were now more pronounced. I reached for my hair, which was wadded up in a makeshift bun on top of my head. It felt dirty and gnarled. "Your hair had to be cut. The nurses did the best they could to take care of it….Look, Dr. Rosen and I will be back later this evening. For now I'm going to put you back to sleep."

Panicked, I looked at him. "No, you can't. I have a million questions. There are things I need to sort out."

He picked up my hand ever so gently. I was beginning to like Dr. Covington. He seemed so understanding and had a sense of when I needed to be consoled. There was a patting on my hand. "I promise you, we'll give you all the time you need to find the answers you're looking for. Right now your mind needs to rest. You need time to process this new information. Your brain needs time to wake up as well."

I was starting to trust this man in the white coat. "Okay, only if you promise." He motioned to the nurse who had been standing behind him to give me the medication. As I drifted off, the words spilled out. "What about Robert?"

Waking up, I turned to see the only light in the room came from a small lamp on a desk that a nurse was seated at. "Is Dr. Covington here?"

She stopped writing and looked in my direction. With a huge smile on her face, she stood and walked toward the bed. She was a slender woman, about my age, with shoulder-length brunette hair. Her friendly welcoming face made me feel safe. "Hi Belinda, I'm Heather Brady. I've been one of your night nurses since you were admitted. You lie there nice and quiet, and I'll go tell the doctors you're awake. I'll be right back."

A few minutes later Heather and the two doctors returned.

Dr. Covington stood at the side of my bed. "I promised I'd be back."

I smiled and pointed to the other doctor, the psychologist. "When does this one stop writing and start talking?"

"She has a wit about her. Dr. Rosen steps in when I'm done. For now he just takes notes. I guarantee he will become well acquainted with you very soon because you'll need help piecing together your memory." Dr. Shane Covington flashed me a huge captivating smile. In the dim lamp light, I was noticing him for the first time. He looked to be about thirty-five years old and was attractive with a boyish manner about him. His sandy-colored hair was tousled about the top of his head, but styled that way. He was neatly dressed with a starched, collared shirt and tie covered by the white lab coat that proudly displayed his name and title in blue thread across the breast pocket. I could tell he kept himself in good shape. His lab coat fit him like a well-tailored suit. On his left ring finger was a plain gold band.

Dr. Rosen looked the opposite. He was casually dressed, had beard stubble, and his hair was a mess. It looked like he hadn't combed it in a week. There wasn't a wedding band and I could understand why. I imagined his house being as untidy as he was. Most likely, his life was the same.

"Belinda, let's get started." Dr. Covington pulled up a chair. "Do you remember anything before the accident?"

"I think so."

"Can you tell us?" He was encouraging more conversation.

"Oh, I've been having the time of my life." I smiled as my thoughts rushed back to Robert and our many intimate encounters. I was embarrassed and could feel myself blushing. "I met the most wonderful man. His name is Robert Pennington." I stopped for a moment. "I can truly and with all honesty say, he is my...my soul mate." I reached over and fingered the gold band on his hand. "Do you love your wife?"

"We're trying to find out about you, Belinda. How I feel about my wife is not important." He was more reserved, as if his privacy was being invaded.

"No, it is important. If you truly love your wife, then you will understand how I feel about my husband." I paused while I tried to think of the words to explain my relationship with Robert. "My husband is the most important person in my life....He is my other half....It's like we reached beyond our own limited existence and found each other. We have this irresistible connection between us that is so strong. I'd gladly give my life for him."

Dr. Covington didn't respond. His eyes met mine and, for the first time, I could see they were a dark brown. They made him look intense as he just stared and studied me.

From the opposite side of the bed, I heard a soft, mousy voice. "Shane...Shane, we need to keep going."

I turned my head in shock. "It speaks!" My tone was sharp because my exchange with Dr. Covington was interrupted. I didn't want anything to do with "The Other Doctor." I was not impressed by him.

"Belinda."

I turned back to Dr. Covington.

"When did you meet Robert?" He furrowed his brow.

"In the spring semester, last April. Why?"

"Belinda." He picked up my hand as he looked at me with intense eyes. "It's now the end of September. How long have you been in a coma?"

At first, his question confused me. I'd been in a coma for the past six months. He knew the answer to his question better than I did....Then I stopped and froze...it hit me. I squeezed his hand as tight as I could. My breathing became irregular as an ache hit me where my heart dwelt. The pain of my revelation was so intense, I almost stopped breathing. Tears filled my eyes as they locked onto his. I shut them as I maintained my firm grip on the doctor's hand. Memories started rushing into my head like waves crashing against a rocky shore. I was an art teacher. I had dated Matt all through college. After we graduated, he left to take a job in California in late September. He gave me Beau before he left. Abbey and Garrett were my best friends and should be married now. I had a car accident leaving Abbey's bridal shower. Taking short shallow breaths, I felt the pain over my heart grow in intensity. *"Robert doesn't exist!"* I shouted out between the sobs. "He's only in my head and in my heart." I wished I had never awakened. If I'd stayed in the coma, Robert would still be real. I couldn't talk for crying so hard. My shoulders heaved as I sobbed. Dr. Covington never let go. He sat holding my hand, offering what support he could, while I experienced some of the most terrifying moments of my life. I realized that I'd just lost my beloved Robert.

My sobbing must've lasted five minutes. The psychologist handed me some tissue and I dried my eyes. I felt dead as I stared into space. My torment was temporarily relieved when Dr. Covington interrupted. "Belinda, we're going to put you back to sleep. Tomorrow is going to be a busy day. Your work with Dr. Rosen is going to start. It won't be easy. You've had multiple losses. It'll take time, but I'm sure you'll overcome this. In the morning, my job will be to put you in touch with a physical therapist. We have to start working on those muscles to get you back into shape. A nutritionist will also come to see you and we'll need to do a swallow test. If you pass that, we'll start to feed you real food. Since the accident, we've been feeding you through that tube that goes into your stomach." He paused from his clinical explanation. "I'm sorry about Robert." I looked at him wide-eyed and surprised. I could swear I saw light tears well in his eyes. He was softer, less reserved. "If I lost my wife, my life would end." He stiffened to regain his composure. "We'll see you in the morning. I'm going to call your parents. I'd like someone you're close to, to stay with you twenty-four hours a day. It will help you reconnect with your 'New Reality.'" I nodded my head to let him know I understood his instructions and concern.

Heather came in and asked if there was anything I needed. What I needed no one would ever be able to provide. Robert was gone in my "New Reality," as Dr. Covington coined it, but I hoped I could find him in my dreams. Welcoming the sedative this time, I wanted to stop the pain and if Robert was a dream maybe I could find him again in sleep.

My mother and Abbey, at my bedside, were the first things I saw as I woke up. Both had grins from ear to ear, looking like Cheshire cats. "Hi, guys. Long time no see," I whispered in my sleepy state.

"Oh sweetie. I missed you so much. Welcome back." My mother started to cry. She turned away from the bed to find a tissue and to compose herself.

"How much do you remember?" Abbey took a seat on the bed next to me.

"Enough to know I missed your wedding. Never a bride and now, never a maid of honor."

Her face lit up and her smile became more exaggerated as she realized I was back. Well, at least part of me was. Due to my debilitated physical state, the simplest task was difficult. I couldn't even sit up without support.

Also there was my mental state. There were things that happened before the real accident that I had trouble remembering. I guess the psychologist was going to be needed after all. Every time I let my mind wander back to Robert, a heaviness came over me.

I was glad Abbey was here. I could always talk to her. She might know if Robert was a real person I met that I didn't remember right now. Maybe he was someone I had a crush on in college. I had so many questions that needed to be answered, and prayed Abbey could help.

"Belinda, you're so preoccupied. What are you thinking about?"

"I'm still feeling the effects of the sedation. I'll be more awake soon." I didn't want to say anything about Robert in front of my mom. I'd have time to talk to Abbey later.

"Your mom and I will be taking turns staying with you for a while," Abbey said in her usual upbeat voice.

"Don't you have to work? You graduated with me and have a job...right?"

She laughed. "Yeah, I have a job. I'm Mrs. Garrett Barnett. Okay, I'm also an art teacher. I'm taking a leave of absence until you don't need me anymore. I'll be on the night shift. I figured that way it would be like old times. Kinda like girls' night in, but without the booze for now. We might be able to get some singing in. That is if the nurses don't quiet us down."

"Sounds good to me! Anything would be a diversion. Maybe you can help me do something with my hair....Wait a minute, do you have a mirror? I want to see what I look like."

My mother and Abbey exchanged a concerned look. "Ah, Belinda, Dr. Rosen asked us not to let you look at yourself yet. He wants to be here." My mother said it softly as if her tone of voice would make me less worried.

Now I was scared. "Did my face get scarred in the accident? Was I burned or disfigured?" My fingers frantically searched my face.

Both of them reached for my hands saying in unison, "No! No! Nothing like that."

"Then what?" I darted my eyes back and forth to each of their faces.

"Sweetie, you're just thin. You've lost a lot of weight....The way Dr. Rosen explained it was...you need time to make adjustments. Your brain needs time to register these changes....He wanted to be here so you could talk with him. He saw how upset you were last night."

I looked at my mother. "He asked you about Robert, didn't he?"

Now mom was sitting on the bed. "Yes he did." She was very serious and, I could tell, concerned.

I saw this as an opportunity to have some questions answered. I looked at both of them. "Well, do either of you know him or do you have any idea how I could know him?" Putting their heads down, they wouldn't answer me. I picked up Abbey's hand. Tears were running down my face. "If either of you can help me, if either of you want to help me, I need to know. This guy was so real. I can remember how he felt. How I felt when he touched me. I was so connected to him. I'm still connected to him….I'm not crazy."

They didn't have the opportunity to answer me. The psychologist walked in and interrupted. "Good morning, Ms. Davies. How are you feeling?"

"How do you think I'm feeling?" I was being as sarcastic as I could. I didn't like this shrink. He was always such a mess.

"She asked us to give her a mirror. She wanted to take a look." My mom offered me up like a sacrificial lamb.

"Okay, I'll go get one so you can have a look." He left the room and returned in a very short time. He placed it face down on the bedside table so I couldn't see the reflective side. "Before I let you take a look, we need to talk. You've changed in the past six months…but it's nothing that can't be reversed. When you start eating you'll start gaining weight. With exercise, your muscle mass will return. That, along with the other therapies you'll receive, should help greatly. Now it's going to be your job to recuperate back to the Belinda you know….Belinda, no one ever expected you to wake up. We all believed you'd be in a vegetative state for the rest of your short life. You need to know you have a second chance here. From now on, the time after you woke up will be referred to as your 'New Reality.'"

My mind wandered back to my life with Robert. I had my second chance when we decided to make our marriage work. No, *Dr. Psychologist*, I would have gladly stayed asleep for however long my life was, as long as I could be with Robert. He was my second chance and now I'd lost him. "Okay. Now can I have a look?"

He turned the mirror over and handed it to me. It was small enough for my weak hands to hold yet big enough for me to see the severity of my affliction. I stared at my reflection. The person staring back looked like me in some ways. I still had striking blue eyes, but now they were sunken. My cheeks were hollowed. My skin color was paler. My long flowing hair was matted and piled on my head with rubber bands. There was a scar at the small hollow place in my throat, I assumed from a tracheotomy. I rubbed my fingers over it, almost in disbelief. I couldn't stop staring. I looked like a concentration camp survivor.

"Belinda, do you have anything to say. Do you want to talk about how you look?" Dr. Rosen waited patiently for my response.

My practical side kicked in. I looked at him. "Yeah, when can I wash my hair and start my physical therapy." I was determined to keep Dr. Rosen from knowing my motivation, but in my heart, I decided Robert was real and he wasn't going to see me like this.

***

My determination to get stronger paid off. After two months of therapy and the right foods, my treatment team was talking about discharge. I had put on at least ten pounds and was walking by myself. I could shower and dress myself.

Abbey was a dream come true, as she had helped me do something with my hair. She had managed to straighten out the gnarled mess. My hair had lost its body due to nutritional deficiencies, but I still had some length on it. It came to below my shoulders, a good four inches shorter than before the accident. I was grateful no one had decided to cut it all off. I later learned my mother had insisted it be trimmed, not cut. She wanted me to wake up with long hair—never giving up hope.

During one of our talks, my mother told me how hard it was for my father and her to take me off the respirator. My parents agreed I'd either breathe on my own or I'd die. They risked the chance of losing their only child. Then again, it wasn't like I was alive to them. When the time came for the machine to be turned off, fortunately, I started breathing. My mom took this as a sign that I'd be back. She has always been in my corner, even on the brink of death.

So here I was, breezing through physical therapy. I was told if I continued at this rate, I'd find myself almost back to where I was before the first accident, the real accident. I'd never recover one hundred percent, but it would be very close and the loss would be negligible. In short, I could live a long healthy life. Not only could it be a good life, it would be a rich one. My parents received a huge settlement from the trucking firm responsible for my accident. No one knew if I'd ever awaken, so a large sum was set aside in a trust to take care of me for the rest of my life, however long that might be. Since I awoke, and seemed to be on the road to recovery, the remaining funds were mine, and they were substantial. It was discovered that the driver who hit me at the intersection of Highway 6 and the Southwest Freeway was smoking weed. The trucking firm knew about their driver's recreational diversion, but needed someone to deliver a load that fateful Sunday evening, the night of Abbey's wedding shower. I just happened to be in the wrong place at the wrong time. If I'd entered the intersection two seconds earlier, I would've never met Robert and my life would've never changed.

With a few more pounds, I'd look as good as my pre-accident self. My body was more shapely and toned from all the exercising and proper eating. In my "Old Reality" and "Dream State," the ways I now referred to my past lives, I never worried about exercising or what I ate. In my "Dream State," I was a natural beauty. My "New Reality," my life right now, was much different. I had to work hard to get back to my goal image. When I found Robert, he was going to see me as a knockout.

***

Dr. Rosen and I met three times a week. I had started out on the wrong foot with him. He had helped me more than I could've ever imagined. With his help, I was working through the insecurities I experienced during my high school years. It seems everything I knew in my "Old Reality," before the real accident, never changed. I'd managed to intertwine that reality with how I wished my life really was in the "Dream State." I fantasized how I would have liked it to be. I figured out from my sessions with Dr. Rosen that my love for Robert was perfect and the problems we had were created from my real feelings or lack of confidence. It seemed I couldn't convince myself that someone like Robert could be in love with me. I kept sabotaging our relationship.

In my "New Reality," I was more settled with who I was and was becoming. My inner self and my "Monster" were at peace. I felt, with the continued help of Dr. Rosen, I'd be saying goodbye to my "Monster" forever.

However, despite all his attempts to "cure" my delusion about Robert, I wouldn't let go. He knew I was determined to keep Robert as a real person in my "New Reality" and that I believed I'd find him again. So in our last session before my discharge, he had finally had it with me, and told me so. "Belinda, you know as long as you hang on to this delusion, I can't say you're alright." Shaking his head, he crossed his arms over his chest.

By now I was very comfortable with this man and felt I could discuss anything with him. "I'll never understand. A man can have all the fantasies he wants about women. Yet when a woman has a fantasy, it's called a delusion, making something wrong with her."

"Belinda, you know that's not what I mean." He shook his head. "We've spent all this time analyzing your life with Robert. You thought you were dying and before that happened, you wanted to experience love, and you did with him. You made up Robert and this whole life around him so you could have those experiences. Since you couldn't be an active participant in the real world, your mind created one. This is what kept you going."

"Robert is what kept me going. I owe my life to him and no matter what you say, I will always feel he is out there somewhere."

Dr. Rosen shook his head and responded, "We still have a lot of work ahead of us."

***

My discharge day was here. I couldn't wait to leave. I was packed and ready to go when Mom and Dad arrived to pick me up. All the staff had been wonderful. This was the biggest bunch of caring people I'd ever met. I loved every one of them right down to Mrs. Franks, who cleaned my room every day. I don't think I could ever repay all of them for the encouragement and support they gave me. I'm sure it wasn't every day that they had a patient leaving in better condition than that in which they arrived. I was the walking, breathing result of all their good work, one of the limited success stories of a long-term care facility.

After the many goodbyes and tears, I sat in the ritualistic wheelchair, my chariot to my parents' car parked under the portico. As I was being wheeled down a corridor, I was imagining how it would feel to be free again, out of the confines of the hospital when I heard a rhythmic beating sound. It was familiar. One I'd heard many times before, but not in this reality. Paralyzed with apprehension, I listened closely to what sounded like Robert's heartbeat. I tensed up and looked around. The orderly asked me if I was alright. Wondering if he heard the sound as well, I took a chance and asked if he could hear the rhythmic thumping noise. He stopped pushing me to listen. "Yeah, I hear it."

I wasn't losing my mind. "What is that?"

"I'll show you. We'll be passing it on the way out."

We came to an open patient room. In it lay an unresponsive man on a bed. The bed was tilting from one side to the other in a methodic, rhythmic motion. With every shift of movement there was a slight soft thumping sound. I asked the orderly if I'd ever been on a bed like that. "All our head trauma patients are on one. The movement helps with circulation."

I froze as I watched the bed simulate what my mind turned into the gentle rocking motion Robert had used to comfort me as he cradled my head close to his beating heart. This was the first sign Robert was only a figment of my imagination. It terrified the hell out of me.

CHAPTER 35

IT WAS GOOD to be home. Mom did the best she could to make my old room comfortable for me. Before the accident, I'd been living in an apartment close to the school where I taught. After the wreck, Mom and Dad cleaned out the place, sold all the furniture, and selectively kept only a few of my possessions. What was left was moved to my old room.

It was still furnished the way it was when I was in high school. Mom hung onto most of my clothes, although I didn't fit into many of the items because I had lost so much weight. I was steadily gaining and suspected some of the more standard articles of clothing would be back in use within a very short time. Right now I lived in jogging clothes, t-shirts, and running shoes.

I was discharged from the hospital on Saturday. Sunday, we made the drive to Brookshire, Texas, a small town west of Houston, to see an old friend. I missed him very much and was excited to see Beau, my horse. When Matt left to take a job in California, he had given me Beau as compensation for not inviting me to join his new life. After three years of dating Matt, I thought we were in love. He had a different view of our relationship and never gave me a second thought when he accepted his new job. I was never a factor in his plans, and that crushed me.

Dr. Rosen and I concluded Matt dumping me the way he did, the car accident, and my perception that I was dying all contributed to my life with Robert. Dr. Rosen always maintained Robert was just a character of my dream, but I could never convince myself of that.

For now, Beau was my consolation prize and I was glad to have him. My relationship with him started in my sophomore year of college. From the first day I saw him and took my first ride, I was in love. Dad told me he couldn't stand to sell Beau because of my affection for him. A close family friend agreed to board him for free after the accident. He wanted to help my father by taking care of Beau until I woke up. I'm sure, at some point, my dad would've found Beau a new permanent home if my coma carried on too long. I planned on moving him closer to Sugar Land as soon as I could find someplace suitable. He'd come in handy for my rehab, but riding, for now, would take place near Brookshire.   It would be great exercise to increase my stamina and coordination.   I'd have to start out slowly and under supervision, but I suspected Beau and I would be on our own in no time.

In my "Dream State," Beau was the reason I attracted the attention of Robert. He was a connection to Robert and I hoped Beau would remember me.

It was the perfect day. There were soft fluffy white clouds scattered in the brilliant blue of the big Texas sky. The air felt crisp and fresh. The wind occasionally gusted into a stiff breeze making leaves rustle as the sunlight darted through tree limbs.

We arrived about one o'clock at the house of Paul and Sarah Jensen. Paul had worked with my dad for years and retired early on a one-hundred-acre ranch near Brookshire. I'd never been there, but my parents assured me it was the perfect place for Beau. The Jensen's had two other horses, so he had company.

"Howdy, young lady!" The burly king-sized man said to me as he put an arm around my shoulder and nearly squeezed the life out of me. "We're so glad you came out of that ordeal. Your mom and dad sure were worried about you. This is my wife, Sarah. She's the horse person around here." He let go of me and walked over to his wife replicating his hold on her. "She does the ridin' and I do the laborin'." He let out a hearty laugh and almost lifted his wife by the shoulders as he gave her a squeeze.

When he released her, she approached me with a warm smile and took my hand. "I'll bet you're anxious to see that big boy of yours. He's such a good-natured animal. Come on, I'll take you to him." As we walked, she explained how well he fit in with her other two horses. She told me she rode him at least twice a week to keep him ready for me. As we approached a grassy paddock, she placed her hand on my shoulder and pointed to just beyond the fence surrounding the enclosure. "There he is. He's alone. I figured you didn't need the other two botherin' you on your first reunion." My eyes drifted from Sarah's face and followed her hand in the direction she was pointing until I saw the figure of a chestnut horse, glistening as he grazed in the sun. "There's a lead rope on the fence. I thought you'd like to spend some time groomin' him. I'm sure he'd enjoy a good bath. After you say your hellos, take him into the barn. You'll find everything you'll need in there....Go on. Go say howdy." She gently nudged my shoulder.

"Thank you. He looks as magnificent as I remember. You took good care of him." Before I climbed over the paddock fence, I took the lead. The gentle breeze touched the top of the tall grass causing it to sway from side to side. Beau got a whiff of my scent. He lifted his head and stood erect with his ears straight up. He snorted at the air, then pawed at the ground as I approached taking small, cautious steps. When I was within ten feet of him, I took the baby carrots I brought for him out of my pocket and extended my hand. "Hey Beau, carrots." He studied me. To my surprise and joy, he slowly relaxed his head and walked toward me. As he approached, he placed his nose in my hand and took the carrots. In a few more steps his head was at my side and I was rubbing him behind the ears.

Thoughts of Robert flooded my memory, and I began to cry.

***

The next several weeks were spent in physical therapy, Dr. Rosen's office, and at the Jensen's with Beau. Sarah was my designated riding supervisor. She knew enough about horses and riding to make sure it was safe for me to be on my own. We quickly became friends and, on weekends, Mom or Dad would drive me out on a Friday then pick me up on Sunday evening. I'd help around the place with chores. The exercise was good for me and gave me something to do. I owed a lot to the Jensen's and didn't mind pitching in.

My first weeks home were busy with my parents driving me to and from all my treatments. I wasn't allowed to drive. I had to be out of the hospital for a month, then more tests needed to be run before I was certified safe to be behind the wheel of a car. As I improved, all the therapy and psychology sessions would decrease.

I was still having trouble with Dr. Rosen. He was convinced Robert was a manifestation of my mind that helped me make sense of the "Dream State." Not for a split second did he believe Robert was a real person. "You have to move on. You can't linger on someone who isn't real," he harped on a regular basis. "How do you expect to move forward with your life if you hang on to his memory? I know it's only been a short time since you woke up, so you need time to mourn his loss. I understand that." His tone was more sympathetic. "We'll be cutting back on our sessions in a few weeks, down to one day a week. Your physical therapy sessions will also be decreasing to two days a week about the same time, and soon you'll be driving again as well." He was calm and reserved, like he always was, as he described my treatment plan. I just listened. "When the time comes, I want you to go back to school to see if you can find any indication that Robert is real."

I looked at him, stunned. "Are you telling me I should try to find him?"

"That's *exactly* what I'm telling you. I know you look for him everywhere you go—always scanning crowds at the mall or looking at the people in the grocery store. You'll continue to do this until you're convinced he was a dream. Once your mind is at peace with that, you'll mourn him and move on." He was leaning forward in his chair trying to make a point. "Do you understand what I'm saying?"

At that moment, I didn't care what he was trying to make me understand. He was giving me permission to search for my beloved Robert. My heart jumped at the thought. If I could prove Robert was a real person, I might have a chance to be with him. "I understand. Do I have to wait until I start to drive?" I hoped to hear the answer I wanted.

"No. I don't think so. You told me he was from Sugar Land. See what you can find on the internet. You're jogging in the evenings—see what you can find. Just be safe and don't do anything foolish."

Barely containing my excitement, I started making a mental list of all the things I could do to look for Robert. Did Dr. Rosen think I was an idiot? I had already utilized my computer, to exhaustion, trying to find any link to a Robert Pennington of Sugar Land. All my efforts led only to dead ends, saddening my heart.

"If this man exists out there, I want you to find proof of it. Go back to your college and see if he was real. You're a stubborn woman, so go find your true love and bring back some proof, because I know you won't be reconciled with this until you're convinced he was only in your head. You'll always be looking for your 'Milk Carton Lover.' So go find him, but I want reports of your progress and you have to balance your search with other activities. I don't want to find out all you're doing is looking on milk cartons."

I couldn't believe my ears. For the past month I'd been told I was delusional. Now he wanted proof. The more I thought about it, the better I liked his idea. I looked over at Dr. Rosen. "Thank you" was all I could say.

I was dismissed from the session with a new hope. My search would start this evening with jogging. Under the ruse that I needed a change of scenery, I'd ask Mom to drive me to the neighborhood where I remembered my in-laws living. When I was finished, I'd call her to pick me up. She'd never know what I was up to.

As planned, Mom dropped me off at a running trail near the subdivision I planned to scope out. Once Mom was out of sight, I changed direction and headed to the route Robert and I drove in my "Dream State."

With every step I took, my heart raced. Knots of anticipation twisted my stomach. I was a block away from the last turn. If I was right, the entrance to the neighborhood I visited with Robert would be right around the next bend. I took a deep breath and rounded the corner, then stopped dead in my tracks. There was no entrance—just the continuation of another subdivision like the one I was in. Taking heavy breaths, I bent over and rested my hands on my knees. Tears clouded my eyes. This was another dead end.

Feeling more defeated than ever, I called Mom and she met me close to where she dropped me off. "Are you okay? You look sad." She could always read me like a book.

"I'm just tired. My session with Dr. Rosen was draining and now with all the running...." I trailed off my sentence as I turned toward the window. The explanation was enough to satisfy her. I didn't want her to know what was really bothering me. The rest of the drive home was in silence. I was starting to doubt myself and the existence of Robert.

We arrived home and I told my parents I was tired. After a quick snack eaten in my room, I showered, and prepared for bed. I didn't want my parents questioning my mood so the sanctum of my bedroom was the safest place for me to be alone and sulk.

***

"Belinda, are you okay?" I opened my eyes and was looking into Robert's clear blue eyes. He had tears running down his face. "Angel." He was cradling me in his arms. He felt so good.

"Robert?" I felt sore with pain all over. "What happened?"

"You've been in a car accident. A truck hit you. Be quiet until EMS has a chance to look at you. You'll need to go to the hospital." He was comforting me. "I was so scared I'd lose you."

"You're crying." I reached up to wipe his tears. "How did you find me?"

"I read your note so I figured I'd come get some bagels. I drove to the bakery and saw you pulling away. I got a chuckle out of us having the same thought. You entered the intersection and I saw the truck run the light and hit you. I was never so scared in all my life." His eyes became more penetrating as they reached deep into my very being. "Please don't leave me." I could feel him gently tighten his hold on me.

I wanted to tell him I loved him and would never leave him. Suddenly I heard a knocking sound followed by, "Belinda, wake up. It's time for breakfast." It was my mother.

I shot up in bed. My respirations were heavy, my heart was racing, my hair wet from perspiration. *Did I just dream about Robert? Was I in his arms?* I embraced my pillow, holding it tight in front of me. I rocked back and forth with my eyes shut tight and sobbed. "He's not real," I repeated over and over again. The pain from my legs overrode my thoughts of him. I'd overworked them the evening before, and they were stiff. The dream was so real and so short. I heard my mother call me again. "I'm up. I'll be right down," I shouted from my bed, frustrated.

This would be the last time I'd ever see him in the world I created for us. I would never dream of Robert again.

***

Everything I needed to do to regain my driving privilege was completed. I made plans to leave for my college on Thursday, returning no later than Saturday. This would be my only chance to prove Robert did exist.

Upon arriving on campus, my first stop was the Registrar's Office. "Excuse me. I'm looking for someone who may have attended this school. Is there any way you could give me that information."

"Are you related to this person?" A well-dressed woman rose from her desk and walked over to the counter.

I didn't feel the need to go through my state of affairs with her and thought if a small lie helped me, then so be it. "Yes, I'm his wife."

She looked at me with a smile that was both puzzled and amused. "You're his wife but you don't know if he attended school here?"

Having nothing to lose, I gave her a brief description of my recent love-at-first-sight romance and fast wedding. Then I dropped the bomb. I told her my husband was killed in a car accident and I was trying to find out more about him. Our life together was so short. Parts of the story were true—I just changed things around a bit. It worked and she asked me to fill out a form giving her enough information so she could look for him.

She left with the paper and returned in about ten minutes. "Are you sure you have all the information correct. I cross-referenced his name, date of birth, and years. I can't find a thing. Sorry." She handed me the paper. Staring at it and afraid to take it from her, I was brokenhearted, but not finished.

Next I went to the library to pore over yearbooks searching for someone who looked like Robert. I went back five years, still nothing, and to my dismay I discovered that there was no mention or pictures of the Delta Lambda Nu brothers in the fraternities sections. With my curiosity piqued, I decided to drive by the Delt fraternity house.

I had turned off the main street toward the frat house when I noticed an old Victorian house that looked very familiar. It was the one Robert and I had lived in. I swerved into the first parking place I could find. Approaching the house, I saw a "For Rent" sign in our old apartment window. I searched for my cell and called. A woman answered and I explained that I'd be attending grad school and wanted to see the apartment. She said she'd meet me there.

Memory upon memory of Robert and our relationship began to overwhelm me while I paced back and forth in front of the house. Just when I thought I couldn't stand the deluge of thoughts, a middle-aged woman approached me. "Are you the lady interested in the apartment?"

"Yes ma'am. I need something close to campus." I lied again.

We walked up the steps. I knew the house could be a memory from my college days. Although I didn't remember having ever been inside this building, my memories of pre-accident events were fuzzy at times. The porch was just as I remembered from my "Dream State." The doors were a little different, more worn but still beautiful. When the realtor opened the door, my mouth dropped as I scanned the interior of the foyer. Everything looked just like it did in my "Dream State." Not one thing about it was different.

My heart was starting to pound. My stomach flip-flopped as I heard the key turn and I entered Robert's and my apartment. My knees started to buckle, but I braced myself against the doorjamb. I could've been back in my "Dream State," for I now stood in the apartment I shared with Robert. I asked the woman if I could look around, explore by myself. She agreed and left.

My eyes filmed over with tears as my life with Robert became something I could touch. Again, as with the foyer, nothing, not one thing, was different. It was like the first time I walked in. I had time to take in the beauty of this small abode and half-expected him to come walking through the door any minute, carrying a box of his packed belongings, like he did the morning he moved in. The memories showered my brain and so did the pain. I walked into the bedroom where I first made love to him. I relived the feel of his touch as I sat on the bed taking in everything I could remember. I missed him terribly. I loved him so much and I cried as I remembered.

Thanking the woman for letting me look at the apartment, I stepped out onto the porch and walked slowly to my car, realizing this proved nothing. For all I knew, I had been at a party and thought the place was so charming I just used it as our first home. I almost started crying again because I hit yet another brick wall, but I still wasn't ready to throw in the towel.

The next morning, I drove straight to where I remembered the Delt house was located. As I walked to the house it struck me how quiet it was. There were no parked cars or frat brothers bustling around the house. To my shock, a little silver-haired lady answered the door. I asked if this was or had ever been the Delt house and she told me no, that it was her residence and she had lived there some thirty years. Her words hit me like a ton of bricks as I realized the fraternity was also just a figment of my imagination. This was the last disheartening dead end. Walking back to my car, I fought back the tears, wondering why my mind created this imaginary life and was playing tricks on me. Why hadn't I dreamed that Matt and I lived happily ever after? That would've been easier to deal with. As I left town in a cloud of tears, reality hit me that my beloved Robert didn't exist in this world. Somehow I'd have to move on with my life alone. Feeling defeated, I dreaded having to explain my failure to Dr. Rosen.

***

"I'm sorry, Belinda, that your trip didn't uncover more information about Robert. Are you willing to start to let go now?" Dr. Rosen leaned back in his chair waiting for my answer.

I didn't want to answer. "It doesn't look like I have any choice." I felt as if I'd had my heart ripped out of my chest. I had never experienced emotional pain like that before. Robert was truly gone to me.

He nodded his head in approval. "If you put 'Dream State' Robert to sleep then you'll be able to move on, make plans for the future, and have a life. You need friends and boyfriends....I'll help you through this."

All I could do was stare blankly back because I knew he was right.

***

It was close to the end of the year. The holidays were approaching. I was making some major changes in my life. Beau would be moving to Sugar Land. I found a good stable next to a gated subdivision. The subdivision consisted of acreage estates so the owners could keep horses on their property or in the stable next door. Trails surrounding it were shared with the stable. The plan was to move Beau just before New Year's Eve.

I'd also been thinking about buying a place of my own. There were some patio homes in the same planned community, close to the stables, but since I hadn't discussed moving with my parents and didn't want to interfere with Mom's holiday plans, this decision would have to wait until after the first of the year.

There was also the matter of a job. I was thinking about going back to teaching high school art. I could start out as a sub then go full-time when something became available. After the first of the year, I would start looking. I would need something to fill my days. A job would do that and make the trust fund last longer.

By now, I'd been released from physical therapy. They could no longer help me. I was fine and progressing very well on my own. As long as I kept up my current physical routine, I'd only improve with time.

CHAPTER 36

I AWOKE DREADING the arrival of the party, December 31. I wasn't quite ready yet to be around a group of strangers. Staying home alone sounded more appealing. I would've loved to call Abbey and tell her I'm not going to Garrett's company's New Year's party, but she'd be upset with me and I *did* need to start socializing again as part of my recovery plan.

I arose, ready for some breakfast, trying to stop thinking about the party. Mom and Dad were sitting at the dining table, finishing their breakfast and reading the newspaper.

Dad took enough time to peep over the top of the Business section. "Good morning, Sleepyhead."

Smiling, I mumbled, "Good morning." I headed to the kitchen to gather up my bowl of cereal and glass of orange juice, then went back to the table and sat next to Mom.

"I'm so glad you're going out tonight. You need to have some fun and meet some single men your age. You never know, you might meet 'Mister Right,' or at least someone to go out with. I really like Abbey and Garrett. It was so nice of them to ask you to go tonight. You know, they truly care about you."

Mom was in her usual form and on a roll. Listening to her, I could understand where I got my ability to ramble. "I know. I'll go and try to have some fun." How much fun could I possibly have at a formal party?

"What did you decide to wear tonight?" Mom looked up at me over the rim of her mug filled with steaming hot coffee.

"That long, pale blue, chiffon dress that I wore to the formal with Matt. It should be perfectly fine for this occasion." Finishing my breakfast, I stood up from the table and took my dishes to the kitchen and put them in the dishwasher. As I passed back by my parents, I told them Beau was arriving today and I had to go to the stables to meet Mr. Jensen.

Paul Jensen was due to arrive with Beau at his new home around two p.m.

on New Year's Eve. I had made all the arrangements for Beau to be moved to the stable closer to home. This was the first change I was making for the start of the New Year. I had planned on his relocation taking place days ago, but Paul couldn't make the trip until today. The box stall was ready and I'd planned on just grooming Beau on his first day. I wouldn't have much time to settle him in before the party.

Paul was running a little late, pressing me for time. If he were much later, I wouldn't have time to wash the horse smell off of me and be ready to leave when my dates arrived.

I walked outside and, for the first time, enjoyed the crisp air of this winter day. In Texas, December can be tricky. There are days when full winter garb is appropriate and others when shorts are the style. Today, however, was perfect. It was overcast, low humidity, with a nice gentle breeze swirling through the now-partially bare trees. I took a deep breath, filling my lungs with fresh air. As I exhaled I saw the F150 and horse trailer.

The truck stopped and Paul hopped out. I was always amazed at the amount of energy he had, given his age. "Howdy, there!" he shouted as he strode to the back of the trailer to release the hatch. He backed Beau out and handed me the lead. "Here's your big boy, as promised." The smile across his face could fill Texas.

"Hey Beau, carrots?" I held the horse's usual treat out for him, then stroked his neck as he ate.

After saying goodbye to Paul, I led Beau to the barn. I tied him just outside his stall then pulled two brushes from the tack box. With a systematic motion, I began to brush the horse's sleek coat, first with one hand brush, then the next, repeating the motion over and over.

I was working on the left side of the animal when a brisk gust of wind swept into the barn. The breeze lifted my hair and it felt as if someone had caressed the back of my head. I stood erect, not moving. In a gentle, barely audible voice, I could swear I heard, "Angel." I turned around, looking over the interior of the barn, but I was alone. Walking outside past the protective covering of the entrance, I stood in the yard and looked toward the woods to the right. I had the most overwhelming compulsion to walk into them. I took a step in their direction. Before taking the next step, I stopped. This was nuts. I didn't have time for this foolishness. I had better things to do, so I turned and proceeded back to the barn, stopping to give the trees one last look. But the feeling continued to linger, invading my thoughts.

The strange feeling I had experienced haunted me as I drove home. For a fleeting moment I wondered what was past the wooded area. I put the incident out of my mind as I drove into the driveway of my parents' home. The stables were only five minutes away. Having Beau this close would be easier and fun. I was looking forward to our first ride. Now it was time to work on my smell and hair. I had a party to attend.

It's amazing how fast time flies when you're *not* looking forward to doing something. It was 6:15, so I decided to start prepping, since Abbey said they'd pick me up around 7:45. The party was supposed to start at eight p.m., and it wasn't far from my parents' home.

I took my time putting on the little makeup I wear. I decided to wear my hair straight and sleek with the ends curled under. That took more time than I had allowed. It was now 7:20. I needed to hurry up if I was going to be ready on time.

I went to my closet and dug through it, looking for the long, blue dress. No dress. I searched again, then yelled, "Mom, where's my blue dress? It's not in my closet." I was starting to feel a little panicky.

"I sent it to the cleaners. Go look in mine. I probably put it in there by accident," she shouted back from the den.

I rushed to her room and rummaged through her closet. To my relief there it was. The plastic dry-cleaning bag rustled when I snapped the hanger off the rod. Holding it up, I took a moment to inspect it. My eyes drifted back to another plastic bag that contained a familiar looking dress. I stared in disbelief. The formal dropped to my feet as I grabbed the second bag and ran to the stairway yelling, "Mom, Mom! Where did this dress come from?"

"What dress?"

"This cream-colored silk dress with the bolero jacket," I rattled off, holding the dress out in front of me.

Mom had walked to the stairway and was looking up at me. "Oh, I forgot about that one. I was on my way to the hospital to see you when I noticed a dress shop with a 'SALE' sign in the window. You know how I am when I see those signs. I stopped and found that dress. I thought you would look so pretty in it. So I bought it for you."

I creased my brow. "You were on your way to the hospital when you bought it?

Mom looked at the floor then back at me. "I always felt that you'd come back to us, even though the doctors kept telling us you probably wouldn't wake up. And if, by chance, you didn't, I wanted you to sleep forever looking beautiful." A few tears escaped and ran down her cheeks. She quickly wiped them away with the back of her hand. "Why are you so concerned about that dress?"

I held it up in front of me, hugging it. "You won't believe me....This is the exact same dress that Robert picked out and bought for me to wear when we married in my dream."

Mom's eyes became big and her mouth gaped open. "How can that be? I brought it to the hospital and showed it to you. But you couldn't have seen it. You were unconscious. I did try to describe it to you. I told you that you needed to wake up so you could wear it, and how pretty you'd look in it." There was a brief silence. "You better forget about it right now and finish dressing, or you won't be ready when Abbey and Garrett arrive."

I carried my "dream" wedding dress into my room and laid it out on my bed, then rushed back to Mom's closet to pick up the pale blue formal. I decided to put the dress on in front of her big, full-length mirror that was hanging on her closet door. I couldn't quite reach the back zipper, so I called Mom for her help. She arrived and zipped the dress. Her eyes opened wide and her hand flew up briefly covering her mouth. "Oh my! You can't wear this dress. The top is too small. You're flowing out of it." She paused. "You wore *this* dress to that frat formal last year?"

"Yeah and I got a lot of compliments. Everyone said I looked gorgeous, and a lot of girls asked where I bought it. I told them you made it."

"You didn't! I'm so embarrassed. I'll bet Matt enjoyed that date, looking down at you all evening." She smiled, shaking her head, and snickered. "I didn't realize you had developed so much."

"I was concerned about the top at first. But then, I kept getting compliments from everyone. So I quit worrying about it." I remembered Robert's face when he saw me and the great time I had that night. Oh. If it had only been real!

Mom was snapping her fingers in front of my face, breaking my trance. "Belinda, come back down to earth."

"Oh. Sorry." I looked at myself in the mirror. "I need some kind of necklace. Do you have one I can wear?" Expelling a long, deep breath, I placed my hand at the base of my neck and remembered the nonexistent diamond double heart necklace that Robert gave me as a wedding gift.

Mom went to her jewelry chest and returned with a beautiful, sparkling, wreath necklace and placed it where his once hung. She pulled some of my hair forward, over in front of my shoulders to cover the exposed part of my breasts. She was shaking her head, but she made me smile. The necklace hit my neck low enough to cover the scar from the tracheotomy.

She left again, heading to her closet. Seconds later, she returned with a long, black cloak. "You'll definitely attract the attention of all the men tonight.

You look beautiful, but you better not let your father see you. He might not let you go looking like this. You know how protective he is of you. Here, put the cloak on before you come down."

I went back to my closet, and found my silver heels and small silver clutch purse. With my cloak on, I headed downstairs to wait for Abbey and Garrett. It was now 7:42 p.m.

As I reached the last step, the doorbell rang. It was my "dates" for the evening. Abbey was wearing a beautiful, long, black-velvet, fitted gown and Garrett had on a tuxedo. They looked very elegant. "Are you ready to go?" Garrett asked with a huge smile across his face.

I held my arms out to the side to show him. "As ready as I'll ever be." Calling out to my parents, I told them I was leaving. Mom said to have fun. Luckily, I missed having Dad see me.

We were on our way to the dreaded party. Garrett said the neighborhood wasn't very far—in fact, it was close to the stables where I was boarding Beau. The GPS directed us right past the stable and along the gigantic stone fence of the gated community next door. We turned between the large stone columns of the entrance and down a winding road where enormous two-story homes appeared. The GPS guided us to a *huge* two-story, Tuscan-style home, set back from the street on a large lot with big oak trees all around. As I gazed wide-eyed at the house, my mouth fell open, my heart sputtered, then started thumping. It looked just like Robert's parents' house, except it wasn't sitting angled on a corner lot. It couldn't be the same house. There were probably a lot of houses that look like it. Anyway, mine was in a dream. It couldn't exist. I didn't say anything about it as I tried to make sense of what I was seeing.

Garrett pulled into the circular drive. There were men, dressed in tuxedos, who opened our doors and helped us out, then valet-parked the car. As we approached the front door, another man in a tux opened it for us. "Welcome, I hope you enjoy yourselves." Who in the world were these people?

Upon walking into the entry, my heart sputtered again. I gasped as I looked around. The inside looked just like the house in my dreams, right down to the two cobalt-blue vases sitting on the two matching Bombay chests. My heart started pounding in anticipation of what else or who I was going to see. My legs started shaking. I gripped Abbey's hand to calm my panicky feeling.

She gave me a surprised look. "Are you okay? You look like you've seen a ghost."

"I'm alright. This house is…fabulous." I was afraid to tell her what I was really thinking.

In the foyer, the stairs and balcony formed a horseshoe shape. At the top, overlooking the living room, a quartet was playing. I took off my cloak. A lady took our coats and purses, placing them in the study to the left of the double staircase.

Garrett's eyes popped. "Damn! You look gorgeous in that dress." Abbey elbowed him in the side.

Garrett sniffed the air and scanned the room, fixing his gaze on the dining room. Evidently hungry, he headed for the food which was to the right of the staircase. It was elaborately displayed. At the top and center of the table was an ice sculpture of an angel blowing a trumpet lined with gold foil. On either side were huge arrangements of red roses. Below and surrounding the ice sculpture, food was arranged on stands at different heights, a tablecloth covering the varying levels with plates of food perched on each. Gold silk fabric was bunched around the stands giving the impression that the plates were floating on a sea of gold. Looking around the room, I remembered the afternoon I spent here with Robert and his parents.

Garrett said he was thirsty and wondered where he could get a drink. I looked around and figured the drinks would be set up in the kitchen. I led the way for Abbey and Garrett. After all, I knew more about this house than they did. I walked through the butler's pantry and into the vast open kitchen area. There was a large island in the middle of the room which was covered with all types of liquor bottles. Garrett asked what we wanted and then started to pour out three glasses of white zinfandel. The bottle went dry after the second glass. He picked up a new bottle and started looking around for a bottle opener. I turned and walked to a lower cabinet drawer, opened it, and pulled out a corkscrew. Walking back to Garrett, I extended it to him. Our eyes met. He looked puzzled, staring at me with it in my hand. He reached out to grab it from me, but before releasing it, I said, "This is Robert's house. I've been here before." Then I let go. Abbey stood frozen in disbelief.

"There's one way to settle this....This place belongs to my boss. I want you to meet him." He took me by the hand and we were off. Abbey followed. Garrett suddenly stopped, looking around the great room. When he found his mark, we were off again, squeezing through the crowd until we stood behind his boss and his wife. Garrett reached for Abbey and placed her on his other side. He cleared his throat and tapped the gentleman on the shoulder. "Excuse me sir, I'd like to introduce you to my wife and her friend." He turned around and before me stood Robert Pennington, Sr. When his wife turned around—it was Sandra. These were my Robert's parents! I took a few deep breaths to calm my rattled nerves.

"Mr. and Mrs. Pendleton, I'd like you to meet my wife, Abbey, and our friend, Belinda. I hope you don't mind that we brought her along. She's been recuperating from an auto accident. Now we're trying to help her get back into the dating scene."

"No, we don't mind at all." They looked at me. "We're glad you came. Enjoy yourself." When Mr. Pendleton smiled, his resemblance to my "Dream" Robert was uncanny. "And I must say, you look very beautiful."

"Thank you…." Pennington??? Pendleton???…I had to ask. "Would your first name happen to be Robert?" The anticipation of his answer was nerve-racking.

"Yes." Mr. Pendleton studied my face. "Have we met before?"

I swung my eyes to Mrs. Pendleton. "And is yours Sandra?"

They looked at each other and then at me. Mr. Pendleton again asked, "Have we met before?"

I didn't know what to say. I couldn't tell them *yes, in my dreams*. "I don't think so. I'm not sure how I know." I lied. "Do you by any chance have a son named Robert?" I held my breath in anticipation of their answer.

Mrs. Pendleton tilted her head. "Yes, we do. Do you know him?"

I gasped at her response. With butterflies taking flight in my belly, I felt the room start to spin. I reached out for Garrett's arm to steady myself. "I met a Robert once who looked a lot like you." I nodded to Mr. Pendleton.

"Robert does look like his father, just a lot younger." Mrs. Pendleton raised an eyebrow and smiled.

"Is he here?" I quickly scanned the room looking for him, almost afraid of the answer.

"No, he was here earlier this afternoon. He left for another party. He said he might stop by here later. If you miss him, I'll tell him you were asking about him. It's Belinda, right?"

"Yes ma'am. Thank you." Now a full-blown beehive was churning where my stomach should be.

Garrett led Abbey and me away. They stopped and stared at me. "Belinda, what's going on? This is really getting a bit strange, even to me." Abbey looked worried.

"I knew he was real. I could feel it. This is the exact same house and they're Robert's parents." A numbing sensation started coming over me. "I'm getting light-headed. I need to sit down before I faint." I took hold of Garrett's arm and he led me over to an armchair where I rested my forehead against my hand until the feeling passed. "I think I need to eat something."

"I'll get you some food." Abbey turned *en route* to the dining room.

"How can all this be happening?" Garrett had a deep look of concern.

"I don't know. It's freaky. Have you met their son?"

"No, but I've heard that he's a nice guy."

"In my dreams, you were best friends and fraternity brothers."

Abbey returned with my food. "You two go mingle. I'll be fine. I don't want to spoil the party for you. Go!" I motioned them away with my hand.

They walked a little ways off to talk to a group of young people. Abbey kept looking back at me. I shook my head.

I finished eating and headed into the kitchen. After refilling my glass to help calm my nerves, I walked around the room looking at things. Everything was familiar. It was like I was back in my dream.

I was facing the cabinets, sipping my wine when I heard a polite voice behind me. "Excuse me. Can I help you?"

I turned around, startled for a second. "No, I was just getting more wine."

A waiter was placing a tray of empty glasses on the island. "Oh, we're here to do that for you. There are waiters circulating around the house with trays of drinks." Again he was polite. "Do you want something?" I shook my head, realizing the kitchen was off limits—the waiters' domain for the evening.

Feeling calmer from the wine, I headed back to the living room. As I passed the island where the waiter was filling more glasses, I picked up a full one of zinfandel and made a toasting gesture to him. He smiled back and nodded. "Have a good evening, madam."

I meandered to the large two-story windows in the great room. As I looked out over the patio, my eyes wandered past the pool to the manicured lawn beyond and stopped at the tree line. As I studied them, I realized they also flanked the stable yard of Beau's quarters. These were the same woods I had the urge to enter this afternoon when I was interrupted by that strange breeze while brushing my horse. If I'd followed that whim, the path would've ended right in the back yard of this magnificent home, just about the same time Robert would've been here. A waiter disturbed my thoughts. "Madam, *hors d'oeuvre*?" I never took my eyes off the trees and shook my head to signal him to leave.

I broke my self-imposed trance by turning and looking at the party participants. People were starting to dance to the slow music. There was soft chatter with the occasional burst of loud laughter coming from different areas. Glasses being raised and clinked together all added to the ambiance of the party. I felt my surroundings weren't real, as if I'd been transported back to a time of the overwhelming love of my dream. It made me wish I were with Robert. It was difficult to believe that the man of my dreams was so close yet still miles away. What if this Robert Pendleton wasn't my Robert Pennington?

If he *was* the Robert I remembered, he wouldn't know who *I* was. I had to be prepared for that. So far no one I met or saw in my coma remembered anything I experienced in my dream. They were there, but only in my head. So if this was my Robert, he wouldn't be the Robert of my dream.

I began searching around for Abbey and Garrett. They were across the room, so I strolled over to them. Garrett introduced me to everyone standing in the group they were socializing with.

Garrett turned to Abbey. "Sweetheart, would you mind if I ask Belinda to dance first?"

"No, I don't mind. Just keep your eyes straight ahead, not *DOWN.*" Abbey was kidding around, making a reference to my bustline.

"Yes ma'am." He grinned as he flashed a quick glance in my direction.

Abbey scowled at him then laughed. "Behave, you bad boy."

Garrett made a face back, and then turned to me. "Belinda, would you like to dance?"

"Sure." He took my hand and led me over to the other dancing couples.

Garrett whispered in my ear, "What are you going to do if it is your "Dream" Robert? He's not going to know who you are."

I whispered back to him, "I know. I can only hope he'll feel the connection we had."

When the music ended, we walked back to Abbey. Several other guys asked me to dance. Thanks to the wine, I was beginning to relax and have fun mingling. My hopes of meeting Robert Pendleton tonight had dwindled away. I met several nice, single, young men who I'd consider going out with if they ever asked. After dancing with Colin for the third time, I decided to join Abbey and Garrett. I wanted to celebrate the coming of the New Year with them, so I excused myself.

As I made my way through the crowd of reveling partyers, the ornamental clock on the wall started to chime the countdown causing increased excitement amongst the crowd. The guests amplified their shouts as the last few seconds of the old year were coming to an end. I had spotted Abbey and Garret across the room when I felt a hand gently rest on my shoulder. I froze in anticipation, as a familiar arousing feeling stirred within me. A male voice spoke in an inquiring tone. "Belinda?"

I slowly turned and looked up. I gasped. Overcome by shock, I felt my knees buckle beneath me as everything went black....

ABOUT THE AUTHORS

Linda Fagala was born and raised in Texas, and currently resides there with her husband. She graduated from Stephen F. Austin State University as an art teacher. She is a member of RWA.

Karen Pugh was born in Chicago, Illinois and graduated from Amundsen-Mayfair City College with an ADN in Nursing. She has had a long interest in writing, practicing the craft with contributions to local newsletters. She is a member of RWA. Currently she lives in Texas with her husband.

Shattered Fate is a fictional love story. The Belinda and Robert saga came to Linda after reminiscing about some of the fun experiences that occurred during her college years and is loosely based on those events. She approached Karen about turning the idea into a romance novel. Karen's experiences in nursing and varied life interests, contributed to the theme of the plot. Combining their talents and ideas, they embarked on their first novel.

Destiny Reborn is the sequel of Belinda and Robert's life, as the two discover the reasons for their attraction.

CPSIA information can be obtained at www.ICGtesting.com
Printed in the USA
LVOW13s0704280514

387572LV00001B/1/P